HANGMAN

Born in St. Louis, Faye Kellerman is one of the most highly considered US crime authors. Her first novel, *The Ritual Bath* (1986), introduced Sergeant Peter Decker and Rina Lazarus. It also won the 1987 Macavity Award for Best First Mystery. Kellerman currently lives in Beverly Hills with her husband and four children.

Also by Faye Kellerman

Blindman's Bluff
Cold Case
The Burnt House
The Ritual Bath
Sacred and Profane
The Quality of Mercy
Milk and Honey
Day of Atonement
False Prophet
Grievous Sin
Sanctuary
Justice
Prayers for the Dead
Serpent's Tooth
Moon Music
Jupiter's Bones
Stalker
The Forgotten
Stone Kiss
Street Dreams
Straight into Darkness
The Garden of Eden and Other Criminal Delights:
A Book of Short Stories

With Jonathan Kellerman

Double Homicide
Capital Crimes

With Aliza Kellerman

Prism

FAYE KELLERMAN

Hangman

HARPER

Harper
An imprint of HarperCollins*Publishers*
77–85 Fulham Palace Road,
Hammersmith, London W6 8JB

www.harpercollins.co.uk

This paperback edition 2011
1

First published in Great Britain by
HarperCollins*Publishers* 2010

Copyright © Plot Line, Inc. 2010

Faye Kellerman asserts the moral right to
be identified as the author of this work

A catalogue record for this book is
available from the British Library

ISBN: 978 0 00 729568 5

Printed and bound in Great Britain by
Clays Ltd, St Ives plc

Mixed Sources
Product group from well-managed
forests and other controlled sources
www.fsc.org   Cert no. SW-COC-001806
© 1996 Forest Stewardship Council

FSC is a non-profit international organisation established
to promote the responsible management of the world's forests.
Products carrying the FSC label are independently certified
to assure consumers that they come from forests that are managed
to meet the social, economic and ecological needs
of present and future generations.

Find out more about HarperCollins and the environment at
www.harpercollins.co.uk/green

For Jonathan – the complete man, from A to Z
And for Lila and Oscar – hugs and kisses

HANGMAN

CHAPTER ONE

THE PICTURES HAD photographed her swollen, battered, and bruised—a puffy lip, two black eyes, a bloated and bright face. Decker found it nearly impossible to reconcile those snapshots with the remarkable-looking woman who sat before him. Terry had changed in the fifteen years. She had morphed from a beautiful sixteen-year-old girl to an elegant, stunning woman. Age had turned her face softer and rounder with the fragile exquisiteness of a Victorian cameo. His eyes traveled from the picture to her face. He raised an eyebrow.

"Pretty bad, huh?" she said.

"Your husband certainly did a number on you." If Decker squinted hard enough at her face, he could see remnants of the thrashing—a greenish tinge in certain spots. "And these pictures are around six weeks old?"

"Around." She shifted her position on the sofa. "The body is a wondrous thing. I used to see miracles all the time."

Being a doctor, Terry would know that information firsthand. How she managed to go through medical school and raise a kid while married to that maniac was a testament to her strength of character. It was hard to see her beaten down like this.

"Are you sure you want to go through with this? Meeting him here in L.A.?"

"I put it off about as long as I could," Terry said. "It really doesn't make sense to hide. If Chris wants to find me, he will. And it's not me that I'm worried about. It's Gabe. If he gets pissed off enough, he may take it out on him. I need to get him to adulthood, Lieutenant, before I make any decisions about myself."

"How old is Gabe?"

"Chronologically, he's about four months from fifteen. Psychologically, he's an old man."

Decker nodded. They were sitting in an elegantly furnished hotel suite in Bel Air, California. The color scheme was a soothing tone-on-tone beige. There was a stocked wet bar off the entry and a marble countertop for mixing drinks. Terry had curled up on the divan opposite a stone fireplace. He was sitting on her left in a wing chair with a view of the private patio lushly planted with ferns, palms, and flowers—an oasis for the wounded soul. "What makes you think that you'll last until Gabe turns eighteen?"

Terry gave the question some thought. "You know how cool and calculating my husband is. This was the first time that he ever laid a hand on me."

"So what happened?"

"A misunderstanding." She looked at the ceiling, avoiding Decker's eyes. "He found some medical papers and thought I had an abortion. After I finally got him to stop hitting me and listen, he realized that he had misread the name. The abortion had been for my half sister."

"He confused the name Melissa with Teresa."

"We have the same middle name. I'm Teresa Anne. She's Melissa Anne. It's stupid but my father is stupid. I still use McLaughlin, like my half sister, because it's on all my diplomas and licenses. He misread the names and he snapped. Not that he cares about children, but the thought of my destroying his progeny made him unglued. I'm just thankful there wasn't a gun within reach." She shrugged.

Decker said, "Why did you marry him, Terry?"

"He wanted it official. I could hardly tell him no since he was supporting us. I could have never finished medical school without his money." She paused. "Mostly he leaves Gabe and me alone. He buries himself in work or booze or drugs or other women. Gabe and I are adept at maneuvering around him. Our interactions are neutral and sometimes pleasant. He's generous and knows how to be charming when he wants something. I give him what he wants and all is well."

"Except when it isn't." Decker held up the photographs. "What exactly do you want me to do, Doctor?"

"I've agreed to see him, Lieutenant, not to go back to him. At least, not right away. I don't know how he'll take the news. Since I can't escape him, I want him to agree to a temporary separation. Not a marriage separation—that wouldn't settle well—just for him to agree to give me a little more time to be by myself."

"How much more time?"

"Thirty years, maybe." Terry smiled. "Actually, I'd like to move back to L.A. until Gabe finishes high school. I found a house to rent in Beverly Hills. I not only have to get Chris to agree to the separation, but I want him to pay for everything."

"How are you going to do that?"

"Watch me." She smiled. "He's trained me, but I've also trained him."

"And yet you feel the need for protection."

"You deal with a feral animal, anything can happen. It's good to take precautions."

"There are a lot of younger, stronger men than me, guys that would probably do a better job at guarding you."

"Oh please! Chris could take any of them down. He's more . . . careful around you. He respects you."

"He shot me."

"If he wanted to kill you, he would have."

"I know that," Decker said. "He wanted to prove who was boss." He blew out air. "More important, Chris likes shooting people. In plugging me, he got a two-for-one."

Terry looked down. "He's boasted that you've asked him for favors. Is that true?"

Decker grinned. "I ask him for information now and then. I'll use any sources I can to help me get a solve." He regarded her face—her milky complexion, hazel-gold eyes, and long chestnut-colored hair. There were a few strands of gray peeking through, the only sign that her life had been a pressure cooker. She was wearing a loose, sleeveless maxidress—something silky with geometric patterns in orange, green, and yellow. Her bare feet stuck out of the hemline. "When's he due in town?"

"I told him to come by the hotel on Sunday at noon. I figured that would be a good time for you."

"Where will your son be when all this goes down?"

"He's at UCLA in one of the practice rooms. Gabe has a cell. If he needs me, he'll call. He's very independent. He's had to be." Her eyes were faraway. "He's so good . . . the polar opposite of his father. Given his upbringing, he should have been in rehab at least a couple of times by now. Instead he's hypermature. It worries me. There's so much inside of him that's been left unsaid. He really does deserve better." She brought her hands to her mouth and blinked back tears. "Thanks so much for helping me out."

"Make sure I do something before you thank me." Decker checked his watch. He was due home a half hour ago. "Okay, Terry, I'll come on Sunday. But you've got to do it my way. I've got to think of a plan, how I want this meeting to take place. First and foremost, you have to wait in the bedroom until I've cleared him. Then you can come out."

"That's fine."

"Also, you have to tell Gabe not to come home until you've given him an all-clear signal okay. I don't want him popping into the middle of a sticky situation."

"Sounds reasonable."

The room was silent for a few moments. Then Terry stood up. "Thanks so much, Lieutenant. I hope the payment is okay?"

"It's more than okay. It's very generous."

"One thing about Chris—he's very expensive. If I offered you anything less, he'd be insulted."

DECKER SAID, "LOOK, if you don't want me to do it, I won't."

"Of course I don't want you to do it," Rina answered. "He shot you, for God's sake!"

"So I'll call her up and say no."

"A little late for that, don't you think." Rina got up from the dining-room table and began to clear the brunch dishes—two plates and two glasses. Hannah rarely ate with them anymore. She'd be starting seminary in Israel in the fall. With three months left of high school, she was as good as gone.

Decker followed his wife into the kitchen. "Tell me what you want?" When Rina turned on the faucet, he said, "I'll wash."

"No, I'll wash."

"Better yet, why don't you use the dishwasher?"

"For two plates?"

Counting all the glasses, utensils, and pots and pans, it was a lot more than that, but he didn't argue. "I should have consulted you before I agreed. I'm sorry."

"I'm not looking for apologies. I'm concerned for your safety. He's a hit man, Peter."

"He's not going to kill me."

"Don't you always tell me that domestics are the most dangerous situations because emotions get hot?"

"They do if you're not prepared."

"You don't think your presence will inflame the state of affairs?"

"It could. But if she doesn't have anyone around, it could be worse."

"So let her hire some other body. Why does it have to be you?"

"She thinks I have the best chance of defusing Chris's temper."

" 'Defusing' is the right word," Rina said. "The man's a bomb!" She shook her head and turned on the tap. Silently, she handed Decker the first dish.

"Thanks for brunch. The salmon Benedict was a real treat."

"Every man deserves a last meal."

"That's not funny."

Rina gave him another dish. "If anything happens to you, I'll never forgive you."

"Understood."

"I don't care what happens to her. I'm sure she's a nice woman, but she got herself into this mess." Rina felt anger rising. "Why do you have to get her out of it? Her asking you for help is *chutzpadik*."

"It's like she's imprinted on me." Decker put the dish away and put his hands on her shoulders. The tips of her black hair brushed against her shoulders, giving her face a breezy look. Rina was anything but. Intense, focused, task-oriented . . . those were the appropriate adjectives. "I'll call her and tell her no."

"You can't do that *now*, Peter. He's due to show up in a couple of hours. Plus if you backed out, you'd look like a wuss to Chris and that's the worst thing you can do. You're stuck." She stood on her tiptoes and kissed his nose. He was tall and big, but so was Donatti. "I think I should go with you."

"Not a chance. I'd rather back out."

"He likes me."

"Precisely why he'd be tempted to shoot me. He has a crush on you."

"He doesn't have a crush on me—"

"That's where you're wrong."

"Well, then at least let me ride over with you into the city. You can drop me off to visit my parents."

"I can do that." Decker looked at the kitchen clock. "Leave the mess. I'll get it when I come back."

"You're leaving now?"

"I want to set up the room before he arrives."

"Fine. I'll go get my purse. Call me when you're done and everything's okay."

"I will. I promise."

"Yeah, yeah." Rina brushed him off. "Isn't marriage about promising to love, honor, and obey?"

"Something like that," Decker told her. "And if I must brag, I'd say I've been pretty good with my vows."

"Pretty good at the first two," Rina admitted. "It's the third that seems to trip you up."

CHAPTER TWO

STRAIGHT OUT OF a Diego Rivera painting, he showed up with an enormous bouquet of calla lilies that took up most of his upper body. Size for size, Decker matched every inch of Christopher Donatti's six-foot four-inch frame.

"You shouldn't have." Before Chris could register surprise, Decker took the flowers, tossed them on the marble counter near the door, and then turned him around, pushing him until he was flat against the wall. Decker's movements were hard and rapid. He pressed the nose of his Beretta into the base of the man's skull. "Sorry, Chris, but she just doesn't completely trust you right now."

Donatti said nothing as Decker patted him down. The man was packing good-quality pieces: the tools of his trade. He had an S&W automatic in his belt and a small .22-caliber Glock pistol in a hidden compartment in his boot. With his own standard-issue Beretta still at Donatti's neck, Decker picked his pocket, tossing his wallet on the counter. He told him to take off his shoes, his belt, and his watch.

"My watch?"

"You know how it is, Chris. Everything these days is micro-mini. Who knows what you're hiding inside?"

"It's a Breguet."

"I don't know what that is, but it sounds expensive." Decker relieved him of the gold timepiece. It was incredibly heavy. "I'm not stealing it. I'm just checking it out."

"It's a skeleton watch. Open up the back and you can see the movement."

"Hmm . . . it's not going to explode on me, is it?"

"It's a watch, not a weapon."

"In your hands, everything's a weapon."

Donatti didn't deny that. Decker told him to keep his hands up and his body against the wall. He slowly backed up a few inches to give himself some room. With an eye on his hands at all times, Decker began to remove the ammo from Donatti's guns.

"You can turn around but keep your hands up."

"You're the boss."

He rotated his body until they were face-to-face. Stripped of his weapons, Chris seemed impassive. There was flatness in his eyes; blue without any luminosity. It was impossible to tell if he was angry or amused.

One thing was certain. Chris had seen better days. His skin was patchy and wan and his forehead was a pebble garden of pimples. He'd grown out his hair from the crew cut he had sported a half-dozen years ago; the last time Decker had seen him in the flesh. It was brushed straight back, Count Dracula style, and trimmed to the bottom of his ears. He was still built lanky but with bigger arms than Decker had remembered. He had dressed up for the reunion, wearing a blue polo shirt, charcoal gabardine pants, and Croc boots.

"I'm starting to get a little pain in my arms."

"Lower them slowly."

He did. "Now what?"

"Take a seat. Move slowly. When you move slowly, I move slowly. If you rush me, I shoot first and ask questions later." When Donatti started to sit on the chair, Decker stopped him. "On the sofa, please."

Donatti cooperated and plopped down on the cushions. Decker

tossed him his watch. He caught it one-handed and placed it back on his wrist. "Is she even here?"

"She's in the bedroom."

"That's a start. Is she coming out?"

"When I give her the okay, she'll come out."

"Where's Gabe?"

"He's not here," Decker said.

"That's probably better." Donatti dropped his head in his hands. He resurfaced a moment later. "I suppose your being here makes sense."

"Thanks for your approval."

"Look. I'm not going to do anything."

"Why the armory, then?"

"I always pack. Can I talk to my wife now?"

Decker stood at the marble countertop of the hotel bar, the Beretta still in his hands. "A couple of ground rules. Number one: you stay seated the entire time. Don't approach her in any way, shape, or form. And no sudden movements. It makes me jumpy."

"Agreed."

"Mind your mouth and your manners and I'm sure everything will go swimmingly."

"Yeah . . . sure." His voice was a whisper.

"You look a little pale. You want some water?" He opened the bar. "Something stronger?"

"Whatever."

"Macallan, Chivas, Glenfiddich—"

"Glenfiddich neat." A moment later, Decker handed him a crystal cut glass with a healthy dose of Scotch. Donatti took a delicate sip and then drank a finger's worth. "Thanks. This helps."

"You're welcome." Decker regarded the man. "Your color's coming back."

"I haven't had a drink all day."

"It's only twelve in the afternoon."

"It's almost happy hour New York time. I didn't want her to think I'm weak. But I am." Another sip. "She knows I'm weak. What the fuck!"

"Watch your mouth."

"If my mouth was my only problem, I'd be in good shape." He handed Decker his empty glass.

"Another?" When Donatti shook his head, Decker closed the cabinet. "What happened?"

"What happened is I'm an idiot."

"That's putting it mildly."

"I've always had reading comprehension problems."

"You're missing a crucial element here, Chris. You don't use your wife as a punching bag even if she did have an abortion."

"I didn't punch her, I hit her."

"That's not acceptable either."

Donatti rubbed his forehead. "I know that. I'm just correcting you because I knew I was using an open hand. If I would have punched her, she'd be dead."

"So you were aware that you were beating the shit out of her?"

"It's never happened before, it won't happen again."

"And she should believe you because . . ."

"I can count the number of times I've lost my temper on one hand. Look, I know she's scared, but she doesn't have to be. It was just . . ." As he started to get up from the couch, Decker waved the gun in his face. He sat back down. "Can I see my wife, please?"

"At least, this time you said please." Decker stared at him. "Let me ask you a couple of theoretical questions. What if she doesn't want to talk to you?"

"She wouldn't have agreed to meet with me if she didn't want to talk to me."

"Maybe she just didn't want to tell you over the phone. That would give you time to plan something dangerous and probably stupid."

"Is that what she said?" Donatti looked up.

"How about if I ask the questions?"

"I'm not planning anything. I was an idiot. It won't happen again. Just let me see my wife, okay."

"What if she doesn't want to see you anymore? What if she asks for a divorce?"

"Don't know." Donatti kneaded his hands together. "I haven't thought about it."

"It would piss you off, right?"

"Probably."

"What would you do?"

"Nothing with you around." His eyes finally sparked life. "Decker, she's not going to ask me for a divorce—at least not now—because, first and foremost, I've got enough money to engage her in a very expensive and protracted legal battle for Gabe. It would be easier for her just to wait me out until he's eighteen, and Terry is nothing if not practical. I've got another three and a half years before I have to confront this issue. I'd like to see Terry now."

He was panting. Decker said, "Another Scotch?"

"No." Donatti shook his head. "I'm fine." He took in a deep breath and let it out. "I'm ready when you are."

Decker gave him a hard look. "I'll be watching your every move."

"Fine. I won't move. My butt is glued to the chair. Can we get on with it?"

There was no sense putting off the inevitable. Decker called out her name. He had placed Terry's chair to the side so he had a clear path from the barrel of his gun to Donatti's brain. Not that he really expected a shoot-'em-up, but Decker was a Boy Scout and a cop and always tried to be prepared. Terry had curled her legs under her long dress, but her posture was erect and regal. Again, she was sleeveless, her long tanned arms adorned with several bangles. Her eyes were on Donatti's face even though he was the one who had trouble meeting her gaze.

"You look good," he told her.

"Thank you."

"How do you feel?"

"Okay."

"How's Gabe?"

"He's fine."

Donatti exhaled and looked up at the ceiling. Then he focused on her face. "What can I do for you?"

"Interesting question," she told him. "I'm still trying to figure that out."

He scratched his cheek. "I'll do anything."

"Can I quote you on that?" Before he could answer, she said, "I'm not ready to come back with you."

Donatti folded his hands in his lap. "Okay. Are you ever going to be ready?"

"Possibly . . . probably. Just not now."

"Okay." Chris glanced at Decker. "Could we get a little privacy, please?"

"Not gonna happen." Decker held up the flowers. "He brought you these."

Terry glanced at the lilies. "I'll call for a vase later." To Chris, she said, "They're lovely. Thank you."

Donatti fidgeted. "So . . . when do you think . . . I mean how much longer do you want to stay here?"

"In California or here in the hotel?"

"I was thinking away from me, but yeah, how much longer are you going to be here, too."

"I don't know."

"A month? Two months?"

"Longer than that." She licked her lips.

"That's getting a little on the expensive side. I mean, not that I'm begrudging you the money . . ."

"It is expensive," Terry said. "I want to rent a house. Technically you'd be renting it. I saw one that I'd like. I'm just waiting for you to write the check."

Decker was amazed at how confidently she spoke, daring him to deny her anything.

"Where?" Donatti asked.

"Beverly Hills. Where else?"

As she started to stand, Decker said, "What can I get for you?"

"I'm a little thirsty."

"You sit back down. What would you like?"

"Pellegrino, no ice."

"Not a problem. What about you, Chris?"

"Same."

"Give him a Scotch," Terry said.

"I'm fine, Terry."

"Did I say you weren't?" she snapped back. "Give him a Scotch."

Donatti threw up his hands. Decker said, "No problem just as long as both of you stay put."

"I'm not going anywhere," Donatti said testily. As soon as the Scotch reached his lips, he seemed to calm down. "So . . . tell me about this house that I'm renting."

"It's in an area called the Flats, which is prime real estate here. It's twelve thousand a month—about as minimal as it gets for that neighborhood. It needs a little work, but it's certainly live-in ready. The main reason I chose Beverly Hills was for the school district, which is a good one."

"No problem," Donatti said. "Whatever you want."

Judging by this conversation, it would seem that Terry was in control of the relationship. Maybe she was most of the time. Obviously most didn't equate to all.

Donatti said, "Do I get a key?"

"Of course you get a key. You're renting it."

"And how long do you intend to live out here . . . in the house that I'm renting?"

"Usually leases are for a year."

"That's a long time."

Terry leaned forward. "Chris, I'm not asking for a legal separation just a physical one. After what happened, that's the least you can do."

"I'm not arguing with you, Terry, I'm just trying to get an idea of how long. If you want a year, take a year. It's about you, not me."

She was silent. Then she said, "You'll know where I am, you'll have a key to the house. Come whenever you want. I'm not going anywhere. Fair enough?"

"More than fair." Donatti forced his lips upward. "It's not bad for me to have a hitching post on the West Coast anyway. It's probably a good idea."

"So I did you a favor."

"I wouldn't say that. Twelve thousand a month. How big is this sucker?"

Terry gave him a smile—a cross between humor and flirtatiousness. "It has four bedrooms, Chris. I think we can work something out."

Donatti's smile turned genuine. "Okay." He took a sip of his booze, then laughed. "Okay. If that's what you want . . . fine. Maybe you'll actually miss me when I'm gone."

"You can dream."

"Very funny."

"Are you hungry?" Terry's eyes ran up and down his body. "You lost weight."

"I've been a little anxious."

"How would you know what anxiety feels like?"

Donatti looked at Decker, his eyes unreadable. "The girl's a wit."

"Are you hungry, Chris?" Terry asked him.

"I could eat."

"They have a world-class restaurant." She glanced at a diamond wristwatch sitting among her gold bracelets. "It's open. I wouldn't mind something."

"Great." He started to stand, but then looked at Decker. "Can I get up without you shooting me?"

"Go down to the restaurant and get something for the two of you, Chris. Get a table next door for me. We'll catch up with you in a minute."

Donatti's expression turned sour. "We'll be in a public place, Decker. Nothing's going to happen. How about a little privacy?"

"I'll be sitting at another table," Decker said. "Whisper if you don't want me to hear. Go ahead. We'll meet you there."

Donatti rolled his eyes. "Do I get my steel back?"

"Eventually," Decker said.

"You can keep the ammo, just give me the pieces."

"Eventually."

"What do you think I'm going to do? Coldcock you?"

"I wasn't even thinking along those lines, but now that you mention it, you are unpredictable."

He turned to Terry. "Do you care if I pack?"

"It's up to him," Terry said.

"They're worthless without ammo." When Decker didn't reply, Chris said, "C'mon. It would show good faith. All I'm asking for is what's mine."

"I hear you, Chris." Decker opened the door. "But you can't always get what you want."

The two men faced off. Then Donatti shrugged. "Whatever." He swaggered through the door without looking back.

Decker shook his head. "That's one icy dude." He regarded Terry. "You handled him very well."

"I hope so. At the very least, it'll buy me some time to think."

Decker noticed she was shaking. "Are you all right, Terry?"

"Yeah, I'm okay. Just a little . . ." Perspiration dripped from her forehead. She wiped her face with a tissue. "You know what they say, Lieutenant." Nervous laughter. "Never let them see you sweat."

CHAPTER THREE

AS LONG AS Decker was in the city—about twenty miles from his front door—Rina made reservations to meet for dinner at one of the many kosher restaurants along Pico Boulevard. They left her parents' house at six, and a half hour later, they were in a booth, sipping glasses of Côtes du Rhône. Although Peter wasn't a big talker, tonight he seemed unusually subdued, so Rina was happy to carry on the bulk of the conversation. Maybe Peter was hungry. She figured he'd join in when the mood hit. But even after polishing off his rib steak, fries, and salad, he remained quiet.

"What's going on inside that cranium of yours?" Rina finally asked.

"Nothing."

"I don't believe you."

"See, that's where you females mess up. Whenever we men don't talk, you ascribe it to some deep inner meditation we're having with ourselves. In my case, I was thinking about dessert—whether it was worth the calories."

"If you'd like, we can split something."

"Which means I eat ninety percent."

"How about we forgo the dessert and just have some coffee. You look a little beat."

"Do I?" Decker stroked his red-and-gray mustache as if he was thinking of something profound. While his facial hair still retained some of its youthful, fiery color, his head hair was more white than orange, but there was still plenty of it.

He smiled at his wife. Rina had changed to a deep purple satin dress that she kept in her mother's closet. Although she was way too religious to ever show cleavage, the neckline did accentuate her lovely throat. He had given her a pair of two-carat diamond studs for her forty-fifth birthday and she wore them every chance she got. He loved to see her in expensive things, even though with his paycheck, that didn't happen very often. "I guess I am a little tired."

"Then let's just go home."

"No, no. I could use a cup of coffee."

"Okay." Rina touched his hands. "You're not just tired, you're bothered. What happened this afternoon?"

"I told you. Everything went smoothly."

"And yet you remain perplexed."

Decker chose his words. "When she talked to him . . . she appeared confident . . . clearly in control."

"Maybe she was with you around."

"I'm sure there was some of that. And he was contrite, so she had a certain amount of free rein. I don't know, Rina. She was bossy almost. When they had lunch, she did most of the talking."

"You could hear them?"

"I could see them. She clearly dominated their conversation."

"Maybe when she gets nervous, she talks."

"Could be. Before we met him for lunch, we spoke a few minutes. All of a sudden she started shaking and broke out in a cold sweat."

"So there you go."

"But there was something else, Rina. If I didn't know any of the backstories, I would have sworn she was acting flirtatious at lunch—downright sexy. Something was strange."

"What's so strange? She likes him."

"He beat her up six weeks ago."

"She knows what he is and there's still something about him that she finds attractive. She makes poor choices. That's what got her into the situation to begin with. No one told her that she had to visit him in jail and have sex with him without birth control."

"She's not a stupid girl, Rina. She's a conscientious mother and she's an emergency care physician."

"Like all of us, she has positive aspects and some blind spots. In Terry's case, her weaknesses are harmful." She leaned forward. "But like I said this morning, Peter, this isn't our problem. You were hired help. She paid you money and you did your job. How about letting go?"

"You're right." Decker sat up and kissed her hand. "We're out to dinner and you deserve a noncomatose husband."

"How about some coffee now?"

"Coffee would be great!" Decker grinned. "I'd even go for dessert."

"How about the peach pie?"

"Peach pie it is. Dare we order it with vanilla ice cream or whatever frozen concoction they make up to simulate the real deal?"

Rina smiled. "Sure, let's go crazy."

THE CELL PHONE went off just as the car had crested the 405 freeway and began to dip into the San Fernando Valley. Mountains on either side made reception spotty. Since Decker was driving, Rina took the phone from his coat pocket.

"If it's Hannah, tell her we'll be home in about twenty minutes."

"It's not Hannah. I don't recognize the number." She depressed the on button. "Hello?"

There was silence on the other side. For a moment Rina thought she lost the party, but then she saw that the phone hadn't disconnected.

"Hello?" she tried again. "Can I help you?"

"Who is it?" Decker asked. When she shrugged, he said, "Just hang up."

"Sorry." The voice was male. He cleared his throat. "I'm looking for Lieutenant Decker."

"This is his cell phone. Who am I talking to?"

"Gabe Whitman."

It took all of Rina's effort not to gasp. "Is everything all right?"

"Who are you talking to?" Decker asked.

"No," Gabe said over the phone. "I mean I don't know."

"Who *is* it, Rina?" Decker said.

"Gabe Whitman."

"Oh Lord! Tell him to hold on."

"He'll be right with you," Rina said.

"Thank you."

Decker maneuvered the car onto the freeway shoulder, turned on his hazard lights, and took the cell. "This is Lieutenant Decker."

"I'm sorry to bother you."

"No bother. What's going on?"

"I can't find my mom. She's not here and she's not answering her cell. My dad isn't answering his cell phone either."

"Okay." Decker's brain was whirling a mile a minute. "How long has it been since you've spoken to your mom?"

"I came back to the hotel around six-thirty, seven. We were supposed to go to dinner. She wasn't here. Her car isn't here, her purse isn't here, but she didn't leave any note or anything. That's not like her."

Decker's stomach dropped. His watch said it was almost nine. "When was the last time you spoke to her, Gabe?"

"Around four. You were already gone. Mom said that everything went well. She sounded fine. She said she wanted to run some errands and she'd be back around six. I don't know if I'm overreacting, but with Chris, I just don't know."

"Where are you now?"

"I'm at the hotel?"

"In the room?"

"Yes, sir."

"Okay. Gabe, I'm turning around and I'll be there in about a half hour. Leave the room and wait for me in the lobby. I want you in a public place, okay?"

"Okay." A pause. "The room's okay . . . I mean like nothing was disturbed or anything."

"That doesn't mean that your dad can't suddenly show up. It wouldn't be good for the two of you to be alone."

"That's true." A pause. "Thanks."

"No thanks necessary. Just walk out that door and don't look back."

Fifteen minutes later, Decker pulled his Porsche into the valet lot. The parking attendants were different from the ones who had been here in the afternoon. When they asked how long he'd be staying, Decker told them that he didn't know.

The resort hotel was fifteen acres of lush plants and tropical foliage set at the foothills in Bel Air. The evening air was sweet from night-blooming jasmine with a hint of gardenia. Broad-leaf palms, ferns, and flowering bushes lined stone walkways and draped over the edges of a man-made lagoon populated with ducks and swans. Decker and Rina crossed over a bridge, glancing at the lake as the birds glided by.

Decker faced her. "Why don't you take the car and go home."

"Hannah's at a friend's house. I can wait."

"I don't know if I want you around in case Chris pops in. I've got a bad feeling about this."

"How about if I wait in the lobby?"

"Would you mind? It may take a while. If I don't find her right away, I'm going to have to do a search of the hotel."

"It's not a problem unless they kick me out." She paused. "What are you going to do with Gabe? You don't know what's going on. You certainly can't let him stay here by himself even if he was of age."

Neither of them spoke.

Rina said, "He can stay with us."

"I don't think that's a good idea."

"I don't think you have any choice."

"He has a grandfather living in the Valley."

"Then contact him in the morning. One night with us won't make a difference."

"You really are Earth Mother."

"That's me," Rina said. "Give me your tired, your poor, your huddled masses yearning to breathe free, et cetera, et cetera. Emma and I had a lot more in common than just our last names."

ALTHOUGH THE ACTUAL hotel was a series of connected low-profile, pink stucco bungalows topped with a Mediterranean red-tiled roof, the lobby was a stand-alone building. Through the window, Decker could see the registration desk with a uniformed woman flipping through files, an empty concierge desk, and a suite of traditional furniture facing a stone fireplace. One of the beige chairs was taken up by a lanky adolescent—*The Thinker* done by Giacometti. He and Rina went inside and the thin kid looked up, then stood up. Decker tried out a reassuring smile. "Gabe?"

He nodded. Good-looking kid—an aquiline nose, strong chin, a mop of dirty blond hair, and gem-quality emerald eyes that sat behind a pair of frameless glasses. Not much bulk, but he had the same kind of wiry muscle that his dad had as a teenager. He appeared to be grazing the six-foot mark.

Decker held out his hand and the boy shook it. "How are you doing?" The kid shrugged helplessly. "This is my wife. She's going to wait here for me . . . or for us. Still haven't heard from anyone?"

"No, sir." He looked at Rina as much as he did at Decker. "I'm sorry to drag you down here. It's probably nothing."

"Whatever it is, it's not a problem. Let's take a walk back to the room."

The woman at the registration desk looked up. "Is everything all right. Mr. Whitman?"

"Uh, yeah." Gabe forced a smile. "Fine."

"Are you sure?"

Gabe nodded quickly. Decker turned to Rina. "See you in a few."

"Take your time."

Decker and his charge went outside into the cool misty air, neither of them speaking as they walked. The pathways looked different at night than they had in the daytime. With the artificial colored lighting slipped between the plantings, the entire complex looked surreal, like a movie set. Gabe twisted and turned from one garden to another until they came to the bungalow he shared with his mother. He opened the door, flipped on the light switch, and the two of them stepped inside.

"Just like I left it," Gabe said.

And not too different from when Decker had left. The flowers that Chris had given Terry had been put into a vase and sat on the sofa table. Donatti's Scotch glass lay in the sink of the bar. The trash had been cleared and the living-room sofa had been folded out into a bed, a room service breakfast menu and a few chocolates left on a silver tray. Water on the coffee table and music coming from a Bose stereo system, the station set on classical music.

"You sleep here?"

Gabe nodded.

Decker walked into the bedroom. Terry's bed had also been prepared. "Were the beds turned down when you arrived here at around six?"

"No, sir, they came in later. Around eight." A pause. "I probably shouldn't have let them in, huh."

"It doesn't matter, Gabe." Decker studied the room. There were a lot of clothes in the closet and a small safe. Decker asked the boy if he knew the combination number.

"Uh, not to this one. But I know the code she usually uses."

"Could you try to open it?"

"Sure."

Gabe punched in a set of numbers. It took him a couple of tries, but eventually the door opened. It was loaded with cash and jewelry. Decker said, "Do you have anything to transport the valuables in?"

"Why?"

"If your mom doesn't come back, you can't stay here alone."

"I'll be all right."

"I'm sure you can take care of yourself, but I'm a cop and you're a minor. I'd be in violation of the law if I let you stay here alone. Plus, under the circumstances, I wouldn't want you alone even if you were eighteen."

"Where are you going to take me?"

"You've got a choice." Decker rubbed his temples. "I know you have a grandfather and an aunt that live in L.A. Would you feel comfortable calling either of them up? I'll be happy to take you over there."

"Is that my only choice?"

"You could spend the night at my house and hopefully things will work out in the morning."

"That would be my first choice. I'd way prefer that to my grandfather. My aunt is nice, but she's a little ditzy. She's not much older than I am."

"How old is Melissa?"

"Twenty-one . . . a very *young* twenty-one."

"All right. So this is what we'll do. You go home with my wife. I'm going to stick around here for a while and try to figure out what's going on."

"Why can't I stay here with you while you try to figure it out?"

"Because it may take a long time. It's best if you go home with my wife and let me do my job. I'll catch you in the morning. If your mom comes home, I'll call you right away. And if you happen to hear from either your mother or father, you call me right away, so I'm not spinning my wheels. Fair enough?"

The boy nodded. "Thank you, sir. I really appreciate it."

"No problem." Decker pulled out a notepad. "I have your mom's number. I'll need your dad's number and your cell number."

Gabe rattled off a series of numbers. "You know that my dad changes phones all the time. A number might be working one day and disconnected the next."

"When was the last time you spoke to your dad?"

"Let me think. Chris called me Saturday morning . . . around eleven. He'd just landed. He told me he was at the airport and was meeting with Mom tomorrow."

"And you said?"

"I don't really remember. Something like . . . cool. Then he asked me how she was and I said she was fine. It was like a two-minute conversation . . . which is pretty typical for us." Gabe bit his lip. "Chris doesn't really like me. I'm an annoyance, something that stands between him and Mom. He rarely talks to me unless it's about my music or my mom. But he's forced to deal with me because I'm what links him and Mom together. It's really messed up."

"Your father's messed up. You wouldn't happen to know his flight number, would you?"

Gabe shook his head.

"Do you know what airlines he usually chooses?"

"When he doesn't fly privately, he takes American first class coast to coast. He likes to stretch out."

"If he left the L.A. area, where do you think he'd go?"

"He could go home. Or he could go to Nevada and camp out there for a while."

"He owns brothels in Elko, doesn't he?" When the boy blushed, Decker said, "Would you know the name of his places?"

"One's the Pleasure Dome." His face was bright red. "The Pleasure Palace . . . he has like three or four places with the word 'pleasure' in them."

"Have you tried calling the places?"

The boy shook his head. "I don't have the numbers. They might be listed. I could call up information if you want."

"No, I can take it from here. Why don't you pack a few things, take out the money and the jewelry from the safe, and then I'll walk you back to the lobby."

"I'm so sorry to be a pain. I feel like a jerk."

"It's no problem." He put his arm around the boy's shoulders. At first the kid stiffened, but then his shoulders relaxed under the weight of Decker's arm. "And don't be too concerned. It'll probably work out."

"Everything works out. Sometimes it works out good. And sometimes it works out bad. It's the bad that concerns me."

CHAPTER FOUR

THE CAR WAS quiet on the way home, the boy staring out at the passenger window, looking like a forlorn puppy. Rina didn't even bother to try to engage him. It took all of her energy to drive Peter's Porsche. He had souped up the engine to God-only-knows-how-many horsepower and the clutch required muscle. Thank goodness most of the ride was on an empty freeway and in one gear.

As soon as she parked in the driveway, the kid leaped out of the car like a caged cat finally set free. His baggage was a school knapsack that he carried by one strap, a laptop, and a small duffel. He was tall for his age, with spindly legs. His pants had a hard time staying on his nonexistent hips.

Rina put the key in the front door lock. "Lieutenant Decker and I have four children, but only our daughter still lives at home. She's seventeen." She opened the front door and yelled out a hello. From behind the bedroom door, Hannah answered back.

"We've got company," Rina said. "Could you come out a moment?"

"Now?"

"It's okay." Gabe cringed.

Rina tried to look reassuring as Hannah came storming out in her pajamas and robe. The two teens took each other in with a quick sweep of the eye. Rina said, "Hannah, this is Gabe Whitman. He's going to be staying with us tonight. Could you show him to your brothers' room and make up the bed?"

"I can do it," Gabe said, pink-cheeked.

"So can Hannah," Rina said.

"I'll do it." Hannah shrugged. "You need anything to eat? I was gonna get myself some cherries. You want to look around the fridge?"

"Uh . . . sure." Gabe followed her into the kitchen and that was that.

Sometimes peer counseling was far superior to the best mothering.

AFTER HANNAH WASHED the cherries, she gave him a handful in a paper bowl. "These are really good. I think my mom got them at the farmers' market."

"Produce is really good out here."

"Out here? Where are you from?"

"New York."

"The city?"

"The burbs." He studied his fruit. "Do you know New York?"

"I have lots of friends out there." She bit into a cherry and spit out the pit. "And my brother goes to Einstein Med School."

Gabe said, "My mom worked at Mount Sinai for a while. She's an ER doc."

"Are you interested in medicine?"

"Not a chance." He finally picked up a cherry and ate it. "You know I'm perfectly capable of putting on my own sheets."

"Fine with me. Can I ask why you're here?"

"My mom's gone . . . like missing. I think your dad is looking for her. He said it was illegal for me to stay in a hotel by myself, so he offered to take me in tonight."

"That sounds like my dad."

"He's a nice guy?"

"He's a very nice guy," Hannah said. "He comes across as very cop, but he has a heart of mush. My mother is even mushier. They're both pushovers. You want something to drink?"

"No, thanks. I should probably get to bed." He put the fruit down on the counter. "Thanks for the cherries. I don't think I'm so hungry."

"Are you going to be able to sleep?"

"Probably not."

"I'll show you how to work the TV. It's a little funky because it's from the Stone Age. My brothers have been out of the house for a while. What grade are you in?"

"I was in tenth. My mom and I just recently moved out here, so I haven't been going to school."

"So you're fifteen?"

"Four months shy. A lot of people think I'm older 'cause I'm tall."

"Yeah, same with me. But I don't mind." She hopped off the counter. "Follow me. And try not to worry too much about the situation. My dad may be a mush ball with me, but he's really tough when it comes to police work. Whatever it is, he'll get to the bottom of it."

"That's good." Gabe smiled weakly. "I just hope that when he gets there, the bottom doesn't drop out."

DECKER'S FIRST CALL was to his favorite detective, Sergeant Marge Dunn. "I've got a situation here. I could use some help."

"What's going on?" In the next breath, she said, "Is it something to do with Terry McLaughlin?"

"She's missing." After he explained the state of affairs, Decker said, "She has a sister and a father in town. I've already called her sister, Melissa—apprised her of the situation. She hasn't heard from Terry in a few days. She also told me not to bother with the father. The two of them are barely civil to each other."

"Did she sound worried?"

"Yes, she did. She told me that Terry would never leave Gabe without a good reason. I told her I'd keep her updated. As far as finding Donatti, I've called up all the numbers I have for him and left messages. That's been a dead end. He owns some brothels in Nevada. I got hold of a receptionist who told me that Chris wasn't due in until tomorrow afternoon."

"That means nothing."

"Of course. I've phoned Elko PD and have asked them to tell me when he comes into town."

"Are they cooperating?"

"Hard to tell. The brothels make a slew of money, so it could be that the department wouldn't be anxious to give up one of their own. I'm trying to retrace Donatti's steps, starting with when he came into L.A. I'm checking commercial airlines, leasing companies, and jet card companies. And rental car companies. He has to be driving something, but I haven't had any luck with that."

"Have you done a search of the hotel?"

"Not yet. If it shakes out that way, I'll call West L.A. It's their district. Right now, I'd like to handle it myself . . . with a little help."

"I'm on my way."

"I came back to the hotel from dinner . . . turned around as soon as the kid called. I don't have any of my kits or evidence bags with me."

"Is something amiss?"

"No, it seems to be pretty much as I left it. There's a drinking glass I'd like to bag."

"I'll bring the stuff down with me."

"I can think of only two reasons why Terry would leave without notifying her kid. Something scared her off or she had a gun to her head. She took her purse, her keys, and her car, but she left behind a wad of money and her jewelry."

"Oy, that doesn't look too good. Didn't you say that the meeting between them went well?"

"I thought it did. But Donatti is unpredictable." He gave Marge the address. "It'll take you about forty minutes without bad traffic."

"Where's the boy?"

"He's with Rina. I'm keeping him at our house for the night."

There was a pause. "Aren't you getting a little overinvolved?"

"You should talk," Decker snapped back. "If you hadn't adopted Vega after that Father Jupiter debacle, she would have been declared a ward of the state and placed into the state foster care program. She would have probably become a delinquent, gotten pregnant ten times, been hooked on drugs, and turned into a prostitute. Instead, you got overinvolved and now Vega is almost done with her dissertation for a PhD in astrophysics. So you tell me if I'm wrong to get a little overinvolved."

There was a long pause over the line. Then Marge said, "Hard day, Pete?"

"A little challenging."

"I'll see you soon."

"Sooner is better than later."

MARGE ARRIVED WITH the kits, the bags, and the gloves. She had put on a little weight in the last year but almost all of it was muscle. At five ten, she was a lean one-sixty and had added workouts in the gym as part of her daily routine. Her face had lines across her forehead and faint spiderwebs crisscrossing at the corners of her brown eyes. Her blonde hair—formerly light brown—was tied back in a ponytail and she had pearl studs in each earlobe. She had dressed in gray slacks and a black sweater, rubber-soled shoes on her feet.

"Thanks for showing up," Decker said.

"Someone has to take you home," Marge told him.

It took the two of them over three hours to conduct a preliminary search of the hotel, first going to the bar and the restaurant, then room to room, and finally checking the spa, the storage areas, and the empty banquet hall. Another hour was spent searching Terry's room. When they had finished bagging whatever paltry evidence there was to be taken, the clock had struck one and Marge saw that Decker was still agitated. The lieutenant was usually the consummate professional. He said, "What am I going to tell that kid?"

"He's probably asleep."

"Would you be able to sleep if you were him?"

"No." A few moments passed. "If he's up, this is what you're going to tell him. You're going to tell him that you've done everything you could do on a Sunday night. Tomorrow you'll call the phone company to see if his mother's cell has been used, you'll call the credit card company and see if there has been any activity, and you'll call her bank to see if there's been any suspicious withdrawals." Marge smiled. "More like you'll assign someone to do it because you're a busy guy and this isn't even your jurisdiction. Have you called in to West L.A. yet?"

"I did indeed. I put in a need-to-locate on Terry's car shortly before you arrived. It's a 2009 Mercedes E550. Somebody has to come back and interview all the personnel. I've only talked to the desk clerk and she doesn't know a thing."

"It's a skeleton crew right now. It'll keep until the morning."

"The desk sergeant told me that someone from West L.A. Missing Persons will call me. Whoever catches the call has to know who they're dealing with."

"So everything's under control. Let's go."

"I'm too worked up to face the kid right now."

"You'll be okay by the time we get back to the Valley. If not, I'll buy you a cup of hot cocoa at one of the twenty-four/seven convenience stores."

Decker smiled. "Hot cocoa?"

"Once a mother, always a mother. Vega may be brilliant, but I still look out for her." Marge patted his shoulder. "We know better than anyone else on the planet that the smartest people can do the dumbest things."

CHAPTER FIVE

AT TWO IN the morning, the house was dark and quiet, just the way it should be. Decker closed the front door as softly as possible, waiting for the kid to emerge out of his sons' room. When he didn't, he tiptoed into his bedroom, undressed, and slid under the covers. Rina rolled over and draped an arm across his back.

"Everything okay?"

"Nothing to report, one way or the other."

Rina was quiet, but then she sighed. "You're upset. I'm sorry."

"Yeah, I'm a little upset. I should have talked her out of the meeting."

"You'd only be postponing the inevitable." Rina sat up. "From what you've told me over dinner, she wasn't planning to leave him permanently."

"You're right, but the fact still remains that she's missing." He rolled over and faced her. "Rina, what am I going to tell the kid?"

"That you're doing all you can and you'll keep him posted. The bigger issue is what we *do* with him. He certainly can stay here for a few days, but if it should drag on longer, we've got a decision to make."

"Well, he has a grandfather living in L.A., but he doesn't like the man. Terry didn't like him. He said his aunt is nice but ditzy."

"How old is she now?"

"Around twenty-one . . . a very young twenty-one is what Gabe told me."

"Ugh, that's way too young to be handling a teenager and probably a troubled one at that. Does she work? Does she go to school?"

"I don't know anything about her except that she recently had an abortion." Decker exhaled. "I'll deal with it in the morning. Let's get some sleep."

"Sounds good." They both slipped under the covers. Peter was out within ten minutes, but Rina lay awake for a long time, haunted by images of a lost, lonely boy.

UP BY SIX, but Rina wasn't the first one out of bed. Gabe was sitting on the living-room couch in the near dark, his head back, his eyes closed behind his rimless glasses, his bags at his feet. He wore a black T-shirt, jeans, and giant sneakers that looked to be around a size twelve.

"Good morning," Rina said softly.

The kid's head snapped up. "Oh." He rubbed his eyes. "Hi."

"Going somewhere?" When he shrugged, Rina said, "Would you like some breakfast?"

"I'm not too hungry . . . but thanks."

"How about some hot chocolate or coffee?"

"If you're making coffee anyway, that would be good."

"Come keep me company in the kitchen."

Reluctantly, the boy got up and followed her. He squinted when she turned on the overhead light, so she immediately turned it off and settled for the under-the-cabinet lighting.

"Sorry." Gabe sat down at the kitchen table. "I'm like a bat in the morning."

"It's too early for a lot of light anyway," Rina told him. "Are you sure you're not hungry? It might be a good idea to eat and keep your strength up." He certainly didn't look as if he had a lot of reserves to draw upon.

A sick smile. "Yeah, okay."

"How about some toast?"

"Okay." A pause. "Thanks for putting me up for the night."

"Were you comfortable?"

"Yes, thanks."

"I'm sorry, Gabe. If you need anything, please let me know."

"So your husband didn't . . . I mean, my mother is still missing?"

"So far as I know, yes." She put two pieces of bread in the toaster. "Lieutenant Decker should be getting up soon. You can ask him whatever you want."

The boy just nodded. If there was a personification of the word "miserable," Rina was looking at it. The toast popped up and she placed the plate in front of him, along with jam, butter, and a cup of hot coffee. "Cream or sugar?"

"Please."

"Here you go."

"Thanks." The boy nibbled at the dry bread. "Do you know where I'm going?"

"Lieutenant Decker told me that you have an aunt and a grandfather in L.A."

He nodded. "So he's gonna call them up or . . ."

"I don't know the procedure. Let me peek in and see if he's up." Rina went into the bedroom just as Decker finished his shower. "Coffee's ready."

"I'll be out in a sec."

"Good. The poor kid's wondering where he's going to stay until things get resolved."

"If they get resolved. He's up already?"

"He's up, packed, and looking wholly dejected. Do you blame him?"

"It's a rotten deal." He put on his pants and shoes.

Rina paused. "Maybe we should put him up for another couple of days . . . just until he gets his bearings."

"And then what?" Decker said. "I feel for him, but he's not our problem, Rina."

"I didn't say he was."

"I know you. You're softhearted. I already got overinvolved with Terry and look where it got me . . . where it got her . . . Lord only knows where it got her. Where's the kid?"

"In the kitchen."

Decker buttoned his shirt. "I'll deal with him and you wake up our daughter." He laughed as he knotted his tie. "I've got the easier assignment."

THE BOY WAS staring at the tabletop. Decker said, "Hey, Gabe."

He looked up. "Hi."

Decker placed a hand on the kid's shoulder. "We haven't found your mother yet."

A forced smile that hid a quivering lip. "What about Chris?"

"We're working on the both of them. We've still got lots to do and lots of options. So the only thing I can say is sit tight and we'll keep you posted."

He blinked several times. "Sure."

"We've got a couple of things to talk about right now, though. I know your father's an only child and an orphan. And we know about your mom's relatives. Before we explore that, do you have anyone in New York that you want me to get hold of?"

"Like relatives?"

"Relatives, friends, buddies . . ."

"I have friends, but no one I'd want to stay with. At least not right now."

"Okay, so that leaves us with your mom's relatives."

"I barely know my grandfather. My mother and he didn't get along."

"So we're down to your very young aunt."

"I guess I could stay with her." He looked down. "What are my options if I don't go with my aunt?"

"On a long-term basis, you'd become a ward of the state—that's foster care. You don't want that." Decker poured himself a cup of coffee. "Tell me why you don't want to live with your aunt."

"She has no money to support me. She's been living off of what my mom gives her. She parties all the time. She smokes pot and her place is a sty. I know she'd let me stay with her. And I actually like her. But she's not very responsible." He dropped his head into his hand. "This really sucks in a life that already sucked!"

Decker sat down. "I'm sorry, Gabe."

"That's . . ." He took off his glasses and wiped them with a napkin. "I'll be okay. Thanks for putting me up." He drummed his fingers across the kitchen table. "You know, I have my own money. I have savings and trust funds and stuff. Do you think a judge would let me live alone?"

"Not at fourteen."

He looked at Decker. His voice was melancholy. "Could I just stay here for another couple of days until things get sorted out? I'm really quiet. I don't eat much and I promise I won't get in your way. I'll be happy to pay you—"

"Stop, stop." The kid was breaking his heart. "Of course you can stay here for a few days. I've already talked to Mrs. Decker. She agrees with me. It was actually her idea."

Gabe closed his eyes and opened them. "Thanks so much. I really appreciate it. I'm sorry to be such a pain."

"You're not a pain and there's no need to apologize. You're in a bind right now. I feel for you. We'll take it one step at a time."

At that moment, Rina walked in with Hannah. Gabe got up. "Excuse me."

As soon as he was out of the kitchen, Decker raised his eyebrows. "He asked to stay here a few more days."

Rina looked at Hannah. The young girl shrugged. "It's fine with me as long as he's not a psycho or anything like that."

Decker blew out air and whispered, "He doesn't appear to be a psycho. But his father is a psycho and I really don't know a thing about him."

"He doesn't want to live with his relatives?" Rina asked.

"Apparently not," Decker said.

"How many days are we talking about?" Hannah asked.

"I'm hoping to locate one of his parents soon."

"So let him stay." Hannah smiled. "Even if he is a psycho, there isn't a lot here to steal."

Decker said, "A couple of days won't make that much of a difference. If it drags on longer than that, we'll reevaluate."

Rina said, "He should be in school."

"Not our school," Hannah said.

"Why not?" Decker said. "It's filled with misfits anyway."

"It's an Orthodox day school, Abba, and I don't think he's Jewish."

"Neither are half the kids in the school."

"That's not true," Hannah said. "Look, I can take him to school. He's real cute and I'm sure all the girls will fall madly in love with him. Just don't blame me if the rabbis have a fit."

Rina said. "Sitting around here is only going to make him feel worse." She turned to Hannah. "Go in and tell him that you're taking him to your school."

"You want *me* to tell him?"

"Yes, I do," Rina ordered.

"I have choir practice tonight. I won't get home until late."

"Take him with you," Decker said. "I seem to recall that he plays the piano. Maybe he can accompany you guys."

"Right!" Hannah snorted and went in to fetch Gabe from her brothers' bedroom.

When she was gone, Decker said, "I hope this doesn't come back to bite us."

"It might," Rina said. "But even God judges us for our present actions only and not on what He knows we'll do in the future. How can we mortals do anything less?"

"That's a nice little speech, but we mortals have to use the past to judge the future because we're not God." He shook his head. "What kind of a teenager doesn't want to live with his young irresponsible aunt who parties and dopes?"

"A kid too mature for his age."

HE SAT ON one of the twin beds, his backpack at his feet, staring at nothing while other people talked about his fate. A position he had been in umpteen times before. The room was filled with athletic trophies, paperback books, comic books, CDs, and DVDs, mostly from the nineties. There were posters of Michael Jordan and Michael Jackson, one of Kobe Bryant when he was about seventeen years old. The CDs included Green Day, Soundgarden, and Pearl Jam.

An utterly normal room in an utterly normal house with an utterly normal family.

What he would give to live an utterly normal life.

He was tired of dealing with a psycho for a father, a totally unpredictable maniac with a violent temper. He was sick of having a psychologically beaten-down mother—recently a physically beaten mother. He feared his dad, he loved his mom, but he was sick to death of both of them. And although he was sincerely passionate about his music and the piano, he detested growing up a prodigy. It drove him to do more and more and more and more.

All he wanted was to be fucking normal. Was that so hard of a wish to grant?

He heard the knock on the door and wiped his eyes. He looked in the mirror and noticed they were red-rimmed. Fucking-A great! The girl probably thought he was a real wuss.

Mom, where the fuck are you? Chris, what the fuck did you do with Mom?

He answered the door. "Hey."

"Hey." She smiled. "You know if you want to hole up here for a few days, you're more than welcome."

"Yeah, your dad already told me that. Thanks. I really mean

that." He bit his lower lip. "I'm sure things will sort out by then. Tell your parents I won't be any trouble."

"I'm enough trouble for the both of us." She smiled. "Hate to tell you this, bud, but my mom wants you to go to school with me."

"*School?*"

"Don't shoot the messenger."

"Right." He laughed. What else was there to do? "Sure. Why not?"

"It's a religious school."

"What religion?"

"Jewish."

"I'm Catholic."

"It's fine. You won't have to do anything against your beliefs."

"I have no beliefs except in the innate evil of human beings." He looked at her. "Except your parents."

"If it's too much for you to handle, I can probably talk my mom out of it."

"No, it's okay." A pause. "I'll deal. Do I need a notebook or something?"

"I'll get you an extra one. You're in tenth grade, you said?"

"I was."

"Algebra two or pre-calc?"

"Pre-calc."

"I'll take care of it. I also heard you play the piano."

His eyes showed a twinkle of animation. "Do you have a piano?"

"My school does. Are you good?"

For the first time, Hannah saw a genuine smile. He said, "I can play."

"Then maybe you can stay after school and accompany our choir. We're terrible. We could use some sort of a lift."

"I probably can help you out there."

"C'mon." She motioned him forward. "I'll guide you through it. You may not know it, Gabe, but you're looking at a BMOC."

CHAPTER SIX

BY THE TIME Decker broke for lunch, he had done enough phone work and legwork to ascertain that there had been no activity on Terry McLaughlin's cell since four o'clock yesterday afternoon. Her major credit cards hadn't been used other than daily charges put through by the hotel, and even those had been earlier in the day. Her name hadn't appeared on any American or United flight manifest—either domestic or international—but Decker certainly hadn't the means and the wherewithal to check every single airline and every single local airport. If the woman had wanted to sneak out, she could have done it in a thousand ways. More to the point, her car hadn't been spotted. All he could do was wait for news and hope it wasn't bad news.

Donatti wasn't picking up his cell, either. According to Gabe, his father switched cells, often using throwaways. It could be that the number that Decker was given wasn't the cell phone he was currently using. Decker did discover that Donatti had arrived on Saturday morning in LAX via Virgin America Airlines, the day before his meeting with his estranged wife. There was no record of his picking up any rental car. As far as locating where he had stayed before he had met with Terry, Decker started calling hotels, beginning on the west with the Ritz-Carlton in the Marina and slowly working his way eastward ho. When he was about to call the Century Plaza, there was a knock on his office door. He put down the phone. "Come in."

Dressed in a wheat-colored shirt, brown pants, and rubber-soled flats, Marge entered his office. Her brown eyes were wide and her face was ashen. Decker felt his heart sink. "What?"

"A foreman at a construction site just found a homicide victim—a young woman hanging from the rafters—"

"Good Lord!" Decker felt sick. "*Hanging?*"

"From cable wire . . . at least that's what I've been told."

"Any identification?"

"Not so far. The uniforms are at the scene, cordoning off the area."

"Has any one cut her down?"

"No. The foreman didn't touch her. He called 911 and the uniforms came quickly enough to preserve the scene. The coroner's office has been notified."

Decker looked at his watch. "It's two in the afternoon. And the foreman just discovered the body? How long had he been at the site?"

"I don't know, Pete."

"What's the location?" When Marge told him the address, Decker's heart started racing. His brain flashed to Terry's face with a noose around her neck. "That's not far from where Cheryl Diggs was murdered."

"I realize that. That's why I'm telling you this."

Way back when, when Chris Donatti né Chris Whitman had been a senior in high school, Cheryl Diggs had been his teen girlfriend. On the night of the senior prom, Donatti had been accused of murdering her, and soon after, he went to jail because of some noble but misguided notion that he was saving Terry McLaughlin from the ordeal of testifying at his trial. It turned out that Chris had been innocent, probably the only crime that he was ever innocent of.

Marge said, "I'm on my way with Oliver. Should I keep you updated or do you want to come?"

"I'm coming." He picked up his jacket, his cell phone, and his camera. "I'll take a separate car and meet you two there."

"Anything I should be looking for?"

"Do you know what Terry McLaughlin looks like?"

"Last time I saw her, she was sixteen. A beautiful girl, as I recall."

"She's matured, but she's still beautiful." Decker slammed his fist into the palm of his hand. "Of course, if it's her, she isn't going to look pretty at all."

CRIME WAS UBIQUITOUS, and while the community policed by the Devonshire substation had its share of assaults, burglaries, and thefts, it wasn't considered high in the homicide department. So when murder did occur, it stood out as an anomaly. Hangings were as rare as L.A. snow.

Decker drove down the main boulevard, twisting and turning until he arrived at one of the more affluent residential areas. It was a planned community and the homes were two-storied with three-car garages and half-acre lots. There were a few architectural styles to choose from: Spanish, Tudor, Colonial, Italianate, and Modern, which was basically an oversize box with oversize windows. Several homes were in the process of being built.

At the given address, a sizable group of gawkers was milling about, craning their necks to see what was going on. One radio van had already arrived and no doubt several more were on the way. Decker parked about a half block away from the hubbub and walked over to the action. He flashed his badge to one of the uniforms and then ducked under the yellow crime-scene tape.

The two-story house had been framed: the rooms had been delineated, the windows were in, and the roof was on. The crowd was gathered toward the back, mostly uniformed officers, but Decker could also see flashbulbs discharging at frequent intervals. Marge, riding with her partner, Scott Oliver, had beaten him to the scene.

Scott was his usually natty self, wearing a houndstooth jacket, black slacks, a black jacquard silk tie, and a starched white shirt. As Decker got closer to the corpse, the air had turned fetid, filled with the stink of excretion. A funnel of blackflies, gnats, and other winged insects was encircling the space.

Oliver was shooing the critters away. "Get lost, bugs. Go eat the carrion."

From his breast jacket pocket, Decker took out a tube of Vicks VapoRub and dabbed his nostrils with the ointment. He waved a hand across his face to disperse the insects as he stared at the body swinging from the rafters. The woman's face was so discolored and bloated that she was almost unrecognizable as human. She was nude, her long dark hair vainly trying to give her some modesty. Cable wire had been looped several times around her neck, the terminus of the ligature knotted on one of the ceiling joists. Her toenails—painted red—just barely cleared the ground.

"Any ID?" Decker asked.

"None so far," Marge answered. "Is it Terry?"

Decker stared a long time. "I'd like to say no, but honestly she's too distorted to tell." He took out his notebook and began to make some sketches. "What cable company services this area?"

"American Lifeline does most of the Valley," Marge answered. "I'll call them up and get a schedule of who's working in the area."

Decker said. "Find out what kind of cable wire they use. Also get someone to start calling electronic shops and computer stores in the area and find out what kind of cable they sell."

"I'll do that," Oliver said.

"No, get Lee Wang to make all the calls. You and Marge start canvassing the area. I'll bring in a couple of other Dees to help you out." Decker continued to study the body. "Do we have any ideas who this might be?"

"Wynona Pratt is making calls to the other station houses, finding out if any young women were reported missing."

Decker rubbed his forehead and turned to the photographer,

George Stubbs, a gray-haired, stocky man in his fifties. "Are you done with her?"

"Almost."

"Did you take close-ups of her neck?"

"I took some. I can take more."

"Do that. Also take several snapshots of the knot on the ceiling where the cable wire is knotted."

Marge had gloved up and was studying the body, circling it like carrion. By law, no one could touch the body until the coroner's investigator gave the okay. "This seems like a bloodless murder. No bullet holes, no stab wounds. No defensive wounds on her hands. Her nails aren't chipped or scratched. Her French polish manicure is like new." She looked up. "Happen to notice if Terry had on nail polish?"

Decker thought back, trying to recall Terry's hands. Then he noticed the hanging woman's feet—bright red toenails. "When Terry first spoke to me, her feet were bare and I don't recall her toenails being polished." A pause. "She could have polished them later, after I left, but how likely is that unless she had it done in the hotel's salon."

Marge said, "I'll call up and ask."

He stared at the face. "It's not her."

"You're sure."

"Almost certain." He regarded her features, then shook his head. "Do we have any forensics—semen, fingerprints, shoe prints, maybe some tire tracks in the area? Lots of dust and dirt, we should be able to pull something from the ground."

"I've been bagging garbage," Oliver said.

"Marking the spots?"

Oliver held up some small orange cones with numbers on them.

Decker said, "What have you picked up?"

"Mostly fast-food sandwich wrappers and junk from the roach coach. S.I.D. is on the way. So are a couple of investigators from the Crypt."

"If it's a construction site, where's all the activity?" Decker asked.

"No activity because they're waiting for the framing inspector to sign off. The appointment was for four o'clock in the afternoon. The foreman, whose name is Chuck Tinsley, arrived here first and was going over the property just to make sure everything looked okay. He was waiting for the contractor and the architect to come down when he discovered the body. He called 911, then immediately called the contractor, who is on his way."

"Where's Tinsley?"

Marge pointed to a black-and-white. "He's ensconced inside. Should I get him?"

Decker nodded as his gaze continued to fix on the swinging corpse. His thoughts were meandering to several places, and none were good.

CHAPTER SEVEN

THE BACK PASSENGER door to the cruiser was open, a uniform standing in front of the space, keeping watch over her charge as well as the set of wheels. If Decker squinted, he could see a figure huddled in the backseat, his arms wrapped around his body as if his arms were straps on a straitjacket. As Decker approached the car, he nodded to the police officer and pointed to the open door. The cop bent down and spoke to the huddled man. When he emerged, Tinsley was average height, a tank of a fellow with long, muscular arms, dark eyes, a strong chin, and a face of controlled stubble. The officer led him to Decker, who glanced at her tag.

"Thank you, Officer Breckenridge, I'll take it from here." He extended his hand to the foreman, whose complexion was ashen behind the darkening of beard. He had brown eyes, a Roman nose, and thin lips. His hair was a nest of cowlicks. He appeared to be in his thirties. "Lieutenant Peter Decker."

"Chuck Tinsley." His voice was deep but held a slight tremble. "This is . . . I'm a little freaked out."

"I do this for a living and I'm a lot freaked out," Decker said.

Tinsley laughed nervously. "If you see a pile of vomit, it's probably mine."

"How's your stomach now?" Decker asked.

He held up a soda can. "Someone was nice enough to give me this. I think it was the lady cop. I'm a little confused."

Decker pulled out his notebook. "Why don't you tell me what happened?"

"Nothing much to tell. I came early to clean up before the contractor arrived." He bit his lip. "I saw the body."

"Can we back it up for a minute?"

"Sure?"

"When did you get to the site?"

"Around quarter to."

"Quarter to what?"

"Oh, quarter to two. One forty-five."

"And when were you supposed to meet the contractor."

"Around three-thirty, four."

Decker looked at his watch. It was nearly three now. "You came early?"

"Yeah, to clean up. You know how it is with construction crews," Tinsley said. "They throw their shit all over the place. I try to get them to clean up at the end of the day, but if it's been a hard one, I let it go. It's easier to clean up by myself when they're not here. That's what I was doing. With the inspection coming, you need a clean site."

"So you came at one forty-five and . . . what did you immediately start doing?"

"Cleaning up stuff. Picking up nails, piling up loose lumber, gathering up tools left behind, throwing away trash . . . lots of trash."

"Did you have a trash bag with you?"

"Yeah, sure."

"Where is the bag now?"

Tinsley's eyes narrowed in confusion. "Not sure. Probably I dropped it when I saw the body."

"When you noticed the body, how long had you been at the site?"

"Maybe five minutes. I saw a lot of flies and figured there was a pile of dog shit that I needed to clean up. Not that I see a lot of dog shit inside the house, but I figured what else could be attracting so many flies?"

"Then what did you do?"

"I think I found a plastic bag or something to pick up the shit with. After that, things got fuzzy. I think I mighta screamed. Then I barfed. Then I called 911 on my cell."

"You also called the contractor?"

"Yeah, I called him, too. He told me he was running late, and hopefully he'd make it before the inspector. But then I told him about the body and that I called the police and that he should cancel the inspection."

"Then what did you do after you called the contractor?"

"I don't really remember . . . the police showed up a couple of minutes later. Someone told me to wait in the car and that someone would be with me in a moment. I said I was feeling a little sick and someone got me a can of soda. And that's that."

Decker said, "Did you touch the body at all? Maybe feel for a pulse?"

Tinsley turned green. "I mighta. I don't remember too well."

"Did you get a good look at the face?"

"I just glanced at it . . . her. It didn't even look human."

"Did you recognize her as someone you know or have seen around the area?"

"Tell you the truth, I didn't look that long."

"Could you glance at the body another time, just to see if you can identify her?"

"I suppose so . . ."

Decker led him over to the corpse. Someone from the coroner's office had given the go-ahead to cut her down. She laid her on a gurney with a sheet over her head. S.I.D. was printing her hands. Decker gently removed the blanket to expose the face. It was still red and puffy, but a bit less distorted.

The foreman stared at the face for a few seconds, and then averted his eyes. He appeared to be holding down his stomach. "I don't know her at all."

"Thank you for trying." Decker guided him away from the scene, the two of them walking toward the cruiser.

Tinsley gave a sick smile. "At least I didn't heave this time. When can I go?"

"We're almost done," Decker told him. "I'd like you to write down exactly what you told me, including that you don't recognize the corpse."

"Uh, sure. No problem."

Decker handed him a tablet of yellow lined paper. "You can sit in the police car while you write. I'll take the soda can if you're through with it. Do you want another one?"

"Yeah, if you wouldn't mind." Tinsley handed the can to Decker.

"It's not a problem. Could you also give me the contractor's name and cell number?"

"His name is Keith Wald. I have to check my cell for the phone number because right now, I'm too shaken to remember it even though I've dialed it a thousand times."

"I'll check your cell for the number. As a matter of fact, would you mind if I looked your cell phone over? I'd like to get the exact times of the calls you made."

"Sure." Tinsley handed him the phone. "You can even look over any of the numbers I used. That's what you want to do, right?"

"If you wouldn't mind."

"I guess it's natural to suspect everyone. Most of my calls are business, but there are probably some to my friends. I'll tell you what number belongs to who. Anything, as long as it takes my mind off of *that*."

Tinsley pointed to the house, assumedly to the body in the house. A moment later, Decker espied a mustachioed, dark-haired man charging across the lot, escorted by Officer Mary Breckenridge. The man's face was all seams, ruts, and pits, with a strong cleft chin and a head of dark thick curls. His eyes were hooded by a jutting brow and he was walking bowlegged. He stood around five eight and seemed to be in his late forties.

"That's the contractor, Lieutenant." Tinsley yelled and waved his arms. "Yo, Keith! Over here."

"What the hell happened?" Wald broke into a jog. "What's going on?"

Decker said, "Officer Breckenridge, why don't you escort Mr. Tinsley into the cruiser so he can write down his statement."

"Yes, sir." Breckenridge gently nudged Tinsley forward. "This way, sir."

"Wait, wait, wait," Wald said out loud. "I need to talk to this man."

"You can talk to him after you talk to me." Decker introduced himself.

Wald stuck out his hand. "Okay. Could you tell me what the hell is going on? Chuck said something about a body hanging from the rafters."

"What else did he tell you?"

"That it was a woman. God, that's horrible." Wald checked his watch. "The city inspector is supposed to come in about an hour."

"You're going to have to cancel that," Decker said. "No one is allowed on the premises until we're done."

"The homeowners are going to blow a gasket. We're already a couple of months behind. Not my fault. Homeowners keep changing their minds."

"Could I get the names of the homeowners?" When Wald winced, Decker said, "They're going to find out. It'll be best if it comes from someone official."

"Yeah, that's true. Grossman—Nathan and Lydia. He's a doctor, so I mostly work with her."

"Do you have a phone number?"

"Yeah . . . hold on." Wald checked his BlackBerry, his mustache twitching as he moved his upper lip. "Here it is."

Decker copied the number on his notepad. "What can you tell me about them?"

"He's around sixty, she's younger . . . maybe forty. They have two teenage boys—fifteen and thirteen. I think he also has a son from another marriage. God, this is awful!"

The dead woman seemed older than her teens, so the boys didn't pop out as primary suspects. Still, they needed to be looked at. "How old is the son from the first marriage?"

"I have no idea." Wald blanched. "Why are you asking?"

"Routine questions. I'll want to contact everyone associated with the spot," Decker said. "Do you know his name?"

"No."

"I'll get it from the homeowners. Could you come to take a look at the body? See if she looks familiar to you?"

"Me?"

"We don't have her identification yet. Maybe she's someone in the neighborhood."

"I don't spend a lot of time checking out the ladies. When I'm here, I work."

"If you'd just take a look at her, I'd appreciate it."

"Oh God." Wald heaved a sigh. "All right."

"Thanks." Decker walked him over to the crime scene and for the second time in ten minutes uncovered the sheet to reveal the face. She was still bloated and purple, but her features were recognizable as those of a young woman. He could now clearly make out the deep purple ligature mark that had cut into her neck at the Adam's apple.

He could now say with confidence that the corpse wasn't Terry McLaughlin.

One less thing to deal with . . . or more to deal with. Terry was still missing.

Wald gagged and slapped his hand over his mouth. "Never seen her before." He turned tail and walked away.

Decker covered her face and caught up with Wald. "Thank you for helping."

"Was that really necessary? Now I'm gonna have nightmares."

"Did you call the inspector?" Decker said.

"Oh yeah, let me do that right now." He punched some numbers into his BlackBerry. Five minutes later, he said, "Can't get hold of the man. Shit!"

"Don't worry about it," Decker said. "We'll take care of him. I'm going to need a list of all the people that have worked here. That shouldn't be too difficult since you're only at the framing stage."

"I've had the same guys for three years. It isn't one of them."

"I'll need that list anyway." Decker looked around for another notepad and gave it to Wald. "Put down anyone associated with this project starting with the homeowners."

"Anywhere I can sit down?"

Decker rounded up Officer Breckenridge. "Could you escort Mr. Wald to a cruiser so he can write down some information for me?" He heard Marge call his name, turned around, and walked over to her and the crime scene. "What's up?"

"Lee Wang called. A nurse who works at St. Timothy's—which is about six blocks away—seems to be missing."

"Oh Lord. What's her name?"

"Adrianna Blanc. According to her DMV license, she's twenty-eight, blue eyes, brown hair, five six, a hundred and twenty-five pounds."

"Married?"

"Single."

"Who reported her missing?"

"Her mother. She went to her apartment to drop off some things this morning and her daughter wasn't there. Her bed hadn't been slept in."

"Maybe she slept somewhere else."

"Her mother has made some calls. Her boyfriend is away with his two best friends on vacation. Her other best girlfriends can't get hold of her. Apparently, Adrianna finished up her shift at the hospital this morning, but no one has heard from her since. Her car is still in the parking lot of St. Tim's."

"That's not good." Decker rubbed his forehead. "Where's Mom?"

"Her name is Kathy Blanc and she's at the station house," Marge told him.

"And Lee's with her?"

"Lee made the call. Wanda Bontemps is with her now."

"Tell Wanda to keep her there. I'll come in and talk to her."

"That's already done," Marge said. "I used a computer in one of the cruisers to bring up her DMV picture to see if we're in the ballpark." She handed him a slip of paper. "Kinda fuzzy, but it's a possibility. We could bring Mom down for identification in person or we could take some of George's snapshots to her."

Decker stared at the DMV photo. A young woman with long hair was grinning full face into the camera. "Do we have any printed postmortem photographs?"

"Yeah, these are from George's camera, printed from his laptop."

Decker flipped through them and compared them with the DMV photo. If he squinted hard enough, he could see that the women were one and the same. "Close enough. I'm sending you and Oliver to St. Tim's. I'll bring the postmortem to Mom. It's kinder than doing an in-person ID. Have you finished canvassing the area?"

"We've just started . . . gone through a couple of blocks when Lee called in."

"Call in Drew Messing and Willy Brubeck and have them canvass the area for Oliver and you. They can direct a team of uniforms around the neighborhood. The first thing I want you and Oliver to do is to go to St. Tim's parking lot with a crime team and work her car over. See if that directs us somewhere. What kind of a car is it?"

"A 2002 burgundy Honda Accord." She gave him the plate number.

"While S.I.D. is working on the car, you go into the hospital and see if you can track Adrianna Blanc's last movements before she disappeared."

"Will do."

"The contractor is writing down names and numbers of everyone associated with the project. The homeowners have two teenage boys together. If it is Adrianna Blanc, she would seem to be out of the boys' age range, but we still need to know where they were last night. There's also an older son by the father's first marriage."

"How old is he?"

"Don't know a thing about him. Call up Wynona Pratt. Tell her to go through the list one by one."

"Sounds like a plan." Marge shrugged. "At least the body's probably not Terry McLaughlin."

Decker exhaled. "All that means is I have to deliver bad news to someone else."

CHAPTER EIGHT

POSITIVELY THE WORST part of the job was bringing bad news to loved ones. It simply sucked. Kathy Blanc's hands were shaking when Decker handed her the first picture and all it took was one look before she bolted from his office. Wanda Bontemps was there to direct her to the ladies' room. Decker sat at his desk with his face in his hands, wondering just how long he could take this kind of stress. And if that weren't enough, there was a fourteen-year-old boy with missing parents, living in his home.

Sometimes it isn't even worth getting up in the morning.

Five minutes later, Wanda Bontemps led Kathy Blanc back into Decker's office and seated her across from his desk. Kathy's complexion had turned the color of eggshell; her eyes were red with black tears streaming down her cheeks courtesy of mascara. Red lipstick had run into the lines atop her mouth. Her body was enveloped with the shakes and she hugged herself in a weak attempt to stop her seizing. The woman's coiffed blond hair framed a long, patrician face now smeared with makeup. She wore pearls in her ears and had on black knitted pants and a red knitted top. Black pumps on her feet.

Wanda Bontemps was at the doorway, her dark eyes looking pretty somber. "How about some water and a wet towel?"

Decker nodded and then faced Kathy Blanc's imploring eyes. "I'm so sorry, Mrs. Blanc. Is there anyone we can call for you?"

"My . . . hus . . . band." She opened her purse, but Decker was quicker. He handed her a Kleenex. "Thank you."

"Do you have a number, ma'am?"

"It's area code 213-827 . . ." Her face crumbled and Decker handed her another tissue. She managed to get out the next four digits. When Wanda returned, he handed her the number and told her to make the call. He gave the water to Kathy along with a damp white towel.

"Is there anyone else you want me to contact?" Decker asked her.

"I can't even think."

Decker nodded. "I want to let you know that we'll do whatever needs to be done to find out what happened. We've got a lot of people working on this. Are you up to my asking you a few questions?"

"I don't . . ." The tears started anew, but she nodded for Decker to go ahead.

"Was Adrianna having problems with anyone?"

Kathy shook her head no.

"How about a boyfriend? You told my detective that there was one."

"Garth Hammerling."

"Any problems with him?"

"Not that I know."

"I don't mean to sound intrusive, Mrs. Blanc, but did you and Adrianna have the type of relationship where she would talk to you about personal things?"

Kathy dabbed her smeary eyes with the towel. When she saw that her makeup was coming off, she whispered an "oh dear." "Adrianna didn't complain a lot." She rubbed her face vigorously to get off all the streaked makeup. "But if something was wrong, I think she'd tell me."

"What do you think about Garth?"

She continued wiping her face. "He seemed all right. I don't think Adrianna was all that serious about him."

"Where'd she meet him?"

"He's a tech at St. Tim's." Kathy looked up. "Why are you asking questions about Garth?" Her eyes filled with moisture again. "Was she . . . violated?"

"I don't know—"

"I don't feel well." She stood up. "I need to use the restroom."

"Detective Bontemps will take you."

"I know where it is." She got up and left. Bontemps stepped into the office.

"Garth Hammerling was Adrianna's boyfriend." Decker wrote the name on a piece of paper and gave it to her. "Check him out . . . although I think Marge said something about his being out of town. Did you contact Mrs. Blanc's husband?"

"Yes, I did. I didn't tell him what was going on, but he knew it concerned Adrianna because Kathy had called him several times."

"Where does he work?"

"Law offices of Rosehoff, Allens, Blanc, and Bellows. Mack Blanc is a senior partner. He's on his way here from downtown L.A."

"We should send a car to pick him up. He shouldn't be driving."

"Didn't get a chance to tell him too much of anything. He hung up on me as soon as I told him his wife was here."

"Give me the number. I'll see if I can reach him. You go into the restroom and make sure that Mrs. Blanc is okay. Well, she's not okay, but make sure she doesn't need medical care. If she does need care, call an ambulance. Have them take her anywhere but St. Tim's."

"THE MOTHER MADE an ID with the pictures," Decker told Marge over the phone. "That means the car is part of an official crime scene. Are the crime techs there yet?"

"Any moment now. Are you coming down?"

"I'm waiting to talk to Adrianna's father. I'll come down after that. Have you talked to anyone at St. Tim's about Adrianna?"

"Oliver's trying to get a time frame. It appears she completed her shift. That would mean she left the building around eight in the morning. Things go blank after that. We did find a nurse named Mandy Kowalski who knew Adrianna Blanc for six years. She's on break in about a half hour and has agreed to speak with us. We're trying to locate a good spot to talk. It looks like the cafeteria is winning the election."

"Who else have you talked to at the hospital?"

"A little of this, a little of that. People are on shift and seem reluctant to talk."

"The hospital isn't cooperating with you?"

"The administration's been all right. We'll see what happens once they find out it's murder. Oliver is getting a list of names of the security officers on duty. There are always a couple of guards roaming the parking lots."

"What about video cameras?"

"We're working on getting the tapes for all the entrances and exits. I don't know if there're video cameras in the parking lots, but I'll find out."

"Has the hospital had trouble with crime in the past?"

"I don't know. We've still got a lot of searching to do. As soon as we get information, we'll keep you in the loop."

"As long as the loop ain't a noose around the neck."

"**WE WENT TO** nursing school together."

Eyes on the tabletop, Mandy Kowalski was staring at bad coffee. Oliver knew it was bad because he was drinking the same swill.

A cute little thing, he thought, dressed in blue scrubs, with a pixie face, bright red hair, and hazel eyes. A dozen moons ago, he would have asked her out despite the forty-year age difference. But a lifetime of bad choices had finally made him realize that sometimes it was best to keep things on the professional level. He was currently dating a middle-school teacher named Carmen who was much too good for him. By the grace of God, she was able to deflect his neuroses and shenanigans with a knowing look and a laugh.

"You're sure she's gone?" Mandy's eyes were still downcast. "Sometimes people just leave without telling anyone."

Marge and Oliver exchanged glances. Marge said, "Mandy, we got a recent update, and unfortunately, the news isn't good. It appears that Adrianna has been murdered."

"Oh God!" Mandy gasped and knocked over her coffee cup with shaking hands. She covered her mouth. "Oh no! Oh my God! How horrible! Oh no!" She looked up and tears had sprouted from her eyes. "That can't be!"

"We got a positive ID from her mother," Marge told her.

"Oh, that poor woman. Poor Adrianna." She buried her face behind her hands. "I'm sorry. I can't . . ."

"That's okay," Marge told her. "Take your time."

Oliver stood up. "I'll get you a glass of water."

Marge tried to distract her. "I noticed you're wearing scrubs. Are you a surgical nurse?"

"Thoracic." She wiped her eyes with a napkin. "Anything to do with the chest."

"Is that what Adrianna did?"

At the mention of her friend's name, Mandy let go with a fresh set of waterfalls. "She's in the NICU. Neonatal intensive care. She's a . . . she was a pediatric nurse. She was great at her job. We used to call her the baby whisperer. But even when she worked with older kids, they loved her."

"I see." Marge took out her notepad. "And you've known Adrianna for six years?"

"Around six years." Oliver came back with water and a new tissue box. Mandy thanked him for both items. "I was just telling your partner that I knew Adrianna for around six years. We went to nursing school together."

"Where at?" Oliver asked. "C-SUN?"

"No," Mandy said. "We went to the Howard Professional School.

Originally Adrianna was just going for an LVN, but I told her that she was smart enough to go all the way for an RN. It was a *lot* harder, I'm not going to lie, but I convinced her that it would be worth it."

"Wow, that was awfully nice of you," Marge told her.

"It was partially for selfish reasons," Mandy said. "We met the first day of orientation and hit it off right away. I figured it would be easier if I had company. I helped her over a couple of rough patches, but she took her own tests and did well."

"You sound like a good friend," Oliver told her.

"At that time, we were very good friends."

"But not so much anymore?" Marge asked.

"You know how it is . . ." Mandy's eyes darted back and forth. "Things change."

"Like what?" Oliver said.

"We drifted apart," Mandy said. "Aside from work, we stopped hanging out."

"What happened?"

"Nothing really . . . just lifestyle issues. Adrianna has . . ." Mandy licked her lips. "She has a lot more energy than I do. She likes to have a good time."

"She's a party girl?" Marge suggested.

"That's making her sound cheap," Mandy said. "She liked her fun. I mean, I do too, but I guess I need more sleep than she does."

"Did her fun include drugs?" Marge said.

Mandy hesitated. "I guess she'd be like a recreational user."

"Did it ever interfere with her work?"

"Never!" Mandy was adamant. "She was a miracle worker with those babies."

"What do you know about her boyfriend?" Marge checked her notes. "Garth Hammerling. What do you know about him?"

"He works here at St. Tim's. He's a radiology tech."

"How well do you know him?" Oliver asked.

"Casual acquaintances," Mandy told him.

But her eyes were elsewhere. Marge said, "Would you know where he lives?"

Mandy looked away. "Why would I know where he lives?"

"Maybe you went to a party there?"

"Can't recall that." Mandy looked at her hands. "I could probably get you his address, but you could probably do it just as easy."

"Not a problem," Oliver said. "Just wondering if you knew it offhand because we need to talk to him." When Mandy didn't answer, he said, "You know we need to ask all sorts of personal questions."

Marge said, "So if I asked you personal information, you shouldn't be offended."

"Because we ask everyone personal information," Oliver said. "Like I could ask you if you had a thing going on with Garth."

"No!" Mandy dried her eyes. "Why would you think that?"

"Just a question," Marge said.

Oliver said, "Because if you had something going on with him, we'd eventually find out about it."

"So now's the time to fess up," Marge said. "Hiding stuff makes you look bad."

"I don't have anything . . ." Again her eyes moistened. "He came on to me, okay?"

"See, that was simple," Marge said. "What could you tell us about it?"

"Nothing happened. I wasn't interested." She shook her head. "It was at one of Adrianna's parties. She had them almost every other weekend. He cornered me in the kitchen and tried to mash me. God, it was embarrassing. He was drunk. So was she." She dabbed her eyes. "It's hard for me to talk smack about her, especially now that she's . . . and we used to be such good friends. It's not that Garth is a bad guy. He's just a player. Everyone knows he's a player."

"Did Adrianna know?"

"Maybe in the back of her mind, she did." She stood up. "I've got to get back to my shift. If you want to talk to me again, please don't do it here. I live in Canoga Park. I'm in the book."

"Thanks, Mandy," Marge said, "you've been very helpful."

"No problem. Just find the bastard who hurt her. Adrianna may have had her issues, but who doesn't have problems?"

"True that," Marge said as she watched the nurse walk away. Then she said, "What do you think?"

"An emotional girl for someone who had drifted away from the victim." Oliver shrugged. "What's going on with Garth?"

"His landline answering machine says . . ." Marge checked her notes. "That Garth, Aaron, and Greg went river rafting and wouldn't be answering calls for a week. If he left a couple of days ago, he's given himself an alibi."

"Some people have perfect timing."

"You know what I think, Oliver?" Marge said. "Perfect timing is always suspicious."

CHAPTER NINE

DECKER GOT THE feeling that Mack Blanc's language was an embarrassment to Kathy, but she was just too numb to stop him.

What the fuck happened!

That's what we're investigating, Mr. Blanc. I'm so sorry.

I don't want your fucking apologies, I want some fucking answers!

Over and over and over and over and over.

The three of them were in Decker's office. Kathy remained silent and seated as her husband paced and swore. Finally, Mack attempted a new line of attack.

"Well, if you don't know what fucking happened, what do you fucking know?"

Decker pointed to the chair. Reluctantly, Mack sat down. As soon as he was quiet, his eyes overflowed. Wordlessly, Decker handed him a tissue.

"Her car is still in St. Tim's parking lot. We're going over it right now."

"Was she . . ." Kathy choked back sobs. "Did it happen in the car?"

"I don't know, Mrs. Blanc. I sure don't want to tell you wrong information."

Mack took her hand and she leaned against his chest, weeping. The hapless man couldn't offer her any words of comfort.

Decker said, "We're also interviewing people at the hospital to get a time frame. Your wife was kind enough to give us Adrianna's cell number and we discovered she made a couple of calls around the time she got off shift."

"She called Sela Graydon," Kathy explained to her husband.

"She and Adrianna have known each other since junior high," Mack answered. "What about the other number?"

"When we called it, no one answered. The voice-mail box is full, so we don't know who it belongs to. We can find out who owns the number and how long the conversation lasted, but that will take a little maneuvering. Also, there's no guarantee that the person who owns the number is the one who answered the call."

"It's not a familiar number to me," Kathy told her husband.

"What about Garth?" Mack said.

"It isn't Garth's number."

"I don't trust that guy," Mack said. "He's cocky. Lord only knows why."

Kathy said, "He's good-looking."

"How could you say that?" Mack said. "Guy had about twenty pierces in his ears and that crazy soul patch. His hair looked like he stuck his hand in a light socket."

"That's the fashion, Mack. All the rock stars have hair like that."

"He wasn't particularly smart. He was always going to Vegas and never invited Adrianna. Lord only knows where he got the money for his excursions."

Decker noticed Kathy's cheeks reddening. He said, "What do you know about the money, Mrs. Blanc?"

Kathy looked up. "Pardon?"

"Had Adrianna ever loaned Garth any money?"

"What?" Mack stared at his wife. "Did she give that loser money?"

"She didn't give it to him, she loaned it to him."

"I don't believe . . ." He jumped up and started pacing again. "*Why?*"

Kathy erupted into tears. "I don't know why, Mack, all I know is that she did!"

"Was she generally a soft touch?" Decker asked.

Mack muttered under his breath and kept pacing. Kathy said, "Softhearted. That's why she became a nurse."

Decker said, "I'm just trying to get a feel for her, so please don't take offense at my questions. As far as you know, did Adrianna take drugs or drink excessively?"

"I wouldn't know," Kathy told him.

"Of course we know," Mack said. "We found weed in her dresser when she was in high school. Twice!"

"She said she stopped."

"She also said the weed wasn't hers." To Decker: "Yes, she probably smoked dope and she probably drank too much."

Kathy wiped her eyes. "She didn't have a problem, Mack."

"I didn't say she had a problem."

"It doesn't sound like she had a problem," Decker said. "She had an important job, and from what I heard, she did it very well."

"She worked in the NICU with all the sick little preemies." Kathy started crying. "They all loved her."

"Good Lord." Mack's eyes moistened. "What the fuck happened?"

Back to square one. Decker said, "What else can you tell me about Garth Hammerling?"

"Met him about a half-dozen times. Didn't trust him." Mack stopped pacing. "Tell you the truth, I didn't always trust Adrianna. Her judgment wasn't the best."

"A good kid," Kathy said. "But she could be a little—"

"She was wild. She was also spoiled. *We* were spoiled by her older sister. That one never gave us anything to worry about."

"Bea was a different child. There's no sense comparing."

"But we do anyway," Mack told her. "More than once we were up at four in the morning, calling Adrianna's friends because her cell was off and we didn't know where she was. When she wanted to be a nurse, I was skeptical. But . . ."

Mack Blanc's voice cracked.

"The girl proved me wrong." He sniffed back tears. "She not only graduated, but got a job with responsibility. Her coworkers love her."

"You met her coworkers?" Decker asked him.

Kathy said, "She had a Christmas party in her apartment two years ago. She invited us and we went."

"I think that's when we first met Garth," Mack told her.

"Do you remember any other coworkers?"

"There was her friend Mandy Kowalski," Kathy told Decker. "They went to nursing school together. I think it was Mandy who set Adrianna up with Garth."

"Mandy set her up with Garth?" Decker repeated.

"I think so." Kathy squinted, trying to bring back memories. "I think she knew a boy who knew him . . . something like that."

"Do you remember the boy's name?"

"No." Mack waved his hand in the air. "We kept out of Adrianna's business."

Kathy said, "His name was Aaron Otis."

"How did you remember that?"

"I just do."

Mack shook his head. "She's a whiz with names."

"That's very good," Decker said. "Aaron Otis. Did you ever meet him?"

"I had to have met him once because I recall he was tall with sandy hair . . . unless I'm getting things confused." She looked down. "That's certainly possible."

"That's helpful," Decker said. "How about the names of Adrianna's other friends?"

"You can start with Sela Graydon and Crystal Larabee. The three of them were a tight little group."

"Did either of them become nurses?"

"Heavens no," Mack said. "I think Crystal wanted to be an actress. At twenty-nine, it ain't gonna happen. What is she? Like a bartender?"

"She's a main hostess at Garage."

"Yeah, waiting to be discovered."

"Be kind, Mack." Kathy regarded Decker. "Garage is the newest Helmet Grass restaurant. It's downtown . . . right near the New Otani."

"Got it. What about Sela Graydon? What does she do?"

"She's a lawyer," Mack told him. "She was always the smart one of the three."

"Do both women live in town?"

"Yes," Kathy said. "I'll get you their phone numbers."

"Do you know anything about Mandy Kowalski?"

"Just that Adrianna met her in nursing school," Mack said. "She seemed nice enough."

"She used to help Adrianna study, especially when finals rolled around. The first time they happened, Adrianna freaked out. I couldn't help her. I don't know the first thing about the nervous system or the circulatory system, but after studying with Mandy, she not only pulled through, she did well. She even got a couple of A's in some of the classes."

The tears came flowing down Kathy's cheek.

"She was so . . . proud!"

Decker gave her another Kleenex and watched the woman sob. There wasn't a state-of-the-art dam in the entire world that could hold back that torrent.

"THERE'S NOT MUCH to come down for." Marge was just outside in the parking lot of St. Tim's because the reception for her cell was better. "The car's being processed and we're just about done with our preliminary interviewing. We spoke to a few of her coworkers. Also, we talked to a woman named Mandy Kowalski. She and Adrianna went to nursing school together, but they don't work on the same floor."

"Yeah, Mandy's name came up when I interviewed the mom," Decker told her. "She thought that Mandy might have set Adrianna up with Garth."

"Hmm. Mandy neglected to mention that. She did say that Garth came on to her."

"Okay," Decker said. "Triangle anyone?"

"Could be," Marge said. "I'll see if I can sort the relationships out. We've also got an appointment to interview Adrianna's supervising nurse tomorrow. She was well liked, did her job, but several people remarked that she liked to party."

"That's consistent with the picture I got from her parents."

"Her parents told you she liked to party?"

"Mostly her father did. He described her—and not kindly—as a party girl."

"Unusual for him to admit that under the circumstances."

"I have a feeling that he's been miffed at her for a long time."

"But she's *dead*, Rabbi. For him to even hint at hostility . . . that's weird."

"People cope in all sorts of different ways. Maybe he figures if he can be mad at her, she's really not dead. Anyway, there's another sister in the family—Beatrice Blanc. She needs to be interviewed separately."

"I'll do it."

"There are also two best friends of hers from high school: Sela Graydon and Crystal Larabee." Decker spelled the names and gave Marge the phone numbers. "Lastly, we need to find out the name of the homeowner's oldest son."

"Did that. Trent Grossman. He's twenty-six. He lives in Boston with his wife and was at a party last night. So he's out of the picture. The two younger Grossman boys were home last night, according to the parents. For verification, they sent e-mails, IMs, and were on Facebook. I haven't dug deeper, but I will if you want me to."

"How old are they? Like fifteen and thirteen?"

"Yep."

"Put them down at the bottom for now. Let's go back to

Adrianna's peers—Crystal and Sela. Set up interviews with them because . . . okay . . . here's the deal."

Decker flipped through his notes.

"Adrianna called Sela Graydon this morning right when she got off of work. Find out what that was all about. Adrianna also made another call, but we don't know the identity of that number. Each time I've called it, the mailbox is full. It's a cell, so our backward directories aren't going to work. We may need a warrant to find out who the number belongs to. Hunt around and see if you can find out if the number belongs to one of her friends."

"Will do." Marge asked him, "Any luck with the canvassing of the area?"

"I haven't heard anything so far. How about we meet up later in the evening and compare notes?"

"Sounds like a plan. Talk to you later."

Marge hung up her cell and started to dial Sela Graydon's number, when a crime-scene tech started walking her way. The woman came up to Marge's stomach. Maybe a little bit higher than her stomach, but she was definitely less than five feet. She was young and Asian and as delicate as a spiderweb, except she had a smoker's voice. Her name was Rebel Hung.

"We're just about done with what we can do here." Rebel snapped off her latex gloves. "I called the truck. We'll tow it to the lab and give it a thorough going-over."

"Doesn't look like this is a crime scene," Marge said.

"I agree," Rebel said. "Who knows if she even made it to her car?"

"Footprints?"

"We've got some partials. We've got lots of latent fingerprints. Maybe something will pop."

"Hope so."

"What about the actual crime scene?" Rebel asked. "Where you found her dangling."

"It's a crime scene, but we're not sure if it's the murder scene. If she was killed there, she didn't seem to put up a struggle. The coroner's investigators haven't found bullet or stab wounds—but she could have been poisoned or sedated before she was hanged. We'll do a tox on her."

"Sexually assaulted?"

"Doesn't look like it, but we'll know more once the autopsy's done."

Rebel pursed her lips. "Hanging's a weird way to commit murder."

"Yeah, someone strung her up for dramatic effect."

"Very dramatic . . . like in serial killer dramatic."

"Yes, indeed, we certainly haven't ruled that one out."

CHAPTER TEN

AS THE FRESHIES set up the chairs, Hannah took Gabe over to the choir director. Mrs. Kent was an energetic, stout woman with a bowl cut of black hair and glasses dangling from a chain.

"This is Gabe," Hannah said. "He plays the piano."

Slipping her glasses over her nose, Mrs. Kent looked the boy up and down. "What year are you in?"

"Sophomore, but I'm just visiting."

"Visiting?" Mrs. Kent let her glasses drop onto her chest. "For how long?"

"Unknown," Hannah said. "Maybe a day or two. I thought if he could play 'My Heart Will Go On' instead of you playing, you can concentrate on the vocals. Although it'll probably take a lot more than that to keep us on key."

"That's very cynical coming from the choir president." She stared at Gabe. "Do you know the song?"

"I can fake it pretty close. It's in E, right?"

"Yes, it's in E. Can you read music?"

"Sheet music is even better," Gabe said.

"It's on the piano." Mrs. Kent told him. "Decker, help the kids set up."

Gabe found a small spinet sitting in a corner, but turned to face the stage. It was a Gulbransen, and while it wasn't exactly the German Steinway, the mark was serviceable. He pushed his glasses up on his nose, and then touched the ivory keys from middle C to two octaves above using his right-hand fingers. With his left fingers, he went from middle C to two octaves below. Then he played the accidental keys. The sound was about as expected from a small-bodied piano. Its tuning was true, although not all the notes were perfect. It would bother him. Anything that wasn't musically perfect bothered him, but he had learned how to live with it. He rarely attended any live rock concerts other than thrash metal, where sound was bent and warped anyway, so who cared about pitch. Pop singers were the worst. Pro Tools notwithstanding, there were very few singers who hit the notes all the time.

He glanced at the music. It needed range. No doubt the choir would massacre it as Hannah predicted. He liked Hannah. She was friendly but low-key. She made conversation but steered away from anything personal. She had self-confidence without being arrogant.

There were twenty-three kids in the choir, lined up on the risers. As soon as the teacher started talking to them, he zoned out. Around five minutes later, Gabe realized that she was talking to him.

"Pardon?"

Mrs. Kent heaved a dramatic sigh. "I asked if you thought you could play the piece."

"Sure."

"Sure?"

"Yeah, sure." Gabe smiled. "It's not Rachmaninoff."

Mrs. Kent eyed him. "You must be related to Hannah. You have the same sense of humor."

Gabe smiled again but said nothing.

"We can start whenever you're ready."

"I'm ready."

"Then start."

Gabe stifled a laugh. When he began the introduction, he saw the choir teacher's eyes go wide. It was stupid that she was shocked. Why would he say he could play if he couldn't? It was a motor skill—impossible to fake.

As rightly predicted by Hannah, the choir was awful; the off-key factor was especially prevalent in the soprano section. It was excruciatingly painful to his ear. Midway through the piece, he stopped playing. The teacher cut off the choir and asked him what was wrong.

"I don't mean to be cheeky, but it's a little high for your voices. Would you like me to take it down to E-flat? Or maybe down a full note to D. I don't like turning songs in sharp keys into songs in flat keys. But that's just me."

Mrs. Kent stared at him. "You can do that?" Without waiting, she said, "I know. It's not Rachmaninoff. Okay, give us a starting note."

Gabe gave them a D and they ran through the number again. It was still terrible, but at least the sopranos weren't straining as much. When Mrs. Kent called for a five-minute break, Hannah went over to the piano. "We've got another hour or so. Sorry it gets out so late."

"I'm not going anywhere. If your dad had something to tell me, he'd call me, right?"

"Yeah, he would. I'm sorry."

Gabe shrugged.

Hannah said, "Your playing is truly amazing."

Gabe laughed. "Any moron who has training could play this."

"Nah, I don't believe that."

"It's true. For as long as I've played, I should be better."

"How could you be any better?"

She had asked the question with utter sincerity. Gabe had to smile. "Thanks. I'll contact you the next time I need an ego boost."

"We're pretty bad, huh."

"It's fine."

Mrs. Kent came over. "How long are you going to be visiting with us, Mr. . . . ?"

"Whitman," Gabe said.

"A day or two," Hannah answered for him.

"Have you ever considered transferring to the school? We do have an orchestra and we always have room for a soloist."

Gabe said, "I'll keep it in mind."

"Have you ever performed any solo pieces?"

There wasn't any way in hell he was going to play for her. He wanted anonymity, not attention. "Not for a while. I'm a little rusty."

"I'd love to hear you when you feel up to it."

"Sure. Another time."

When the teacher left, Hannah whispered, "I'm so sorry. She's relentless."

"She's just being a teacher." He paused. "Hannah, if I have to come back with you tomorrow, do you think I can practice when no one's using the room? I mean it's really silly for me to be in your school trying to learn anything. My time would be better spent practicing. I mean, it's not that I *have* to play. But playing calms me down."

"I'm sure it's okay, but you'll have to ask permission from Mrs. Kent." Hannah raised her eyebrows. "I'm warning you that if you do, you'll make a deal with the devil. In exchange, she'll make you come to orchestra while you're here."

"So I'll come. As long as I don't have to solo."

"Got it. But you might want to reconsider about orchestra. We are truly bad! Worse than the choir."

"It's fine, Hannah. I've gone through a lot hairier things than a few bad notes."

"If it were just a few, I wouldn't say anything." She wagged a finger at his face. "And stop looking so cute. You're distracting the entire soprano section. And in case you haven't noticed, they have enough trouble staying on key."

AFTER THE BLANCS had left his office, Decker felt as if he had taken off a winter jacket in an overheated room: twenty pounds lighter and he could finally take a deep breath. Kathy Blanc had told him that her daughter's apartment appeared in order, but she admitted that she hadn't looked too closely.

Decker started working on scheduling his time. He'd manage a quick stop at home for dinner and then he'd go over to Adrianna's place . . . or maybe he should go down to St. Tim's and see what Marge and Oliver were doing. His mind was elsewhere when his cell rang and he neglected to pay attention to the caller ID number. Didn't matter because the number was blocked, but the voice told him who it was in the single word.

"What?"

Sounding more annoyed than anxious, but that was typical Donatti. Decker's heart started jogging. "Your cell out of order, Chris? I've been calling you for the last twenty-four hours."

"You know how it is, Decker. Sometimes you just don't want to be disturbed."

"Where have you been?"

"Where have I been?" A laugh over the phone. "What difference does it make?"

"Just wondering what could have kept you so preoccupied that you wouldn't bother checking your phone calls."

Another laugh. "You sound pissed."

"Where have you been?"

"Now you sound like you're interrogating me. I don't like your tone. Matter of fact, I don't like you. You've got two seconds to tell me what you want before I hang up."

"You don't want to call me back, fine. But I would think you'd answer your son's calls. He was so upset that he called me." There was the expected pause. It could have been real or staged. "We've got ourselves a big problem, Chris. Terry's missing."

This time the pause was much longer. "Go on."

The anger was gone, but his voice remained flat. Decker said, "That's it. Terry's missing."

"What do you mean, *missing*?"

"We can't find her—"

"I fucking know what the word 'missing' means. What do you mean that *she's* missing?"

Donatti had gone from zero to sixty in five seconds. He was clearly agitated, but that could be staged as well. The veracity of his emotions was impossible to read over the phone. "You need to come into the station house, Chris. We need to talk."

"Not until you tell me what the fuck is going on?"

"Your son called me yesterday around nine in the evening. He was distraught. When he got back to the hotel at seven, Terry was gone. She wasn't answering her cell phone, so he called you. When he couldn't get hold of either of his parents, he called me. So I took him in for the night because he didn't want to sleep at his aunt's house. So now I'm responsible for your kid until you get here. Where *are* you?"

"I'm in Nevada. My receptionist told me you called."

"You need to come to L.A. We need to talk."

"What the hell happened?"

"I don't know and that's why we need to talk—"

"So fucking talk!"

"Not over the phone," Decker said calmly. "In person. You've got to come here anyway. Your son is here, remember?"

"Okay, okay, lemme think a moment." He was muttering to himself. "When did she . . . I mean how long has she been missing?"

"Long enough that there may be a problem—"

"Is her car gone?"

"Chris, I can't tell you over the phone. How soon can you return to L.A.?"

"Shit! What time is it?"

"Around six."

"Fuck!" The sound of something crashing over the line. "Fuck, fuck, fuck! When did this happen? Yesterday?"

"Yes. Chris, I'll fill you in once you're in L.A. How soon can you get here?"

"I'm two hours out of Vegas. I drove in, so I don't have my plane. By the time I get to McCarren and into LAX, I wouldn't make it before eleven or so. Driving would take five to six hours . . . fuck! Let me see if I can lease something at the local airport. I'll call you back." Donatti disconnected the line.

Decker put down his cell and drummed his fingers on his desk, waiting for further information. But his mind was on a particular thought.

I drove in, so I don't have my plane.

I drove.

Lots of empty land and deserted highway between California and Nevada. The vast, unpopulated tracks that cut through the Mojave, with their infinite miles of nothingness, had always made for fertile dumping grounds.

CHAPTER ELEVEN

EVEN THOUGH IT was beyond happy hour, the bar was packed. Ice was one of those trendy restaurants with its walls and ceilings composed of lit-from-behind panels of pastel colors that changed hues over the course of an evening meal. The tint of the moment was aqua, giving the place the appearance of an igloo. The temperature inside sure could have used a little of the North Pole's arctic blast. The day had been unseasonably hot and yucky. Even though Marge had dressed for the heat in beige linen pants and a white cotton blouse, she felt sticky, like her clothes had been taped to her body. Over the phone, Sela Graydon had said that she'd be wearing a gray suit, red blouse, and black pumps, so the woman was easy to spot.

The lawyer was draped by a mane of brown, wavy hair that fell to her shoulder blades. Her pose was head down, eyes staring at the bar top, with her chin in her hands. She was being chatted up by a thirty-something man with a gilding of blond stubble. Every so often, Sela would lift her head, make a swipe at her eyes with her fingertips, and then lower her head and continue to stare at nothing. Marge wriggled through the crowd and snagged the seat next to hers. "Sela Graydon?"

The woman glanced up at Marge's face. "You're the police?"

"Sergeant Marge Dunn. We spoke over the phone. Thank you for meeting me on such short notice."

Sela bit her lip but didn't say anything. The blond man extended a hand to Marge. "Rick Briscoe. I work with Sela at Youngblood, Martin and Fitch." Marge took his hand in the briefest of shakes. "I didn't think she should be alone."

"Nice of you." To Sela, Marge said, "How about if we take a corner table. Little more private."

Sela looked around. "They're occupied."

"My partner, Detective Oliver, is saving one for us."

"Go ahead, Sela," Rick told her. "I'll wait here until you're done. I'm working on the Claridge depositions anyway. Just give a holler if you need something."

Sela nodded, slid off the stool, and stood up, her height being around five four. Marge brought the lawyer over to table where Oliver was nursing tonic water. He introduced himself and asked if she was hungry.

"No . . ." She sat down and tears leaked from her eyes. "I can't think about food. Kathy called me, asking me to come over. I said of course, but I don't know why. I'm still in shock. I'm sure I'm not going to be any help to her."

"Kathy is Adrianna's mother?" Oliver asked for confirmation.

"Yes, sorry. She's almost like a second mother. It's going to be so awful."

"Sometimes the best thing to say is nothing," Marge told her. "You spoke to Adrianna this morning."

"I didn't speak to her," Sela said. "She left a message on my cell."

"The call was almost two minutes."

"She left a *long* message."

"What about?" Oliver asked her.

"I wish I could tell you all of it." A big sigh. "The truth is that sometimes Adrianna kind of rambles and I don't pay attention. Actually I deleted it before I heard all of it."

"What was the gist?"

"Something about us getting together tonight because Garth is out of town, but not that his presence would stop her anyway 'cause he's always gone. Then she started saying that it's good that he's gone, and if she was really smart she'd ditch him because he was a drain on her emotionally and financially. And he never appreciates a single thing that she does for him and there were lots of fish in the sea and blah blah blah." Wet tracks were streaking down her face. "I erased the message when I got to the blah-blah-blah part."

Oliver said, "You called her back, Ms. Graydon."

"Is that a statement or a question?"

Marge said, "We have her cell phone, so we know you called her back."

"I did call her back. I left a very short message. I was busy tonight. How about we meet for brunch on Sunday. It's always easier dealing with Adrianna in the daylight."

"Meaning?" Oliver asked.

Sela's smile was achingly sad. "Don't take this the wrong way. I loved Adrianna with all my heart. But sometimes . . . especially if she's feeling low . . . she has trouble knowing when to stop." Again, she wiped her eyes. "She was never a mean drunk . . . but she could get careless with her words."

"Can you give me an example?" Marge asked her.

"Let me think how exactly to say this," Sela said. "When Adrianna drank too much, she started giving advice—that I needed to get out more, that I needed more exercise. She'd try to fix me up with people I loathed. I knew she was tipsy but I could tell that she was saying what she really thought. It got on your nerves."

Marge nodded.

"She could be really ridiculous." A flush had come to the lawyer's cheeks. "I don't mean to sound snobby, but we're in different places. And Adrianna kept on equating our stations in life. I didn't care about that. But even when she wasn't tipsy, she would say things. Like the time I was complaining to her that I had overbooked a couple of clients and I didn't know what I was going to do. So instead of being sympathetic, Adrianna said to me, 'Oh, you have clients. Isn't that cute.' I swear I wanted to slug her."

The table fell silent.

"Oh God, that's awful of me!" Sela started to cry. "She could be difficult, but she was also the nicest person in the world. I really loved her."

Marge put a hand on her shoulder. "Of course you did. You were close. And close people know how to push each other's buttons."

"It's horrible that she died in such a tragic, brutal way," Oliver said. "But you're not required to extol everything she's ever done. Mean people die, too."

"She wasn't mean, she was just careless."

"She could be a handful," Oliver told her. "Her own father said so."

"She didn't get along with him."

"We gathered that. What did they fight about?"

"What difference does it make? He didn't kill her. I can guarantee that."

"Just trying to get a complete picture," Marge said. "Like when Garth was out of town and Adrianna had too much to drink, did she hook up with men?"

There was a long pause. Finally, Sela said, "She didn't go missing from a bar, she disappeared from work."

"But maybe she was meeting a pickup from the previous night," Marge said. "From what she was telling you about Garth, it sounded like she was mad at him."

"She was always mad at him. But she always went back . . . one of the reasons I tuned out her complaining. She'd never *do* anything about it."

"Maybe cheating was her way of doing something about it," Oliver suggested.

"How could she cheat with a guy? She worked last night."

"She didn't go on her shift until after eleven P.M.," Oliver pointed out.

"She wouldn't go to a bar before she worked." Sela's eyes were moving back and forth. Oliver could tell she was nervous. "She was dedicated in her job. I didn't see her last night if that's what you're asking."

Oliver said. "Would you know if Adrianna went out for dinner or a Coke at a bar before she went in to work?"

"I told you, she wasn't with me."

"That doesn't answer the question," Marge said. "What we're asking is do you know if Adrianna went out last night."

"Okay, here's the deal." A sigh. "I found out after the fact. Because Crystal called me. Crystal Larabee. The three of us were inseparable all through school. God, that seems like ages ago. Anyway, she told me that Adrianna was at Garage last night and she was flirting with someone. But Crystal insists that they didn't leave together . . . that the guy went on to other women after Adrianna left for work. And since Adrianna showed up at work, the guy was probably a dead end. So Crystal didn't want to say anything, especially to the police, because she didn't want to get in trouble."

"Why would she get in trouble?"

"I can't say for sure, but I suspect she was comping Adrianna. Maybe even comping the guy along with Adrianna. She's done it before. Crystal probably didn't want the manager to find out she was giving away free drinks."

"So why does she continue to comp people?"

"Because Crystal is Crystal. The point is that Adrianna didn't leave with anyone, so it's probably nothing."

"What if Adrianna and the guy she was talking to decided to get together the following morning?" Marge said.

"From her phone call to me, it didn't sound like anyone was waiting in the wings. She was tired and pissed. She'd just gotten off shift, so she probably wasn't at her best."

"Crystal isn't at work," Oliver said. "We've already called Garage looking for her."

"She took a sick day off," Sela told him. "When I spoke to her, she was at home and in bed."

"We stopped by her place," Marge told her. "She wasn't in."

"Any idea where she might be?" Oliver asked.

"I don't know. I don't routinely spy on my friends."

"We're just asking if you know where Crystal likes to spend her free time," Marge said. "We need to talk to her."

Oliver said, "But she's not answering her cell phone."

Marge said, "Maybe she doesn't like taking calls from a blocked number. So I've got an idea. Why don't you call her up and ask her where she's at?"

"You want me to fink on her?"

"It's not finking," Oliver said. "It's . . . locating someone, that's all."

Marge said, "And we know, Sela, that you want to do everything possible to find Adrianna's killer."

Sela made a point of massaging her temple. Then she picked up her cell and punched in some numbers. "Hey, where are you? . . . No, I can't come over, I have to visit Kathy Blanc. Have you called her yet? . . . Yeah, I promised. I'm sure she'll want to see you, too . . . No, I'm not telling you anything, I'm just suggesting . . . No, it doesn't have to be now, just . . . Crys, how wasted are you? . . . No, I'm not insulting you, but . . . I know you feel . . . oh dear . . . stop crying, okay . . . I'm *sorry*, okay . . . I feel like shit, too, but I can't come down and drink. I have work tomor—I'll call . . . okay . . . okay . . . okay . . . okay, I will. Bye." Sela turned to the detectives. "Now I've pissed her off. Happy?"

"Where is she?" Marge said.

"At the Port Hole in Marina Del Rey."

"Thank you very much, Ms. Graydon."

"It's Sela and I feel like a fink." She stood up and picked up her purse. "If she asks you how you found her, don't mention my name."

THE MINUTE HANNAH pulled into the driveway, Gabe's stomach dropped. Although the school was not his school, it was a familiar environment—kids, teachers, classrooms, lockers. At her house, he was an alien. He didn't want to have to make conversation with her mom. She seemed nice enough, but like most moms, she was a normal mom. His mom was different: part mom, part peer, part protector, part co-conspirator. The two of them were always figuring out ways how to avoid pissing off his dad. Most of the time, they were successful. Sometimes they weren't, and a pissed-off Chris Donatti was a dangerous thing. Several times, when Chris was drunk or stoned, he'd taken potshots at Gabe for fun. His dad would always say the same thing.

Stop looking so scared. If I had wanted to kill you, you'd be dead.

He loved his mom—really he did—but she had made some poor life choices. He wasn't too scornful, though. He wouldn't have existed had she been wiser. There was even a part of him that loved his dad. His parents were his parents. And now they were both gone and he was once again in limbo. In a perverse way, this day had been one of the easiest that he could remember, not having to deal with either of them.

Hannah shut the motor. "You okay?"

"Yeah." He took off his glasses, cleaned them on his T-shirt, and perched them back on his nose. "Sure."

"Uh, I think my sister and brother-in-law are here. I mean I know that they're here. That's their car."

"Okay."

"Just wanted to let you know. My mom is a great cook. It's probably going to be a shebang with Cindy and Koby staying for dinner. Don't feel obligated to eat everything."

"I think I forgot to eat today. I'm kinda hungry. How old's your sister?"

"Midthirties. She's from my father's first marriage. She's a cop. Koby's a nurse. He's a great guy. I think my sister may be pregnant. Maybe that's why she's here. I hope this isn't overwhelming. "

"It's fine." Gabe pulled the door handle on her ancient Volvo.

The two of them walked to the door and went inside the house. The sisters looked alike—both of them tall with long, wild red hair, a long face, and a strong but not unfeminine chin. Both had almond-shaped eyes. Cindy's were brown, Hannah's were blue. Cindy was taller by a couple of inches—around five nine—but Hannah probably still had growing to do. The dude was black. That surprised him, although he didn't know why. Koby was taller than him but shorter than his dad—around six two.

Hannah said, "Cindy, Koby . . . Gabe."

Koby stuck out his hand and Gabe shook it.

"Dad should be home any minute," Cindy told Hannah.

"A family meal?" Hannah looked at her sister's stomach and detected roundness. She smiled inwardly. "What's the occasion?"

"The occasion is I haven't seen Dad in two weeks." Cindy smiled at Gabe. "I hope you're hungry. Rina cooked enough for an army."

"She cooks like an angel," Koby said.

"Great." Gabe gave him a forced half smile. "I think I'll wash up."

After he left, Hannah let out a sigh. "Oh man."

Koby said, "Has it been hard for you?"

"No, he's a nice kid. It must be strange for him. I get the feeling his life is strange."

"Nice of your mom to let him stay here," Koby said. "I'll see if she needs help."

"I'll join you in a minute." After he left for the kitchen, Cindy said, "I think Dad located the kid's father, but don't say anything, all right."

"Okay. That's good news."

"I hope it's good news. I think his dad's a whack job."

"In what way?"

"I'm not sure. Did he talk to you about his dad?"

"He didn't say much . . . which is what I would do if I were him."

They both heard the car pull up. Decker unlocked the door and broke into a smile when he saw his girls. "How are my two favorite daughters?" He kissed both of them on the cheek. "To what do I owe this honor?"

"You sounded grumpy over the phone," Cindy said. "Being totally narcissistic, I figured my presence would cheer you up."

"It does." He faced Hannah. "How was your day?"

"Uneventful."

"How'd it go with Gabe?"

"Fine. He's in his temporary room. Any luck with his parents?"

"Nothing with his mother, but his father called me."

"That's good," Hannah said. "Any reason why he called you and not Gabe?"

"No idea. I'll talk to Gabe in a minute. Where's Koby?"

"In the kitchen with Eema."

Decker headed for the kitchen and came in just as Koby was lifting an oversize iron-clad casserole from the oven. "Something smells incredibly good."

"Good and heavy," Koby said.

"Chicken-and-sausage paella." Rina kissed her husband's lips. She was wearing an apron festooned with butterflies and her black hair was pulled into a ponytail. "I love one-dish meals."

"There is also a salad." Koby plopped the hot casserole onto the stovetop.

"Two-dish meals, then."

"And all the appetizers. And dessert." Koby grinned. "Don't worry, Rina. I will eat it all. I always do."

"How do you eat so much and stay so thin?" Decker asked.

"I don't know, Peter. I would say that most Ethiopian men are thin, but most of us in Africa are also on a subsistence diet. I think it's genetics and luck." He patted his stomach and picked up a stack of dishes. "I'll set the table."

"I can do that," Decker said.

"You stay with Rina and play sous-chef. My wife and sister-in-law will help. They will probably relieve me of my table setting duties anyway, which is fine with me. I haven't read the paper today."

"It's on the dining-room table," Rina told him.

After Koby left, Decker regarded his wife's inquisitive bright blue eyes. She was bathed in a sheen of sweat and looked incredibly sexy. He said, "I've found Chris Donatti. Rather, he found me. He's driving in from Nevada and should be in town by midnight."

"That's good . . . I think."

"We'll see. I've got to talk to the kid."

"I haven't seen him yet."

"He and Hannah came home about five minutes ago. He's in the bedroom."

"Okay," Rina said. "Will your chat take long?"

"I suspect not. Do you need any help?"

"I was going to ask you to choose a bottle of wine, but I can do it. How about a Sangiovese?"

"Anything as long as it has alcohol." Decker paused. "But not too much. I've got some work to do with a fresh homicide and then I have to deal with Donatti. I need to be on my toes."

"Yeah, the hanging. That's horrible. How's it going?"

Decker blew out air. "It seems the girl enjoyed partying. Nothing wrong with that, but risky behavior widens the net of suspects. We've barely scratched the surface."

"It's going to be a long evening for you."

"When is it ever not?" Decker pulled his wife into his arms. "Lucky for me, I've got an understanding wife who cooks like a demon."

She gave him a lingering kiss. "Let me ask you this. What's more important to you? The understanding part or the cooking part?"

"Depends how hungry I am. Right now, you could be mean to me and I wouldn't care a fig. Just so long as I get my fair share of paella."

LYING ATOP ONE of the twin beds, his hands behind his head, Gabe felt his eyes close a few seconds before he heard the knock. It wasn't tentative, it wasn't overly strong. It was a detective's knock. He sat up. "Come in."

Decker came in and sat down on the twin opposite. "Nothing on your mom, but your father called me about an hour ago from Nevada. He couldn't get a flight out that made sense, so he's driving in. He should be here around midnight."

Gabe felt his voice catch in his throat. He nodded.

Decker said, "How do you feel about that?"

"It's fine."

"Is it?" When the boy didn't answer, Decker said, "No sense being coy. We both know who and what your dad is. How safe do you feel being with him?"

"Safe. He's okay."

"He beat up on your mom. Has he ever beat up on you?"

"No." Gabe paused. "It was the first time he ever beat up on her, you know."

"Maybe," Decker said. "But I also know that your dad has way more sophisticated methods than his fists to intimidate. If you really knew your father, you'd be scared to death of him."

"I know my father." Gabe licked his lips. "I can handle him."

"No one should have to live in fear. That's just basic."

"The thing is . . ." He bounced his leg up and down. "If my mom remains missing, my dad's not gonna stick around to raise me. Even when he's home, he does his own thing. I'm like a nuisance to him. Besides, I don't need anyone to raise me. All I need is a place to live, access to a car and driver, and a piano teacher. Chris will give me money."

"You have other options, Gabe."

"I barely know my grandfather and I'm not living with my aunt. She's a slob and I'm obsessive-compulsive. Her habits bother me way more than my dad's temper. At least he's as neat as I am."

"Okay," Decker said. "If you need anything, just give me a call. You're certainly welcome to stay here a few days to figure it all out."

"Thanks." He took off his glasses and cleaned them on his shirt. The boy mustered a smile even though his eyes were on the brink of tears. "Thank you very much. I take it you haven't heard anything about my mom."

"You'll be the first to know." Decker stood up. "We're about ready to eat. Lots of food. I hope you're hungry."

"I am. Be there in a few."

Decker closed the door and gave the kid his privacy.

He pretended not to hear him cry.

CHAPTER TWELVE

HANNAH KNEW SOMETHING was going on when Cindy didn't drink the wine and Eema kept pushing food on her.

"How about some more cobbler?" Rina asked.

"If I eat another bite, I will explode," Cindy answered.

"Then how about a care package for later. I'll also give you some paella." Rina got up from the dining-room table and went into the kitchen before her stepdaughter could protest. Cindy looked at her watch. It was after nine.

"That went fast. We've got to go. I'll go help her pack up."

"I'll help you pack up." Hannah raced after her sister and met up with her in the kitchen. She said, "Are you sure you don't have anything you want to tell me?"

Cindy felt her face go hot. "Aren't you nosy?"

"Yes, no, maybe?"

Rina said, "Hannah, you're acting entirely inappropriate."

"Puh-leeze?"

"Keep your voice down," Cindy said. "The answer is yes, but I couldn't very well say anything in front of the boy."

Hannah clapped her hands with the tip of her fingers. "When?"

"End of December."

"Do you know if it's a boy or a girl?"

Rina said, "Hannah, that's enough!"

She turned to her mother. "How long have *you* known?"

"As long as Cindy's wanted me to know. And keep your voice down, please."

Cindy said, "Your mom is right. Let's keep it low-key."

"Can I come shopping with you for cribs?"

Rina said, "You can shop with me for a crib. We'll keep one here."

"I can't believe you and Abba kept it from me." Hannah paused. "I can believe that you kept it, but not Abba. He must be so happy!"

"That's an understatement," Rina said. "It hasn't been all that hard because you two rarely intersect with your busy schedules."

Hannah couldn't keep the grin off her face. "I'll help Eema pack up for you. You go sit and relax."

"I'm feeling fine, I'm not a cripple. *You* go sit. Every time you leave the table, that poor boy looks like he's swallowed lye. Do him a favor and ask to be excused so he can be excused."

"Okay." Hannah gave her sister a giant hug. "I love you."

Hannah pranced back into the dining room, where she exchanged wide, knowing smiles with her father. Gabe didn't appear to notice. He and Koby were talking about music. It turned out that Gabe played a zillion other instruments. He said to Decker, "I noticed that your sons have a couple of cases in the closet. Mind if I have a look?"

"It's a guitar and a bass," Decker said. "I don't think either one of them has been played much. Knock yourself out."

"None of us have any musical talent," Hannah said. "Koby has a beautiful voice, but that's only because he isn't a blood relative. Can I be excused?"

"I still see dishes on the table," Decker said.

Hannah sighed impatiently and started gathering the dessert dishes. When Gabe got up to help, Decker said, "You're a guest. She can do it."

"I don't mind, Lieutenant. It makes me feel normal."

Decker nodded his assent. Fifteen minutes later, the couple were gone and the door to his son's room was shut. Actual music was coming from behind the walls even though the amp was turned way down. Decker listened for a moment as notes flew out in rapid succession—bent, twisted, warped. Atonal riffs, but interesting. When Decker knocked softly, the music stopped. Gabe opened the door a crack. "Too loud?"

"Not at all. I just want to tell you my schedule if you need me. Your dad's due in around three hours from now. I've still got a little work left to do. I'll be back here around eleven. I want to be here when he comes to pick you up. I've got to talk to him anyway. If you need to reach me earlier, give me a call on my cell, okay?"

"Thanks. I'll be okay."

"You're all packed up?"

"I will be. Not much to pack."

"Do you need anything?"

"No, I'm fine. Thanks." The teen paused. "Thanks for everything."

"Gabe, if you want a few days to think about things, I can make that happen. You don't have to go with him right away."

"I'll be fine."

"Just so you know, all right?"

He nodded.

Decker said, "I haven't heard anything bad about your mom or her car. Maybe she just needed a few days to think by herself."

Gabe swallowed hard as he nodded.

Decker put his hand on his shoulder. "You're a tough kid. But even tough kids need help every now and then. Don't be shy about calling."

"Okay."

"See you later."

"Sure. Bye." The door closed gently.

The music that followed was soft and melancholy.

———

THE PORT HOLE was a waterfront restaurant/grill/sports bar boasting free hors d'oeuvres during happy hour, weekday specials, and local sports games broadcast on a ten-foot flat screen. True to their ad, the ginormous TV was airing the Lakers-Nuggets game with Kobe Bryant at the line, his magnified sweaty face revealing every open pore. There was such a thing, Marge thought, as too much high resolution.

Sela Graydon's description of Crystal Larabee was as follows: blonde, blue-eyed, good body, probably garbed in sexy clothes, and she drinks cosmopolitans. There were three candidates, all of them at the bar: a blonde in the sequined tank top and jeans, another blonde in the red tee and lamé miniskirt, and lastly, a blonde wearing a strapless black tube and low-rise jeans whose thong was visible.

"My gut says number three," Oliver said.

"I'm with you, partner."

The two of them snaked their way into the three-deep crowd at the bar until Marge was looking over Crystal's shoulder on the right and Oliver was on her left. She was practically falling out of her tube top and her mascara was as thick as tar. She was talking animatedly to a bullnecked block of man who had his hand on her lower back, a finger slipped under her thong. He looked a good ten years older than his prey.

"Crystal?" Oliver said.

"Hey . . ." She slowly turned to face him. "Who're you?"

Her voice was slurred. A dollop of drool sat at the corner of her mouth.

Oliver took out his badge. "Police. I'd like to talk to you."

Her heavy lids were halfway closed. "Wha's goin' on?"

"Yeah, what's going on?" Block Man echoed.

Marge took out her badge. "We need a little privacy. Give us a couple of minutes and we're out of your hair."

"S'right," Crystal said. "I'm tired anyway." She tossed on a black sweater and slung her purse over her shoulder. "I'm outta here."

She slid off her bar stool and tripped. Oliver caught her before she hit the ground. "How about we take a little walk?"

"I don' need a walk . . ." She fished out her keys.

Marge gently took them away. No resistance. "I really think you need a walk first."

She stared at Marge, blinking several times. "Who're you?"

"We're the police," Marge said. "We need to talk to you about Adrianna Blanc. You remember her. She's one of your best friends."

Immediately, Crystal burst into tears.

Marge put her arm around her and Crystal leaned her head against her chest and sobbed. "I know, honey. It hurts."

"It hurts so bad!" Crystal wailed.

A sleek, dark Latino bartender looked up. "Can you get her out of here, please?"

Oliver took one arm and Marge took the other. Together, they led Crystal out of the restaurant, crossed over the asphalt parking lot, took her down a half-dozen steps until they reached the boardwalk. It was an overcast night and the sporadic streetlamps emitted muted yellow light haloed by fog. They schlepped her along the rickety wooden esplanade, passing boat slip after boat slip after boat slip, the spaces holding everything from medium-sized motor cruisers to mega-sized yachts with antennas and satellites. There was a gentle saline breeze coming off the ocean.

In her wedgies, Crystal was having trouble standing erect. "Why, why, *why*!"

"That's what we're trying to figure out," Oliver said. "And you can help us, Crystal. But you've got to focus."

"I don' wanna focus." She wiped her eyes on her arm, tattooing the skin with a black ribbon of mascara. "I wanna go home. I wanna sleep!" She sniffed and began rooting through her purse for her keys.

"Where do you live?" Marge already knew the answer. She and Oliver had gone by the place earlier in the evening.

"In the Valley."

"How convenient! I live there, too. Why don't I take you home and Detective Oliver will drive your car for you."

"I'm . . . okay."

"I know, honey, but this way you can rest." Marge was already steering her back to the parking lot. "Where's your car, honey?"

She squinted. "I think . . ." She tottered and stopped.

Marge said, "What car do you drive?"

"A Prius. Gotta be like . . . econonological."

There were a number of them in the lot. "What color?"

"Blue."

"I see it." Marge tossed Oliver the keys. "See you later."

"Good luck."

Marge helped her into the passenger seat of the unmarked Prius and buckled her seat belt. "Comfy?" No answer. Marge started the motor and drove toward the freeway.

Crystal snored all the way home.

CHAPTER THIRTEEN

ADRIANNA MADE HER home in a block-long complex of three-story dun-colored buildings, planted with ferns and palms, illuminated at night by colored spotlights. Her apartment number was 3J, and Decker walked quietly through the two-bedroom, two-bath unit. She might have been a wild party girl, but she had kept her place tidy. Maybe that was the nurses' training. When he was a medic in the army, he found that organization was not only handy, it was imperative. Lives depended on it.

It was an open-concept design. The living room/dining area was furnished with the basics—a sectional couch with a chaise, a couple of end tables, and a trunk for a coffee table. There was a square dining table and four chairs. The kitchen was tiny with beige tiled countertops and newer white appliances. A flat screen had been mounted to the wall opposite the couch. The place could have belonged to anyone USA except for the only revealing item in the space—a bookshelf.

Not many books but lots of DVDs. More important were the framed pictures of Adrianna in life. She'd been an attractive woman with long brunette hair and a wide smile. She stood on the slopes holding her skis with a goofy grin, she posed with her girlfriends at a restaurant holding up a margarita glass, she stood tall in a cap and gown, with her parents on either side. There were several shots of her with the same man—average height, spiky sandy-colored hair, light eyes, and several piercings in each earlobe. Good-looking guy. Probably Garth Hammerling. Decker placed one of his pictures in his briefcase.

He moved on to the bathroom—OTC analgesics, face creams, birth control pills, and a nice-size bag of weed. He left everything as is and went on to the spare bedroom, which Adrianna had set up as an office. There was a cheap desk that held a Dell laptop and a printer, a rocking chair, and a foldout sofa bed.

A computer was a valuable thing. He unplugged the laptop, closed the lid, and gently slid it into a carrying case. Then he began to rifle through her desk—pencils, papers, receipts, paper clips, rubber bands, tape, Post-its, and dozens of loose photographs.

He flipped through some of the pictures.

Adrianna had an orderly mind. On the backs of most of the photos, she had labeled the people and dated them. The same names and faces kept coming up: Sela Graydon, Crystal Larabee, Mandy Kowalski, Garth Hammerling—the cute guy in the framed, living room picture—and a few of Garth's friends, Aaron Otis and Greg Reyburn. Again, Decker selected several pictures and stowed them in his attaché.

Not much else inside the desk. One drawer was dedicated to printing paper; another contained a tangle of cable cords. He got up and surveyed the clothes closet. It was used as a spare, holding heavy winter coats, a set of skis, a boogie board, six black party dresses, and a set of luggage.

Her bedroom was also neat. A pink paisley comforter sat atop a queen bed. Two night lamps on either side sat on two identical nightstands, which held a clock radio, a land phone, and a pad and pencil. Decker picked up the blank pad of paper and the pencil. Using a light touch, he rubbed the side of the pencil tip against the pad, the indentations revealing a former grocery list. He put the pad down.

A flat screen had been placed atop an open console. Her clothes closet, on the other hand, was jammed. It was neat-ish but not compulsive. Different sections for blouses, shirts, skirts, pants, and dresses, but not color-coded. Formal wear sat with casual wear. She had lots of shoes and lots of running shoes. Dozens of purses, belts, and scarves, and ten pairs of sunglasses. Nothing designer, just mega-quantity.

Decker checked his watch. It was time to get back, just in case Donatti decided to be a speed demon and come in early. He didn't want Chris picking up Gabe without his being there. He gave the bedroom a final once-over. On impulse, he walked over to the right nightstand and pulled out the small top drawer. It was crammed with a Sudoku book, several mechanical pencils, a nail file, several Tampax, and a pad of Post-its. The left nightstand drawer had a wheel of birth control pills, the remote control for the TV, and a latched leather-bound book. Decker picked it up

A diary.

Didn't come across those too often. How lucky is that?

He stowed the diary in his briefcase.

His bedtime reading.

CRYSTAL LARABEE'S APARTMENT was a two-story white stucco building of sixties vintage. She was on the second floor and Marge pitied the person who lived below her. It was amazing how much noise she could make wearing cork-sole wedged shoes. As soon as she kicked them off—with a thud—Marge realized that Crystal was a very petite woman, about five feet tall. The cuffs of her jeans dragged along the floor. She plopped down on her couch and threw her legs on a glass coffee table.

"What time is it? I wanna go to sleep."

"It's not late," Marge lied. "We'll only be a few minutes."

She yawned. "I'm tired."

The doorbell rang.

"Who the hell is that?" Crystal said.

"My partner."

"The guy?"

"Yeah, the guy." Marge got up and opened the door. "This is Detective Oliver. He drove your car home from the Port Hole."

"He did?" Crystal rubbed her eyes and noticed black on her fingers. "I gotta wash my face." She ran her tongue over her teeth and grimaced. "My mouth is yucky. I don' feel so good. Can't this wait?"

"How about if you wash your face, I'll put on some coffee," Marge said. "You do have coffee, right?"

"Yeah."

"So I'll make some coffee, okay?"

"Whatever." She disappeared into a bedroom.

Oliver rolled his eyes. "How much do you think we'll get out of her?"

"At this point, I'm just aiming for the name of the hunk that Adrianna was flirting with. Or maybe he was flirting with Adrianna."

The two detectives took in Crystal's living space. The carpet hadn't been vacuumed for a while and the blinds were speckled in dust. Copies of *Cosmo*, *People*, and *Us* magazines were strewn on tabletops and littered the floor. Furniture was simple: sofa, an ottoman, end tables, a dinette set, and a flat screen on a stand. Messy but not filthy.

The kitchen was another story: dishes in the sink, sticky countertops, grit on the floor, and an overflowing garbage can under the sink. Marge found some coffee in the fridge and milk that was fortunately not beyond its expiration date. She brewed up a pot of strong coffee, found some clean mismatched mugs—she rinsed them out anyway—and poured a cup for Oliver and for herself.

It was taking a while for Crystal to make her appearance. Marge got up from the couch. "Let me see what's going on."

She found Crystal in her bedroom, stripped to her skivvies and fast asleep atop her comforter.

"Oh boy." Marge gave her a gentle shake. "Crystal, we need a few minutes." Another shake. "Wake up, honey."

Crystal opened her eyes. "Wha?"

"Last night, honey," Marge said. "We need to talk about last night."

"I was at the Port Hole."

"Not tonight, Crystal, last night. At Garage . . . where you were working."

Crystal rolled over. "I took the day off."

Marge shook her. "I want to talk about Adrianna, Crystal. She was flirting with a man at Garage. I want to talk about that man."

Crystal turned over and faced Marge. "Huh?"

"Last night at Garage. You were comping them both free drinks. You could get into trouble for that."

That got her attention. She sat up. "You're not gonna say something?"

"Not if you talk to us," Marge said. "Put on a robe, come out into the living room, and let us talk to you for a few minutes. Then you can go to sleep."

"Okay." Crystal blinked several times. Her lids, freed from the crushing weight of the mascara, could move. With a scrubbed face and no makeup, she looked far more vulnerable. "I'll be out in a sec."

"We'll be waiting in the living room."

A sec was fifteen minutes, but she did come out, and when she did, Marge gave her a cup of coffee. "Drink."

Crystal obliged. Her voice was shaky. "You can't tell my boss . . . about the drinks." She rubbed her eyes with her right fist. "If he finds out, I'll get fired."

"For comping a few drinks?" Oliver asked her.

"It wasn't like . . . the first time." Another sip of coffee. "It's not like it's such a big deal. Jeez, they dilute the shit anyway. I'm mostly comping them water."

"You're a good friend," Marge said.

Crystal's eyes swelled with tears. "I wasn't expecting her last night. She just popped in, but I shouldna been surprised. She does that a lot when Garth isn't around."

"Does what?" Marge asked.

Crystal appeared to be deep in thought. "When he's gone, she gets lonely. She likes a little fix of company. She usually doesn't come to Garage because it's expensive—the bar is. But she knew I was working and she knew I'd give her a break."

"Do you know the guy she was flirting with?"

"Don't recall knowing him," Crystal said. "He's not a regular."

"Did you get a name?"

She thought hard. "I mighta heard someone calling him Farley."

"Is that a first or last name?"

She shrugged.

"What does he look like?" Oliver asked.

"I dunno. Medium height, medium weight . . . real big shoulders."

"Good-looking?" Marge asked.

"Not too bad."

"Kind of a hunk?"

"More like the Hulk . . . 'cause of his shoulders."

Marge nodded. Sela Graydon said that Crystal had referred to him as a hunk. Maybe she misheard "hunk" for "Hulk." Or maybe Crystal had reassessed in the light of day. "Were the two of them hitting it off?"

Crystal took another sip of coffee. "Maybe he thought so. Adrianna wasn't serious about a hookup that night. She had to work."

"What time did she leave Garage?"

"Around ten."

Oliver said, "Did Farley seem pissed off when she got up to leave?"

"I don't know if that's his name, Detective."

"We'll just call him that for right now. Did he seem angry when she left the bar?"

"Not at all. I think they mighta even shook hands."

"Could they have planned to meet up later, after Adrianna's shift?"

"Don't know." She finished her coffee. "She left and he moved on to other women. He mighta even left with one. And even when

Adrianna takes it to the next level, it's not serious. She's really into Garth."

"What's the next level?"

A big sigh. "It's not serious with Adrianna, not in her mind at least, but you know how it is. Love the one you're with. Garth is gone a lot."

"I've heard mixed reviews about her boyfriend," Oliver told her.

"He's real cute and he knows it. He takes advantage of her."

"In what way?"

"He's always borrowing money from her. I think he might have a problem. Could I get another cup of coffee?"

"I'll get it for you." Marge went into the kitchen and made a fresh cup for her. When she came back she said, "What is Garth's problem? To me, that means drugs."

"He smokes weed, but that's not what I meant. He borrows money for weekend trips. He goes to Vegas a lot."

Oliver said, "He gambles."

Crystal said, "Yeah, that and maybe he's fooling around on her."

"Maybe they have an understanding," Oliver said. "She fools around on him, he fools around on her."

"She only fools around on him because he's gone all the time." Crystal thought a moment. "Adrianna told me that sometimes Garth has a little trouble in the love department. She blames it on his pot smoking—he does smoke a lot of weed—but I'm wondering if it isn't because he's getting it somewhere else."

"So you're saying that Garth is basically leeching off Adrianna."

"Maybe that's a little strong."

Oliver said, "He borrows money from her, smokes a lot of pot, and gets his jollies with other women. Does the guy have any good points?"

"He's cute."

Marge said, "We're trying to get hold of Garth, but he's on a river-rafting trip."

"Yeah, right!" Crystal was scornful. "It just so happens that the rafting trip happens to be near Reno."

"Really," Marge said. "How do you know?"

"I'm friends with Greg Reyburn, one of Garth's friends. He told me that they are going river rafting, but they're also making a detour to the casinos. He also told me not to tell Adrianna."

"Did you?" Oliver asked.

"I wasn't gonna tell her. But then she looked so lonely. So I mighta said something about Garth not being entirely truthful with her and she should just have a good time and forget about him." Crystal looked up at the ceiling. "I think that was a mistake."

"Y'think?" Marge said, "How did Adrianna respond?"

"She asked what I meant. So I said, I heard the boys were also going to Reno for a little R and R. Then she said, how did I hear that? Then I said, I heard it from Greg. So she said, why didn't I tell her? Then I said, I told Greg that I wouldn't. So she said, well then, why did I just tell her? And I said, I thought she should know the truth so she could have a good time."

Crystal's eyes darted to the left.

"She was pissed. She told me she loaned him five hundred bucks because he told her he was river rafting, not gambling. If she would have known they were going to Reno, she wouldna lent him the money. But then she got up and started talking to Farley or whatever his name is. She started laughing and gave me a thumbs-up. I dunno. I still felt guilty. So I comped them both a few drinks."

"Garth sounds like a real loser," Marge said. "Any idea why she didn't break up with him a long time ago?"

"Like I said, he's cute. Better looking than Adrianna, honestly. And she told me that when they actually did it, he was good in the sack. So maybe that was enough. Or maybe he was good arm candy and that made her feel good. Some girls really like that kinda shit."

Marge said, "Crystal, I want your opinion on something. After you told her about Garth's deception, could she have called him up and broken up with him?"

"I dunno. Check her phone records."

"We have," Oliver said. "She didn't call him, but she placed a call to two different people when she got off shift. One was Sela

Graydon. The other number is a mystery to us, but we do know it's not Garth's cell phone."

Marge said, "Maybe you can help identify it."

When she read off the digits, Crystal shrugged. "Don't know it. It's not Greg's number, that's for sure. What happens when you call it?"

"The mailbox is full without any identification. Sounds like the person hasn't checked for messages in a while."

"Maybe that person is away on a rafting trip," Oliver said. "What about Garth's other friend—Aaron Otis."

"I don't know Aaron's cell number. I could find it out for you. I have to make a few calls."

"That's fine. We'll wait."

"Why would she call Aaron?"

"To get to Garth."

"Why wouldn't she just call Garth?"

"I don't know, Crystal. We're just exploring all avenues right now."

"You know even if Adrianna did call up Garth and break it off, I don't think Garth would care. He wasn't that into her, you know."

"He might not care about her, but he might care about the money," Oliver said.

"And you never know about people, hon," Marge said.

"That's true." Crystal put her mug down. "It's like what I learned in science way back in high school . . . that usable energy—you know, energy that does stuff—it wants to turn into chaos. Well, that's real true with people, too. Sometimes we get it right and it all makes sense. Mostly we just screw up and everything turns to shit."

CHAPTER FOURTEEN

OVER THE LINE, Marge said, "Crystal Larabee got us an ID on the mystery number. It's Aaron Otis's cell phone."

Decker made a face, although Marge couldn't see it. "Garth's river-rafting buddy?"

"That's the one. Otis's mailbox is still full, so it makes sense that he might be in the middle of nowhere, but Crystal has her doubts."

"What do you mean?"

"One of the other buddies, Greg Reyburn, told her that the guys were also headed to Reno for a little R and R." She recapped their interview. "It seems Garth likes his games of chance and all the vice associated forthwith."

"Interesting." Decker was sprawled out on his bed, talking on the extension on his nightstand. "When are the boys due back in town?"

"According to Garth's phone message, it should be in a few days," Marge said. "Adrianna was apparently angry when she found out about Garth's detour. Maybe she was thinking about finally calling it quits."

"If Adrianna wanted to break up with Garth, why call Aaron and not Garth?"

"Maybe she knew that if she called Garth's number, he wouldn't answer."

"Or maybe she was having a fling with Aaron."

"Cheating seems to be a pastime with the two of them. Any indication in her diary of something between Adrianna and Aaron?"

"Not so far, but I've only skimmed it. Her last entry was dated five days ago and all it said was that Garth was going out of town on a river-rafting trip. Reading the entire diary carefully is going to take time." Decker looked at the nightstand clock. It was a little after midnight and Donatti had yet to even call. "I might have a lot of that. I'm still waiting for Chris Donatti to pick up his son."

"Is he late?"

"Not yet, but until he gets here, I'm skeptical. Anyway, most of what I've read so far buttresses what Crystal told you about Adrianna and Garth—that her sex life was lacking and she wondered a few times if he was getting it elsewhere."

"Was she angry?"

Decker paused. "More disillusioned than anything else."

"Any candidates for Garth's fling in her diary?"

"None so far, but I've been thinking about Mandy Kowalski. Didn't you tell me that Garth came on to her?"

"That's what she told us. She said that Garth was a player and she's probably right about that."

Decker said, "If Garth was a player, why did Mandy set him up with her friend, Adrianna?"

"No idea."

"Ask her about it. And find out where she was the morning of the murder."

"She was working."

"Get a time line on her. Maybe there're some unexplained absences."

Marge said, "The CI was pretty convinced that Adrianna died from asphyxiation. She had petechiae in the eyes and face. Mandy's a nurse. She could have poisoned Adrianna, but I don't see Mandy having enough strength to choke her to death, then string up the body. Deadweight, no pun intended, is very heavy."

"Maybe she had help," Decker said. "That's why you need to talk to her again. And what's with this Farley guy, the man that Adrianna met at Garage? Is that a first or last name, by the way?"

"We don't know, Pete," Marge told him. "Crystal was pretty hammered when we spoke, so everything is suspect. We'll take another crack at Garage tonight."

Decker checked the nightstand's clock radio for the time. "I should get off the line in case Donatti's trying to call."

Marge said, "How are you feeling about handing the kid over to Donatti?"

"He's the parent. I'm legally handcuffed unless I can prove abuse, and I can't."

"And nothing on Terry?"

"Not a peep."

"That's disturbing."

"Yes, it is. Get some sleep, Sergeant. I'll see you tomorrow." Decker sat on the edge of the bed and put on his shoes. He went into the living room, where Rina was lying sideways on the couch, a pillow behind her head. She was doing a crossword puzzle and looked up when he came in.

"Can I make you some coffee?"

"No, I'm all right. Where's Gabe?"

"In the boys' room. I haven't talked to him in a while. I figured if he wanted something, he'd ask. I suspect he wants his privacy."

Decker sat down and placed Rina's feet on his lap, rubbing the soles. "Why don't you go to sleep?"

"I hate to leave you alone with him . . . just in case he tries something."

"He's not going to try anything."

"Peter, you butted into the man's personal affairs with his wife. You acted as her protector against him. You listened to them argue. You took away his guns, and that's equivalent to castrating him. In other words, you humiliated him. And you don't think he's going to try to get revenge?"

She had made some good points. "He has other things on his mind—like finding his wife."

"If he didn't already kill her. He's probably seething inside. I bet he's setting you up."

"As pissed as he may be at me, he's still answering my phone calls. Besides, he's a professional hit man. If he wants to get me, he will."

"That's very encouraging."

He smiled. "He's not going to hurt me."

"How do you know?"

"Because if he didn't kill her, he's worried about her and he knows I can help him. If he did kill her, he's going to want to sound me out, find out how much I know about it. Either way, I'm better to him alive than dead."

"Do *you* think he murdered her?"

"It's a possibility."

"And you're handing Gabe over to him after you think he murdered his wife?"

"If Gabe wants to go with him, I have no choice."

"Gabe only wants to go with him because he doesn't want to go with his aunt or his grandfather. Maybe he wants to stay here."

"Rina, if Donatti wants his son and Gabe's willing to go with him, I'm not stepping in the way. That would be unnecessary provocation. Right now, all I want is for him to get here. Got a lot of questions for him."

"He's not going to confess to you, Peter."

"No, of course not. And there is that possibility that he didn't do it. Donatti has made lots of enemies. Maybe Terry's disappearance has to do with one of them."

Rina thought about his words. "That makes sense."

Decker kissed her forehead. "Go to bed. Let me get this over with, all right?"

"I won't be able to fall asleep until you're beside me."

"Then you'll probably be up all night. It's going to take a long time."

"It's okay. I'll wait up." She held up the magazine. "This book contains fifty killer crosswords and I'm only on number four."

AT THREE IN the morning, Decker got up from the couch and knocked on the door to his stepsons' bedroom. After a few seconds, Gabe opened the door. "He's here?"

"You sound surprised." When Gabe didn't answer, Decker shook his head and said, "No, he's not here and he hasn't called. I have a feeling that he might be a no-show."

Gabe went back into the room and perched on the edge of Sammy's bed, folded his hands in his lap. Decker sat facing the boy, on Jacob's bed. The two twins were separated by a nightstand. "I'm sorry."

"I'm not," Gabe said. "I'm relieved."

"You're relieved."

The kid nodded.

"I told you that you didn't have to go with him."

Gabe said, "Actually, yes, I would. Chris says go, you go. By not showing up, he made the choice. For once, I caught a break."

"Now you put me in a bind. What should I do if he does show up?"

"Lieutenant, if he wanted to be here, he'd be here by now. My father's obsessive. That includes being punctual. He's not going to show."

"So you're okay with that?"

"Yeah, I'm *really* okay with that."

Decker stared at the teen. There were bags under his eyes and he looked gaunt despite the big dinner. "You're sure he never hit you?"

"Nope. Never. But just because he hasn't hurt me doesn't mean that I want to live with him—especially without my mom. He's crazy."

"So why didn't you tell me this in the first place?"

"Because if Chris wanted custody of me, that would be it. I'm not about to piss him off. That's suicide." Gabe took off his glasses and rubbed his eyes. "If he wanted me, he'd come get me. He's dumping me on you, Lieutenant. You know that's what he's doing."

"I asked you to stay here, Gabe. You weren't dumped anywhere."

But Gabe knew the truth. Although he wasn't completely without recourse, his future was bleak. So what else was new? "Knowing my father, he'll send some money. That would be his style. He thinks money makes everything okay." Gabe looked up at Decker. "So what's next?"

"I don't know, Gabe. I haven't thought that far in advance."

"I am *not* living with my grandfather. My mom hated him." He looked upward. "I suppose it's my aunt Missy. She's nice . . . infinitely better than foster care."

"Nobody's going to put you in foster care, Gabe. That's not on the table. You can stay here until we have this figured out."

"Thanks." He made a swipe at his eyes then put his glasses back on. "I really mean that. Is that okay with your wife?"

"She's a softer touch than I am. It's too late to start thinking about solutions. Let's both go to bed and things will be clearer in the morning." Decker smiled. "I've got work and you've got school."

"I've got to go to *school* tomorrow?"

"Yep."

"It's three-thirty in the morning."

"So you'll be a little tired. I'm sure you've suffered worse things." That got a smile out of him. "You need school because you need to be in a normal environment—although Hannah may debate my definition of 'normal environment.' If you're there, I'll know where you are and you'll be supervised just in case he does show up."

"I feel real bad about dragging you into this."

"Your mother is missing. It's a police matter. So you didn't drag me into anything." He put his hand on his shoulder. "Get some sleep, okay?"

"Right. Thanks for everything."

"You're welcome."

Gabe bit his lip. "For what it's worth, my mom really likes you,

you know. She always talked about how she wished you were her father."

"Your mom is a good kid."

"And I think, in a weird way, Chris likes you, too."

" 'Like' isn't the right word." Decker thought a moment. " 'Respect,' maybe."

"Yeah . . . that's a better word."

Decker stood up. "I'll tell you one thing, Gabriel. When your parents were kids—not much older than you are now—they were madly in love. It's easy to see your mom falling for your dad. She was young and naive and your dad was not only good-looking and talented but a real charmer. But, honestly, your dad fell just as hard for your mom. He was completely in love with her."

"He still is. He's absolutely obsessed with her. That's why I don't think he'd hurt her. I know he beat her up, but I think that was a fluke. As much as I think he's crazy, I don't think he'd kill her."

Decker nodded, although he knew the truth. The first time was always the hardest. The subsequent times went much easier.

Gabe had a faraway look in his eyes. "I was my father's meal ticket to get to her, you know. If it hadn't been for me, she might have escaped." He stared at the ceiling. "Poor Mom. She was just sixteen. She never knew what hit her."

CHAPTER FIFTEEN

TRUDGING INTO THE kitchen with a load of clothes under his arm, Gabe was living on borrowed time. Despite his best efforts, he couldn't fall asleep and he gave up by six in the morning. He was surprised to find Mrs. Decker up and about. She was dressed in a denim skirt and a long-sleeved T-shirt, and her head was covered with a kerchief. Hannah had explained to him that married Orthodox Jewish women dressed modestly.

A bit different from what he was used to.

The mothers of his friends were cougars, decked out in wife-beaters or tank tops and miniskirts or sprayed-on jeans. Sometimes they wore dresses as tight as a second skin. They all had had boob jobs. They all grew their hair long and plastered their faces with makeup. The idea was to seduce as many teenage boys as they could. He was always *the* trophy among trophies because he was Donatti's kid. They tried and tried and he rejected and rejected.

They called him queer but not to his face.

Mrs. Decker gave him a cheery good morning, relieving him of the bundle he was carrying. It was great to be around an older woman who wasn't trying to grab his crotch. He was in a terrible mood—enraged, abandoned, sick to his stomach—and wanted to hit something. Just beat the crap out of whatever was in his way. Instead, he decided it was more profitable to wash his smelly clothes when he thought no one would be up. "It's really okay, Mrs. Decker. I do laundry all the time."

"So do I." Another smile. "Gabe, you look exhausted. Would you like to sleep in this morning and I'll take you to school in the afternoon?"

"I'll be fine. But thanks."

"Are you hungry?"

"Not really." Silence. "Maybe I'll just rest for a half hour or so."

"That's a good idea."

"Okay." He paused. "Thanks for putting me up and everything."

"It's not a problem. The beds are going empty anyway."

"How old are your sons?"

"They're in their midtwenties. My oldest son, Sammy, is graduating med school and will be doing his residency in New York. I don't know about Jacob. He's got a degree in bioengineering but he's working as a legal aid. He's always marched to his own drummer."

Gabe nodded. "Yeah . . . anyway, thanks again."

At that moment, Decker walked in. He looked at the boy. "You're up early. Or maybe you just never went to sleep."

"I'm all right." An awkward silence. "I think I'm gonna lie down for a little bit."

"Are you sure you don't want to sleep in?" Rina asked him.

"Can't." He smiled genuinely. "Lieutenant's orders."

"You know that there's a rank above lieutenant," Rina said. "It's called wife."

"Thanks, but I'll be fine. See you in a bit." Gabe left the room, knowing that as soon as he was gone, they'd be deciding his fate.

"Coffee smells good." Decker sat at the kitchen table.

"Lucky for you I made enough for both of us." She handed him a steaming cup. "What can I get you for breakfast?"

"How about a working brain?" He hit his forehead. "What was

I thinking, getting involved with Terry like that? Stupid, stupid, stupid."

"You couldn't let her flounder, Peter. Sometimes you need to get involved. And isn't it good that you did? Your conscience is clear and Gabe has a place to stay." She sat down next to him. "Did I ever tell you that my parents took in one of my friends when I was fifteen?"

"No, you didn't. What was that about?"

"I had this friend. Her father was long dead and her mother committed suicide when I knew her. She had an older brother and a younger sister. The brother was on his own and the younger sister was farmed out to some relatives, but the middle one, my friend, had nowhere to go. I asked my parents if they could take her in."

"And they said?"

"Yes, without a moment of hesitation. She lived with us for a year. Then she went back east for two years. Then she came back and lived with my parents for another six months after I got married. It wasn't easy having her. At times I was mad at my parents for agreeing to take her in, even though I had asked. Sometimes I felt like my space was invaded. But I was never sorry I had asked. And my parents did it because they're wonderful people and probably, being Holocaust survivors, knew what it was like to be lost."

"What happened to the girl?"

"Strangely enough, I don't know. We lost contact. Her name was Julia Slocum. She wasn't even Jewish. I had met her at an art class after school when we were like twelve. We became fast friends because she was goofy and smart and always laughing. It must have been very hard on her, but she never let it show."

"Your parents rock."

"They do rock." Rina paused. "I do know that she got married and had kids of her own. I know nothing beyond that and I guess I was never curious enough to pursue something more. It was a relationship for that time. My parents felt morally obligated to help and help they did."

"I know where this is leading."

She took his hand. "You did the right thing by getting involved." She paused. "Now on to the problem at hand. What do you want to do with the boy?"

"Right back at you, darlin'. What do you want to do?"

"There are two solutions—a short-run quick fix and a long-run, more permanent resolution. The short one is that we keep him here and hope his situation takes care of itself—that his mother or father or both show up and take him home."

"Sounds okay. How much time passes before short-run quick fix becomes a long-run problem?"

"I'd say a month."

"And if we're still in the same position after a month?"

"Then I'd say at least wait until the school year ends. And then we reevaluate."

"It'll be a little late in the game to kick him out by then."

"So obviously we're not going to kick him out. But there may be other possibilities. I bet he has money. Maybe he could become legally emancipated."

"Not at fourteen."

"No, not at fourteen. More like sixteen or seventeen. If he wanted to live in a place of his own, like his dad did, he could do that. Or he could live part-time with his aunt and part-time with us. I don't know what the solution would be. We may not even get that far. Could be he'll hate it here and take off for parts unknown. Let's ride it out for a while and see what happens."

"What are you going to do about his schooling? He's not Jewish."

"I have to talk to the school. I'd rather him go to Hannah's school than send him to public school. More quality control. He's obviously not going to attend the religious classes, but I don't think it would be a big deal to let him finish up the year in his secular studies."

Decker didn't say anything.

"What are your thoughts?" Rina asked him.

"I'm still thinking long run, Rina. I was looking forward to retirement, grandchildren, and travel once Hannah left for college."

"I'm sure his aunt would take him whenever we were away. And how much are you going to want to be away with a grandchild coming?"

"That's not the point. If he wants to stay with us, it's three more years of child rearing. It's taking in a troubled adolescent. You're young, but I'm not."

"Whither you go, I go, buster. We have to be a solid front on this decision because it's a big one. However, it's one that we don't have to make right now. So let's just tell him that he can stay here until things settle down. He needs to feel that he has some stability. The rest we'll figure out later."

"Do we include Hannah in this decision?"

"Her life will be disrupted, but I think the decision is ours alone." Rina kissed his forehead. "How about the morning paper?"

"As if I'm not depressed enough." But he took the paper anyway, reading about a world far less organized than his own life. Five minutes later, Gabe came back into the kitchen.

"Hi there," Rina said. "That was quick."

"I'm a little antsy."

"Understandable. How about some toast?"

"Do you have any more coffee?"

"I do. Sit down. Maybe you can cheer up the lieutenant. He looks a little bothered this morning."

"You gave me the paper," Decker muttered behind the broadsheet. "How am I supposed to feel after reading all this depressing news?"

"You take things too much to heart," Rina told him. "Sit down, Gabe. Take some cereal." She plunked a bowl of Cheerios in front of him. "Eat."

A few minutes later, Hannah came into the room, sleepy-eyed and half dressed in her school uniform. She had on the blue skirt but was still wearing her pajama top. She regarded Gabe. "You're still here." A statement, not a question.

"Sorry about that."

Hannah sat down. "What happened?"

"My dad didn't show up," Gabe said. "Big shock."

"You can stay here if you want." She looked at her parents. "I mean that's okay, right?"

"We'll talk about that one a little later," Gabe said.

"You can stay here, Gabe," Rina said. "The lieutenant and I have already talked about it. We'll enroll you in Hannah's school in the meantime."

"Poor you," Hannah said. "Going to my school and you're not even Jewish."

"No pressure to stay, Gabe," Decker said. "It's your decision. We're here to accommodate. Think about it and tell us what works for you."

"I'm okay here." Gabe took off his glasses and rubbed his bloodshot emerald eyes. "I like it. Thank you very, very much."

Decker got up from the table. "See you all tonight, providing that the good people of my district behave themselves."

"Bye, Abba. I love you."

"Love you, too, Pumpkin." He kissed her flaming hair. "Drive carefully. Oh, and you might want to change your top."

"Ha ha."

"I need to sort through a few things on my computer before I go to work." Rina kissed her daughter. "I'll see you both later at school. Drive safely."

"Bye." When her parents were gone, Hannah turned to the boy. "Are you okay?"

"Tired, but I'm okay."

"A bummer about your dad."

"Honestly, it's better. I've known your dad for two days and I like him a hell of a lot better than my own dad."

"He's a good guy—my dad."

"You're really lucky, having a normal mom and dad and brothers and a sister and a regular dinner and all those kinds of normal things."

"I am lucky. I love my family. But we're not normal, Gabe, because there's no such thing as a normal family."

She pulled her chair closer to him so she could drop her voice without her mother hearing.

"My sister is from my father's first marriage, my brothers are from my mother's first marriage. My mom and her first husband got married when my mother was only eighteen. Then he died of a brain tumor when my brothers were real little. My father adopted them. Actually, my father is adopted. My grandparents from his side are like really religious Baptists who probably think I'm going to hell because I'm Jewish. But they love me and I love them and Grandma Ida makes the best pies in the entire world. My father's brother, my uncle Randy, has been married like three or four times. My mother's parents are Holocaust survivors, so there's always that ghost in the background. My mother's brother lives in Israel and is a religious fanatic. Her other brother is a doctor and he and my aunt are nice folk. Their first two kids are doctors as well, but the youngest one has been in and out of rehab since he was sixteen. If I dug deeper, I could probably even pull up more pathology."

She shrugged.

"Sorry to disillusion you, but as far as our family goes, you'll fit right in."

CHAPTER SIXTEEN

HOPING TO FIND some quiet time to read Adrianna's diary cover to cover, Decker had arrived at his desk by seven-fifteen and began sorting through pink message phone slips, most of which could wait but a few needed to be dealt with. There was a call from the coroner regarding Adrianna Blanc, two calls from Kathy Blanc wondering when the body was going to be released, two calls from Melissa McLaughlin, Terry's half sister, and one call from West L.A. regarding Terry McLaughlin.

He made the LAPD call first, to Detective Eliza Slaughter in Missing Persons, who was handling the case. At this hour, he was lucky to find her at work.

"No body, no car, nothing," she said. "Where can I get hold of her husband? I'd love to talk with him, and the number I have for him doesn't work."

"Do you have a few minutes?" Decker said. "I need to bring you up to speed and give you an idea on what and who you're working with."

With questions and answers, the few minutes took twenty.

"Oh my, my," Eliza said. "That's a story and a half. This guy is really a hit man?"

"So I've been told."

"So why hasn't he been caught?"

"He's excellent at what he does."

"And you talk to him on a regular basis?"

"Not on regular basis, but we've communicated on and off over the years. Like I told you, he was supposed to come in last night and pick up the kid. I don't know where he is, but somewhere in the future, he'll contact me or his son or both."

"This is a little much for me to absorb this early in the morning. You say he owns brothels?"

"He owns some legit ones in Elko, Nevada. He used to have others scattered throughout the States that were illegal. Maybe he's cashed those in for the legal ones. I haven't kept track of his business ventures."

"How'd he get a license to run legit brothels if he's a felon?"

"It's all in his wife's name: one of the reasons why they got married."

"Should I call up Elko PD?"

"You know, I've been thinking about that. If Donatti thinks he's going to be cornered, he's gone. My feeling is the best thing to do is wait him out. But it's your call."

"What if he killed his wife? Why would he stick around for you to wait him out?"

"He could have killed her, but the fact that he called me back says maybe he didn't. Did you get a chance to talk to the staff yesterday at the hotel?"

"I talked to the desk clerk and the concierge . . . hold on, lemme get my file." It took a few moments. "Harvey Dulapp and Sara Littlejohn. They both knew Terry pretty well since she's been there for a while."

Decker took out a notebook. "When was the last time they saw her?"

"Neither one remembers seeing her Sunday. She's paid up for the month. Any time you want to go back in the room and look around, that's not a problem."

"Did you talk to anyone in the parking lot? Maybe someone remembers seeing her leave . . ."

"Didn't get a chance to speak to the valets on duty. There's also a self-parking area that has an attendant. That's probably where she left her car. I'd like to go back today and see if anyone remembers her leaving after the kid spoke to her. Wanna meet up at the hotel?"

"I have a big whodunit on my desk. I can make time in the afternoon."

"That would work. I'm trying to get a time line for Donatti on Sunday. What time did you leave the hotel?"

"Around two-thirty. Chris and I walked together to the lot. I saw him pull out. He was driving a black 2009 Lexus, either a GS 10 or an ES 10. Like an idiot, I didn't get the license."

"And he didn't come back?"

"If he did, Terry didn't call me up and tell me. But maybe after meeting him and having things go her way, she felt secure enough to meet with him alone."

"We really need to talk to him, Lieutenant."

"First we need to find him. He's a big, big fish, Detective. If we try to reel him in too fast, he'll break the line and get away. You've got to tire him out."

"Okay, Lieutenant, you've not only got the rank, you've got the history. I'll take your word on this one. When would you like to meet at the hotel?"

"How does two in the afternoon sound?"

"It sounds doable. I'll meet you in the parking lot. I'll also keep a need-to-locate on Terry's car. You know, if this guy is the asshole you say he is, maybe she decided to cut out."

"It's possible, but I can't see her leaving her son." Decker paused. "She definitely wouldn't leave him in Chris's possession. I could see her leaving Gabe with me."

"That may be why you have him now. I'll see you at two."

She cut the line and Decker rubbed his temples. Next on tap was

Melissa McLaughlin. She picked up after two rings. "It's Lieutenant Decker, Melissa. How are you?"

"Nothing about my sister?"

"If I had information, I'd call you right away. She's still missing."

"He killed her! I just know it! The bastard finally did it!"

The bastard who has been supporting his sister-in-law for the last four years since Melissa has been living on her own. Decker could hear her pacing in the background. "Have you heard from Chris?"

"What do you mean?"

"Has he called you?"

"Why would he call me?"

Go slow. "Melissa, there is a very definite possibility that he killed her. There is also a possibility that he didn't do it and is looking for her. He might call you for information."

"What kind of information?"

"Have-you-heard-from-Terry kind of information."

"Why would I hear from her if he killed her?"

Decker sighed to himself. "Maybe he didn't kill her. Maybe she disappeared on her own."

"She would never leave Gabe. She was constantly afraid of what Chris might do to him."

"Did he abuse Gabe?"

"Not that she told me, but Chris is capable of anything."

Approach the subject from a different angle. Decker said, "Melissa, if Terry were to run away—and I'm not saying she did—but if she were to escape, any idea where she might go? Did she have a favorite place where she liked to vacation?"

"Vacation! Hah! The guy wouldn't let her out of his sight. She had no freedom. Her one stab at freedom was moving out here after he beat the shit out of her. And now she's gone."

"So you don't know of any place or country where she might have escaped to."

"You're not hearing me. She wouldn't leave Gabe . . . could you excuse me? I've got a call on the other line."

"Sure." Decker rolled his eyes. Patience. She was just a kid herself.

She came back on a minute later. "Hi. I've got to go. Just find the bastard, okay?"

"Okay. If the bastard happens to contact you, can you let me know?"

"If he comes anywhere near my door, I'm calling 911."

"Probably a good idea. If Terry happens to contact you, let me know as well."

"If she contacts me, it'll be during a séance. 'Cause the way I see it, the only way she's gonna talk to me is from the grave." She hung up.

Kathy Blanc was next in Decker's long line of obligations.

"When can we give her a proper burial?" the grieving mother asked.

"I have a call in to the pathologist," Decker said. "I'll call you as soon as the release comes through."

"And when will that be?"

"Not too long. Probably by the end of the week at most."

"That's a very long time."

"I'll try to speed things up. Thanks for being patient."

"Do I have a choice?" When Decker didn't answer, she said, "How is my daughter's case coming along?"

"We're going through her friends and acquaintances."

"What if it wasn't one of her friends or acquaintances?"

As in a stranger murder. "We're exploring everything including the possibility that the crime was done by someone she didn't know. I'm sending a team out to canvass her apartment complex. Had Adrianna ever complained about someone bothering her . . . maybe stalking her?"

"Like someone who lived in her complex?"

"Someone who lived in her complex, someone at work, anything like that."

There was a moment of silence. "I don't recall her ever mentioning a stalker. But she was a very friendly person. It's possible that someone mistook her sociability for something deeper."

"Of course," Decker said. "Would you happen to know any of her favorite hangouts?"

"She loved movies."

"How about restaurants?" More like restaurants with bars, but Decker didn't amend the statement.

"Her friend Crystal worked at Garage downtown. She'd go there sometimes. Also, I know she liked the Marina."

"How about restaurants closer to work? I know her friend Sela Graydon sometimes goes to Ice."

"I really don't know, Lieutenant. We were mother and daughter, not drinking buddies."

"That's fine, Mrs. Blanc. I just need to ask. Is there anything else that I can help you with right now?"

"Just find out . . . when we can pick her up."

"I will. Call me if you need anything else."

"I need a lot of things, Lieutenant, but I doubt you can help with any of that."

MARGE KNOCKED ON the frame and walked into the open door. She was dressed for summer even though spring had just begun—ecru linen pants, a white blouse, and white sneakers. She plunked a cup of hot coffee on his desk. "For you."

Decker picked up the mug and sipped without looking up. "Good stuff." He raked his fingers through his hair and smoothed his mustache and then smiled at his favorite sergeant. "Thanks for the brew."

"You're welcome. You look exhausted and it's only ten in the morning."

"Catching up on my phone calls." He pointed to a chair and Marge sat down. "Adrianna died from asphyxiation. But there was nothing on her body other than the ligature marks from the cable wire: no bruises, no scratches, nothing under her fingernails. My opinion? She was drugged or strangled before she was hanged—or both. The cable wire around her neck could have obliterated manual marks."

"What about the stomach contents?"

"At the time she died, she didn't have much undigested food. We did test the blood for alcohol and that was negative. There didn't appear to be any cocaine or pot in her system either. For the more exotic drugs, we'll have to wait until the lab work comes back."

"Any evidence of sexual assault?"

"No semen found, but these days our psychos are getting very clever about leaving evidence behind. He could have worn a rubber."

"Any indication of sexual activity?"

"Nothing forced."

Marge said, "I have Lee Wang going through old cold cases to see if we have any unsolved hangings. There isn't anything that pops up."

"It's a weird way to die unless it's suicide or erotic hanging and that's usually more a guy thing than women. And usually with rope, not with cable wire. Did you find a stool or a box that she could have stood on?"

"Nope," Marge said. "But there were piles of lumber around her feet. I tell you what I did find. The cable company called back. They claim that no one was in the area yesterday."

"That sucks. Where are we on locating Aaron Otis?"

"Funny you should ask."

Decker sat up. "You found him?"

"He finally decided to clear his mailbox. I just got off the phone with him."

"So what's going on?"

"Aaron actually talked to Adrianna on the phone and—according to Aaron—this is what she told him." Marge turned to her notes. "He said that Adrianna told him—Aaron—to give Garth a message. The message was—and I quote—that he could fuck himself. Adrianna then went on to say that she was tired of giving him money that he spent on vacations without her. She also said that Garth shouldn't bother calling her back now or ever. She would just hang up on him. When Aaron offered to give the phone to Garth, she did hang up. The conversation, according to him, lasted about two minutes. According to the records, it was two minutes fifty-two seconds."

Decker thought a moment. "If she wanted to break up with Garth, why not call Garth?"

"I don't know, Pete. Aaron felt that maybe she was using him as a messenger of bad news."

"Did he give Garth the message?"

"He did, and this is where it gets interesting."

"Go on."

"The boys were supposed to go on a weeklong river-rafting trip. But they decided to shorten it to five days and spend a few days in Reno for some R and R."

"So that squares with what Crystal told you last night."

"It does. Aaron got Adrianna's phone call a few hours before they were supposed to leave for the rafting trip—at about eight in the morning."

"That also squares with the records."

"At first, Aaron didn't tell Garth right away because he figured . . ." She flipped through her notes. "And again, I quote, 'Why ruin the dude's good time?' But then he thought it over and figured it was better to tell him before the trip in case he wanted to call Adrianna. Once they got deep in the mountains, their cells wouldn't work."

"And?"

"Garth's reaction was unexpected. 'The dude flipped out!' was what he told me. He immediately wanted to go back to L.A. But the other guys didn't want to go back. They had planned the vacation for a while and tried to convince Garth to come along. But he was adamant about returning home. Garth's reaction shocked Aaron. They've been friends for a long time and he really didn't think that Garth cared that much about Adrianna."

"Okay. So what did he do?"

"According to Aaron, Garth packed up on the spot and left in a taxi to go to the airport."

"So Aaron thinks that Garth came back to L.A.?"

"That was Garth's plan."

"Does Aaron know what time it was when Garth left?"

"He thinks around nine in the morning. Aaron and Greg packed their car and left for the mountains about an hour later. Within a few hours their cells were out of range, so he wasn't answering the phone."

"So that was around . . . noon, maybe one in the afternoon?"

"Something like that," Marge said. "When they finally got to the spot where they were supposed to camp, they both realized that the river was really swollen. Plus, it was bitter cold. They changed their minds about rafting. They camped overnight and decided to go back to Reno. As soon as his phone was in range, Aaron checked his messages. So did Greg. They found out about Adrianna roughly the same time because everyone was calling them. They freaked. Aaron was especially scared because he got a call from us—the police. They've both tried to call Garth, but he hasn't been picking up his cell or his house phone. Aaron says he's in total shock about the murder."

"Where are Aaron and Greg now?"

"They're driving home from Reno. I've already informed them that they need to come to the station house. This is a serious police matter. So far both boys have been cooperative."

"And they don't know where Garth is?"

"No idea. I've made a couple of calls to the airlines, Oliver's been calling up Garth's family and friends, and Brubeck and Messing are staking out his apartment." Marge got a buzz on her BlackBerry. She looked at her phone. "Hmm . . . this is good."

"What?"

"Just a text message. Yesterday there was a Mountaineer Express flight from Reno to Burbank that left at ten-ten A.M., getting into Bob Hope at eleven forty-five. That was the woman from the airlines. She's agreed to check the manifest to see if Garth was on the flight." She stowed the phone in her pocket. "I'll call back in a little bit."

Decker said, "If Garth was on that flight, he didn't have a lot of time to act."

"All it takes is about six to nine minutes of strangulation before the person expires," Marge said. "According to my calculations, that's plenty of time."

CHAPTER SEVENTEEN

WITH AROUND HALF the classes being Jewish subjects, Gabe had lots of free periods—all in all a pretty sweet deal.

At 7:35, there was Morning Prayer.

He was excused from that.

There was something called Gemara: Hannah explained it as interpretation of scriptures.

He was excused from that.

English was English. The only difference was that the class was rowdier than he was used to. If his friends mouthed off to their teachers in the way these Jewish kids did, they would not only have been expelled, they would have had the crap beat out of them by their fathers. St. Luke's was supposed to be a Catholic prep school, but it was mostly a holding ground until the boys went off in their fathers' businesses and the girls got pregnant, married, and divorced—uh, excuse me, annulled. There were some smart kids who made it to the Ivies, but most went to State provided that their gray matter wasn't completely pickled in alcohol or drugs by the time they graduated.

So far, the new place was okay. No one tried to mess with him and he kept to himself.

After English, there was Jewish History. Since that class was given in English, they told him to go and try it out. It was all about the Holocaust: he actually found a situation that was far worse than his. They were talking about the Warsaw Ghetto, which he had never heard about.

American History was American History.

And after attending Math, it was clear that the place prized brains over brawn. He could compete on that level, but why bother? It wasn't that the kids were assholes, it's just that his unstable life had turned even more temporary, so it didn't make any sense to try to integrate. The girls ran the gamut between ugly and cute. Not a lot of blondes. About half of the brunettes had pale pink skin, the other half were olive-complexioned with curly black hair—Mediterranean-looking, which he liked because he grew up with a lot of Italians. The girls glanced at him with stealthy looks and half-closed eyes. He wasn't interested, and even if he was, what was the point? The only real redheaded girl he'd seen was Hannah.

He liked Hannah. She was easy to be with, didn't ask questions, had a wicked sense of humor, and there was absolutely no sexual tension between them. It was like she was an instant big sister. He was amazed that she was so accepting of his intrusion. He knew that if the situation had been reversed, he wouldn't have been nearly so magnanimous.

His next class was Bible and that was taught in Hebrew, so he was excused from it. He wanted to go somewhere and sleep for twelve hours, but since he was dependent on Hannah for wheels, he had no choice but to stick around. Besides, if he didn't show up at Biology, someone might say something and he didn't want to cause any problems.

During his breaks, he'd been playing a lot of scales, but the instrument was off tune and it was killing his ears. He didn't mind banging out an off-pitch "My Heart Will Go On," but Chopin deserved a lot better. Since tuning a piano was a specialized skill, he finally gave up.

There was a café across the street and he could use a cup of coffee. Technically, sophomores weren't allowed off campus, but the guards were a joke. Within seconds, he easily slipped out of sight and into freedom—whatever that meant.

He hadn't walked more than a few steps when he heard the whistle—a melodic slide that went from G to C-sharp. It was always the same whistle—always the same tempo, the same duration, and the same pitch.

Gabe's ear didn't come from nowhere.

He stopped walking, his stomach acid churning as his brain went momentarily black. No sense pretending he didn't hear—clearly he had heard because he stopped walking—so now it was just a matter of choosing the right car so he wouldn't look like a doofus.

There were three cars parked along the curb. The Honda Accord was out of the picture—too pedestrian and no pickup. The Jaguar was too flashy and in the wrong color—no way he'd drive a powder blue car. The last one was a black Audi A8—2008. Good car with enough pickup, and most important, probably enough room in front to accommodate his long legs and his six-foot-four frame. The windows were tinted but not dark enough to arouse suspicion.

In a single motion, Gabe yanked up on the passenger-door handle and slid inside. Once there, he stared out the windshield, counting the seconds as they ticked by. He knew that the only way to handle Chris Donatti was to roll with the punches. It took his father a good five minutes before he uttered a sound.

"You okay?"

Gabe nodded, his eyes still fixed ahead. "Fine." He could hear his father breathing hard. No boozy smell; the man was sober and that made him scarier. A moment later, a manila envelope plopped on his lap. It was closed with a metal clasp and taped several times around the flap.

Donatti said, "Your birth certificate, your passport, your Social Security card plus about ten grand in cash, two debit cards, and your bank account numbers. You've got one account that's active with about fifty grand in it. You can write checks off of it or use your debit card. The second account is all the paperwork for your custodial account. That's yours when you're eighteen. There's about a hundred grand in it. The last account is paperwork for your trust fund. You've got access to it when you're twenty-one: you've got about two mil in that one. The bank's the trustee. If you need anything before you turn of age, you gotta go to them.

"I don't know how long fifty grand will keep you, but I'll be checking in from time to time. If you need more, I'll know about it and deposit cash into the account. You should be okay."

Gabe still hadn't touched the envelope. He nodded.

"Any questions?"

Gabe looked down at the envelope, his lifeline to the world. "Are you leaving the country?"

"Gabe, right now I am so fucked up, I don't know what the hell I'm doing."

The admission made him glance at his father before returning his eyes to the windshield. Chris rarely looked healthy, but now he looked exceptionally gaunt. His face was covered by a swatch of blond stubble. His eyes were patriotic—red, white, and blue. Sometimes it was impossible to believe that Chris was only thirty-four. Then there were other times, when his father was cleaned up, off the booze, and had a good night's sleep and proper nutrition; people thought they were brothers.

Donatti said, "I figured the best thing I could do for you was to get your affairs in order in case something happened to me."

"What would happen to you?" Gabe asked.

Donatti let out a small laugh. "Are you serious?"

Silence.

Donatti said, "Look at me, Gabriel." When the boy obeyed, he enunciated his sentence word by word. "I . . . *didn't* . . . kill . . . her."

Gabe looked away. "Okay." Silence. "I believe you."

"But . . ." Donatti shoved a fist into his mouth and took it out. "But it's complicated."

Silence.

"I came back to the hotel . . . after Decker left . . ." A pause. "How's he treating you?"

"He's okay."

"Has he talked to you about me?"

Gabe shook his head no.

"I don't believe that."

"I mean he asked me to tell him if I heard from you. But I hadn't, so . . ."

"So what do you talk about?"

"With Decker?"

"Yeah, with Decker."

"Nothing really. If we talk at all, he asks me about Mom. Did she sound upset when I last spoke to her—"

"Did she?"

Gabe looked at his father. "Not really, but I wasn't paying attention." His heart was beating in his chest. "What happened, Chris?"

"I came back after he left . . . Decker." Donatti squirmed in his seat. "She let me in. We fought. It was a bad one, Gabe. I lost my temper."

"You *beat* her up again?"

"No, no, no." He paused. "I didn't beat her and I certainly didn't *kill* her. She was alive when I left the room. She was scared shitless, but very much alive."

"Why was she scared?"

"Because I told her if she didn't get her ass back where it belonged, I'd drag it back dead or alive."

Donatti wiped drool from the corner of his mouth. He lit a cigarette.

Chris only smoked when he was frazzled.

"I must have been yelling. You know me, I never yell."

"No, you really don't."

"No one can get me as angry as your mom. She knows how to push my buttons and she was pushing every single one of them that day. Fuck, I just blew. I was loud and it was bad."

He took a drag on his cigarette.

"What made it really bad was that one of the fucking gardeners or maintenance men or whatever the fuck he is overheard me screaming. He knocked on the door, asking if everything was okay."

"Did he call the police?"

"No. Your mother answered the door and told him everything was fine. But you'd have to be a moron to believe that. The guy was clearly on the brink of saying something. So I made an appearance and flashed him some money. About a grand."

Donatti laughed.

"He took it, making the problem go away . . . temporarily." He took another drag on the cigarette. "Now, I don't like Decker. I think he's an arrogant self-righteous son of a bitch who gets his kicks out of torturing me. But he's a good detective. How long do you think it'll be before he locates that stupid fuck?"

Gabe was silent.

"He's going to find out that I fought with her. He's going to find out that I threatened her. And now she's gone." Another puff. "Circumstantial evidence . . . because there's no body and without a body you don't get good forensics. It would be hard to prove a case against me. My lawyer would argue that she ran away and went into hiding. That's a two-way street, given the most recent interaction of my fists and your mother's face. Hiding makes sense, but also my killing her would make sense. Juries are unpredictable and I'm not willing to risk it."

He flicked ash into a paper cup.

"If she split to get away from me, I'll find her. She doesn't stand a chance."

Gabe glanced at him, then averted his eyes.

Donatti exhaled out loud. "What I meant is that I can find anyone. And when I do, I'm not going to hurt her. I just need for her to hear me out. I need . . . you know . . . to make it right."

Gabe nodded, although he doubted that they held the same definition of "make it right."

"But there's also the possibility that something bad happened to her . . ." Donatti finished the cigarette and dropped it into the cup. There must have been liquid in it, because it sizzled. "I have to know what happened to her, and if it's bad, who the hell did it. Exact my own kind of revenge on the motherfucker. If I'm locked up, how the hell am I going to do that?"

Gabe stared at the manila envelope—his life summed up in a paper packet.

"You understand, right."

"Of course."

"And you're going to keep quiet about this?"

"Of course."

"Look at me and say that."

Gabe locked eyes with his father. "If you didn't hurt Mom, I would never ever betray you. You're my father."

"Whatever that means."

"It means something to me."

"Do you hate me?"

"Sometimes. And sometimes I love you. Most of the time, I try to keep out of your way."

Donatti regarded the teen's face. "You know you were an accident, but I wasn't unhappy about it."

"Thanks . . . I think."

"So how are you going to explain that to Decker?" Donatti was pointing to the envelope.

"Before I left the hotel, I took stuff out of the safe and shoved it into my backpack."

"What kind of stuff?"

"Some of Mom's jewelry and a lot of cash. The point is that the lieutenant doesn't know what I took."

"How much cash?"

"I don't know. I didn't count it."

"Take a guess."

"Maybe like five thousand dollars. It's in hundreds. You want it back?"

"No, I don't want it back." Donatti lit another cigarette. "If she left behind cash, that isn't good." He inhaled deeply on his smoke. "On the other hand, how far would five grand get her? Shit! This is really messing with my mind. I can't sleep, I can't eat, I can't do business, I can't think. I probably can't even shoot straight. I've got a lot of enemies, Gabe. I'm always looking over my shoulder. I've got to be alert. I've got to know what happened to her. I just can't function until I have this behind me one way or the other." A pause. "You'll keep quiet about this talk, right?"

"Of course."

"I don't believe you," Donatti said. "Not because you're dishonest but because you're too honest. It's gonna slip out."

"I know how to lie." He looked at his father. "I've learned from the best."

"You think?" Donatti laughed. "You're your mother's son. If your ear wasn't as good as it is, I'd swear that your mom fucked some other tall guy while I was penned up. Your face is easy to read, and if I can read you, Gabe, so can Decker."

"I swear I won't say anything. What more do you want from me?"

Donatti was silent for a minute or two. Then he said, "Give me three days to disappear. I can make my trail go cold in three days, okay."

"Okay."

"After that, I want you to tell him that we talked. Tell him I came so I could give you all the shit that I gave you. And tell him I didn't do it. But don't tell him about the fight and don't tell him about the dude who I paid off. Let him figure it out himself. Agreed?"

"Whatever you want, Chris. You call the shots."

"That's what I want."

"I'll do and say whatever you want me to do as long as you didn't hurt Mom."

"When I left her, she was alive. I swear on my mother's grave, that's the truth."

"Then it's a done deal."

Donatti laid a meaty hand on the boy's shoulder. "You'll be okay?"

"I'm fine." In fact he was relieved by his father's admission. Of course, his mom was still missing. But at this moment in time, it suited him best to believe Chris.

Donatti took a final puff on his second cigarette and dropped it into the cup as well. "You know you're in good hands. Better than with me. We both know that."

"I'd be fine with you, Chris. I'm okay wherever I am."

"That girl you're hanging with . . . She's Decker's daughter, right?"

"Right."

"You should fuck her."

Gabe felt his face go hot. "I don't think so."

"Why not?" Donatti paused. "Are you queer?"

"No, I'm not queer."

"I wouldn't care if you were."

"I know you wouldn't." The truth. His father was probably bisexual. Often, when his mom was working late or out of town, Gabe saw Chris taking the young boys as well as the young girls who "worked" for him into the bedroom. Chris Donatti fucked anything that moved.

"You still a virgin?"

"Can we talk about something else?"

"Yes or no?"

"Chris, no guy over fourteen at St. Luke's is still a virgin." That was also the truth. It was a ritual: one of the upper-class girls from St. Beatrix would do you in her car. His first time had about as much complexity as a piano rendition of "Heart and Soul." She had liked him and offered to do him again. She was funny-looking but he still said okay. He, like his dad, never had trouble getting girls.

Chris was talking to him. " . . . don't you want to fuck her?"

He faced his father, staring at cold, dead eyes. As impossible as it seemed, they became even more frigid whenever Chris got angry. "You know, Dad, it isn't always about sex."

"You're wrong, Gabriel." Donatti stroked his grizzled face. "It's *always* about sex."

CHAPTER EIGHTEEN

THE SELF-PARKING LOT sat across from the hotel, elevated and paved, a square of asphalt spread onto the mountain like butter on a muffin top. Undeveloped land in Bel Air was valuable and it was only a matter of time before some conglomerate crunched some numbers and came up with a new development scheme.

And it appeared that the time had come.

Decker read the sign posted at the valet station. It announced the closing of the hotel for renovations and thanked its loyal clients for their patronage. He asked an aqua-shirted valet about the shutdown. He was tall and young and named Skylar.

"They're going to modernize the hotel. It's going to take a couple of years. Can I help you with something, sir?"

"I'm waiting for someone." Then Decker recognized that the valet had been on duty last Sunday. "But as long as I'm here . . ." He pulled out his badge. "I'm trying to locate a woman who was staying here with her son." He pulled out a few snapshots he had downloaded off Gabe's Facebook page. They weren't the best, but they showed Terry and Gabe full face. "She's been here for six weeks."

Skylar regarded the badge and then the pictures, his jaw moving furiously as he worked a wad of gum. "That's Ms. McLaughlin."

"Yes, it is."

"And you're trying to find her?"

"Yes, I am."

"Is she missing?"

"She could be missing or she might have left town on her own. We're still in the investigation stage."

"Why are you investigating her?"

"It's at her son's request."

"Oh." Skylar handed the pictures back to Decker. "She was lovely." A pause. "I mean lovely in her personality. She was good-looking, but she was so nice. She used to tip us even though she never used the valet. A couple of times I helped her carry things from her car in the lot across the street to her suite. Then she'd tip me double even though I told her it wasn't necessary."

Decker had taken out his notebook. "When do you first recall seeing her?"

"I don't know . . . maybe like a month ago."

"How did she appear to you?"

"Appear to me?" He didn't wait for clarification. "She had a couple of fading bruises on her cheeks and under her eye . . . and her lip was swollen. People often come here to relax after they've had plastic surgery. I don't know what she looked like before, but the surgery must have been a real success. She was beautiful."

Decker didn't bother to correct the misconception. "How'd you find out her name?"

"She introduced herself. She told us she was staying here for a while for rest and relaxation. I'm so sorry she's . . ."

Decker nodded. "Did she ever seem preoccupied . . . worried?"

"Not so far as I could tell. She was always friendly."

"Did you ever see her with anyone other than her son?"

A silver Rolls-Royce Phantom drove up to the station. Skylar excused himself, greeted the driver, and parked the grande dame in a coveted spot. He came back a moment later. "What did you ask me?" Decker repeated the question and the valet gave it some thought. "No, I don't remember seeing her with anyone other than the boy. He's about fifteen, right?"

"About."

"Quiet kid. She used to chat us up, saying things like 'Hey, Skylar, how are the auditions going?' or 'When am I going to see your name in lights?' Just stuff to let us know that she regarded us as human. The son . . ." The valet thought a moment. "His name was Dave?"

"Gabe."

"Yeah, that's right."

A classic red Ferrari roared into the parking lot. Skylar was there with the ticket and a smile. After he parked the bucking horse, he jogged back to Decker. "The kid was quiet. Whenever his mother made small talk, he'd stand there looking embarrassed . . . you know, like teens get when they're around their parents. He was a good-looking boy." He snapped his fingers. "He played the piano."

"How'd you find that out?"

"We have a piano in our main hall. The management would let him play it when no one was around. I heard him a couple of times. Man, he was unbelievable—a real pro." Skylar's expression became perplexed. "She's really missing?"

"At the moment, we're trying to locate her."

"What about Gabe?"

"He's being cared for." Decker showed him a picture of Donatti. "What about this man? Have you ever seen him before?"

Skylar studied the face. "I might have seen him a couple of days ago."

"That would be what? Saturday? Sunday?"

"Maybe Sunday."

"Do you remember what time?"

"Maybe around noon. We have brunch then and it's usually pretty busy with the cars. I don't think he had a car. He probably self-parked."

"Do you give out tickets for the self-parked cars?"

"Yeah, but not for long-term guests. If that's the case, you get charged daily on your room, so what would be the point of the ticket?"

"But for someone using the restaurant, say. He'd get a ticket?"

"Yeah, most likely."

"Take a look at the picture again. Can you tell me anything about him."

Skylar stared at the photograph. "He was tall . . . carrying flowers maybe?"

That was Chris. "Did you see him leave?"

"I don't think so." He eyed a plum-colored Aston Martin coming through the entrance driveway. "But I get off at three, so he might have left afterward. Why don't you talk to one of the self-park attendants?"

"Who was on duty that Sunday?"

"Either Trent or Alex. I think Alex will be on at three. Excuse me."

As Decker waited for the valet to tend to the Aston Martin, he noticed a small brunette waving at him. He returned the gesture even though he wasn't sure that he was the targeted recipient. She wore a black suit and a red blouse with low heels on her feet. She carried a briefcase, marching through the lot at a fast clip. When the valet returned, Decker said, "Is there anyone else that Ms. McLaughlin talked to besides you?"

"She talked to all the valets. Probably other service people, too. She was friendly."

"Okay. And one last question. When was the last time you remember seeing her?"

"Oh gosh . . ." He thought hard as he turned over the parking ticket in his hands. "I don't recall seeing her Sunday." He looked at Decker. "But I'm not sure. Sorry."

"You've been a real help." Decker shook his hand. "Thank you very much, Skylar. I hope they save your job for you."

"They're firing everyone," the valet said with a combination of bitterness and wistfulness. "Trying to de-unionize the staff and the only way they can do it is by closing two years. But don't worry about me. Like Ms. McLaughlin said, one day you'll see my name in lights."

UP CLOSE, ELIZA Slaughter was maybe five feet tall, ninety pounds, and had bones as delicate as a songbird. "Yowser," she exclaimed. "How tall are you? About six five?"

"Six four."

"I look like one of your ski poles. Sorry I'm late." Her head was craned upward. "Traffic was a bitch."

"Not a problem."

Her face was equally elfin. She had short, feathery hair, hoops in her ears, and pink cheeks. She wore very little makeup and her fingernails were clipped almost to the quick. He introduced her to Skylar, who excused himself and met up with a Maserati. "The guy was very helpful."

Decker recapped the conversation as the two of them crossed over the bridge, walking down a pathway that cut through a tropical jungle's worth of potted and planted foliage in full spring bloom. The scent varied from pungent to sweet, the rich verdant leaves dripping water from a recent misting.

He said, "Since Terry seemed to be friendly, we should talk to the staff—even those who were off on Sunday. Maybe we could get a list from someone in the lobby."

"I don't know if they're going to be cooperative. Violating their guests' rights kinda thing."

"If the hotel administration wanted to play hardball, yes," Decker said. "On the other hand, the place is closing down, so maybe they'll give us a little latitude. We'll ask for a list of all the employees, which we won't get. Then we'll ask for just a list of the people working on Sunday, which we'll probably get. Let's stop by the office once we've looked at Terry's suite. Who we really need to talk to is Alex or Trent, the self-parking lot attendants. Now that Terry's an official missing person, I want to see if (a) someone remembers Terry leaving in her car; (b) if someone does remember her leaving, was she alone; (c) if she wasn't alone, who was she with; (d) does anyone remember Chris Donatti coming in and leaving and coming back; and (e) if they do remember all this, what was the time frame?"

"That's a lot to remember."

"Maybe the attendant wouldn't pay too much attention to Chris, but I'm betting an attendant would remember Terry. She'd been holed up here for a while, and like I said, she seemed to be an amiable person."

They stopped at the door to Terry's suite. Since she had paid up until the end of the month, the card key that Gabe had given him still worked. On the night of Terry's departure or disappearance, Decker had given the hotel instructions not to go inside and clean the suite. It was a compromise reached between a reticent clerk and Decker. In exchange, Decker agreed not to string up crime-scene tape across the door.

The rooms were exactly as Marge and he had left them. It smelled a little stale in the heat. Decker opened the patio door and stepped outside. He examined the planting area that surrounded the brick pad—azaleas, impatiens, gardenias, and camellias. He was looking for anything that signaled a fight or a struggle: broken branches, crushed bushes, footprints in the dirt. The space was impeccably manicured and in full bloom. He came back into the suite.

Eliza was in the bathroom. "Medicine cabinet is empty."

"We bagged the contents."

"What did you find?"

"Advil, Tylenol, Benadryl, a recent prescription for Ambien, and a prescription for Vicodin. The bottle was dated two months ago and it was half full. I don't think she'd been using it recently. You want me to drop the stuff off at West L.A.?"

"No, you can keep it in your evidence room," Eliza said. "What about birth control?"

Decker raised his eyebrows. "Didn't find it."

"How long had she been with her husband?"

"I don't know exactly when they married, but they've known each other for around sixteen years."

"She must have been taking something to prevent future babies, don't you think?"

"As a matter of fact, that's what caused Donatti to snap. He thought she had aborted his baby. It turned out she was paying for her half sister's abortion."

"So, they've been trying or . . ."

"Who knows? He obviously didn't want her having an abortion." Decker thought a moment. "Terry was going to rent a house in Beverly Hills. She got Donatti to agree to pay for her living arrangement even though he was probably not going to live there."

"And her controlling hit-man husband agreed to that?"

"Chris was feeling contrite." Decker smoothed his mustache. "Terry did make a strong point of telling him that he'd have the key and that he could come whenever he wanted. She implied that they would still share a bedroom when he was in town."

"So she was probably on birth control if their relationship was ongoing."

"Or she wanted Chris and me to believe that it was ongoing."

"You think she was scamming you?"

"No, not scamming me. Maybe she was trying to convince people like me that something happened to her. Maybe she's been planning this, she knew she was never going to see Chris Donatti again, and she threw away her birth control."

"And you think she'd just get up and leave without her kid?"

"Yeah, that's the rub, and it's a big one. It's certainly possible that Donatti came back and got her."

"Got her? Like offed her?"

"Maybe. I don't know. He seemed okay with her renting the house when I was around, but it could have been an act." He glanced around the room. "If Terry left the hotel with Chris, she didn't leave me any signs that she left in distress."

"Do you think he could kill her here and not transfer any kind of evidence?"

"Usually something is left behind, but he's . . . good at what he does. Marge and I examined the carpets, the walls, the baseboards, the shoe moldings. We scoured the bathrooms and sinks and tub drain. We didn't find even a hint of blood. Nor did we find any evidence that someone had cleaned up. No smells of disinfectant, no towels missing, no used boxes of Kleenexes."

"Her car is gone," Eliza said. "If she disappeared for good—as in dead—she might have left behind her birth control."

"Yeah, she could have run off with another man. Donatti pretty much stalked her, so I don't know how she'd develop a relationship."

"But even the most diligent stalker isn't there all the time. What does her son have to say about that?"

"He seems genuinely perplexed by her disappearance. Maybe she didn't tell him her plans."

"Or there were no plans," Eliza said. "Donatti came back and murdered her."

"Or someone else killed her. Until we find her body, we don't have a clue as to what we're dealing with." Decker gave the room a final glance. "I don't think we're going to get much more out of this. Let's see what the staff has to say about friendly Dr. McLaughlin and her quiet son, Gabe."

CHAPTER NINETEEN

THE ONE GREAT thing about playing was that it was all consuming. When he was into it, Gabe simply didn't have the psychic energy to deal with anything else. Playing transported him to another place. He was so focused on what he was doing, he was able to shut out the world. Unfortunately he had only one hour of intense solitude before Hannah and the others would come in for choir practice. The way his nerves felt—raw and discharging at whim—he would have done well with an entire week of isolation—just him and Mr. Steinway.

Hannah was the first to arrive. She immediately walked over to him. "Hey." She sat down at the piano bench next to him. "Where'd you disappear to?"

Gabe felt his skin go hot. "Someone noticed I was gone?"

"Yeah, *I* did. You had me worried."

"Worried?" He was mystified. "Why?"

Hannah was puzzled. "After what happened to your mom, I'd think you'd want to be a little cautious."

"I just got a cup of coffee. I'm fine. Do me a favor and forget about me, okay."

She was silent. "I don't mean to look over your shoulder, Gabe. It's just that my dad's a little concerned about you."

"Why? What does he think's gonna happen?"

"He's probably a little uneasy about what Dad could do."

Again, Gabe felt his face warm up. "I keep telling *your* dad that *my* dad doesn't give a shit about me." His fingers danced up and down the keyboard. "See, your dad is thinking like a dad. My dad doesn't think that way. Unless I have something he wants, he has no use for me. When I was attached to my mom and we came as a package, he wanted my mom, so he was stuck with me. But now my mom's gone. Ergo, he doesn't give a rat's ass about me."

"I'm sure that's not true."

"Rest assured that my dad is out of the picture." He turned back to the keyboard, hoped his lies—well, half lies—were convincing.

When he was little—before his parents married—Chris used to come visit them in Chicago, where his mom was going to med school. He and Chris used to spend a day together. They'd go to the park in the morning, have lunch at a restaurant, then they'd go back to the apartment, where Chris would sit him down at the piano for a two-to-three-hour lesson. Even though Chris wasn't a pianist, he was a musician and knew brilliance in any instrument.

He was one of the best teachers that Gabe had ever had.

After his parents got married and they moved to New York, things rapidly went downhill and escalated into chaos. No one could live with that man full-time.

"I'll talk to your dad," Gabe told her. "And stop worrying about me. I can take care of myself. I've been doing it all my life."

A few more kids started to filter in.

Gabe got up. "I'll help you set up the chairs."

Hannah put her hand on his shoulder. "Don't be mad."

"I'm not mad, I'm just . . ." His jaw was clenched so hard, his teeth ached. "Sometimes . . . the enormity of what happened just hits me, drags me under like this giant wave . . . and it's just real hard to stay afloat 'cause the water keeps coming and coming and coming. And every time you surface and you catch your breath, there's still another giant wave to deal with." He faced her. "I have so much *rage* inside of me." He realized he was scaring her and he forced out a smile. "But then it passes and I'm fine."

She let her hand slide from his shoulder. "You don't have to be happy, Gabe. What you're going through sucks."

"I'll be fine."

She studied his face. "You know, that's why you don't judge people on first impressions. You're real good-looking and you're really gifted and all the girls in the school keep pestering me about you. And the boys all ask about you because you come across as this real cool guy with this swagger."

"I don't swagger."

"Yes, you do."

Gabe laughed. "My father swaggers. I don't swagger."

"Yes, you do."

Mrs. Kent's voice broke through the debate. "Decker, you have plenty of time to flirt after choir. Now kindly set up the chairs."

"Right away." She took a pack of folding chairs and began to set them up. To Gabe, she said, "I'm not a cougar. I don't flirt with young boys."

"I know. That's what I like about you. You're very . . . like . . . sisterly with me."

"That's me." Hannah sighed. "I'm everyone's perennial big sister."

"I didn't mean it like that."

"I'm just teasing you, Gabe."

"I mean I think you're very pretty."

Hannah was grinning. "You can stop now."

"I'm sure all the boys have crushes on you. I mean I have a crush on you."

"Is that your own grave you're digging?"

"It's just that I need a friend *way more* than a girlfriend."

"I get it." She placed her hands on his shoulders. "For your information, I'm already spoken for. His name is Rafi. We went to camp together last summer. He's in Yeshivat HaKotel, but he's doing Shana Bet so we can be together in Israel next year."

"I understood everything you said except for the last sentence."

"No matter. It means as far as my availability goes, Whitman, you're out of luck."

"Well . . . all right, then."

"And don't you dare get all mopey. You just said you considered me a big sister."

"I do consider you that way. And I'm not mopey. And even if I were mopey, it wouldn't be because of you. I'm just mopey because I'm in a bad situation. So stop trying to claim ownership of my mopeyiness."

"Well, excuse me!"

They both broke into laughter.

Mrs. Kent was glaring at them. "Perhaps you'd like to share with the rest of us what you find so hilarious, Ms. Decker?"

Hannah stifled another round of the giggles. "Why are you picking on me, Mrs. Kent? He was laughing just as much as I was."

"You are the president of choir. You have to set an example."

She began putting up the last row of chairs. "So I get reprimanded and he gets off scot-free?"

"Indeed, Ms. Decker, the world isn't a fair place."

"You just like him better because a mediocre alto is way more replaceable than a spectacular accompanist."

"You're treading on thin ice, young lady."

"I know, I know," Hannah said. "The truth hurts, but that isn't your fault. Between the two of us, I'd choose him as well."

Mrs. Kent's eyes softened. "Hannah, you're a one-of-a-kind and totally irreplaceable." She clapped her hands. "Everybody take your seats. Ms. Decker, since you were duly elected president, would you like to lead us in a rousing rendition of the national anthem and 'Hatikvah'?"

Hannah beamed. "Mrs. Kent, it would be my pleasure."

ALEX—THE SELF-PARKING LOT attendant—was in his sixties, a tall man with white hair who looked spiffy in his aqua shirt, white pants, and white slip-on shoes. He sat behind a podium shaded by a beach umbrella. At five in the afternoon, the sun was low and hot. Decker recognized him as the man who gave him a ticket on Sunday. That meant Alex was on duty when Chris arrived and left.

When Decker showed him Terry's photograph, he identified her immediately.

"She's a real nice woman. Always smiling and slipping me a few bucks every time she took her car in and out even though she didn't have to."

"When was the last time you saw her?" Eliza Slaughter asked.

"Last time I saw her?" Alex frowned. "Something happen to Ms. McLaughlin?"

"She appears to be missing," Decker said.

"Missing?" Alex grimaced. "Oh my, that's not good."

"She may have left on her own," Decker said. "That's why we're trying to retrace her steps. When was the last time you remember seeing her?"

"Golly, must have been a couple of days ago. Maybe Sunday." He studied Decker's face. "I've seen you before."

"I was here on Sunday, too. I left around two-thirty."

"Aha."

"When I left, Ms. McLaughlin was still at the hotel. Do you remember if you saw her after three in the afternoon?"

"No, sir, I was pretty busy."

"But you remember the lieutenant?" Eliza said.

"He's a hard man to miss."

Decker showed Alex a picture of Donatti. "What about this man?"

Alex looked at it for a while. "This guy . . ." The attendant tapped the picture with his fingers. "He was here on Sunday. He was carrying a bunch of flowers. Who is he?"

"Ms. McLaughlin's husband."

"She's married?"

"Yes," Eliza said. "Does that surprise you?"

"Yeah, a little. She just seemed so carefree to be married." When both Decker and Eliza erupted into laughter, Alex said, "I didn't mean it like that. Been married for forty-two years—"

"I'm happily married, too," Decker said, "but I know what you mean."

Eliza said, "So you remember this guy carrying flowers. Did you give him a ticket?"

"I give everyone who's not a long-term guest a ticket. They got to get it validated at the hotel or restaurant. Otherwise they can't park here."

Decker said, "Do you remember what time he arrived?"

"Sunday's brunch is between eleven and four. It gets real busy." He snapped his fingers. "But I'll tell you something that might help. Every time someone comes in here, I write down the license number on the ticket. That way, at the end of the day when I turn in the tickets, the folks in accounting can reconcile the validations with the cars."

"A license plate would be handy since I didn't bother taking it down myself," Decker said.

"Do you know how long accounting keeps the tickets?" Eliza asked.

"Nah, you'd have to check with them."

"What time did you get off work on Sunday?" Decker asked.

"Me? Around five."

Eliza said, "And you don't remember Ms. McLaughlin coming into the lot to pick up her car?"

Alex thought very hard. "Can't say yes or no. I don't want to say something that might mess you up later on."

"That's fine," Decker said. "We'll see if we can get her husband's ticket. Thanks, Alex, you've been a big help."

"Wish I could be a bigger help," the attendant said. "But you know how it is, you can't pay attention to everything."

"Nor are you expected to pay attention to everything," Decker said.

Him, on the other hand. He was a friggin' lieutenant. Why hadn't he taken down Chris's license plate?

A rather big omission.

He thought about it for a moment, tried to put himself back in time.

He saw the car driving away. Then he remembered. The front and back plate were paper. "Hey, Eliza."

"What?"

"The Lexus that Chris was driving. It had paper plates. So either he switched them out or the car was new and it was rented."

WHILE ELIZA JOTTED down the local car rental services, Decker checked his cell. There was an urgent message from Marge. He called her back, and when she answered, he said, "Tell me you found Garth Hammerling."

"Not yet," Marge told him. "But I just heard from Aaron Otis. The two boys will be in town in about an hour."

"Marge, I can barely hear you. There's a lot of static on the line."

"That's because I'm in a parking lot . . . hold on, Pete." She quickly ran up the stairs until she was on ground level. Then she walked outside. "Better?"

"Much. What parking lot?"

"St. Tim's. We're in the process of pulling the videocassettes from the security cameras in the parking lot. The head guard told us that the cassettes are erased and replaced once a month."

"Tell me good news."

"We just squeaked by, Rabbi. They were due to be changed in a few days. How clear the recording is, or if Adrianna or her car is even on the film, is another thing altogether."

"How many cameras would pick up the area around Adrianna's car?"

"One camera definitely works that area. We might get a peripheral view from another one. We're also pulling the tapes from the entrances and exits to the parking lot to see what time Adrianna left the hospital. We'll probably view them all in a little bit."

"At the station house?"

"No, at the security station here at the hospital. The guards are watching over the cassettes like hawks."

"Good for them. It's just too bad they weren't as diligent with Adrianna."

CHAPTER TWENTY

THE WOMAN BEHIND the reception desk was named Grace. She was in her early forties with a pale face and soft, honeyed curls. She wore a black suit and a button-down aqua shirt with the name of the hotel emblazoned over the pocket. Her brown eyes turned sad when she spoke about the closure.

"I started working here when I was twenty-three, fresh out of hotel management. I was so green that on my first day my voice shook. I sounded like I was gargling."

Eliza smiled. "I'm sure you did okay."

"I was awful," Grace said. "But management had patience back then." She rolled her eyes. "They knew how to nurture a career."

"How long have you been here?" Decker asked.

"Twenty-two years."

"Do you have any future plans?"

"Take a long vacation. Then who knows? The hotel business isn't so hot right now, but like everything, it cycles. Maybe by the time I start looking, opportunities will present themselves." Grace gave a practiced smile. "You're not here to listen to my issues. How can I help you?"

"We're looking for one of your guests."

"Ms. McLaughlin. Someone called here yesterday to ask about her."

"That would be me," Eliza said.

"I've thought about it. I haven't seen her since maybe the middle of last week."

Eliza said, "That would be around Wednesday?"

The phone rang. Grace held up a finger, answered the call, and transferred it to the dining room. "Wednesday . . . maybe Thursday."

"And you didn't see her over the weekend?"

"I didn't work the weekend."

Eliza went through her notes. "That was Harvey Dulapp and Sara Littlejohn. They didn't see Terry that Sunday, but we know she was here."

Decker said, "I was told that Ms. McLaughlin was a very friendly person. Did she ever drop in just to say hello?"

"Not just to shoot the breeze," Grace said. "If she dropped in, it was to collect her mail or pick up her messages. Um . . . I remember a few weeks ago, there was a maintenance issue with her toilet. She came in personally to tell us about it. And she was very friendly."

"Do you know who serviced her toilet?"

Grace smiled. "Is that important?"

"Anyone who went in and out of her suite is important to us," Decker told her.

"I'll call maintenance and see if they have a record of who answered the service call. I must tell you that they're down to a skeleton crew. If something breaks, we've been given the orders to transfer the guest into another room and just black out that problematic room."

"Did they move Ms. McLaughlin to an upgraded suite?" Eliza asked.

"No, she was in a premium unit. They had to fix her toilet. All I'm saying—" The phone rang. "Excuse me."

Grace was several minutes on the phone. When she came back,

she gave the detectives a weary look. "Vis-à-vis our conversation, one of the TVs isn't working. I have to find another room for this guest. Excuse me, what did you want again?"

"The names of anyone who went in and out Ms. McLaughlin's suite."

"You mean the maintenance people."

Decker said, "Maintenance, housekeeping, room service. It might be easier if you gave me a list of employees. That way Detective Slaughter and I can go through them and check them off one by one."

"I'm sorry, Lieutenant, I can't give you that. You'd have to talk to someone in senior management. Besides, so many of our employees have already left."

Decker appeared to think a moment, but he knew what he was going to ask for. "Well, could you at least call maintenance and housekeeping and find out who was working on Sunday afternoon when she disappeared."

A big sigh. "I can probably get you that, but it may take a little bit of time."

"Is there someone we could talk to in maintenance and house-keeping to ease the burden?"

"That's sweet. I'll call up housekeeping and maintenance for you."

"Thanks so much," Decker said. "One more thing. The lot attendant in self-service parking told me he turns the day's parking tickets into accounting when he's finished. Where would we find that department?"

"It's not a department anymore, it's a person. Debra's in the back. Would you like me to send her out?"

"It might be easier if you send us in," Eliza said.

"I'll ask her if she's busy," Grace said.

"Thanks. It's important that we find this woman. She has a son."

"Yes, the boy . . . Gabe. What a shame." Grace shook her head. "This is terrible. Nothing like this has happened here before. It really gives the hotel a black eye." She paused. "Then again, the whole place is being shut down for at least two years. Lucky for the new owners that people in this town have very short memories."

THE HOSPITAL'S SECURITY office was in the basement of St. Tim's—a futuristic, windowless area filled with black-and-white monitors, alarms, sensors, cassette and DVD players, and a wall-size panel of buttons. The cameras shone on the institution's entrances and exits, the elevators, the stairwells, the interior hallways, and all the class-three drug cabinets. The space was cavelike: compact and dimmed to see the monitors. Marge hated dark and small, her abhorrence courtesy of a horrendous raid years ago when she was forced to crawl through a tunnel in order to evacuate children from a cult and a homicidal maniac. One of the superb things to come out of that mess was her adopted daughter, Vega. Oliver knew of this foible and gave her a reassuring pat on the shoulder.

The head of security was a Russian fellow named Ivan Povich. Currently, he was sharing the warren with a uniformed guard named Peter, who continually stared at the monitors and had yet to utter a sound. Povich spoke with a slight accent. "We also have a smaller security room on each floor."

Marge was studying the images on the screens—people going in and out. It calmed her down. "But here's where you monitor all of the hospital's entrances and exits."

"Yes," Povich said. "And we always have someone watching them at all times. We take the job seriously. Usually it's Peter."

Peter gave a wave.

Oliver said, "What about lunch and bathroom breaks?"

"Whoever is on duty calls for a relief person before he or she leaves. That way, we always have a pair of eyes. If there was a problem, someone would have seen it."

"Who was on duty yesterday morning?" Marge asked.

Peter waved again.

"How long have you worked here?" Marge asked him.

"Forever," Povich answered. "He is my best man. I have no trouble with any of my men and women. If I have trouble, they're out." He handed Marge a box. "Here are the cassette tapes from yesterday. Usually we just reuse them, but I already put new ones in the cameras, so you can take your time looking at them. If you need something, ask Peter and he'll call for you. Before you get started, do you want coffee or water?"

"Water would be great," Marge said.

Povich said. "And you, sir?"

"Coffee—as strong as you can make it."

"No problem. You know how to work this cassette machine?"

Oliver said, "I'm sure we can figure it out."

"You need help, you can ask Peter."

"Does the man talk?" Marge asked.

"Only when he has something to say."

Ten minutes later, the two detectives were staring at a black-and-white tape. They had rewound the first cassette to around ten-thirty the previous Sunday night, then they fast-forwarded the tape. But not too fast not to notice the people on it. At 10:50, a Honda pulled into a parking spot.

Marge said. "That's the car."

Oliver slowed the tape to normal speed as they both watched Adrianna get out of the driver's seat, her eyes focused straight ahead until her image disappeared from view. They rewound the tape several times to make sure they didn't miss anything. When they were satisfied that they had noted all that could be noted, they allowed the tape to move forward, the image of Adrianna's parked Honda in the middle of the monitor.

As the tape kept rolling, they continued to stare . . . and stare . . . and stare.

DEBRA FROM ACCOUNTING was cooperative, handing over the parking tickets once Decker explained that all they wanted to do was match each license plate number on the ticket with a name. He assured her that he wasn't interested in any of the guests except one—Chris Donatti, Terry McLaughlin's husband.

She said, "Even so, I'd appreciate it if you wouldn't tell anyone where you got the information from. When will you give them back to me?"

Eliza said, "I'll go through them as quickly as I can. If you need anything, I work at West L.A. I can come back here on a moment's notice."

"Thanks, I appreciate that."

Decker said, "How would I get to the maintenance and house-keeping offices?"

"I could tell you, but it's easier if you ask Grace for a map."

"Thanks for your help."

"Sure. I'd say anytime, but I'll be out of a job in a few weeks," Debra said. "But don't worry about me. My kids are delighted, my husband is delighted, and my aging mother is really delighted." She smiled. "My former housekeeper and my former personal trainer, who were paid from my salary . . . them, not so much."

AS THEY WALKED through wooded pathways, Eliza scanned the batch of parking tickets. "Some of them don't have license plate numbers."

"Probably during a busy time and he got a little careless." Decker shrugged. "Nothing we can do about it."

"Hey, Lieutenant." Eliza was enthusiastic. "We've got two time stamps per ticket. One coming in and one going out. That's a break. If we find Donatti's Lexus, we'll know when he came in and when he left."

"If the attendant was smart enough to mark it as a Lexus with paper plates."

"If Donatti was going to do something bad, would he have parked his car in the parking lot? Much more likely he'd be noticed."

"Unless it was an unplanned thing, although Donatti isn't usu-ally rash," Decker said. "But he did beat up his wife . . . using only an open palm . . . he was quick to tell me that. Like that was sup-posed to impress me."

"What a scumbag."

"A scumbag and a psycho," Decker said.

"How's the kid?"

"Quiet . . . unobtrusive. It's hard to tell what he's thinking. My daughter seems to have developed a rapport with him."

"Uh-oh."

"Yeah, I've thought about that," Decker said. "He's a good-looking kid. But she's seventeen and has a boyfriend and will be out of the house in several months. He's only fourteen." A pause. "If he were a couple of years older, I know I wouldn't have let him stay with us."

"Genetics, huh? Sins of the father."

"Especially when it comes to my daughter. Hannah is smart but naive. I don't know much about Gabe, but I suspect he's way more streetwise than she is."

They walked a few more moments in silence until they arrived at the maintenance office. The door was open and they crossed the threshold. The space inside was hot and confined. A swarthy man at the desk was sweating profusely. "Yes?"

"We're looking for Gregory Zatch."

"That's me."

Decker brought out his badge and identified the two of them as homicide detectives.

"Homicide?" Zatch said. "Someone got killed?"

"Someone is missing," Eliza explained. "Sometimes we're given those cases. We're here because a couple of weeks ago, maintenance was called for a plumbing problem in suite 229. A leaky toilet." She fanned herself with a handful of parking tickets. "We'd like to know who serviced the unit."

"The missing someone was in 229?" Zatch said.

"Yes."

"How long has the person been missing?"

"Since Sunday night," Eliza said.

"Teresa McLaughlin," Decker said. "Have you ever met her? We hear she was a friendly gal."

Zatch thought. "I don't remember."

"She has a fourteen-year-old son," Decker said. "We don't think she would have left him alone voluntarily."

"Ah, the boy. I remember him. He plays piano like a master." He shook his head. "It does not sound promising . . . her being missing. And you think that one of my men had something to do with it?"

Decker said, "This is routine, Mr. Zatch. We're just checking who went in and out of the suite while she was staying there."

Zatch's expression was sour. "You notice how hot it is in here?"

"Hard not to notice," Eliza said as she continued to fan herself.

"Management has turned off the air-conditioning in the office."

"That stinks."

"I've complained. They say if we don't like the working conditions, we should leave. And you know what? Most have left. We're down to four . . . no, not four. Three men. One of them just quit yesterday morning. That means the lone survivors are working double shifts. None of us hurt your lady. Too busy answering calls."

"Did the guy who serviced the toilet in 229 quit?"

"I have to check . . . when was the date of the call?"

"I don't know the exact date. The call was a couple of weeks ago."

Zatch sighed. "What was the unit number? Two twenty-nine?"

"Yes."

He consulted his books. It took around ten minutes to find the call in the service book. "That was Reffi Zabrib. He left about two weeks ago. Most of the people left then because the new management offered two weeks of free salary if they'd leave one month before the closure. Most of my men took the money and began looking for new jobs. I need the money and need overtime. Otherwise I'd go, too."

"Then who would be in charge of maintenance?"

"No one, because there's nothing to maintain. All I do is answer calls. If something breaks, it stays broken unless it's a major pipe. Then I call a plumber. It's stupid—to sit around answering calls, looking at the problem, and then doing nothing."

Decker said, "So your guys are busy but you're not doing anything?"

"We're busy answering calls. If it is a simple problem—like plugging in a TV—we fix it. If not, we hem and haw and then the front desk moves them to another room. Still, we have to answer every call we get. And since nothing has been fixed in over three months, we get lots of calls."

"Could we have his phone number anyway?"

"Whose phone number? Reffi?"

"Yes."

"He's probably back in Europe, but I'll give you whatever number I have."

"Thank you very much. Also you said someone just quit yesterday morning?"

"Yes. Eddie Booker. He just made it under the wire for his free lunch. I thought he needed the money, but he said he was out of here. I don't blame him."

"Could I have his number, too?"

"Sure." He searched a list, wrote down the numbers, and gave them to Decker.

"Thank you. Can you tell me who was working here on Sunday?"

"It wasn't me." He checked the books. "It was Booker. Ah, this makes sense. He completed his shift, worked through the night, and clocked out Monday morning. Then he quit." Zatch looked at Decker. "Eddie's a good man. He's been married for twenty years and has children. He goes to church."

That meant nothing. More than one serial killer had been a deacon. What caught Decker's attention was Booker's timing. Not only that he worked the night Terry had disappeared, but that he quit the next morning.

"Thanks for your help," Decker said.

"No problem, Detective. At least I do something useful other than sweat."

———————

ADRIANNA'S HONDA REMAINED parked in its spot, undisturbed, until the tape's time read 2:14 Monday afternoon—the time that Adrianna was found dead. At that point, Marge turned off the machine. "She never made it to her car."

Oliver stood up and stretched, blinking to bring moisture to his dry eyes. "Could she have left the hospital from a different door?"

"Only one way to find out." Marge held up the cassette tapes.

"What time is it?"

"About ten to five."

"Aren't we supposed to meet up with Aaron Otis and Greg Reyburn?"

"I've got to check my messages. They're supposed to call me when they get into town. My cell is dead in here."

"So they could have called and you wouldn't have known about it?"

"Exactly. Let's take a break. I'll check my phone."

Just as Marge stood up, Povich returned. "Any luck?"

"We've gone through the most important tape once," Oliver said. "We did see Adrianna park her car and go into the hospital at around quarter to eleven. We didn't see her coming back to her car on this tape."

"That doesn't mean she didn't leave," Marge said. "But now we need to check all the other hospital entrances and exits. That's going to take a long time. It would be helpful if we could view the tapes at our station house. That way I could put a lot of people on them and move this along at a quicker pace."

"Eventually the hospital is going to have to give them to us," Oliver said. "They're evidence."

"Evidence to what?" Povich said. "There was no crime here."

"We don't know that," Marge said. "If we check all the other tapes and maybe see her *leaving* through another exit—not only would it be helpful to our investigation, it might clear the hospital of any wrongdoing. But since we haven't seen her leave, we need to view all the tapes."

Povich drummed the table. He said, "You take a break. I'll call management and see if you can take them. But one thing. If you view them at the police station, I want to be there. Then I think I can talk them into it."

"No problem." Marge shook his hand. "You're welcome to come with us."

Oliver said, "We'll miss Peter, but somehow we'll have to get along without him."

With his eyes glued to the monitor, Peter gave a wave.

CHAPTER TWENTY-ONE

IT WAS AFTER seven by the time Decker made it back to the station house. The squad room was quiet with a few stragglers, including Wanda Bontemps, a recent transplant to Devonshire homicide. She and Decker had worked together on the Cheryl Diggs case back when Chris Donatti had been not much older than Gabe. Chasing down a killer had led Decker into Wanda's district. There had been tension between them at first, but by the time the case had been solved, Decker had been won over by her professionalism. He'd gone to bat for her when she had wanted to transfer into the detectives' division, and she'd been loyal to him ever since.

In her late forties, Wanda was five six with a spread around the middle. She had recently taken to push-ups and it showed in her muscular arms. She had mocha skin, dark eyes, and very close-cropped salt-and-pepper hair with just a touch of blonde.

"Have a second, Loo?"

"Sure." Decker took out his keys and unlocked his office door. "Come on in." He sat at his desk and Wanda sat opposite with papers in her hands. "What's up?"

Wanda checked her notes. "I've been looking through hanging deaths. Almost all have been suicides or accidental—autoerotic asphyxiation. It's really rare as a method of suicide for women. I was able to find two homicides by hanging, but both of them old, old cases done in South Central."

Decker had taken out a notepad. "Open cases?"

"Yes. The wisdom at the time was that it was a serial killer because both of the women had been prostitutes."

"How long ago are we talking about?"

"Twenty-five years."

"Doesn't sound like a good match to Adrianna's case."

"That was my feeling."

"What about hangings outside of L.A.?"

"That was my next step. To murder someone that way is really weird, so maybe it's a serial killer who recently moved into the area."

"Lovely," Decker said. "But valid."

"Also, even though no one from the cable company was in the area on Monday, I did find out from the foreman that a private audiovisual company was wiring the house for flat screens and computers. His name is Rowan Livy. I have a call in to him."

"Good. And who told you about him?"

"The foreman."

"Chuck Tinsley or Keith Wald?"

"Tinsley."

"The one who found the body," Decker said. "We should talk to him again. Maybe he'll remember something when he's not as frazzled. And first on the scene is always suspicious."

"Agreed. I also had a chat with Bea Blanc—the victim's sister. She and Adrianna haven't been close for years. Bea's a stockbroker—married with a couple of kids—and the two of them lead very different lives. She didn't know much about Adrianna's personal comings and goings."

"Did you detect any animosity between them?"

"Not when I spoke to her. She seemed pretty broken up."

"So as a source of information, she's a bust, and as a suspect, she's way down on the list."

"Exactly."

"Okay. Good work. Anything else?"

"Not at the moment. I thought I'd join the others in the view room and look at the tapes of St. Timothy's exits and entrances. So far it appears that Adrianna never made it back to her car. Marge and Oliver want to know if Adrianna left the hospital at all."

"I thought the hospital wasn't going to release them to us."

"Apparently they had a change of heart. You want to come in and take a look?"

"Maybe in a minute. I've still got a couple of calls to make. Tell them I'm here in case anyone wants to talk to me."

"Will do."

After Wanda left, Decker started calling maintenance personnel from the hotel. His first call went out to Eddie Booker. A kid whose voice sounded like he was in the throes of adolescence answered the phone. "My mom and dad just left for vacation."

"Do you know when they'll be back?" Decker asked.

"I dunno. You can talk to my grandmother. She'll be back in an hour."

"Can I leave you my number and have her call me at her earliest convenience?"

"Uh, I don't have a pencil. Should I get one?"

"Please." Decker gave him the number, thanked the kid, and hung up, knowing that there was a good chance that Grandma wouldn't get the message. His next call was to Reffi Zabrib. Gregory Zatch, the head security guard, had said that Zabrib had gone to Europe. So Decker wasn't surprised that the line had been disconnected. Since Zabrib had quit when Terry was still around and about, he wasn't high on the list.

There were still six more people to call from maintenance as well as fifteen from housekeeping. Decker was about to make another phone call when there was a knock on his door frame. Marge came in, rubbing her eyes.

"We're taking a break. Want to see the movies?"

Decker checked his watch. "I think I'll drop by my house and see if my wife still remembers me. What's the status? Wanda told me that Adrianna never made it back to her car."

"We saw her pull up, park, walk to the elevator door."

"And that's the last you've seen of her?"

"So far we haven't seen her walking through any of the hospital parking lots. She wound up at the construction site. At some point, she had to leave the hospital. The problem is that the cassettes aren't that clear. There are plenty of people going in and out that we can't identify."

"Or someone carried her out under the radar. Adrianna seemed to have suffered a bloodless death. That's strangulation or poison. There are lots of ways to get hold of potent chemicals inside a hospital."

"Povich said that there are cameras on the narcotic cabinets. I'll take a look at them. See who's been checking out the strong stuff. When are the tox reports due in?"

"Not for another couple of weeks," Decker said. "What's happening with Aaron Otis and Greg Reyburn? Shouldn't they be in town by now?"

"Their car broke down about fifty miles north of Santa Barbara. It'll take until tomorrow to fix it. It's almost easier for Oliver and me to drive up than to wait for them to come down, but I figured it would be more professional to interview them here."

"It can wait until the morning. Have you had any luck locating Garth Hammerling?"

Marge shook her head. "What about this, Pete? What if after Adrianna called Aaron, Garth called her back and told her that he had cut short his vacation just to talk to her. Maybe she didn't want to meet with him at home, so they agreed to meet at the hospital."

"Go on."

"They meet and they talk and then they fight. Something bad happens and Adrianna dies. Garth panics, and somehow gets rid

of her. I bet he'd know how to get her out without being noticed."

"But a call from Garth didn't register on Adrianna's phone."

"So maybe he called Adrianna at the hospital because he knew
she wouldn't answer his calls on her cell."

"It took him at least three, four hours to come down to L.A. If
she was waiting that long for him in the hospital, someone would
have seen her at that time."

"Could be that she was dog tired and went to sleep in an on-call
room while she waited."

"Go back to St. Tim's and try to find out if someone saw Adrianna
after her shift ended."

"We need to do that anyway." Marge paused. "If that did happen,
one of the security cassettes should show Garth entering the hospital. So I probably should be looking for him as well."

"Yep."

"Except I have no idea what Garth looks like except for a crummy
DMV photo."

Decker opened his desk drawer and took out some pictures. "I
borrowed these from Adrianna's apartment. Try Facebook and
see if Garth is a member. We can probably pull up some more
recent snapshots from the computer. Also . . . and I don't know
why I didn't think of this before. See if the guy posted anything
recent."

"That's a good idea," Marge said. "People are always exposing
themselves metaphorically. These days privacy is as quaint as a Victorian swoon."

HE PULLED UP at eight-fifteen, noticing that Hannah's car was absent
from the driveway. When Rina greeted him at the door, he said,
"Just the two of us?"

"Make that three. Hannah's gone, but we've got a boarder."

Decker frowned. "Where is she?"

"At Aviva's."

"So why didn't she take him with her?"

"I don't know, Peter. Maybe she needed a little alone time. Why don't you come in and close the door and we can talk inside. It's okay to do that because you live here."

The two of them walked hand in hand into the kitchen. Decker sat down where his dinner awaited him. It was hot and delicious: a Reuben sandwich complete with nondairy soy cheese, coleslaw, and a big juicy sour pickle. All too quickly, it was gone.

"Man, that was good."

"You want another one?"

"No, one was quite enough." Decker heard a lilting melody wafting through the air. He'd never heard electric guitar played so beautifully. "How's the kid doing?"

"I fed him. He said thank-you."

"Not much in the conversation department?"

"No, there was a little social banter. I asked him if the school was comfortable for him. If not, I'd look into something else, but he said he was fine with it, especially because everything was temporary." She laughed. "He told me that it wasn't all that different from Catholic school."

Decker laughed. "How's that?"

"Just that the rabbis reminded him of the priests. He said everyone was nice enough. Then he thanked me for the sandwich and started to eat. I told him I had a few calls to make. He said, don't let me stop you. I figured it had to be a strain for him to make small talk, so I left him alone. When I came back, he thanked me and said the sandwich was terrific. Then he excused himself and has been playing Yonkie's guitar for the last two hours. The kid has stamina."

She poured both of them two cups of coffee and sat down.

"Have you made any progress finding Terry?"

"I'd let you know if I had." Decker sipped coffee. "I interviewed several workers at the hotel where she and Gabe were staying. Everyone told me that the boy plays piano like a professional. Is having him here a strain?"

"Not really."

"Rina, you must tell me. If you get any kind of bad feeling about him, we can send him to his aunt's apartment. Because we really don't know a thing about him except that he's musical."

"He seems to be okay. Maybe we should rent a piano for him."

"A piano?"

"Why not?"

"Don't you think that might be getting a bit overinvolved?"

"You brought him home." When Decker didn't say anything, she said, "Why don't you talk to him and find out how committed he is to his playing? I'd hate to be the one to stall his progress, especially if he was one of those prodigy kids."

"His development is not our responsibility."

"It will be if he stays here."

"And do we have to stop at a piano? What about a teacher? And what if he needs a special teacher who costs a fortune?"

"Why don't we start with a piano," Rina said.

"How much does renting one cost?"

"I don't know. I'll find out."

"And what do we do with a piano if his mother suddenly shows up, or if his father shows up, or if he decides to pick up and leave?"

"I took lessons when I was little. I'm not getting any younger. I think it's time to get reacquainted with my creative side."

WHEN DECKER KNOCKED, the music stopped. A moment later, Gabe answered the door. "Hi."

"You got a minute?" Decker crossed the threshold and sat on one of his sons' twin beds. "How are you doing?"

"I'm fine." Gabe laid the guitar down and kneaded his hands. "Is anything wrong?"

"Nothing's wrong, but we haven't made much progress. We've talked to several people at the hotel today. Your mother was a friendly gal, especially to the staff, which might make our job easier."

"How's that?"

"They remember her." Decker paused. "Maybe if I talk to enough of them, someone will remember something that you didn't know about."

"Like what?"

"Like your mother bringing a guest to her hotel room." Gabe didn't answer, so Decker said, "Do you remember her making contact with anyone other than family . . . maybe calling up an old friend?"

The boy shook his head no. "But I wasn't always around. She rented a practice room for me at UCLA, so I was gone probably six hours a day."

"So it's conceivable that your mother had a life that you didn't know about."

"Like what are you saying? That she ran off with someone?"

He was clearly upset. Decker said, "I'm just saying since you weren't around all the time, she could be hiding things from you."

He nodded. "Mom could be secretive. But she wouldn't just run off. First of all, if Chris found out, he'd kill . . . he'd be real angry. Probably he'd find her and get her back anyway, so what would be the point? Second, she wouldn't leave without telling me."

"That's probably true. I've heard from everyone how devoted she was to you."

Gabe was silent and sullen. Clearly Decker had hit a raw nerve. "I'll keep you up-to-date. I'm sorry I don't know more." The boy was still sulking. "Wow, six hours a day. That's a lot of practicing."

"It's about average." Gabe shrugged.

"Did you practice that much back home?"

"I only went to school until one." He paused. "Fine with me because almost all of high school is a total waste."

"I think Hannah would agree with you there. Are most kids like you homeschooled?"

"Yeah, but I didn't want that. My father's a night owl and often sleeps in to midmorning. He's real sensitive to noise. When he sleeps, he needs quiet, so it was good for me to be out of the house."

"So how serious are you with your music?" Decker said.

The boy took off his glasses, wiped them on his shirt, and put them back on. "I don't know how to answer that."

"Do you want to be a professional musician? *Are* you a professional musician?"

"I think you're asking me if I want to be a concert pianist. That's an interesting question. You should probably ask my teachers if I have the chops."

"Who were your teachers?"

"I went into the city three days a week at Juilliard. You know, with regards to the whole thing of where I should live. I could apply to Juilliard in the fall. My last teacher is a professor there and told me I could come whenever. I could probably squeeze in this fall. That would take care of my housing problem if this thing doesn't get settled."

"Is that what you want?"

"I'd like it better than living with my aunt, that's for sure." He drummed his fingers. "I was kinda hoping that I could go to a regular college—like Harvard or Princeton. It's too late to apply for next year, but I know they take younger kids with special talents. I'd have to take the SAT, I suppose."

"Have you taken the PSAT?"

He nodded.

"How'd you do?"

"Two hundred ten, which is okay, but irrelevant in my case. I could get into one of the Ivies on a music scholarship. I've won enough of the petty competitions to look impressive and know how to audition to look like I play better than I do. I'm real good at flash."

Decker said, "How would you feel about living alone at sixteen?"

"I've lived alone most my life, so it's no biggie there." Gabe paused. "That's not entirely true. My mother has been a factor in my life." His eyes watered. "I miss her. Anyway, in answer to your original question, I'm good enough to be a professional classical musician. I could play chamber music and small companies. But that's very different from being a concert-quality pianist. My teacher in New York wanted me to enter the Chopin competition in Warsaw when I'm old enough five years from now. I love Chopin and happen to interpret him very well. But it would really help if I had a teacher." He laughed. "It would help if I had a piano."

"Rina and I were talking. She asked me if you think we should rent you a piano."

"Man, I'd love that!" His face lit up. "You wouldn't even have to pay for it. I have all that money from my mom. I'll pay if you were willing to put one in the house."

Decker looked at him. "Gabe, I didn't ask you at the time because it seemed too intrusive. But I'm going to ask you now. I'd like to see what your mother left behind in the safe."

"It was just some cash and papers."

"I'd like to see the papers."

The boy grew nervous. "Okay, but it isn't much. Just my birth certificate and my passport and maybe some bank accounts."

Resistance. "What about *her* birth certificate and *her* passport?"

"I don't know, Lieutenant. I just separated the cash from the rest of the stuff and put it away for safekeeping."

"I'd like to see what papers you have. Bank accounts would tell me a lot."

"Uh, sure." Gabe stood up. "Give me a few minutes to find them and I'll bring them out for you."

In other words, get out of the room while I do this.

Decker stood up. "I'm not trying to pry into your finances, but how much cash did she have in the safe?"

"Around five thousand dollars."

"That's a lot of cash considering she paid most of her bills with credit cards."

Gabe shrugged.

"Do you have a credit card?"

He nodded.

Dragging information out of him. "Are you the primary card-holder?"

"What do you mean?"

"Who pays the credit card bill? Your mother or your father?"

"Chris pays for everything."

"Okay. Your mother worked, right?"

"Yeah."

"So she had some money of her own."

"Probably."

"Did she give her money to Chris?" A shrug. The kid was stalling. "Would you mind if I looked at your credit card receipts?"

"I haven't charged anything except a couple of cups of coffee and some books."

"I just want to see the pathway. I'm still trying to locate your father, and if he pays for everything, maybe the bank might have some information on him."

Gabe looked down. "Lieutenant, it might be better to leave my dad out of it. If he didn't have anything to do with it, why bug him and get him all pissed? And if he did do it, I wouldn't want to know about it."

"So that would be a no about into looking at your credit card receipts?"

Gabe cringed. "Can I think about it? I don't like Chris, but I wouldn't want to send him to jail or anything like that."

"Even if he murdered your mother?" The boy was quiet. Decker said, "Look, you seem to be a little hesitant about the papers. For all I know, your father's contacted you and has given you instructions on what and what not to do." He paused and regarded the kid as his cheeks pinkened. He was putting the boy in a bad position. "Gabe, I'm a cop. I'm going to ask. But you don't have to do anything that'll make you sorry. Just think about it. I want to do what's best for your mom. You do, too."

"I'll think about it. Thanks for being understanding."

"Who says that I'm understanding?" Decker tousled his hair. "Your dad is on my to-do list and nothing's going to dissuade me from finding him. But you're not me and you don't have to give him up. I understand split loyalties."

His smile was angry. "Story of my life."

CHAPTER TWENTY-TWO

WEDNESDAY MORNING, EIGHT A.M., Decker was in his office, sipping cappuccino courtesy of an espresso maker and Marge's recent barista skills. She had brought in the machine about a month ago and squad-room coffee had never been the same. Currently, she held the number one spot as the most popular detective. She was the only one who knew how to froth milk.

"You looked at all the cassettes?"

"I did." She sipped and gave herself a milk mustache, which she licked off with her tongue. "I was getting eyestrain toward the end. Povich said we can keep them for another day, so I'll look through them again."

"You saw her go in, but you didn't see her go out."

"Like I told you yesterday, there were lots of unidentifiable people. That's why I'd like to see them again."

Decker said. "What about Garth Hammerling?"

"Didn't notice him if he was there, but ditto on lots of unidentifiable people."

Oliver walked into the open door. "Smells good. I'd love one of those."

"I'll make you one, but only if I can teach you how to do it," Marge said.

"I'm inept when it comes to coffee."

She made no attempt to move. "I was just telling the Loo that we didn't see Adrianna after she left her car and came into the hospital Sunday night."

Oliver pulled up a chair. "Yeah, all that eyestrain and I wasn't even watching porno."

Marge said, "I had a dream last night."

"Was I in it?"

"No, you weren't, but Adrianna Blanc was."

Oliver took the coffee cup out of Marge's hand. "Pretty please?"

"Finish it. I'm on cup number two anyway."

"Your dream?" Decker asked.

"Yeah, my dream. All night long, I kept seeing the tapes—grainy black-and-white people walking through the frames . . . then I jerk myself awake with something sticking in my brain. I'm not even sure if it's real or a ghost from a bad night's sleep."

Oliver sat up. "What'd you see?"

"Was there a series of frames where we saw a woman in scrubs go outside from the main entrance about six in the morning? She was looking down at her cell phone, and then she took out something from her pocket that looked like a second cell phone, then went back inside."

Oliver scrunched his brow. "Yeah . . . you think that was Adrianna Blanc?"

"It stuck with me. Why didn't we think it was her?"

"We didn't rule her out, Marge, we just couldn't see her face. Also Adrianna was in the hospital until around eight-fifteen. So even if it was her, it doesn't help us much."

"I'd like to see the cassette again," Marge said. "I'm wondering why someone would leave the hospital and then immediately turn around and come back in. And why would she be carrying two cell phones?"

Decker said, "She might have gone outside to make a call on her cell because she works in a dead spot in the hospital."

"Okay. That would explain one cell phone. Why two cell phones?"

"Maybe the second cell phone was a pager and she looked at the number and returned because she was needed."

Marge nodded. "I suppose the sensible thing to do would be to find out if Adrianna was paged at the time."

Oliver said, "She didn't have any outgoing call on her cell before eight-fifteen."

"Something distracted her. Who would she call so early in the morning?"

Decker shrugged. "Maybe she was about to make the breakup call to Garth, but she got paged and had to go back in."

"But why make the breakup call at that time?"

Oliver said. "She had a few minutes and she wanted to get it over with."

Decker said, "What's on your mind, Marge?"

"I'm wondering if she didn't meet someone at Garage who finally gave her the courage to break up. And then maybe she and Mr. Right hooked up the following morning and that's who murdered her."

"But how would she hook up with someone when we didn't see her leave the hospital?" Oliver asked.

"She had to come out. We just missed it. If we can enhance that woman who keeps running through my brain, we could at least see what she looked like the day she was murdered."

"Give it a try," Decker said.

"The murder is weird," Marge said. "The killer made no attempt to hide the body. Instead it was presented in a dramatic way . . . like shown off. And it sounds planned. She didn't seem to struggle. It just doesn't sound to me like an argument between girlfriend and boyfriend gone south."

Oliver said, "You're really into this deadly hookup thing."

"Just want to find out who Adrianna was talking to the night before she died."

"Go back to Garage and work the crowd for an ID," Decker said.

"You know I've said this before. It's possible that you didn't see Adrianna on the tapes because she never left the hospital alive. My guess is that she was sedated or poisoned before she was strung up. Go back to St. Tim's. Get a more precise time frame. That will tell you a lot."

Marge said, "She had to leave at one point, Rabbi, because we found her dead at the construction site."

"Corpses are removed all the time from hospitals by funeral-home cars, hearses, and coroner's wagons," Decker said. "Could be someone took her out in a body bag."

OVER THE PHONE, Eliza said, "I got a hit for Donatti. One of the tickets had a 2009 Lexus with a paper plate that came from Luxury Cars and Vans in Westwood. It's about a fifteen-, twenty-minute ride from the hotel. The rental contract was filled out by Donatti. According to his parking ticket, he came in at twelve-eighteen and left at two forty-seven. Donatti returned the car to the rental office at three twenty-seven in the afternoon."

"Great job."

"The bad part is the trail gets cold after that. He needed some form of transportation from the rental company to wherever he went. I called up the local cab companies. The closest pickup the company had on the books was about a half mile away at four-oh-five. I'm trying to get hold of the cabdriver. See if he remembers Donatti. But the pickup may not have been him. And I don't see him taking the bus."

"Probably not. What about hotels? Chris came in Saturday morning. Where did he stay?"

"I've tried all of Westwood and am now doing Beverly Hills—Montage, Beverly Wilshire, the Beverly Hills Hotel. So far, no luck. Maybe I should try smaller places."

"Maybe he slept in the park . . . Jeez, that man is hard to locate." Decker raked his hair with his hands. "Gabe spoke to his mother at four in the afternoon. He said that Terry sounded fine. He returned to the hotel suite at around six-thirty, seven, and she was gone. If Donatti did something to Terry, he only had a two- or three-hour-max window; meaning he would have had to return immediately after he left. Was there any record of any livery service dropping him back off at the hotel?"

"No cab, but I haven't tried the car services yet."

"Maybe he had a second vehicle and was planning all along to sneak another visit in with his wife after I had left."

"Would she be stupid enough to let him in?"

"They parted on relatively good terms. He seemed okay. Maybe she was caught off guard."

"Or maybe he never returned," Eliza said. "We're focused on him, but we ought to consider that Terry was a friendly woman. Maybe the wrong type of guy misinterpreted her friendliness for something more."

"Then there would have been some sort of struggle in the hotel room. Besides, her car is gone and so are her purse and keys." Decker thought a moment. "Cars don't disappear as easily as people. You think we might have found the car by now, and the fact that we haven't makes me wonder."

"I'll check out some local garages and storage areas," Eliza said.

"Good idea. I'm just wondering if she's long gone. I think her son found his passport and birth certificate in the hotel safe, but not her passport or her birth certificate. Maybe she took them and took off."

"Sounds plausible." A pause. "What do you mean by you *think* that he has his ID?"

"I asked to look through the papers left behind in the safe and Gabe was reluctant to show them to me. When I asked about his mother's passport and birth certificate, he was quiet. He's hiding something. Sooner or later, I'll get it out of him."

Eliza paused. "So you haven't taken a look at his birth certificate?"

"No. Why?"

"Just wondering if she listed Chris as the father. Maybe Terry was hiding a deep secret and Chris found out about it. I mean, we always know who the mother is. But we don't always know who the father is."

"I don't know about that. She was sixteen and a virgin when she met him."

"So he took her virginity. It doesn't mean he knocked her up. Didn't you say he spent some time in jail? Maybe she got bored of waiting."

"Maybe." Decker paused. "He would have killed her if he found out the kid wasn't his."

"You said it. Maybe the true father is on the birth certificate. Or maybe she's hiding a DNA test. You know how it is, Lieutenant. Hell hath no fury like a hit man scorned."

THE WOMAN ON the line sounded elderly. She identified herself as Ramona White. "I'm looking for Lieutenant Detter."

"This is Lieutenant Decker."

"Oh, is it Decker? I can't read my grandson's handwriting so well."

"How can I help you, Ms. White?"

"It's Mrs. White. I'm returning your call."

"Regarding . . ."

"I don't know what it's regarding. I just got a message to call you."

Decker had to think for a moment. Grandson . . . grandmother. "Oh yes. I'm calling about your son-in-law, Eddie Booker. Do you know where he is?"

"He and my daughter are on a cruise."

"Do you know when they'll be back?"

"In a couple of days. They went on a cruise to Acapulco. They invited me to come with them, but I get seasick. Besides, someone has to watch the monsters at home."

"Do you know what cruise line?"

"Seacoast or Seacrest. Something like that."

"Any way of reaching them?"

"Probably through the company. They left me an itinerary some-where. Is it an emergency?"

"No, it isn't. If Eddie checks in with you, could you leave him a message that I'm trying to reach him?"

"What's going on? Is Eddie in trouble?"

"Not that I know of. Has he been in trouble before?"

"Not that I know of, but you never know. I've been married three times. In the beginning, they were all angels. By the end, they were pond scum. So forgive me if I'm cynical. Men just do that to me."

NO MATTER HOW much the tape was slowed, the detectives couldn't make out a face. The woman who left the hospital at six in the morn-ing only to go back inside a few moments later would remain a mys-tery.

Oliver flipped on the lights. "That was a bust."

"It was indeed. We could go through the tapes one more time."

Oliver looked at the wall clock. "Aaron Otis and Greg Reyburn are coming in about a half hour. Why don't we review the tapes after we've interviewed the lads."

"Sounds like a plan." Marge checked her cell phone. "Hmm . . ." She called her voice mail and listened to the messages. "That was St. Tim's. Someone named Hilda or something. Adrianna was paged at six-oh-seven. So maybe that second phone was a pager."

"And that would mean the lady in the video was probably her," Oliver said.

Marge said, "Who was she trying to call?"

"Probably Garth, but it didn't register on her phone records. It probably never connected. How about a coffee break?"

"Decker gave me Adrianna's diary. I'm going to look through it before we talk to the boys. See if I can find out a hint of a love con-nection between Aaron and her. But you're welcome to use the ma-chine."

"You know I don't know how to do it."

"And that's my problem because—"

"All right, all right." He stood up. "I'll bite the bullet. Teach me how to foam."

"Now it'll have to wait, Scott. I've got things to do."

"How long would it take?"

"The truth is, it probably wouldn't take too long, but that's not the point. I was willing to put myself out this morning, but you didn't want to."

"How about if I beg?"

She got up. "If you're going to demean yourself, ask for more than a latte."

"Sweetheart, I've demeaned myself for a lot less. At least a latte won't slap my face when I'm done drinking."

CHAPTER TWENTY-THREE

MARGE WAS OLD enough to remember when a tattoo meant something, that the skin art went hand in hand with felonious behavior and an affiliation with a badass gang. Back then, the only other acceptable tattoos, like MOM enclosed in a heart, were associated with men of the U.S. armed services. The rest of the male population went without. Nowadays ink was completely accepted and worn like permanent jewelry. Tattooing had almost become, dare she say it, *conventional* ornamentation. The really *handy* thing that came out of the craft was identification because no two images were exactly alike.

Aaron Otis was festooned with multicolored swirls up and down his left arm, while his right arm had been inked in a series of armbands that included—but was not limited to—a circle of razor-tipped barbed wire, a bangle of Japanese writing, a snake bracelet, and an array of bullets in an ammo belt. The only place that showed Aaron au naturel was his gaunt face—tan, craggy, and blond—as if he'd spent his life in the outback. He wore a black T-shirt and beige cargo pants. Loafer Vans encased his sockless feet.

Greg Reyburn was a little more discerning in his choice of body pictorials, but his skin still contained enough ink to pen a novelette. He was average height and build. The young man had a head of black curls, high cheekbones, and a pointy chin. His eyes, like those of his fellow traveler, were saggy and red-rimmed. He had on jeans, a black polo shirt, and sandals.

Marge had put them into two separate interview rooms. While Scott worked his magic on Greg Reyburn, she'd take Aaron Otis. She brought him a soda and sat down next to him, leaning forward, trying to appear maternal. "You look tired."

"Exhausted." Otis took the soda and thanked her. "It's been a hell of a few days." He drank greedily. "Between the car repairs and the vacation, I'm flat broke." He made air quotes over the word "vacation." "The whole thing was a bust. Plus, now you're looking at me with voodoo eyes!"

Marge took out a notebook. "Why do you say that?"

"Because Adrianna called me and not Garth. If I would've known she was going to die, I would've . . . well, I don't know what I would've done. It's just creepy. Talking to her and then . . . you know . . . it's creepy."

Marge nodded.

"I mean, like what happened? She was fine when I spoke to her . . . I mean like she was pissed off royally, but . . . like it's so weird."

"What do you do for a living, Aaron?"

"Me?"

"Yeah. How do you earn money?"

"I'm a GC."

"General contractor? Like you build houses?"

"Mostly I'm a framing foreman for bigger companies."

"Okay." Was it a coincidence that Adrianna was found in a construction sight? Not that Otis could have done it himself if he was miles away. "How'd you meet Garth?"

"We went to school together. I've known him since seventh grade."

"What can you tell me about him?"

"He's a good guy . . . a little vain, but hey, why not?"

"You two are pretty tight?"

"We're good friends. Good enough for me to be shocked if—" He stopped himself.

Marge said, "Has he contacted you since he took off?"

"No." A beat. "I'm nervous about that. Where would he go if he didn't go home?"

"That's what we're wondering. We've checked the airline manifests. He deplaned at Burbank airport, but we lost track of him after that. He's your friend. If he wanted to hide out, where do you think he'd go?"

"I don't know." He flexed a bicep. His bracelets expanded then contracted. "His family is here. Have you tried them?"

"First thing. His mom thought he was still with you."

"It looks bad for him . . . to suddenly disappear."

"Or it could be something bad happened to him. I'd like to find him to make sure he's all right."

Otis's eyes widened. "You think he's . . . dead?"

"Don't know, Aaron. We know Adrianna was murdered. It would grieve me to think that Garth met with the same fate."

"Wow." He scratched his swirling-colored arm. "That's really weird. I was thinking like . . . you know . . ."

"No, I don't know. Tell me."

"That you thought Garth was like a suspect. Although I don't know how he'd do anything. By the time he left Reno, he wouldn't have enough time."

Marge didn't argue. Garth had enough time, but it would have been tight. She said, "Tell me about Garth's reaction when you told him about Adrianna's phone call."

"He was upset."

"What did he say?"

"I don't remember his exact words . . . something like . . . he hates when she gets like this. He was going to have to go home to talk to her because a phone call won't cut it."

"When she gets like this? She's broken up with him before?"

"Yeah, they fought all the time."

"About what?"

"Things. Guy/girl things."

"Can you give me an example?"

"He complained that Adrianna was overbearing . . . checking up on him too much. And she had no business doing that 'cause she really wasn't an angel herself." Otis looked at his lap. "I really shouldn't talk for Garth."

"What about her side?"

"I don't know about her side. I'm friends with Garth."

"And yet she called *you* to say that she was leaving him. What does that mean?"

"That she had my phone number and didn't want to talk to Garth."

Marge leaned in closer. "It's more than that. I think Adrianna and you were pretty tight yourselves."

"Not at all." Eyes averted.

"Maybe you want to think about that statement, Aaron." Marge pulled back to give him a little breathing room. "Did you know that Adrianna kept a diary?"

A blush ran through the man's face. Although Adrianna talked about trysts with other men, she didn't use names. Marge had no idea if one of the assignations had been with Aaron, but if Otis was like most men, he would deem himself important enough to make an entry.

"Aaron?"

"It wasn't serious."

"It was more than a one-night stand," Marge lied.

"It was a one-night stand that happened maybe three or four times. It meant nothing to either one of us. She'd get mad at Garth and fool around because Garth was fooling around on her."

"So why didn't they just break up?"

"Obviously she did break up with him. Or at least was *gonna* break up with him."

"What took her so long?"

"I dunno. They've been having problems for a while."

"Well, why do you think Garth stayed with her?"

"Because she was hot. At least that's what I think."

"You know that from firsthand experience?"

"C'mon, cut me some slack."

"She's dead, Aaron. I need to know everything. Why do you say she was hot?"

The young man seemed to wilt. "She'd do things that a lot of girls wouldn't do. Nothing was off-limits. Plus, she gave Garth money."

"She sounds like the perfect girlfriend. Why would he cheat on her?"

A lopsided grin. "'Cause guys are dogs."

An adequate if not totally fair summation of the opposite sex. But Adrianna had her lapses as well. "If she was so hot, Aaron, why only three or four times?"

"It was her idea to stop."

"Were you upset by that?"

"Nah, it was cool."

"So why was she upset if Garth fooled around when she was fooling around?"

"I dunno. I'm tired, Sergeant, I can't think too clearly right now."

"Did she tell you why she broke it off with you?"

"She said she'd gotten it out of her system, if you know what I mean."

"I'm not sure I do know. Explain it to me."

"Look, Sergeant, I wasn't the first of her revenge fucks and I wasn't the last."

"How do you know about her revenge fucks?"

"'Cause she'd tell me whenever she picked up a guy that Garth didn't know about."

"Sounds like you two were good friends if she told you about her love life. Why do you think she confided in you?"

"I dunno. Maybe she thought I'd tell Garth and he'd get jealous."

"Did you?"

"Hell, no. If I started saying things, I'd be on the chopping block."

"You think Garth would get pissed at you even though he fooled around?"

"I guess on some level he cared about her. Otherwise, why would he cut his vacation short just to calm her down?"

"I don't know, Aaron. Frankly, I'm wondering what might have happened if he didn't calm her down."

"I don't know. The whole thing is weird."

"Maybe the relationship had less to do with sex and more to do with Adrianna giving Garth money. How did you know that Adrianna was financing his excursions to Vegas?"

"I asked him about it . . . that he always had money for Vegas. He said she gave him spending cash."

"And what did you say to that?"

"Something like sweet deal or some shit like that."

"She worked as a nurse. Where'd she get money to give him?"

"Probably from her mom. Her parents have money."

"Did she tell you that she got money from her mom?"

"She might have. The point is both of them always had enough cash to buy some drinks and shit and make a party. She loved to party." His eyes moistened. "It's horrible, thinking of her hanged to death. Who would do that?"

Marge sighed inwardly. It was a rhetorical question. Still, she could have given him a half-dozen answers and all of them would have been creepy.

"INTERESTING . . . OTIS being a contractor." Decker thought a moment. "Is it relevant?"

Marge pulled out a chair and sat down, throwing her head back until she was looking at the ceiling. "I'll check and see if he had anything to do with the Grossman project where Adrianna was found."

Oliver said, "Contractors are guilty until proven innocent in my opinion."

Decker said, "Speaking of which, have you gotten hold of Keith Wald and Chuck Tinsley?"

"I got hold of Wald," Marge said. "We set something up. Tinsley hasn't returned my call." She turned to Oliver. "What does Reyburn do?"

"He's a grip for WB studios in Burbank."

"How'd he meet Garth?" Decker asked.

"The three of them were friends from seventh grade on."

Decker said, "Do you think that if one of them were in trouble, the others might help him out?"

"Three Musketeers' kind of crap?" Oliver said. "Maybe, although you have to wonder about loyalty when your friend is screwing your girlfriend."

Marge said, "I'm wondering if Greg Reyburn made it onto Adrianna's fuck list."

"Don't know because I didn't ask him."

"Is he still here?" Decker asked.

"No, he left an hour ago. I can ask him, but we know that Adrianna slept around and that Garth sleeps around. One more isn't going to change the balance sheet."

Marge said. "I was thinking that if his friends felt guilty about sleeping with Adrianna, they may have been willing to help him out with the body."

"How would they help him out if they were miles away?" Oliver said.

"Maybe Aaron told Garth to dump the body at the Grossman house."

"If Aaron was associated with the project, he'd have to know that it would come back to bite him in the butt."

Marge said, "I don't mean to cast aspersions on Mr. Otis, but he's not exactly Harvard material. Maybe Garth called him up in a panic and Aaron gave him the first dump spot he could think of."

Decker said, "Check out with Wald if Otis is associated with the job. When are you two going to St. Tim's? You need to retrace Adrianna's movements."

"Next on the list," Oliver said. "Right after a coffee break."

"I think I'll pass," Marge said. "Help yourself to the machine, Scott."

Oliver said, "Last time I tried, I burned my hand."

"Practice makes perfect." Marge stood up. "But I'll show you one more time. Who woulda thunk a little machine could be so addictive?"

"It's not an addiction, it's a preference."

"And so goes the denial until it's a habit," Marge said. "Maybe we should set up coffee rehab centers, guys. Who among us hasn't had a caffeine headache? If people are willing to plunk down five bucks for something that cost about forty cents, we can sell them on the idea that they have an addiction that needs breaking. It's all part of the modern philosophy of passing the buck. Take all of the credit but none of the personal responsibility."

CHAPTER TWENTY-FOUR

DECKER HAD HIS feet up on his desk. His door was closed and it was one of the few times he had allowed himself a breather. He needed to regroup after hanging up from an emotional call to Kathy Blanc. The desire to get a solve in a murder case was like a persistent itch he couldn't scratch. Now he was on the phone with Eliza Slaughter and could barely make out her words.

"Where are you? I'm getting static on the line."

"I'm . . . the field. Hold on. I'll walk . . . my car. I'll . . . you back."

She disconnected the line. While waiting for the call, Decker sorted through his phone messages. He had spent most of the morning talking to what was left of the hotel employees. It was hard doing interviews over the phone and a few of them might have to be visited in person. He had also had a brief conversation with the pathologist. Adrianna Blanc's autopsy report showed her death to have been caused by asphyxiation from the hanging. There were also bruises and marks on her skin consistent with dragging the body.

The phone rang and Decker picked it up.

Eliza said, "Is this better?"

"Much. What's up?"

"Show-and-tell time. I've spent most of today checking local garages, chop shops, and junkyards. Since garages and storage bins need keys and owners' permissions to open them up, I started with what was accessible—the junkyards. No one seems to mind if you sift through the piles of junked cars. I'm on number three. They're all in the Valley."

"East and north Valley. I used to work in Foothill."

"The one I'm at is in your district. Are you familiar with Tully's Scrap Metal?"

"It's off Rinaldi."

"You should come down. Something caught my eye."

"Something like a 2009 Mercedes E550."

"That's what I'm thinking, although it's hard to tell the make and model when the vehicle's stripped and gutted. It is silver."

"When did it come in?"

"The kid who's here now isn't sure. He thinks a couple of days ago. Right now, we're trying to locate the owner of the lot. He has the records."

"I'm about a half hour away."

"See you then." Eliza waited a beat. "Terry went to school in the west Valley, right?"

"Correct."

"So it's possible that she might be familiar with the place."

"Anything's possible."

"You have your doubts."

"I don't know, Eliza. I think the bigger issue is that Chris Donatti—Chris Whitman back then—went to school in the Valley. And he drove a cool muscle car when he was a teen. Terry, on the other hand, walked or took the bus."

CAPPUCCINOS HAD A soothing effect on Oliver. Maybe it was something in the milk, because Scott was sipping it with almost orgasmic delight. He had not only learned how to use the coffee machine but had finally mastered the art of foaming. The two of them were on their way to St. Tim's: Marge was driving and Scott sat shotgun.

Oliver said, "I'm turning into a girly man."

"Drinking lattes doesn't make you a girly man. Italian men drink cappuccinos and lattes all the time." Marge smiled. "Of course, they don't drink them in the afternoon. They drink espresso because milk coffees are breakfast drinks."

"Are we in Italy, Marge?"

"I'm just saying—"

"Last I checked, the official language wasn't Italian—"

"Just giving you a little culinary history."

"You know, Dunn, I see a cable TV show in your future. You, in full uniform, steaming soy milk while telling your viewers how to prevent an ADW. We'll call it *Cop Does Coffee*."

"Sounds like a porn movie."

Oliver smiled. "That would work as well." He finished his latte. "So what's the plan?"

Marge signaled for a right turn. "First we return the tapes to Ivan Povich."

"Talk to him yet?"

"I left a message, asking him for the tapes from the cameras in the emergency vehicle areas."

"Why didn't Povich give them to us in the first place?"

"Don't know. Betcha when we asked him the first time, he assumed we had wanted only the pedestrian entrances and exits."

Oliver said, "So you like the theory of Adrianna being carried out in a body bag?"

"Maybe." Marge paused. "If the murder did occur inside St. Tim's, I'm thinking about what could have gone wrong? Who, besides Garth, was close enough to Adrianna so that an argument would end in murder?"

"Why do you think the murder was done by someone she was close to?" Oliver told her. "From what Aaron and Greg told us about Adrianna, she could have been having a fling that went bad. Maybe she was fooling around with a married doctor or administrator. Maybe she threatened to expose him."

"But then why would she suddenly decide to start exposing her hookups?"

Oliver said, " 'Cause she was pissed off at Garth but taking it out on other men. That's what women do."

"As opposed to men?" Marge laughed. "Think serial killers who hated their mothers?"

"I'm just trying to get your goat." He waited a moment. "Although if someone tried to kill her, you'd think she would fight back."

Marge turned left. "Unless the two of them were stoned. What if she was blitzed?"

"No cocaine, no booze, no pot in her system. We know that much."

"It could have been something more exotic. Who would have better access to drugs than someone in a hospital with free rein over all the locked medicine cabinets?"

"They don't have free rein," Oliver said. "I think they have to sign in for them. We should check the drug logs. It would buttress our case if some weird drug was checked out and she had it in her system."

Marge said. "Problem is that sometimes you have to know what you're looking for to find it in the tox screen."

Oliver opened the thermos and licked the foam with his finger. "You're looking skeptical. What's bothering you?"

"That Adrianna's hookup would suddenly turn deadly. What could have been said or done that made it go so terribly wrong?"

"You know how these things work, Margie. It starts off as something stupid and ends up as something tragic."

ONCE AGAIN, MARGE and Oliver sat in space control central at St. Tim's. What was even more amazing was that Peter was still on duty. "Does he ever go home?" Oliver asked Ivan Povich.

"He goes home, he comes back." Povich pulled the cassette tape. "I got your message, Sergeant. This is from the emergency vehicle area. We have cameras everywhere. You ask for entrances and exits,

I don't think about emergency areas. My mistake. I would have given this to you."

"No problem," Marge said.

"We are lucky. It was just about to be taped over. But I have what you need."

"Small favors are good," Marge said.

Povich popped the cassette into the machine and fast-forwarded it until the tape displayed last Monday's date. The three of them watched the monitor. Ambulances coming in with hapless patients hooked up to IVs, strapped onto gurneys. In the time frame they watched, it was mostly the same people in the same vans, even though different emergency vehicles came from lots of different places.

No body bags but Marge did see something interesting. At 11:13, a civilian car was backing up toward the docks and then it disappeared from the camera's eye. She kept watching for another minute or two, then her eyes widened.

"Stop the machine!"

"What is it?" Oliver asked.

Marge didn't answer. "Go back a few frames."

"What do you see, Marge?" Oliver asked.

"I'm not sure. That's why I want to look again."

The tape was rewound, the black-and-white figures jerking and jumping as they moved from frame to frame.

"Stop!" Marge pointed to a small, lone figure standing at the docks. "Can you enlarge this image?"

Povich said, "Peter, come here. Can you enlarge this over here?"

Wordlessly, Peter got up and took control of the monitor, and the small figure grew. With each enlargement, the image lost clarity.

Marge told him. "Look familiar, Scott?"

"No. All I see is a blur."

"Make it smaller, Peter." The mute security operator took it down a few notches. "How about now?"

Oliver stared at the figure. "Nothing."

"Don't look at the face. Look at the scrubs, then look at the size and build of the person."

"Mandy Kowalski."

"Could be right."

"Maybe."

"What's she doing out there? Watching gurneys being loaded in and out of ambulances?"

"Only one way to know," Oliver got up. "Let's find her and ask her about it."

CHAPTER TWENTY-FIVE

TULLY'S SCRAP HAD been a fixture in the west hills for almost forty years. It was currently under the care of Caleb "Audi" Sayd, a twenty-eight-year-old dude whose ancestry might have once been Egyptian, but now he was pure California twang. He stood around six feet, a hundred eighty pounds, black hair, and dark eyes. His uniform of choice was low-rider jeans, a white T-shirt, and combat boots. He stood with his arms folded across his chest, his hands tucked under his armpits. He shook his head when Decker showed him the picture of Terry McLaughlin.

"Never seen her before," Audi said.

"You're sure?" Eliza Slaughter asked.

Audi hit the picture. "That face . . . I'd remember her if I saw her."

They were standing in an ocean of junked, gutted, and flattened cars. Most of them hadn't seen any road time in many a moon. The piece of metal that they were interested in was a gutted and compressed silver frame that gave hint to a Mercedes E550 in a former life. It had jumped out at Eliza like a frog on meth.

Decker viewed the hunk of metal. "What can you tell me about it? From the lack of rust, it looks like a new one."

"It is new," Audi said. "That got my attention. You don't usually scrap a good car."

"So you were suspicious," Eliza asked.

"Of course I was suspicious. It wasn't brought in by one of my main contacts."

"Do you know who brought it in?"

"Never seen the guy before. But he had the pink slip and I checked it out with the DMV before I gave him an offer. It was all legit."

"You have a name?" Decker asked.

"The paperwork's in my office." Audi pointed to a trailer. "Last name was Jones."

"First name?"

"Don't remember. Don't know if I ever knew it."

"What'd he look like?" Eliza asked.

"Dark complexion. Dark straight hair, brown eyes. Shorter and thinner than I am."

"Hispanic?"

"Could be. He had a slight accent, but I couldn't place it."

"Mideastern?"

"No, ma'am, that I would be able to place."

"When did he bring it in?"

"Uh, last Saturday or Sunday. I have the date."

"*Saturday or Sunday?*" Decker asked.

"Yeah, it was over the weekend."

That certainly threw a monkey wrench into Decker's thinking. Now he was wondering if he even had the right car. "How was he dressed?"

"Like a mechanic—overalls, T-shirt. But his nails were clean. Hands were soft like he'd never done manual labor in his life. Odd, but hey, we're always getting stories."

"So what was his story?"

"Something about the car being a heap of bad memories with his ex-wife or girlfriend. It sounded like bull, but like I said, everything checked out with his ownership."

"So you didn't question?" Eliza asked.

"In this business you deal with a lot of weirdos. Who else deals in car parts and scrap metal?" He began to tick off his fingers. "If the car hasn't been boosted, hasn't been used in a crime, hasn't been owned by someone associated with crime, and the ownership is legit, you don't question. I don't want any trouble, Detective."

"How much did you pay him?" Decker said.

"I gave him a lowball offer and he took it. He didn't care about the money, what he wanted was the car trashed and junked ASAP. He came back to make sure it was done and asked me to hide it in the middle of the lot. I told him that would cost a little extra and he agreed. After he got what he wanted, he walked away from it."

"What did you do with the parts?"

"He towed in the shell. Don't know what happened to the car's guts."

"And you never did business with him before?" Eliza asked.

"I'd tell you if I did."

Decker said, "Could you look up Mr. Jones for me? A first name would be helpful."

"Sure." The three of them walked over to the trailer and stepped through the door. Inside it was hot, with several humming fans going at once. Furnishings included a desk that held several neat piles of paperwork, a desk chair, four folding chairs, and a bank of files. Audi sat down and drank water out of a Big Gulp cup. He picked up one of the stacks of paper and found what he was looking for right away. He handed the yellow invoice to Decker. "Here you go."

"Thanks." The first thing that Decker noticed was that the date corresponded to last Saturday—the day before Terry had disappeared. So maybe he was off base. The client's name was Atik Jones. "Unusual first name."

"What is it?"

"Atik," Decker said.

"Doesn't sound familiar. He probably didn't tell it to me."

"So how'd you write it down on the invoice?"

"I got it from the pink slip. I'll get it for you." Audi swiveled his desk chair around and began rooting through files. A moment later, he was puzzled. "I can't find it. I musta misfiled something. Give me the invoice again."

Decker handed it back to him. Audi wrote down some numbers and again hunted through the files. "I goofed up something. Man, that's annoying. Let me start at the beginning of *J*. It may take me a few minutes. I got a lot of them."

"We'll wait," Eliza said.

After several minutes, Audi said, "Okay, okay, here we go. I got the name wrong on the invoice. I could have sworn he told me Jones."

He gave the pink slip to Decker. The name wasn't Jones but Jains. Atik Jains. Decker thought a moment. "Could this guy have been Indian?"

"Like a Navaho?"

"Like an Indian from India. Jain or Jains is an Indian name."

Audi nodded. "Yeah. Yeah, that's what he was. He was from India."

Decker looked at the pink slip. "Can we get a copy of the pink slip and the invoice from your fax machine?"

"Sure." As Audi copied the papers, Decker spoke to Eliza. "Jains owned the car for six weeks. And then he junked it on Saturday."

"Saturday?"

"That's what the invoice said."

"If he owned the car for six weeks and junked it before Terry disappeared, do we even have the right car?"

"I don't know. But I do know that Teresa McLaughlin moved out here six weeks ago," Decker said. "We have the VIN number from the pink slip. That should help trace its history."

Audi handed Eliza the copies. "Anything else?"

"Yes, actually." Decker pulled out a picture of Chris Donatti. "Ever see this guy before?"

Audi's gaze shifted to the photograph then back to Decker's face. "Tall guy about your size?"

Decker felt his heartbeat quicken. "Yep."

"Yeah, he was here . . . looking older than the picture."

"He is older than the picture. When was he here?"

"A day or two ago. He was poking around when I came into work."

"What did he want?"

"I don't know. He didn't buy anything, didn't sell me anything. Just looked around. When he left, he gave me a fifty for letting him hunt around." He grinned. "Just peeled it off a big wad like he'd done it a thousand times before. I expected him to tell me to keep his visit between the two of us, but he didn't say anything like that. Just gave me the fifty and said thanks."

"How long was he here?"

"About an hour."

"And he didn't tell you anything about the purpose of his visit?" Eliza asked.

"Nope. Another weirdo, but I'm used to them."

"If he comes again, can you give me a call?" Decker gave him his card and Eliza did likewise. "And unlike Mr. Donatti, I'm telling you to keep this visit between us. Don't tell him that you've spoken to either Detective Slaughter or me."

"Donatti?"

Decker nodded.

"Guy's Italian?" Audi made a face. "He sure didn't look Italian. Is he like a criminal Mafia guy or something?"

"Right now, he's just a person of interest," Eliza said.

"Interested in what?" Audi said. "The card says you're from homicide."

"That's why you don't tell him anything," Decker said. "He might react funny."

"Funny how?"

Decker made a finger gun and pulled an imaginary trigger.

"So he's dangerous?"

"Especially when riled. And right now, knowing what I know, I'd say he's pretty worked up."

"MANDY'S NOT WORKING today."

Oliver and Marge were talking to Hilly McKennick, the head

nurse on the eighth floor, which housed the thoracic/cardiac care unit. Hilly was in her forties, a gamine-like woman with wide-set brown eyes, a thin nose, Cupid's-bow lips, and boy-cut short platinum hair. Mandy Kowalski had been doing Intensive Care for the last six months and Hilly had only laudatory things to say about her.

"When was the last time she was on shift?" Marge asked.

"I think she did a double shift on Sunday/Monday so she could have yesterday and today off."

"Why did she change her schedule?"

"I don't know. She just asked for the time and I was able to accommodate her. Mandy never asks for any favors. In general, she works like a dog, picking up the slack when I need it. Since she asked for this one favor, I figured I'd help her out."

"You like her," Oliver stated.

"We're not friends per se, but she's dedicated." Hilly paused. "Too much, I think. Most of us who work intensively need a break. Gardening is my refuge. I'm a fixture at the local camellia nursery. Camellias are my passion. Janice loves to ski. Darla sings at a local bar where she lives. Mandy was all work. No hobbies, not even a boyfriend that I've ever met. Since she asked for a few days off, I was hoping that maybe she had something brewing. But I didn't ask."

"What about girlfriends?" Marge asked.

"Well, I know she and Adrianna went to nursing school together. I've seen them eating lunch together, so maybe they were close. I know that when she heard about Adrianna, she broke down. I asked her if she wanted time off, but she declined."

Hilly looked pensive and Oliver asked her about it.

"I was worried," the head nurse said. "I felt a little strange having her work such an intensive unit when she was upset. But she did her usual fine job and left."

Marge showed Hilly a black-and-white snapshot. "Would you say that this woman is Mandy Kowalski?"

Hilly stared at the black and white. "It's fuzzy."

"It was taken off of a tape from a security camera."

"Maybe." Hilly studied it carefully. She picked her head up. "Why?"

"This was pulled from a camera in the emergency vehicle area," Oliver told her. "If this is Mandy, we're just wondering what she was doing there."

"I have no idea," Hilly said.

"So she wasn't assigned to that area."

"No, not at all. So maybe it isn't her. But even if it is her, why would it matter?"

"Just trying to place everyone on the Monday of Adrianna's death," Marge said. "This picture was taken on Monday. We're trying to narrow down the time frame from the end of Adrianna's shift until the body was discovered."

Oliver said, "Right now, we've got a blank between eight in the morning and two in the afternoon." The head nurse appeared troubled. Oliver asked her what was on her mind. "Now's not the time to hold back."

Hilly bit her thumbnail. "The day of Adrianna's death, the two of them were having coffee together . . . in the cafeteria. So it's not like it was a secret or anything."

Marge shot Oliver a look. "Do you remember the time?"

"It was morning. I remember smelling the bacon."

"Did you say anything to them?"

Hilly looked down. "This is so strange to remember this just now. I didn't say anything to them, but I was annoyed. Mandy shouldn't have been on break. It was actually my break time. I remember being short-staffed because I couldn't find her. I figured she just went to the bathroom because she's usually so responsible. So I went downstairs to grab a bagel. I was starving. When I saw her talking to Adrianna, I was peeved. I pointed to my watch and Mandy got up right away. She apologized later on and I told her to forget it. I knew she was working a double shift and chalked it up to fatigue, that maybe she needed a caffeine pit stop."

Marge was scribbling on her notepad. "Is there any way you can approximate a time?"

"Let me think . . . I signed back in at nine-fifteen. So it was around then. Does that help?"

"We just gained another hour!" Marge said in triumph.

"Any idea what they were talking about?" Oliver asked Hilly.

"No. But I do remember Mandy looking sheepish when she saw me, probably because I had silently reprimanded her." Again, Hilly paused. "You know, now that I'm thinking about it, I don't know what they were talking about, but the conversation was intense. When I first walked in and saw them together, Mandy didn't even notice. And when she saw me, she blushed. Clearly, she knew she shouldn't have been on break."

"Intense in what way?" Marge said.

"Mandy was leaning over the table and Adrianna was talking with her hands. But I only had a chance to observe them for a couple of seconds."

"And Adrianna was doing the talking?"

Hilly nodded. "She seemed upset. Maybe that's why I didn't come down too hard. Mandy, as usual, was trying to help."

"Would you have Mandy's home address?" Oliver said. "If Adrianna was upset, maybe Mandy could tell us what was upsetting her."

"Didn't you already talk to Mandy?"

Marge said, "We did. But Mandy didn't mention having coffee with Adrianna. Now we're curious why."

Hilly said, "It was out in the open. It wasn't clandestine or anything like that."

"Which makes us all the more curious why she didn't mention it to us," Oliver said.

"I suppose even if I didn't give you her address, you could get it from another source," Hilly told them. "So I might as well make it easy on you."

"That would be lovely," Oliver said.

"You've been very open," Marge said. "We appreciate that."

"That's my family style . . . to be open. It has pluses and minuses. Often, I put my foot in my mouth. But the flip side is I'll never get a stress ulcer."

CHAPTER TWENTY-SIX

OVER THE PHONE, Marge said to Decker, "She's not answering her cell and she's not answering the door."

"Where does she live?"

"She has a condo about two miles from the hospital."

"She's entitled not to be home at five in the evening. Maybe she went out for an early dinner and turned off her phone." He paused. "It's warm outside. Do you smell anything weird?"

"Just the faint hint of cat piss outside the door."

"Can you see inside at all?"

"Window shades are drawn. No pry marks on the front door and windows."

"Leave your card," Decker said. "If you don't hear from her in a couple of hours, you can go back."

"Oliver and I are going back to Garage. We'll grab some dinner there."

"You're going to question Crystal Larabee again?"

"That and hunt around for the mystery man that Adrianna was talking to. Maybe someone will remember him."

"It's a little early for the bar crowd," Decker remarked.

"That's the point," Marge said. "The earlier we arrive, the more likely we'll find gray matter that hasn't been obliterated by alcohol."

BY THE TIME the two of them had put away all the chairs and cleaned up, Hannah's Volvo was the lone car in a poorly lit parking lot that sat across the street from the school. She jingled her keys.

"I have to lock up the gate." She tried to find the correct key by feel. "Man, I'm tired."

"You're the president," Gabe told her. "Can't you assign an underling to put away the chairs?"

"Yeah, I probably should have done that at the beginning of the year."

They waited at the traffic light. When it turned green, they trudged across the street.

"What time is it?" Gabe asked her.

"Seven-thirty. I should call home. My parents are going to start to worry. I'll do it from the car. I just want to get out of here."

She walked over to the wrought-iron gate and gave it a push, struggling to slide it across the track. "Can you help me get this on track?"

"Shouldn't we do it after we pull out the car?"

"I just want to get it on track first."

Gabe tucked his briefcase under his arm and said, "You get the car. I'll do . . ."

And it was at that moment when he heard the noise, felt something in his ribs before he actually saw the small shadowed figure to his right. An ominous voice talking to him while trying to grab his briefcase.

But he really didn't hear what the figure was saying to him. Because all Gabe could fathom was his paltry life—summated by official forms and bank accounts—being ripped away. So not only would he be parentless, he'd have no identity. Because to replace everything stolen would require contact with Chris, explaining to his father why he had allowed some motherfucker to snatch his briefcase.

And he thought of all of this in half of a split second as he crashed his briefcase atop the mugger's head while simultaneously knee-dropping him, sending whatever was poking into his ribs skittering to the ground. As Gabe kicked it with his left heel, sending it into the bushes behind him, he pummeled flesh—pounding and pounding and pounding until the figure was on his knees, crying and begging.

But he really didn't hear the figure's pleas.

What he heard was Hannah screaming at him:

Stop, stop, stop!

And like a dog that had been elevated to red-zone status, the screams suddenly snapped his mechanical throttling, drawing his attention back into the present. At once, he felt a throbbing pain in his left hand and cursed his stupidity. He let go of the mugger's shirt until the man crawled away on all fours then got to his feet and ran off.

Gabe's hand was raw and wet. He wiggled his fingers. Nothing broken.

God was a benevolent being—this time.

Hannah was still shrieking. He tried to project his voice over her hysteria. "It's okay, it's okay, it's okay."

She screamed, "Are you crazy!"

He was confused. In his mind, he had just done a good thing. Why was she still yelling at him? "He had a gun to my ribs."

"He had a gun? He had a *gun*? You could have gotten killed!"

"But I didn't, okay." He was still clutching his hand. Nothing broken, but man, it was sore. "I'm fine."

"You're fine?" she yelled. "You're *fine*? You are not fine! You're crazy!"

"I should have just let that motherfucker rob me?"

"Exactly. Why didn't you just give him the damn briefcase?"

"Because I didn't want to!"

The excuse sounded lame even to his ears. And for just the briefest of moments, he thought about confiding in her. That he'd met his father yesterday afternoon, that Chris gave him all this shit—his bank accounts, his checks, his estate papers, his passport—and he had forgotten to take them out of his briefcase because he was an idiot. And because he had been an idiot, he would have had to go back to Chris and admit that some lowlife mugged him. And he wouldn't ever be able to look his father in the eyes again. It was better to die than to face contempt. He wanted to tell her that. But he couldn't confess without betraying his father.

He'd simply have to wait another couple of days.

In his book, a fucking promise was a fucking promise.

"You didn't *want* to?" Hannah yelled. "And that's worth *dying* over?"

"It's mine. Why should I give it to him?"

"What was it there that's so valuable that you risked your life for it?"

"Nothing much. Just my sheet music."

"You're absolutely insane!" she said with disgust in her voice.

"You're screaming at the wrong person!" Her yelling was beginning to piss him off. "I didn't mug anyone, he did. And if I want to take a chance and get myself blown away, that's my business!"

"Hah!" She breathed out. "You are sincerely crazy!"

"Stop calling me crazy! I'm not the one you should be mad at!"

"On the contrary, you're the perfect person to be mad at. You nearly got yourself killed over a stupid briefcase filled with sheet music. What if he tried to shoot me?"

"That's why I *stopped* him—"

"And on top of that, you look like you wrecked your hands. How stupid is that!"

"You know, I have enough shit in my life without your telling me I'm stupid, okay?" He waved her off. "Fuck all of this! I'm outta here!"

He charged down the street in the darkness without knowing where he was or where he was going. He heard her running after him. She grabbed his arm.

"Let's just go home."

"You go home, Hannah." He was still walking. "See, you have a home. At present, I'm homeless, remember?"

"Gabe, stop. Stop!" She yanked at his arm. "Stop walking!"

Now she was sobbing.

He stopped walking and groaned.

Another ridiculous, sobbing female who couldn't keep it together. His mom, whenever she was desperate, turned on the waterworks. His aunt was absolutely a nutcase, always weeping about something real or imaginary. Sometimes it was easier to deal with his dad's fury than his mom's hysteria.

It was dark and he was starved. If he was going to leave to be on his own, he figured he'd do it on a full stomach. "Fine, Hannah. Let's go back to *your* home and see *your* parents and eat *your* dinner that was prepared by *your* mom!"

"Stop making me feel guilty!" she yelled.

"Stop screaming!"

In a huff, Hannah headed for the car, but Gabe hesitated. "I want to look for the gun. It's a bad idea to leave it for some kid or another motherfucker to find."

Hannah stopped walking. "Good idea. I'll help you."

"No, *I'll* do it. You turn the car around and shine the headlights into the bushes so I can see, okay?"

She complied with his wishes. When she realized it was taking a while, she got out and helped him search. They were both on their knees moving through brush that stank of trash, rotten food, and dog excrement. It felt positively yucky to be touching anything. "Maybe it wasn't a gun, Gabe. Maybe he held you up with these disgusting chopsticks over here."

"It wasn't chopsticks, it was a gun."

"And you know what a gun feels like?"

"You'd better believe it."

She didn't say anything. Sometimes it was best not to continue a conversation. A few minutes later, Hannah saw something glint. "What's that?"

"Where?"

"Under that bush over to the right of the McDonald's wrapper."

Gabe dropped onto his stomach and crawled under a bush. "Good eye. Go in the car. I'll get it out."

"I'll wait with you."

"Hannah, in case it discharges, you shouldn't be around. Just go in the car, okay?"

"I'll stand back, but I'm not leaving you here alone." It was bad enough being bossed around by her dad; she wasn't about to take lip from a kid three years younger than she was.

"Fine, just move out of the way." Gabe carefully extended his left hand under the brush. Of course, it had thorns. His fingers were normally very long but the swelling had turned his digits to sausages. Eventually, his fingers wrapped around the butt of the weapon and retrieved it from the brush. He stood up and carefully took out the magazine. "Nine-millimeter semiautomatic. That ain't no chopstick, sister." He stowed the gun in his briefcase, then tried to close the gate and winced.

"I'll do it," Hannah said.

"It's heavy."

"As long as it's on the track, I can slide it. Just take care of your hand." She closed the gate, locked it, then got into the driver's seat and turned on the motor. "I'm sorry I yelled at you." She had tears in her eyes. "I was just scared."

"Forget it. I'm sorry if I scared you."

"You were scarier than the mugger." She eased onto the roadway. "God, I thought you were going to kill him."

"Better him than me."

"That's for sure. Where's the gun?"

"In my briefcase."

"We'll give it to my dad. Maybe he can find out who it belongs to. Let me tell him what happened. I don't want him to freak out. I can handle the situation more calmly."

"You can handle the situation more calmly?" Gabe asked.

"I'm calmer now."

The next few minutes were spent in silence.

Gabe said, "Your dad wouldn't have let himself be mugged."

"My dad has been a police officer for like forty years."

"It doesn't matter. Either you're that type of person or you're not."

"Fine. You're a superhero."

"Jesus Christ, I'm not saying that—"

"Just let me tell my dad, okay?"

"Do whatever you want, okay. It's your father. I'm just an abandoned outsider."

"Stop trying to make me feel bad."

"I'm not." But he really was. He exhaled. "I think I'll call up my aunt and stay with her this weekend. I should see her anyway."

Hannah didn't argue. "How are your hands?"

"My left one is killing me." He looked upward. "He was down at the first count. I didn't have to beat the shit out of him. That was stupid."

"You're left-handed?"

"Right-handed, but it just seemed easier to hit him with my left. Actually, that was probably a good thing. "

"We're going to pass a 7-Eleven. I'll get you a bag of ice."

"I'll get it. You stay in the car."

She pulled into the parking lot. He got out, and five minutes later, he was carrying a five-pound bag of ice. Once he was seated, he ripped it open and plunged his left hand into the frozen water, kept it there until it was almost numb. Then he pulled it out and did it again. "I didn't break anything. It's just a little sore."

"That's good."

More silence until they got home. They both got out. She opened the door and Gabe went inside first. Decker was sitting on the couch reading the paper. "You're home late." He looked at Gabe's hand and the bag of ice. "What happened to you?"

The boy didn't answer, going straight into his temporary shelter.

Hannah said, "Don't freak, okay?"

Rina stepped into the living room. "What's going on?"

"We're fine . . . I'm fine," Hannah said. "Someone tried to mug us."

"Oh my God!" Rina rushed over and hugged her daughter. "Are you hurt?"

"No, I'm okay."

Decker stood up. "Did you call 911?"

"No."

"Why not?"

"The guy got away—"

"You still should have called 911. You should have called me."

"Abba, everything was okay, so—"

"It's not okay. He's not okay," Decker scolded her. "He's obviously hurt. You should have called me right away. What were you thinking?"

"Could you please not yell at me?" Hannah burst into tears.

"It's all right, Chanelah," Rina cooed. "You're okay. You're safe."

Decker plopped down on the couch and held out his hands to his daughter. "You're right. Now's not the time. Come sit down, Pumpkin. Please." Hannah sat between her parents. "Could you tell me what happened?"

"I don't even know what happened." She dried her tears on her shirt. "Gabe and I were closing the gate to the parking lot—"

"Why were you closing the gate?" Decker wanted to know.

"Because we were the last ones in the school to leave."

"It's not your responsibility to lock up," Decker said. "I'm calling up the school—"

"Abba, no!"

"What do you mean, *no*?"

"Peter, can you just let her finish?" Rina said.

Decker clenched and unclenched his hands. "I'm sorry. Go on. You were closing the gate."

"We were closing the gate. The next thing I knew, Gabe was on top of this guy, beating the crap out of him. I didn't know exactly what happened until afterward."

"What happened afterward?"

"He said the guy tried to steal his briefcase. Gabe fought back. He's a scrappy kid."

Rina and Peter exchanged glances. Decker said, "That's how he hurt his hand?"

Hannah nodded.

"So the guy didn't have a weapon?" Decker asked.

"Uh, he had a gun. He stuck it in Gabe's rib cage."

"He had a gun and Gabe *attacked* him?"

"Yeah, pretty stupid, huh. He should have just given the guy the briefcase. It all happened so fast. It was really scary. But don't yell at him. I've already done enough of that for both of us. He feels pretty stupid right now."

"He should feel stupid," Decker exclaimed.

Hannah didn't say anything.

Rina looked at her husband. "What should we do?"

"What do you mean?" Hannah asked.

"She means his stupid judgment could have gotten you both killed."

Hannah said. "He just like . . . overreacted. You know how it is when adrenalin kicks in. Tell you the truth, Abba, I could see you doing that."

"I'm a trained police officer, Hannah."

"I bet you'd do it even if you weren't."

Decker didn't address her statement. "You're his defense attorney, all of a sudden?"

Again, Hannah felt her best option was to say nothing.

Decker turned to his wife. "What should I do?"

"Why don't we talk to him and ask what happened."

"I'm really not interested in a therapy session. Do we let him stay or do we send him to his aunt's and wash our hands of this whole entire mess?"

"You're worried that he's violent?" Rina said.

"It's occurred to me. We don't know a thing about him except he has bad genetics on his paternal side."

"He's not violent," Hannah said.

"You just said he beat the crap out of this guy."

"He beat the mugger, he didn't beat me. For goodness' sakes, he might have saved my life. He's not rash. As a matter of fact, he's tightly wound. And anyone would be considering the circumstances he's gone through. I can't tell you what to do, but you know that he's basically homeless."

"He has relatives, Hannah, but that's not the point," Rina said. "Do you punish a kid for acting altruistically—"

"Stupidly," Decker said.

"Maybe, but maybe not. We don't know what happened. And maybe in his circle, you fight or you get your derriere kicked by your friends and by your father."

"Not when there's a weapon involved," Decker said.

"You know . . ." Hannah stopped herself.

"What?" Decker said.

"Nothing."

"Tell me, Hannah. I need to know everything if I'm going to make a sensible decision."

Hannah said, "We went looking for the gun afterward. Gabe didn't want to leave it around in case the mugger returned."

"Technically he was a robber."

"Whatever, Abba. Gabe didn't want to leave the gun around like in case a little kid was playing in the bushes and found it."

"Well, that was smart," Rina said.

"I'm not impressed," Decker said.

"Anyway, we were looking on the ground for it and I found a pair of chopsticks. Then I jokingly said maybe he was held up with chopsticks. Then Gabe said that it wasn't chopsticks, that it felt like a gun. Then I asked him if he knew what a gun felt like. And he said, 'You'd better believe it.'"

No one talked for a moment.

"Like he's had experience with weapons," Hannah said. "So maybe that's why he reacted. Maybe guns don't scare him that much."

"That's the problem, Hannah. Guns should scare him." Decker blew out air. "But knowing his father, there's truth in what you said. Are you sure you're okay?"

"I'm fine."

"Where's the gun?" Decker asked.

"Gabe has it."

"Well, first things first." Decker stood up. "Let me get the weapon out of his hands."

CHAPTER TWENTY-SEVEN

I N THE EARLY evening, most restaurant bars tended to be quiet, but Garage's happy hour was lively. Half-price drinks and free bar snacks must have brought in a white-collar trade because the place was brimming with suits of both sexes. If Marge had to guess, she'd peg most of the pack as lawyers because the downtown courthouses were just blocks away. The souls who weren't involved with the legal system were probably bankers, stockbrokers, and accountants from old established L.A. firms. The majority were on the young side—late twenties through late thirties.

Finding a table proved to be a challenge, but with her eagle eye, Marge spotted one in the corner. She and Oliver sat down and perused the drink and food menu. Eventually they ordered a hummus plate and a couple of club sodas from a cocktail waitress named Yvette. She had blue eyes and shoulder-length platinum hair with long legs and a pneumatic chest. Her head looked very small in proportion to her body, reminding Oliver of a blowup doll.

She placed napkins on the table. "I'll be right back with your drinks."

Oliver asked, "Do you know when Crystal is due in?"

"Crystal?" As if the name momentarily stumped her.

"Crystal Larabee," Marge clarified. "She works here as a cocktail waitress."

"She took a few days off."

"Because her friend was murdered," Oliver stated.

Yvette nodded. "She was pretty upset. I mean, who wouldn't be?"

Oliver took out his badge. "We're investigating the homicide. Could we talk to you for a few minutes?"

"Um . . . I'm kinda busy. Let me take care of my business. I'll come back."

"Thank you." Marge turned to Oliver. "Mandy takes a few days off, Crystal takes a few days off . . . coincidence, I ask?"

"Everyone's entitled to a vacation."

"Call up Crystal's cell. Let's get a location on her."

He dialed the number and hung up after ten rings. "No answer."

"Again, I state: Mandy is not home, Crystal is not home."

"Want to take a ride over to Crystal's apartment?"

"I think we should," Marge said. "I'm getting a bad feeling about this, Scott, especially since Garth is missing."

"Like the Loo said, they have a right to go out to dinner."

"So you think it's nothing?"

"I don't think, therefore I am."

Yvette, the small-headed waitress, returned with the sodas and the hummus plate. In addition to the chickpea spread, it came with olives, onions, pickles, tomatoes, and a plate of grilled pita. Marge suddenly remembered that she was hungry. "This looks good. Can we get another one of them?"

"Certainly."

"But first have a seat," Oliver told her.

"Only for a minute," Yvette said. "Really, I can't tell you anything because I don't know anything."

"How about we start with the basics?" Oliver said. "We know that Adrianna was in Garage the night before she was murdered."

"That would be Sunday night," Marge specified.

"I know that," Yvette said. "I was here, too. Weird."

"Weird in what way?" Oliver asked.

"You see a person and then she's gone." Her eyes misted. "Crystal was comping her drinks. I told her not to, that the boss would get mad if he found out, but she did it anyway."

"Was Adrianna drinking?"

"Yes, of course."

"Hard stuff?"

Yvette thought a moment. "I don't know. Why?"

Marge said, "She didn't have any booze in her system. We were told she was only touching the soft stuff because she had to go to work."

"That could be. I wasn't paying attention. But whatever it was, Crystal was comping both Adrianna and that hunky guy that Adrianna was talking to. I'm sure he was drinking."

"What was he drinking?"

"Beer. After he'd gone through a couple of refills, I finally told Crystal to quit it or I'd tell the boss." A pause. "She got pissed at me. But it didn't matter anyway. Adrianna left. And then about a half hour later, the hunk left."

"What time was that?" Marge asked.

"Around nine-thirty."

"Did they look like they were enjoying each other's company?"

"They were talking. Beyond that, I couldn't tell you."

Oliver said, "Did the hunk have a name?"

She shrugged. "I didn't catch it."

"Does the name Farley sound familiar?"

"Farley?"

"Crystal remembered the hunk being called Farley," Oliver said.

When Yvette's response was a confused shrug, Marge said, "Or maybe it was Charley?"

"Beats me," Yvette said.

"What did he look like?"

"Beefy. Big chest, big arms . . . like he worked out a lot. You put him in a gay bar, he'd fit right in. He wasn't wearing a suit, but he was wearing a jacket."

"What kind of a jacket?"

"Like a blazer. Black jacket, black T-shirt and jeans. He wore sandals on his feet."

"Sounds more Hollywood than lawyer or stockbroker," Oliver said.

"Good call. He did seem Hollywood. Or pretend Hollywood."

"Do you think you could identify his face?" Marge asked.

"I got a decent look at him. He had a square jaw, masculine features. Dark eyes."

"Could you come down to the station house tomorrow and work with a police artist?" Oliver suggested.

"I suppose."

"That would be great," Marge said. "Thanks so much. You've been very helpful. Do you have a number where we could reach you?"

Yvette rooted through her pocket and gave them a card.

THE YVETTE JACKSON BAND

SPECIALIZING IN JAZZ, ROCK, AND THE OLD STANDARDS

LIVEN UP YOUR NEXT COCKTAIL PARTY WITH THE REAL DEAL

SPECIAL WEEKDAY RATES

There was a cell phone and an e-mail address. Marge said, "You're a singer?"

"Singer, dancer, musician. I studied at the Western Conservatory School of Music for five years. I majored in classical guitar, but I'm done with that. No one wakes up in the morning and decides to become a cocktail waitress. But the pay is pretty good if you suppress the ego and do the job. I've got a nice smile and big boobs. So far, most of the patrons remember my attributes when it's tip time."

"Thanks for the card," Marge said. "Maybe I'll hire you one day. I happen to love classical guitar."

"So do I, but it has its drawbacks. We're about as much in demand as a typewriter. There's an old joke. What's the difference between a classical guitarist and pizza?"

"I give up," Oliver said. "What's the difference?"

She got up from the table. "A pizza can feed a family of four."

———————

THE KID WAS on his cell when Decker came in, his clothes neatly spread out on the bed. From his tone of voice, he sounded agitated. "It's fine, Missy, we'll make it another time . . ." Gabe rolled his eyes. "I think I'll pass, but thanks for asking . . . yes, I'm sure. It's fine. Okay . . . okay . . . okay, I'll call you when you come back. Bye."

He hung up, threw his phone on the bed, and regarded Decker. "Hi."

Decker looked at the clothes. "Going somewhere?"

"I thought it might be a good idea to spend some time with my aunt. But she's going to Palm Springs for the weekend." Gabe plopped down on the mattress and lowered his head into his right hand while dipping his left in and out of the ice bag, now a mixture of cold water and slush. "My mother has been supporting her since she left her house three years ago. My mom's missing. She might be dead. You'd think that my aunt might feel a little abashed partying with the girls in Palm Springs."

Decker didn't say anything.

"I don't know," Gabe said. "Maybe she has the right idea. Maybe Chris has the right idea. Because it's certainly easier not to give a shit."

Decker said, "Make sure your hand doesn't get too cold."

"You're right." Gabe took it out and flexed his fingers. They were stiff but he could move them. He rotated his wrist.

"How does it feel?"

"I'll be okay." He looked up. "I'm sorry, Lieutenant."

"For getting held up?"

"I should have just given him my briefcase."

"That might have been smart. What was in there that was so valuable?"

"Sheet music." Green orbs averted Decker's stare. "The gun's in there now. I took out the magazine."

"Can I take a look?"

"Sure."

Decker retrieved the valise from the bed, pulled out the weapon and the magazine, and dropped them in a paper evidence bag. He sat down on the opposite bed. "The guy wasn't fooling around. Why'd you decide to take him down?"

Gabe said. "I didn't think. I just did it."

"Over sheet music?"

Again, the boy looked away. This time he said nothing.

"Gabe, your father was in town yesterday."

The boy said nothing.

"This is what I think," Decker said. "I think he contacted you. I suspect that Chris gave you stuff and that stuff was in your brief-case. And that's probably why you reacted like you did. So I'm ask-ing you again, what was in there?"

Again, Gabe didn't answer.

"Okay, we'll get back to that one," Decker said. "What did Chris tell you?"

"Why do you think Chris was in town?"

"Because we're both looking for your mom and we're going in the same direction. He's just a few steps ahead of me because he can devote full-time energy to this."

"So you saw him?"

It was Decker's turn to sidestep the question. "We think we might have located your mom's car."

Gabe looked up. "You did? Where?"

"It's been junked at a scrap-metal dealership. We've got the pink slip and the VIN number. We're trying to tie that car in some way to the car your mother drove. Because the one we found didn't belong to her."

"So why do you think you found her car?"

"How many new Mercedes are sold for scrap?"

The teenager paused. "Who owns the car?"

"Atik Jains. Does the name sound familiar?"

"No."

"He's Indian . . . Indian Indian. Jainism is a religion common in India. Does your mother know any Indians?"

"No," Gabe told him. But his cheeks pinkened.

"You know you're blushing?" Decker paused, then said, "Gabriel, we both have the same goal. To find your mother. We need to work together."

"I have no idea if she knows any Indians. I didn't follow my mother's social life. As far as I knew, she didn't have much in the way of friends."

"And yet you blushed when I asked about her knowing any Indians. What's that all about?"

"It's probably nothing."

"Tell me anyway."

The boy squirmed. "It was a while back. I was waiting at the hospital for my mom to finish up. The place was swarming with guys in turbans. I thought it was like a terrorist threat or something. When I asked my mom about it, she said it was nothing, that some really rich maharaja was getting heart surgery and all those guys were his bodyguards."

"How long ago was this?"

"I have to think. It was when I first started taking lessons at Juilliard. So it must have been two years ago."

Decker took out a notebook. "Okay. What else?"

"Nothing else," Gabe said. "I think I made some wisecrack about India having a billion people and the maharaja had to come to New York to find a surgeon. My mom told me that the maharaja's son was a visiting cardiac surgeon in the hospital and he wanted his father to have the operation where he could keep an eye on him."

The seconds ticked on.

"That's it."

"So you were around twelve?"

"About. I only remembered it because it's not every day you see like twenty guys in turbans."

"Did your mother say anything else about the maharaja or his son?"

"No." He averted his eyes and began to ice his hand again. "But she knew him . . . the maharaja's son . . . who is actually an old guy, like in his fifties."

Decker smiled. "Go on."

Gabe sighed. "I took lessons in the city, so I was in Manhattan a lot. I used to take the bus in from my house, and after my lessons, I'd walk over to the hospital and my mom would drive us home. One time, this was about a year ago, I finished early—which never happens. My ex-teacher was a slave driver, but he wasn't feeling well. Anyway, I walked over to the hospital and I saw my mom talking to this guy who looked like a little Zubin Mehta—graying hair, well dressed, dignified."

"Okay," Decker wrote. "Did they look like they knew each other well?"

"Like they weren't touching or anything, but they were talking . . . a lot. And she was smiling—my mom. Then he got paged and that was that. Then my mom saw me and we went home. I did ask her who she was talking to. She said that he was the cardiac-surgeon son of the maharaja who had all the bodyguards."

When Gabe didn't elaborate, Decker said, "Did she seem embarrassed to be talking to him in front of you?"

"No," Gabe said. "She was very matter-of-fact. But I remember it because it was rare to see her comfortable around a man. She usually avoided men even when my dad wasn't around."

"So she didn't seem flustered?"

"No." Gabe collected his thoughts. "Lots of times we'd do stuff and not tell my dad. Go out to movies or to restaurants when he stayed in the city. Once I went to a Christmas party with her. If she wanted it kept private, she'd say to keep it between us. She didn't say that. So I forgot about it."

"Did you ever see the surgeon with your mom again?"

"No." He looked at Decker. "If I'd seen her with him again, that would have been weird. So you're thinking that the surgeon is the Indian guy who owned the car?"

"Gabe, I have no idea. But I'd like to find out the surgeon's name."

"So if it is the same guy . . . like do you think like he kidnapped her or . . ."

"I don't know." Not even entertaining the notion that she might have taken off with him. Decker paused. "Maybe we should have someone look at your hand."

"I'll be fine."

"Just in case." Gabe was quiet. Decker said, "Look, son, I'm going to level with you. I know that you saw your dad. You don't want to be holding material evidence that could implicate your father in your mom's disappearance. You're nothing like Christopher Donatti. Don't go down for him."

Gabe wouldn't meet his eyes. "How do you definitely know my father was in town yesterday?"

"I told you. He was at the junkyard. We missed each other by thirty-six hours. He wouldn't call you on your cell. That would show up on your phone records. But I know he got in touch with you. And I know he gave you some stuff. I just want to make sure it's nothing that was used in a crime."

Gabe held his head, his mind racing about the cleanest way to get out of it. "I saw him for about five minutes. He gave me my passport, my birth certificate, and some cash." *Don't tell him about the bank statements. Those are traceable.* "That's it."

"That's a start," Decker said. "What did he tell you?"

"He said, 'Here's stuff you might need. Good-bye.'"

"And that stuff was in your briefcase?"

Gabe nodded.

"Where is that stuff now?"

Gabe pulled out his birth certificate, his passport, and a wad of cash from his backpack and gave it to Decker. "If this is material evidence in a crime, keep it."

"It's not material evidence." Decker paged through the kid's passport. He'd been to England, Belgium, Germany, Austria, and Poland. "How'd you like Europe?"

"I was at piano competitions, so I didn't see much."

"How'd you do?"

"Win some, lose some."

Decker said, "Gabe, if this is all he gave you, why didn't you tell me this yesterday?"

The teen shrugged. "I don't know."

"You're holding back."

"Look, Lieutenant, if I thought he killed my mom, I'd kill the bastard myself. But I don't think he hurt her. So I'd rather you just leave him alone. I know you're not going to do that. But if Chris didn't do it, why should I help you?"

"If Chris didn't hurt your mom, I could clear him. I've done it before."

"Maybe he doesn't trust you."

"You want to know what I think?" A pause. "That maybe you're right. That maybe he didn't kill your mom. Maybe your mom ran away from your dad. And if Chris is looking for her, God help her if he finds her. I understand your loyalty to your father, Gabe. But it's better if I find her before he does."

"I agree, but I can't help you. I don't know where she is. I don't know where he is."

"So your father just gave you stuff and said sayonara?"

"Exactly. It's clear he doesn't want any connections to me. And that's fine."

"And yet you remain loyal to him."

"He said he didn't kill her." Gabe was adamant. "I believe him. Then he gave me the stuff and left. That's it. I don't have anything else to tell you."

Decker pocketed the birth certificate and his passport. He thumbed through the cash. It was all in hundreds, and a lot of them. He offered the wad back to the teenager.

"Keep it," Gabe said. "Rent."

"Stop it." Decker waited. "My arm's getting tired. Take the money."

Gabe relieved him of the wad. "I really need to be alone for a while. My aunt left a key to her place under the doormat. I think I'll just hole up there for the weekend."

"You can't stay in her apartment alone. If you want to move in with your aunt, then you'll have to wait until she comes back from Palm Springs."

"What am I going to do there, Lieutenant? I don't drink at all, I don't take drugs. If I wanted to mess myself up, I could do that here as well as there. I don't know anyone in the city, but I guarantee you I could probably find a dealer in about an hour."

"I have no doubt."

"So let me just get out of your way and move into my aunt's and everyone will be happy."

"You're too young, Gabe. I can't let you do that."

The kid growled. "Fine. I'll leave on Monday."

"I'm not kicking you out."

"I can't stay here. You're hunting down my father. You're the enemy."

"I'm not the enemy. Your dad wouldn't let you stay here if I was the enemy. He knows who I am and he knows that I'll take good care of you. But he also knows I'm going to ask you lots of questions because your mother is missing, and right now, that's my first priority. Not your feelings; your mother's welfare. If you want to move in with your aunt on Monday, I won't stop you. But don't put it on me."

Gabe rubbed his eyes under his glasses. "This is so fucked up!"

"Don't curse. Why do you think that your father didn't kill your mother?"

The teenager was confused. "I dunno. He seemed sincere."

"Your dad's a pathological liar."

"I know. But still, he seemed really upset. And now you tell me that he's hunting for her. I mean, why would he do that if he killed her?"

"I have a couple of questions for you." Gabe waited. "Did your mother use the car over the weekend?"

"Let me think . . . it seems like ages ago."

"Take your time."

"Saturday morning I was practicing. I went back to the hotel, and then we walked into Westwood, saw a movie, and ate dinner. Sunday I was in a practice room all day. I don't know if my mom used the car, but she didn't drive me anywhere. I think she said something about wanting to stick close to the hotel because Chris was coming in."

"What about Friday?"

"Honestly, I don't remember."

"Try."

"Friday, Friday . . . I was practicing from like . . . ten to four." A sigh. "We ate dinner at the hotel. What did we do after that?" He paused. "I went swimming. It was a warm night. When I came back to the room, she wasn't there. She returned an hour later in her gym clothes, so I guess she went to the fitness room. We watched TV and then went to bed. Really swinging time. Why are you asking about the car over the weekend?"

Decker was taking notes. "Because the owner of the junkyard said that the car came in on Saturday."

"So . . . that means it's not my mother's car since she disappeared on Sunday, right?"

"She disappeared on Sunday. It doesn't mean she drove off in her car on Sunday. No one remembers seeing her leave. She could have sneaked out."

"Why would she do that?"

"Maybe the meeting with Chris didn't go as well as I thought it did. Maybe she felt threatened by your father and took the opportunity to leave once and for all."

"She told me she was renting a house in Beverly Hills."

"That's what she told your father. But we've checked with most of the real estate agents in Beverly Hills. None of them had ever heard of your mother."

"I don't understand . . ." The boy was confused as well as saddened. "Why would she lie?"

"If she did lie, I'm sure she had her reasons."

"You think she left without me on purpose?"

"I don't know, Gabe, but if she did, she must have felt very threatened."

His words were little solace to the boy. He looked devastated . . . dejected.

"It could be that things didn't go well with your father . . . that your mom jumped right after Chris left, figuring now or never."

Gabe shrugged. "Is that what you think?"

"It's a possibility."

Or, Decker thought, she had planned the whole thing long before Donatti's arrival . . . which is why she junked the car on Saturday. She knew she wouldn't need it again. Figuring that if she made Donatti feel secure, he'd go back home.

After he left, she jumped ship.

Meaning she knew she'd be leaving without her son.

So maybe that's why she'd called him up in the first place. Her ultimate purpose was not hiring Decker for protection, but rather giving her son a safe haven after she left for good.

If that were the case, Gabe wasn't the only one who had been duped.

CHAPTER TWENTY-EIGHT

"**W**E'RE ZERO FOR two." Oliver disconnected the line. "Mandy's not picking up her phone and neither is Crystal."

"Crystal's a party girl," Marge said. "I'm not surprised that she's not answering her landline, but she should be answering her cell."

"Maybe she's in a crowded bar and can't hear it."

They were driving north on the 5 with Griffith Park on their left—an inky vast track of foliage and trees donated to L.A. as recompense after Colonel Griffith shot his wife. God only knew what kind of animals were hiding in the dark—four-legged as well as two-legged. They had managed to avoid most of the evening commuter traffic. Nighttime fog was settling in as they hit the higher elevations going over the hill and back down into the Valley.

Marge said, "Call up Sela Graydon. Find out if she can get through to Crystal."

"Sure." Oliver paused. "What do you think about Mandy Kowalski going AWOL?"

"From what we've been told, the girl is as reliable as sunrise and suddenly she's not answering any of her phones. What do you want to do if she doesn't answer her door?"

"What time is it?"

"Eight-thirty."

"Do we know if she has any friends or relatives that might have a key?"

"She didn't seem to have much in the way of a social life," Oliver said.

"I'm getting a weird feeling about it. She may have heard one too many confessions, know what I'm saying? Do you know what kind of car she drives? I'd like to see if it's in the condo parking lot. And if it's there and she's not answering her bell, we could justify coming into her place without her permission."

"I'll call up the DMV. Do you want me to do it before or after I call up Sela Graydon?"

"Get the car info first. That's an easy fix."

Oliver talked to the DMV as Marge made a descent into the Valley, going parallel to the cement bed of the L.A. River. At this time of night, it was a dark abyss on her right. She passed the exit for the L.A. Zoo merging onto the 134 West, ripping past Forest Lawn Cemetery.

"It's a 2003 Toyota Corolla, black." Oliver recited the license plate number. "Do you have Sela Graydon's phone number?"

"Not on me."

Oliver made a second call and within minutes had the digits he needed. When he called it, she didn't pick up. He left his phone number. He regarded Marge, who appeared deep in thought. "What's on your mind?"

She paused. "I was just thinking."

"That's always dangerous."

"Remember when we were talking to Yvette Jackson, the waitress? I asked her if she knew anyone named Farley. And then I said it might have been Charley?"

"Yeah, she didn't know either one of them."

"I gave myself an idea. Maybe it was Charley . . . as in Chuck Tinsley." When he didn't answer, she said, "Yes, no, maybe?"

"Interesting," Oliver said. "The Loo told us to interview him again. Let's do it."

"Why don't we get a picture of Tinsley, put it in a six-pack, and show it to Yvette Jackson?"

"Do you think he'd be stupid enough to string her up in the property he was supervising and then report her dead?"

"We've gone through a lot of criminals in our years on the force," Marge told him. "Personally, I've never met one who qualifies as an intellectual light."

RINA KNOCKED BUT didn't wait to be invited into the room. "I just called up Matt Birenbaum. He'll fit us in tomorrow."

Decker said. *"Him?"*

"I know he's a little bit of an eccentric, but he's also a top-notch hand surgeon."

Gabe realized they were talking about him. "I'm okay, Mrs. Decker. Nothing's broken."

"That may be, but you need to be looked at. Even if you weren't a pianist, I'd do it. *Kal v'chomer*, I should do it for someone who needs his hands for a career."

Gabe didn't understand everything she was saying but he felt his best defense was not to argue.

"*Kal v'chomer* means I should *especially* have you looked at," Rina said. "I forgot the English legal equivalent. We've got an eleven o'clock appointment. Dr. Birenbaum prides himself on his piano playing, so at least he'll know what your needs are."

"He thinks he's Mozart," Decker said. "He's terrible and I don't even have an ear."

"He's a bit full of himself, but that's what you want in a surgeon." She looked at his clothes spread across his bed. "Are you going somewhere?"

"I thought I'd visit my aunt for the weekend but she's not going to be home. Lieutenant Decker was nice enough to let me stay until she comes back on Monday."

"You're moving out?"

"It might be better. Thank you so much for your hospitality. One day, maybe I can repay it."

"No payment necessary. But you're not going anywhere until you've had your hand checked out. After you've seen the doctor, you can go to your aunt's. Agreed?"

Gabe nodded.

"Peter, go get him a proper ice pack."

"Yes, ma'am." Decker stood up and smiled at the boy's forlorn expression. "She didn't single you out, Gabe. She's tough on everyone."

"That shouldn't be a problem for him. He should be used to tough women." After Decker left, Rina sat on the twin bed opposite the boy. "How is your hand? An honest answer, please."

"Sore."

"That's why boxers wear gloves. Let me see it." He took his hand out of the ice bag and gave it to her. She looked it over with care. "You have some nice bruises. You can move your fingers?"

"Yes."

"You're lucky."

"It was stupid."

"It might have been stupid, it might have been smart. I don't know. I wasn't there. Everything turned out okay, so I'm going to leave it at that. Are you hungry?"

"Not really."

"Neither is Hannah, but both of you need dinner. Once you start eating, you'll get your appetite back."

"Is Hannah mad at me?"

"She's been acting as your advocate, so I'm guessing the answer is no. Dinner will be ready in about ten minutes. Are you right- or left-handed?"

"A righty with a strong left . . . at least, I used to have a strong left."

"You'll be okay. Being as you're right-handed, your schooling shouldn't be impacted." She waited a moment. "After the appointment,

I was going to take you to look for pianos to rent. But if you're going to move in with your aunt, that wouldn't make much sense."

The boy was silent.

"If you want to live with her because she's your aunt and you'd be more comfortable there, I'm fine with your decision. It's hard living with strangers. But don't leave because you think we're mad at you. Knowing your father, you should be able to stomach a little conflict without buckling."

"It's not conflict. I am used to that." Gabe looked away. "I'm tired of being a burden."

"If you were a burden, you wouldn't be here. I don't do burdens, Gabe, I'm too old. Besides, I don't have burdens, *you* have burdens. I'm doing great. And don't worry about my stress level. I've raised two boys. They were always getting into scrapes, although I must admit that I don't think anyone ever held a gun to their ribs."

The teen shrugged. "I'm a magnet for trouble. Things just seem to happen when I'm around."

"It's not smart to be in a parking lot in that area in the dark. I'm going to call up the school. At the very least, they can put up some decent lighting." Rina looked at him. "Knowing your father, you've probably been around guns all your life."

He nodded.

"Do you have a gun? If you have one, give it to me and I'll put it in our gun safe."

"I don't have a gun."

"You wouldn't be fibbing me, would you?"

"No. I swear. I wouldn't have used my fists if I had a gun."

"You might not have been packing, but that doesn't mean you don't have a piece."

"I don't. Check the room."

"I might just do that when you're not around," Rina said. "I wouldn't read your personal material like mail and papers, but I'm not beyond looking under mattresses and other hard-to-find places for guns or drugs."

"I'm not a druggie. I've never bought the stuff in my life. I certainly don't drink. My father's an alcoholic and my grandfathers on both sides were alcoholic. It's in my genes, so I don't go there."

"And you don't have a gun?"

"I don't. Feel free to look around."

Rina shrugged. "But you know how to shoot, right?"

"Yep." A pause. "Chris took care of that."

"Are you a good shot?"

"Not as good as Chris, but I've got a decent aim. Honestly, I hate guns."

"That makes two of us. But I also know how to shoot. I learned because my husband thought it might be a good idea."

"Same with Chris." He was thoughtful. "My dad has lots of enemies. He said that I needed to learn to protect my mom and myself. He used to drill me. He used to shoot at me just to get me used to the sound of whizzing bullets."

"That's insane."

"My dad's insane." The boy smiled. "Maybe they were blanks. He never said."

"That's outrageous, Gabriel."

"Yeah, it was pretty bad. Chris wouldn't have been my first choice in fathers." A shrug. "I guess he's a step up from his own dad. Chris never abused me."

Rina raised her eyebrows. "You don't consider getting shot at child abuse?"

"I mean physical abuse. Chris's father used to beat him. Normally I'd think that Dad was lying, but I've seen the scars." He regarded Rina. "I'm sick over my mom. I really miss her. But there's this tiny part of me that misses Chris, also. Is that weird?"

"Not at all. I'm sure you miss your old life."

"Yeah, probably. It wasn't pretty, but at least I owned it."

IT TOOK ABOUT fifteen minutes before the gate opened to the condo's parking lot. Marge followed the car inside, freaking out the woman driver. After she and Oliver displayed their badges, she calmed down. The driver was in her thirties with a mocha complexion. "You scared the life out of me."

"Sorry about that," Oliver said. "Would you happen to know Mandy Kowalski? She's a nurse at St. Tim's."

"What unit is she in?"

Marge gave her the number. "She's usually at home at night, but she isn't answering her door."

"Maybe she's soaking in the hot tub."

Mandy didn't appear like the hot-tub type. Marge said, "Do you know her?"

"No, sorry. There are lots of units here."

Marge gave her a card. "If you see her, give us a call."

The woman threw the card into her purse. Marge and Oliver watched her until she disappeared behind a door leading to the elevators. Then Marge scanned the parking lot for Mandy's car. "About forty double spaces?"

"Yeah, but a third are half full," Oliver said. "You take the left, I'll take the right."

"And I'll be in Scotland afore you," Marge quipped.

Twenty minutes later, they met up, neither of them claiming success at locating Mandy's car. Oliver said, "It's past nine. I'm not liking this."

Marge said, "Let's try her condo again."

"Her car's not here, what makes you think she's in her condo?"

"Just have a peek, okay?"

They rode the elevator up to the third floor. As soon as they stepped out of the lift and into the open, Oliver's phone rang. He looked at the number and shrugged. "Looks familiar but I don't know who it is." He depressed the talk button. "Detective Oliver."

"It's Sela Graydon returning your call."

"Yes, Ms. Graydon, thank you very much. We're trying to locate Crystal Larabee. Would you happen to know where she is?"

"No. I was actually going to call you about that. I can't seem to get hold of her. She hasn't answered any of my calls. It's making me a little nervous."

"How many times have you called her?"

"About four . . . maybe five."

"When was the last time you spoke to her?"

"Around nine or ten yesterday morning. We mentioned something about getting together for coffee and that was the last I've heard from her. I was thinking about going over to her place, but I don't want to seem ridiculous. I mean, she is a grown woman."

Oliver said, "How about if we meet you there?"

"You know where she lives?"

"I do. We could probably be there in twenty minutes."

"It'll take me about a half hour."

"So we'll see you in a half hour."

"So you don't think I'm being ridiculous?"

"Caring about your friend's welfare is never ridiculous. Do you know anyone who might have a key to her place?"

"I have a key. I don't know if it works. I never used it."

"Bring it—just in case."

"In case of what?" Sela asked.

Oliver didn't answer, choosing to disconnect the call instead.

CHAPTER TWENTY-NINE

MANDY STILL WASN'T answering her door, but with her car gone, Oliver and Marge were less worried than they were curious. Maybe the woman had asked for a few days off to soak up the sun on some close-in Mexican beach. Of greater concern was Crystal Larabee. When the friends got worried, it was time to sit up and take notice.

The two-story dingbat that Crystal called home was lit with hot white spots throwing the occasional patches on the white-fade-to-gray stucco. Sela Graydon was waiting outside, dressed in a fiery red suit with an enormous black leather purse perched on her arm. She was pacing and jingling her keys, but stopped when she saw Marge get out of the car. Her attempt at a smile was a dismal failure.

"Hi." Sela adjusted her purse over her shoulder and held out a hand. "Thanks for coming. It makes me feel less crazy."

Marge shook her hand. "Your friend just passed on a few days ago. You have every right to feel concerned."

"I'm a nervous wreck. I can't concentrate at work. I have to read everything over twice." She bit her thumbnail. "I'm very sad, of course. It's so horrible. I keep wondering what Adrianna got herself into."

Marge said, "Until we know, it's good to be cautious."

"Cautious about what? I mean, this doesn't have anything to do with me, right?"

"Can you think of a reason why Adrianna's death would have something to do with you?" Marge responded.

"No. I mean just because we were friends doesn't mean that we were involved in the same things." A long pause. "Should I be worried?"

"One step at a time," Oliver said. "Do you have the key to Crystal's apartment?"

Sela held up a ring with about a dozen keys on it. "Help yourself."

"Crystal gave you the key," Marge said. "With it, she gave you implicit permission to enter her property. So we'll let you do the honors."

The trio walked upstairs. When they reached Crystal's door, Oliver knocked hard. "Crystal?" Another knock. "Crystal, are you there?"

Sela bit her thumbnail. "Is it my imagination or am I smelling something yucky?"

"No, something stinks," Marge said. "Could you open the door?"

"I don't want to go in."

Oliver said, "Tell us that you called us and wanted us to check out her apartment because you suspect something might not be right."

"I called you to check out her place. I suspect something might not be right."

"Great," Oliver said. "Unlock the door and we'll take it from there."

With a shaking hand, Sela managed to insert the key and turn the dead bolt. As the door fell open, the stench blew stronger. Not exactly the stink of a rotting body; more like overripe garbage.

Sela was ashen. Marge said, "How about if you wait downstairs in your car?"

"Good idea." She swooned and Oliver caught her arm. "Let me help you down the stairs."

"I'm . . . okay."

"I'm sure you are, but the steps are steep and you're wearing heels."

She offered no resistance as Oliver guided her to the first floor. A minute later, he came bounding back up. Marge was already inside, scoping out the kitchen. She had put on latex gloves and had opened one of the two bags of garbage stacked against the wall. "Whew, that's strong! I should have brought up a face mask."

"Shoulda, coulda, woulda." Oliver put on gloves as well, shooing away a couple of buzzing flies—never a good sign. "Find any body parts?"

"No, just a lot of slimy vegetables." She looked up, waved a fly away, and wrinkled her nose in disgust. "As long as I started the dirty job, I'll finish it up. Why don't you look around and tell me if you find something interesting."

He waved air in front of his face with rapid hand movements. "I won't argue."

Marge continued to rifle through the trash. In addition to decomposed produce, there were several discarded cartons of milk, a discarded carton of orange juice, moldy cheese, and old green-tinged deli meat. She tied up the bag and opened the next one. Its contents included a slew of half-used condiments including but not limited to ketchup, mustard, mayo, soy sauce, hot-dog relish, a jar of crystallized strawberry jam, vinegar, wasabi horseradish, maraschino cherries, pearl onions, and pimento-stuffed olives.

Oliver returned to the kitchen about twenty minutes later, just as Marge was tying up the second bag. "There are clothes on the floor and the bed's unmade."

"Any signs of a struggle?"

"More like she's a slob than a crime scene."

"How about recent sex?"

"No used condoms. The room didn't smell particularly clean, but it didn't reek of sperm. The bathroom is also messy, but nothing overtly gruesome like bloody towels or wall spatter. How about you?"

"For a slob, she just did a major cleanup on her kitchen."

Oliver looked around. Like the first time, there were crusted dishes in the sink and the counters were dirty. "What do you mean? The place is a sty."

"She cleaned out her refrigerator." The two of them looked at each other. "Or *someone* cleaned out her refrigerator." She wrapped her gloved hand around the handle of an old white Amana and gave it a yank.

An arm flopped down.

No body followed.

The two detectives peered inside. The nude body of Crystal Larabee had been crammed in so tightly that even gravity had failed to dislodge her from her gelid tomb. Shelving had been removed to make room for the corpse. She had been folded into accordion pleats. Her feet had been bent forward at the ankles, her legs folded at the knees so that her thighs sat on her stomach and chest. Her head had been pulled forward, turned to the right, and was smashed between her knees and the top nonremovable shelf.

Oliver blew out air. "You call it in to the coroner's office. I'll get the crime-scene kit from the car."

Marge took out her phone. "While you're down there, talk to Sela Graydon. We should keep an eye on her."

"As a potential suspect or a potential victim?"

"Right now I'm thinking victim." Marge punched in Decker's phone number. "We don't know what's flying. We certainly don't want a case of two down and one to go."

SELA WAS IN the backseat of the unmarked car. The poor woman had thrown up her dinner. Right now she was shaking and sobbing. "Why . . . is this . . . happening?"

"It must seem like a nightmare," Marge said.

"It is a . . . nightmare!" Sela sobbed into a Kleenex. "I'm scared. What if it's like one of those horror movies? Someone . . . from high school is getting back at us with a vendetta?"

"Do you live alone?"

"Yes."

"Is there someone you could stay with for the night?"

"My parents . . ." She broke into a fresh round of sobs. "I want to go home!"

"Where do your parents live?"

"In Ventura."

About forty miles away from L.A. Marge said, "I don't think you're in a good state to drive right now. How about if I call them up and have them come fetch you."

"I need my car." Sela blew her nose. "I have to go to work in the morning. I'm already behind because I've been so distracted . . . because of Adrianna."

"Are your parents married?"

"Yes, of course."

"Maybe they can drive down together and then drive back to the house separately."

Sela dried her eyes. "I'll call them up now."

"Before you do, I want to ask you a couple of questions." Marge took out her notebook. "Who should I call about Crystal?"

"Oh God!" The tears started up again. "I guess her mother. She doesn't live in L.A. anymore. She moved away."

"Do you have her number?"

Sela shook her head.

"How about a name?"

"Pandy Hurst." Sela spelled it. "It's short for Pandora."

"And you have no idea where she lives?"

"I'm sure her phone number is on Crystal's cell phone."

"Okay. We'll find her." Marge paused. "Can you think of a reason why someone would want to hurt Crystal and Adrianna?"

"The only thing I can think of is that guy that Adrianna was talking to in the bar. Maybe he's a serial killer."

"Yes, we're looking into him. On a more personal note, we still can't find Garth Hammerling. From what we heard, the man wasn't true blue. Could he have had something going with Crystal on the side?"

"It's totally possible. Garth's a jerk."

"What about Aaron Otis? He had a brief fling with Adrianna."

"I don't know him well . . ." She suddenly paled. "I think I feel sick again."

She threw open the door and heaved on the curb, retching and coughing. In the background, Marge heard the approach of wailing sirens.

"Excuse me for a moment." Marge got out of the backseat and met up with the two black-and-whites, giving the four uniformed officers orders to block off the street and secure the apartment building. A crowd was gathering and Marge needed their help. Oliver was already upstairs cordoning off the apartment.

Sela had stopped vomiting and was sitting in the backseat with her head between her knees. Slowly she brought her head up and then wiped her eyes and face. "God, I'm a mess!" She was drooling and dabbed the corners of her mouth with a tissue. "It's funny." A pause. "Not ha-ha funny but ironic funny. For the last year or so, I've been trying to distance myself from those two. And now they're gone . . . and I feel so horrible! Like I caused it by wishing it."

"You didn't cause anything, you know that." Marge had slid into the backseat of the car. "You're as much of a victim as they are."

"Except I'm still here."

Survivor's guilt. "Thank God for that. I'll call your parents now if you want."

"I'll do it. I can handle this." Sela was talking as much to herself as to Marge. She punched in the numbers, but as soon as her mother answered, she burst into sobs. Her mother started shrieking, loud enough for Marge to hear.

"I'm fine, I'm fine, I'm fine," Sela sobbed out.

Marge took the phone and introduced herself.

Another heart-wrenching phone conversation.

Another long night.

CHAPTER THIRTY

TWO BLACK-JACKETED CORONER'S investigators had gently removed the body from the refrigerator and laid it on a blanket. The older of the two investigators—a female Hispanic in her forties named Gloria—turned to Decker. "We need to let the body warm up before we unfold her. If you've ever worked with raw cold beef, you know that it isn't as pliable as room-temperature meat. We don't want to tear anything."

"Got it." Decker squatted down to study the body. Freed from the confines of the icebox, it had unfurled a bit. Crystal was now in the fetal position. Her polished nails appeared intact, although the paint was chipping off of them. The coroners would clip them to determine if there was foreign or biological material present. She had been placed in the fridge for a while, because lividity had taken place, the blood sinking down into the lower halves of the woman's calves, thighs, and torso. With his naked eye, Decker couldn't see any gunshot or stab wounds. Her skin tone hovered around bluish-tinged gray, with her lips being a deep indigo. He regarded her neck. There appeared to be some purple dots—

petechiae—around the portion of her neck that was visible. That usually meant strangulation.

He stood up and scrutinized the inside of the refrigerator. It hadn't been scrubbed down in a while. There were particles of rotted produce clinging to the walls and in the crisper along with a few spills and splotches on the bottom and sides.

He took out a presumptive blood kit and swabbed several stains with Q-tips. Most of them turned blue, indicating the probable presence of blood. No surprise there. Raw meat defrosting in a refrigerator on a plate often sat in its own blood. If one handled the plate carelessly—and Crystal didn't seem to be the meticulous type—the slush often splashed onto the walls or dripped down. Given the amount of stains, Decker would bet that the blood was animal rather than human. In his mind, Crystal, like Adrianna, had died a bloodless death.

Oliver came into the kitchen. "I bagged the sheets, the towels, the clothes on the floor, the crap on the floor, the garbage in the bedroom and bathroom, the toothbrush, and the hairbrush. Anything else you want from the bed and bathroom?"

"What about flies and maggots?"

"A few flies. Didn't find a pile of maggots. I guess the girl was smart enough not to leave raw meat around."

"Or someone was smart enough to put her in the fridge so she wouldn't attract flies." Decker blew out air. "Not to mention messing up our time of death."

"Sela Graydon talked to her yesterday morning." Oliver checked his notes. "Crystal suggested that they go out for coffee, but then never got back to Sela."

"What about Crystal's cell phone?"

"We haven't found it."

"Does she have a landline?"

"No."

"Did you find any personal effects?"

"Just a lot of trash. No purse with any ID in it. Her car is still in the parking space."

"Makes sense. Let's get her cell phone records."

Marge joined up with Oliver and Decker. She snapped off her gloves. "The lady was a slob. Makes it hard to distinguish between evidence and trash." She looked at the body . . . slowly unfurling. "Golly, that's sad. Looks like someone broke her neck."

Decker said, "I'm thinking that she might have died by strangulation."

"Yeah, she has the petechiae." Marge blew out air. "Adrianna died from hanging . . . which is strangulation."

"So what are the links between the two girls?" Decker asked.

Marge ticked off the possibilities on her fingers. "They were best friends, they were both at the bar at Garage the Sunday night before Adrianna died, they both were talking to the same strange man at the bar, and they both knew Aaron Otis and Greg Reyburn."

Oliver said, "Didn't Aaron admit that he fucked Adrianna?"

Marge nodded.

"Could he have fucked Crystal as well?"

"Maybe," Marge said. "Maybe Greg fucked them both. Crystal and Greg were good friends."

"Did Garth fuck Crystal?"

"Don't know."

Decker said, "Get Aaron Otis and Greg Reyburn back for more interviews. See what they have to say about the latest developments."

Oliver looked at his watch. "It's after eleven. Want us to do it tonight?"

"They'll keep until daylight. We still have things to do around here."

"I'll call them first thing in the morning," Oliver said. "By the way, Marge had an interesting idea."

"What idea was that?" Marge asked.

"Farley, Charley."

"Yeah, yeah." She turned to Decker. "So Adrianna was being chatted up by this mystery guy at Garage. Crystal thought she might have heard someone call him Farley. I was thinking that maybe she heard 'Charley' instead of 'Farley.' As in Chuck Tinsley."

Oliver said, "We interviewed a woman named Yvette Jackson a few hours ago who works at Garage. She said she thought that she could identify the guy Adrianna was with. We were thinking about making a six-pack with Tinsley's DMV picture and see if she could point him out."

"Does Tinsley have a record?" Decker asked.

"He's not in the system. But I didn't check beyond LAPD."

Decker shrugged. "Give it a go."

No one spoke as three pairs of eyes looked down at the body. Gloria, the Hispanic CI, came over and felt her skin with a gloved hand. "She's still cold."

"How long is it going to take for her to warm up?"

"A while."

Decker spoke to his detectives. "I'll wait here. Why don't you two start canvassing the complex. Not too many apartments, so it shouldn't take too long. I'll give you a buzz when they're ready to move the body."

"You bet." Marge looked at her boss and longtime friend. "Are you all right, Rabbi?"

"Just tired."

"How's the kid?"

"He's still parentless." Decker messaged his temples. "I feel bad for him. I also feel stupid for getting involved in his mother's life." He gave them a minute recap of his day. "I don't know if she's legitimately in trouble—in which case I'll feel guilty for being mad at her—or if she played me, using my home as a safe place to dump her kid while she reinvents herself."

"And you haven't heard from Donatti?"

"I haven't but the kid admitted to me that he saw him yesterday."

"So he's in town or . . ."

"Probably long gone. Donatti gave Gabe his passport, his Social Security card, and a wad of cash. Probably gave Gabe other things but that's all the kid will admit to. It's clear to me that Donatti isn't coming to pick up his progeny any time soon."

"Doesn't his aunt live in L.A.?" Oliver said.

"His aunt and his grandfather."

"So he has options. Why are you shouldering the burden?"

"He's offered to go to his aunt's. But he'd rather stay with me."

Oliver said. "It isn't his choice, Rabbi, it's yours."

"I know. I should let him leave. But my conscience tells me that putting him into the custody of an irresponsible kid herself is not the right thing to do."

"See, that's your problem," Oliver said. "You're listening to your conscience. I can tell you from personal experience, Deck, that no good ever comes from that."

BY TWO IN the morning, the body had been removed, the scene had been dusted, evidence had been taken, and a padlock was placed on the apartment. Decker didn't need to wait with his two crack detectives but decided to do so anyway. Before he had been called down, he had managed to eat some dinner, although it was tense with the two kids picking at their food. When Marge phoned him the news of Crystal, he was shocked, but part of him was relieved to get away and do something productive.

"See you in the morning," Decker said. "I'll be in around eight."

"Take care." Marge jingled the keys. "I'd like to go by Mandy Kowalski's place."

Oliver checked his watch. "Do you not know what time it is?"

"I'm not going to bang on her door. I just want to check if her car is in the lot."

"The lot is gated. How do you propose to get in?"

"So I'll peek through the bars. Look, Scotty, she lied to us about having coffee with Adrianna in the cafeteria. Now Crystal's dead. I just want to see if her car's there."

"You want me to go with her, Oliver?" Decker volunteered.

"Nah, I'll go," Oliver grumped. "We're just having our usual spats. I mean, who needs sleep anyway?"

"Sleep is highly overrated," Marge said.

"Since when have you become such a night owl?"

"Since my daughter moved out. It's sometimes hard for me to sleep. I keep wondering about her."

"But you adopted her when she was a teenager. You lived without her for years."

"That was then and this is now. I can't help it if I worry."

Decker said, "Kids are like heroin—an injection of pain when they're around, but even when they're not around, it's like that next fix. You just can't stop thinking about 'em."

WHEN THE CLOCK struck six, Decker gave up. Through the curtains came the hint of light dulled by gray overcast. He slipped out of bed, put on his robe, and decided to start the coffee. Get a little solitude before the onslaught, but it wasn't meant to be. Gabe had beaten him to the sunrise. He was wearing a T-shirt and jeans, sitting at the breakfast table, his laptop open but off to the side. He was reading Decker's morning paper. "Hi."

"Hi," Decker answered—a bit sullenly, he decided. Or maybe he was just weary.

"I took the liberty of making coffee. You want a cup?"

"Thanks. I'll get it. How's your hand?"

The boy put down the paper and wiggled his fingers. "Sore. I guess now it's just like going through a process. I'll be all right."

"Just take care of it. You're up early."

"I couldn't sleep. I heard you come in last night. It was late. Is everything okay?"

Decker smiled inwardly. No one in his family thought twice about his hours. "Just work." He poured a cup of coffee and sat down. "How are you?" This time he was sincere with the question.

"I'm okay. Is there anything I can help you with?"

Decker smiled for real. "Your mother said you were a good kid. She wasn't lying."

"That's me." He pushed his glasses up on his nose. "You can put it on my gravestone. I was a good kid."

"If I were you, I'd be seething with anger."

Gabe looked up at the ceiling. "I guess it comes out. Like brawling with that idiot last night." He shook his head and pulled a sheet of paper out of his back pocket. "Since I couldn't sleep, I played with my computer. I went into the hospital's Web site."

"Which hospital is that?"

"Yeah, that's right. You can't read my mind. The hospital where my mom worked."

That got Decker's attention. "Find anything?"

Gabe handed him the piece of paper. "I wrote down all the Indian names that have passed through cardiology or cardiovascular surgery in the last eight years. Before then, my mom and I lived in Chicago. I think some of the names might be women. I don't know if any of these guys was the guy my mom was talking to, but I wasn't doing anything anyway, so . . ."

Decker regarded the surnames: Chopra, two Guptas, Mehra, two Singhs, Banerjee, Rangarajan, Rajput, Yadav, Mehta, and Lahiri. "None of them sound familiar?"

"Just Mehta, and only because of the famous conductor. Like I said, she didn't tell me the guy's name."

"Would you recognize him from a picture?"

"I don't think so." He took a sip of coffee. "If you want, I could Google the guys, one at a time, and see if any of them had maharajas for a father. I'm not going to school today. It would give me something to do."

Decker studied the boy. "And what would you do with the information?"

"Give it to you."

"How about giving it to your father?"

Gabe crossed his arms in front of his chest. "Why would I do that?"

"Why wouldn't you do it? He's looking for your mom, too."

"Lieutenant, if he's looking for her, it means that's he's as in the dark as we are. If he can find her quicker than you, why would that be bad?"

"Are you serious?"

"He won't hurt her."

"He already has hurt her."

"Well, I don't think he'd do it again."

"Is that what he told you when you saw him?"

"Yes, as a matter of fact."

"And you believe him?"

"Yes, I do." His eyes grew angry. "But he isn't calling me up for help and I can't reach him, so this whole discussion is moot. If I had wanted to give Chris the information, I could have mailed it to one of his places. But I didn't. If you want help, I'll look them up for you. If not, that's okay, too."

Back off, Decker. Chris is still the kid's father and you're not going to change that bond ever. "Talk about looking a gift horse in the mouth. Anything you can help me with is appreciated. So sure, look them up for me. And for the future, what you do with your dad is your own business."

Gabe was quiet. Then he said, "I don't know why I'm defending the bastard."

"He's your dad. He's got all the history with you."

"Yeah, and most of it's bad." A pause. "That's not entirely fair. He has some good points. He just chooses not to show them very often." He looked at Decker. "I don't trust my dad. I never have. But I wouldn't want to be the one to put him in jail."

"Totally understandable." If Decker wanted an ally, he had to start treating the kid like one. He held up the list. "This is very helpful. I'll make a copy and both of us can see what we come up with, all right?"

"Sure."

"Gabe, my main objective is finding your mother, not screwing your father."

"I know. But I also know that if it came down to it—that my dad hurt my mom—you'd go after him without any consideration for my feelings."

"That's true."

"I'd do the same thing. I mean, if I were you, I would."

"How about if *you* were you?"

"I don't know, Lieutenant. Like my therapist would say, perhaps it's not a good time to visit that issue."

Decker laughed. "You know the lingo."

"I've always had an excellent ear."

CHAPTER THIRTY-ONE

MARGE PLUNKED A latte in front of Oliver. "Maybe this will help. You look tired."

"I am tired. By the time we were done being Peeping Toms, it was past three."

"And I told you that you didn't have to come. Let's drop it. And you're welcome for the coffee."

Oliver groused out a thank-you.

Marge rolled her eyes. "Mandy Kowalski still isn't answering her cell. I also called the hospital and spoke to Hilly McKennick—the head nurse. Mandy was supposed to come back today, but she didn't show up for rounds."

"That's not good." Another sip of coffee. "Since it is now daylight, I will be happy to go over to Mandy's condo and see what's going on."

"We can do that now."

"What's going on with Aaron Otis and Greg Reyburn?"

"Greg hasn't called me back, but I did speak to Aaron. He's coming in at ten. It's only eight. We have enough time to go back and forth."

"Did you tell Aaron about Crystal?"

"Broke the news to him twenty minutes ago. He's acting totally freaked."

"He probably is. So why wait until ten to bring him in?"

"He's at work and wanted to get a few things squared away. I figured it's best to let him set the time frame, use him as an ally instead of a suspect, even though he is one. I have uniformed officers on him and at Greg's apartment in case either of them decides to run. It's all under control." She slung her purse over her arm. "Ready?"

Oliver finished his latte in one gulp. "Man, you were a busy bee this morning. How do you function on so little sleep?"

"I never went to sleep. I knew it would be hell waking up after three hours, so I decided to make myself useful. I found out where Crystal's mother lived. You'd think it wouldn't be difficult to find a woman named Pandora Hurst, but it took me the better part of an hour. I called Mom at six in the morning—eight her time. She's coming in from Missouri."

"Not a good way for you to start the morning."

"It was a very bad way to start the morning, but it had to be done. Also, I made a six-pack from Chuck Tinsley's DMV photo for Yvette Jackson. All that jazz took up another hour."

"Surely you haven't called Yvette Jackson yet."

Marge checked her watch. "I'll do it when we're on the road to Mandy's condo. Let's go."

"Aren't you exhausted?"

"At the moment, I'm jacked up on coffee and Red Bull. If I were to kick at this moment, I'm sure my heart would go on beating hours after my demise—like a pithed frog. Even so, I'm willing to admit that my spatial perception might be a tad off." She handed him the keys. "So would you mind?"

Oliver took them. "Thanks for dealing with everything. I owe you. How about dinner tonight?"

"How about one day without your complaining?"

Oliver shook a finger at her. "Let's not push it."

ONE NAME STOOD out: Paresh Singh Rajput. He had been a visiting cardiovascular surgeon for two years in the right time frame—when Gabe was about twelve. The name—which means "son of a king"—was a warrior name and the royal family to which it belonged had ruled a number of princely states between the ninth and eleventh centuries. There were around five million Rajputs in India, mostly in the central region of Uttar Pradesh but also in the northern regions.

From the Google information Decker had pulled up, it was hard to ascertain if Rajput's father was a maharaja because most of the articles centered on Dr. Rajput's professional achievements—which were many. He had renowned skills as a surgeon, but he had also devoted a significant part of his time to working in poor communities. He was also active in Doctors Without Borders.

The biographical information told Decker he was in his early fifties with two adult sons, both of them doctors as well. Further information revealed that Rajput's wife, Deepal, had died three years ago—around the time he took a visiting position in the States. He was currently single.

Decker managed to pull up several pictures of Rajput. The snapshots showed a well-built man with chocolate skin, a thin nose, full lips, thick eyebrows, black eyes, and a head full of salt-and-pepper hair. He wore beautifully tailored Western suits, as well as traditional Indian garb. In those photographs, his fingers sparkled with stones big enough for Decker to notice. It seemed that a man who dressed that well and devoted that much time to the underprivileged didn't have to worry about money.

The information led to some interesting possibilities if Terry was alive. It wasn't hard to imagine Terry, after being trapped for years in a relationship with a psychopathic and abusive man, finding a savior in a wealthy older widower who routinely used his money, knowledge, and power to help out the downtrodden.

And it wasn't hard to picture Dr. Paresh Singh Rajput coming to the rescue: a wealthy older *lonely* widower liberating a brilliant and gorgeous damsel in distress. Terry was more than just stunning. She had this wounded beauty that melted any male heart on impact, her exquisiteness made all the more intoxicating because she never flaunted her most marketable asset.

Together they would go back to India and Terry could start a new life.

If this were the case, it would be the end of the trail for Decker. Maybe Donatti would pursue it, but Decker wasn't about to tackle a country of a billion people to look for a woman who wanted to get lost.

In either scenario, with Terry dead or alive, Gabe was still out a mother. Poor kid. Not even fifteen and on his own. His parents gave him the brains, the looks, and the talent, but their own shortcomings failed to deliver to the teen any sense of security. They both had abandoned him into the care of strangers.

It was enough to make you want to wring someone's neck.

"SHE'S NOT ANSWERING her cell and her car's not here," Marge told Decker over the phone. "Do we break the lock or not?"

"And you're sure she was supposed to show up for work today?" Decker said.

"According to the head nurse, yes. She's concerned."

"Have you tried calling her parents?"

"I've left a message with her mother. She hasn't called me back."

"When was the last time you called the mother?"

"Ten minutes ago."

"What about a father?"

"Don't know if he's in the picture. I don't have a number for him."

"Friends?"

"Other than Adrianna, I'm in the dark. Hilly didn't have any help with that one."

Decker thought a moment. "I don't know what she has to do with Crystal Larabee, but she was one of the last people to see Adrianna alive. Break the lock."

"What do you want us to do once inside?"

"Look around. See if her walls talk."

"That's going to take some time. Aaron Otis is supposed to come into the station in a half hour. Do you want to interview him?"

"Sure. What happened the last time you talked to him?"

Marge gave him a recap of the conversation as best she remembered. "We know he had a fling with Adrianna. He knows Crystal, but I don't know how well. I do know that Greg Reyburn is friends with Crystal. I phoned him and left a message, but he hasn't returned my call."

"If you have his number, I'll call him again."

Marge read out the digits. "Last I heard from Tim Brothers, the officer on watch detail, Reyburn's car is still in the parking lot of his apartment house. I could tell the officer to go knock on Reyburn's front door."

"That might be a good idea. How you handle it from there is up to you."

"Will do." She paused. "The whole thing is odd, Pete. Adrianna kept loaning Garth money for him to take mini-vacations without her. Then she'd sulk and screw other guys including Aaron Otis. Maybe Greg Reyburn as well."

"Did anyone ask Reyburn if he had a relationship with Adrianna?"

She gave the cell to Oliver. "The Loo wants to know if Greg Reyburn admitted to screwing Adrianna."

Scott took the phone. "Reyburn claims he never fucked Adrianna."

"What about Crystal Larabee?" Decker asked.

"There were booty calls. Mostly they were friends."

"So let me get this straight. Garth and Aaron screwed Adrianna, Greg screwed Crystal, but not Adrianna. Did Garth ever screw Crystal?"

"Don't know."

"Did Aaron ever screw Crystal?"

"Don't know."

"And how does Mandy Kowalski fit into all of this?"

"Mandy worked with Garth," Oliver said. "She complained he came on to her."

Decker said, "I'm writing all of this down. Trying to get some kind of flowchart." He waited a beat. "Also, Kathy Blanc told me that she thought that Mandy was the one who set Adrianna up with Garth. So there's another connection. We've got more arrows than I thought. Okay. I'll take Aaron, see what he has to say."

"It would be very convenient for him to admit that he screwed Crystal."

"Yes, indeed. Not that it's against the law to have had sex with two girls who wind up dead, but after looking over this flowchart, I can tell you that it doesn't look too good on paper."

THE WORLD MIGHT be an artist's canvas, but Aaron Otis used his own body as one. The guy was inked from the neck down, leaving his face a monotone mask. Tan skin, tan hair, light brown eyes, and lots of wrinkles indicating a life outdoors. His hair was wild and curly. He looked like a multicolored lion.

"This is totally freaky." He was gripping a coffee cup with trembling hands. "Like a crazy coincidence."

"A coincidence?" Decker repeated.

"Or like maybe not."

"Both of the girls were friends of yours?"

"Acquaintances, sure."

Decker had many acquaintances. He only had sex with his wife. "I'm trying to find Greg Reyburn. He isn't answering his door and his cell goes straight to voice mail. Would you know where he is?"

Aaron rubbed his face. "We were partying last night. I left the bar at one."

"Where?" Decker took out his notebook.

"Wild Card . . . it's on Cahuenga just past Ventura."

"Okay. You left the place at one. What about Greg?"

"I don't know. He was talking up a girl. Maybe he hooked up with her."

"But his car is in his apartment parking-lot space."

"I drove last night. When I left, I asked Greg about a ride home; he told me he was cool. So he could be at someone else's house sleeping it off. It isn't that late."

It was ten after ten. Decker had been up for four hours. "Let's go back a little bit. Why don't you start at the beginning of your trip."

"You mean my trip with Greg and Garth?"

"Yes, that's exactly what I mean."

"That's way back."

"It's less than a week ago."

Aaron was hesitant but eventually got out his story, basically a recap of what he told Marge. As they were preparing for their camping trip, Adrianna called him. Aaron delivered the message to Garth—that she was breaking up with him. Garth panicked, and went back to L.A. to talk to her. Garth left for the Reno airport in a taxi while Aaron and Greg went on their trip. But it was too cold in the mountains for them to stay.

"There was snow on the ground. We brought fleece and stuff, but it was way colder than we were prepared for. So we turned around the next day and came back."

"How far did you travel by car?"

"Musta been like, I don't know . . . two hundred miles. It took all day to get there. The roads are really windy."

"They have gas stations along the way?"

"Yeah, but not a lot. You gotta be careful of your gas tank."

"Did you stop for gas?"

"Sure."

"Where?"

"Several places. I told the lady detective that I put all my purchases on my credit card." Aaron paused. "I was far away when Adrianna died. My credit cards prove it."

"It certainly does prove that your credit cards were far away. Anyone see you at your pit stops?"

"Yeah, sure. We went into a convenience store. We got some snacks. I remember the store clerk. She had blonde hair and brown eyes and had a nose pierce. She was cute. I think her name was Ellie or something like that."

Decker knew that most convenience stores had video monitoring. If he could pull Otis's credit card records, he could contact the store and probably get the video verification if the clerk hadn't erased the tape.

Aaron said, "We also stopped there on the way back. Same clerk, by the way."

"Can I pull your credit card receipts to get the name of the convenience store?"

"Sure. Whatever you need to prove that I wasn't anywhere near L.A."

"Okay. If everything checks out, you probably weren't involved directly in Adrianna's murder. So let's move on to Crystal."

"I'm not friendly with Crystal . . . I mean I'm not unfriendly with her, but she's much better friends with Greg than me."

Decker looked up from his notebook and made eye contact with the lad. "I'm going to ask you this and I want an honest answer. If I find out you were lying to me, I'll be much less forgiving of your statements. Do you understand?"

Aaron put down the coffee cup. "I'm not lying to you."

"I haven't asked you the question yet." Decker's eyes bored into his. "Have you ever had sex with Crystal Larabee?"

Aaron's eyes shifted focus. "Yeah, like a long time ago . . . like two months."

Decker had to stifle a smile. "Not so long ago to me. How long did the affair last?"

"It wasn't an affair. She came over to Greg's house and I was there. Greg had to go to work and . . . one thing led to another."

"How long did your affair last?" Decker repeated.

"We did it like maybe six times. It was real casual. Crystal got around."

"And the last time you were intimate with her was about two months ago?"

"Maybe even three."

"Why'd you stop having sex with her?"

"We didn't stop officially . . . the opportunity just didn't come up. It's not like I made booty calls to her. Once in a while, we'd find ourselves together and it would happen." He rubbed his face. "Honestly, I haven't seen Crystal in at least a couple of weeks."

"Okay," Decker said. "Tell me what you did yesterday. Recount your day."

"I got up around seven . . . went to work." A shrug.

"When do you go to work?"

"Around eight."

"Go on."

"I was at work all day. I came home around five. I ordered in a vegetable pizza from Muncher's. I left to go to Wild Card around eight-thirty." A pause. "That's it."

"Did you call anyone while you were home?"

"I called Greg. I called Garth again, but got no answer. My mother called. Like the usual stuff."

"On your cell phone or on your landline?"

"I only have a cell."

"Can I look at those records?"

"Sure. Absolutely."

Decker said, "How do I say this? It seems to me that you have a lot of casual sex—with Adrianna and now with Crystal Larabee."

"Why not?" The boy's face was absolutely guileless.

"You weren't bothered by screwing Garth's girlfriend?"

"It was a casual thing . . . like when Garth wasn't around . . . which was a lot. He spent a lot of time in Vegas."

"Without Adrianna."

"Yeah, without her, yeah. It was weird."

"In what way?"

"That she financed his Vegas trips without her. I mean it's not like she liked it. She complained about it. I asked her why she kept doing it."

"What'd she say?"

"She said you can't keep guys pinned down. They get resentful, which is true . . . So she did it and then *she'd* get resentful. When we'd have sex, she'd say things like, 'I wouldn't do it except that Garth's away so much.' She messed around a lot. I know I wasn't the only one."

"Who else did she mess around with?"

Aaron realized that he had just put his foot deep down his throat. "I mean she told me she messed around a lot."

"You didn't answer my question. Who else did she mess around with? And please don't bullshit me."

Aaron threw up his hands. "Yes, she screwed Greg. She loved screwing Garth's friends. I guess she thought it gave her some kind of revenge."

"Did Garth know about it?"

"He knew something. He didn't seem to care."

"But according to you, he cared enough to cancel his trip and fly out to see her."

"True that. He freaked when she said she was dumping him. It surprised me."

"Why?"

"Because he didn't seem to care that much about her."

"Maybe he cared because he stood to lose his interest-free bank."

Aaron didn't talk for a moment. "That might be. He did go to Vegas a lot."

"Garth goes to Vegas, Garth goes to Reno. Does Garth have a gambling problem?"

"Garth?" Aaron laughed. "He plays two-dollar tables and quarter slots. Sometimes he plays the poker machines. I rib him about it all the time. I once told him that he was the only guy I knew who could make fifty bucks last a weekend."

"So why does he go to Vegas so much if he really doesn't gamble?"

"You're kidding, right?"

Decker didn't answer.

"You know the saying," Aaron replied. "What happens in Vegas stays in Vegas."

"What happens in Vegas?"

"Nothing too spectacular." But Aaron looked very uncomfortable. "I mean, it's just that Garth likes women. They're notches on his belt, you know what I'm saying."

"What kinds of women?"

"See, that's the thing. He doesn't have a certain kind. He likes them all: young, old, black, white, Asian, Hispanic, fat, skinny, blonde, brunette, redhead, bald, you name it. He told me it's his goal in life to screw every kind of female in the world. I told him that was impossible because everyone was different. Then he said that that's the point; he'd never get it all, so he'd have to keep going."

"What did you say to that?"

"I dunno. We just laughed or something. C'mon, Lieutenant. We're guys. That's what you do when you're young and single and that's certainly what you do in Vegas."

"Do you know if Garth was into kinky?"

"According to Garth, he was always up for anything new." Aaron pressed his lips together. "Call me old-fashioned, but it turns me on when I get a girl off. Garth didn't care about that. He told me several times he likes it back door. He told me that with back door, the guy has a grip and doesn't have to look the girl in the eye. He made a point of saying that with back door, the guy's always in control."

CHAPTER THIRTY-TWO

MANDY KOWALSKI DIDN'T decorate with heart.

The place appeared staged for max sale, done up in good taste, but very generic. The color scheme was muted. The furniture included a taupe Ultrasuede sofa, a teakwood coffee table, and an armchair and ottoman. Off to the side was a dining table with four upholstered chairs. A freestanding bookcase held paperbacks, DVDs, and professional nursing books. Scattered among the shelves were candles and a half-dozen very well-focused nature photos. A distinct lack of any personality, with nothing to suggest that Mandy had a mother, father, sibs, or friends.

The kitchen was small and spotless—clean sink, clean counters. Oliver opened the fridge. "There's a salad bag in the crisper." He took it out and regarded the greens. "Still good." He took down a carton of milk. "This still has a week to go."

"Anything else in there?" Marge asked while checking cupboards.

"Coffee, condiments, a package of baloney." He closed the door. "Not a whole lot to make a meal. Maybe she ate at the hospital."

"From what we've been told, she spent a lot of time there. Did you call the hospital again to make sure she hasn't shown up?"

"Yes, I called, and no, she hasn't clocked in for work." Oliver leaned against the fridge. "She's only been gone for a little over a day. Can't really call it a missing person case. No one called it in."

Marge thought a moment. "Mandy was way down on our suspect list until she lied to us. And there's the video. What was she doing on the emergency vehicle dock?"

"Is it her?"

"I think so, but I'm not proof-positive." Marge shrugged. "We have a few good reasons for wanting to talk to her. So even if no one's reporting her missing, we still need to find her."

"Well, wherever she is, we're not getting any answers in the apartment."

"We've still got the bathroom and bedroom." Marge stepped into the only lavatory in the condo. It, like the rest of the living quarters, was tidy and clean. No unusual drugs in the medicine cabinet—Advil, Tylenol, bandages, Neosporin, one percent corticosteroid cream, toothpaste, dental floss, and a nail file. The one thing that Marge did notice was that almost everything in the cabinet was sample-size packets instead of retail bottles. One of the perks of working in a hospital: free drugs. The towels were hung neatly, the bathtub and toilet were clean.

Mandy's bedroom was large, with a big picture window and a door leading to a small balcony that overlooked some rooftops. Her bed was made and her nightstand tops were clear except for a phone charger and a clock. Her closets were organized by color. Marge searched through her hanging clothes, then went on to the dresser drawers, which were as orderly as the closet. "If she took off, it doesn't look like she packed a lot of clothes. There's lots of stuff left behind."

Oliver got up off his knees after looking under the bed. "I haven't found any luggage. The head nurse said Mandy was planning a vacation of sorts. Maybe she decided to extend her trip."

"And not call in to her boss?"

"Yeah, she hasn't been portrayed as the spontaneous sort."

"Maybe she has a dark side." Marge started talking to herself. "Okay, dark side, if I were you, where would I hide? If I were into drugs, maybe I'd hide in the freezer or in the toilet tank."

"I'll give it the old college try," Oliver said. But he returned a few minutes later empty-handed. "We're wasting our time. I could request a warrant for phone records, but since she hasn't been reported missing, I don't know if I could get it."

"Does she have a MySpace or a Facebook? Sometimes they post things that may help us out."

"I wouldn't know. I'm too old for that nonsense."

"You mean you don't want a thousand Facebook friends?"

"*Au contraire*, I'd love to lose a few that I already have. Call the Loo and let's get our next move."

But Marge wasn't ready to leave. She went back into Mandy's closet, checking the walls and floors.

"What are you looking for?" Oliver asked.

"Maybe a safe . . ." She sighed. "One more shot, Scotty, just for the heck of it."

"Sure, why not. I'll go over the living room—again."

Marge started rummaging through Mandy's clothes a second time. The dresser was just low enough to hurt her back. And if she dropped to her knees, she couldn't look into the top drawer properly. She decided to take the entire drawer out and put it on the bed, going through the items while seated, starting with the bottom drawer filled with bulky sweaters and sweatshirts. Mandy was neurotically meticulous, tucking tissue paper inside every sweatshirt and sweater to keep each article from wrinkling. The clothes crackled static as Marge went through them, piece by piece by piece, unfolding them, and then folding them back up. When she got to a thick green cable knit, she felt something a little more solid between the front and back of the sweater.

Inside was a double-ply plastic bag.

"And what is this?" She regarded the contents. Then her eyes widened. "Oliver?" No answer. "Yo, Scott."

"What?" he yelled from the other room.

"You need to come here now," Marge said. "We've found her dark side."

He came bolting in as Marge spread the photographs on top of the bed. In several snapshots, Mandy was on all fours, garbed in black fishnets, garter belt, and a leather bustier. A spiked dog collar was pulled against her neck by a taut leash. The man who was restraining her was masked and shirtless, with ripped muscles and a six-pack. Even though his facial features were obscured, he had plenty of identifying tattoos. Didn't look like Aaron Otis's ink work, but she'd definitely have a look at the young man's arms again.

Both she and Oliver had seen lots of pictures of this sort of thing. Mostly the photos looked like silly sex games. Not this time. The pose was menacing enough, but there was something about Mandy's expression that told her it wasn't a joke. The cat-o'-nine-tails that the man was gripping in his right hand sealed the deal.

"Quick question," Marge said.

"Tell me."

"The pictures look pretty well focused, no?" Marge said.

"Yeah, you can make out detail. Why?"

"They don't look like they were shot with a timed camera on a tripod. So my question is—who took the pictures?"

A KNOCK ON the interview-room door, then Wanda Bontemps came inside. "Sergeant Dunn on line three. She says it's important."

Decker nodded and stood up. "Excuse me for a moment, Aaron. Would you like something to drink? Some coffee or soda?"

"Water would be great."

"I'll get it for him," Wanda volunteered.

Decker closed the door behind him and took the call in his office. "What's up?"

"Did Aaron Otis ever come in?"

"I was just finishing up with him. What's up?"

"Can you take some snapshots of his arms?" Marge explained why. "I don't think it's him, but I'd like to make sure."

"I can hold him here for another twenty minutes or so. If you bring in the photographs, maybe he can identify the tattoos."

"Maybe. Or maybe he was there, Rabbi. The photographs looked staged and that means someone snapped the poses. If Garth and Aaron were swapping girls, why not Mandy?"

"Good point. Aaron just confessed to me that Garth likes to do it from the back because he likes to be in control."

Marge squatted down and slid the bottom drawer back into the shelf. "I would say with a hundred percent certainty that the guy in the photograph likes to be in control."

"Get here as soon as you can with those pictures."

"And what's our justification for taking personal stuff from Mandy's apartment?"

"We have two brutal homicides and we can't find Mandy Kowalski anywhere. Then we see these pictures, so now we're really worried about Mandy's safety. It's imminent danger. And that's no lie."

ALL HE WANTED to do was fade into the woodwork.

Instead, as he sat in the doctor's office, he realized he was a supreme pain in the ass.

"My hand's fine, Mrs. Decker. This isn't necessary."

"Call me Rina, and how do you know what's necessary?" She took in her charge. Gabe was neatly dressed in a clean white shirt and jeans. Athletic shoes housed big feet. His face looked tired, his eyes dragging behind his glasses. He had broken out all over his forehead. His hair was hanging into his eyes and brushing the top of his shoulders. Nice hair—thick and shiny.

Gabe wiggled his fingers. "Nothing's broken."

"You have nerves and tendons, right. I'd be derelict if I didn't check it out."

"Why would you be derelict? You don't owe me anything."

Rina gave him a stern look. "I'm not your mother. I'm not your father. I'm not even your legal guardian. I barely know you. But for some reason, providence has dropped you into my lap. And I shall take care of you until otherwise directed."

The boy said, "My dad's around somewhere. I'm sure he'd sign papers for me to go to a boarding school next year."

"Is that what you want?"

"I dunno." A pause. "It's a little late in the year to start applying, but I'm sure I could get in anywhere. Talent trumps all."

"Any specific school in mind?"

"Doesn't matter. I told the lieutenant that I could get into Juilliard when I'm sixteen, so I guess all I have to do is hang in for a little over a year. As far as a high school, they're all the same." Gabe made a face. "It would be helpful to find a piano teacher."

"Where would I find the kind of teacher you need?"

"There are two really good ones at USC. I'd have to audition. Probably should wait until my hand is a hundred percent."

"Okay. Let's get you healed up and we'll take it from there."

Gabe flicked hair out of his eyes. "I really appreciate you letting me stay with you." A pause. "I do like my aunt. She's a real nice person but she's immature and very sloppy. I get physically ill when I'm in messy surroundings."

Rina laughed. "My sons' room has never looked so neat. Can I sic you on my daughter's room?"

"I can't go in there," Gabe said. "It makes me nervous."

The boy was dead serious. The nurse called his name. As he stood up, the nurse said to Rina, "You can come in with him if you want?"

Rina shrugged. "Up to you."

Gabe said, "I don't care. It's just my hand."

The two of them were seated in an examining room. Twenty minutes later, Matt Birenbaum came in: a short man in his fifties with wiry gray hair styled in a bad comb-over. Rina stood up from the chair.

"Sit, sit. I'm fine. How's the family? What's the Loo been up to?"

"The usual mayhem. How are the boys, Matt?"

"Josh is starting Penn Med School in the fall."

"Mazel tov. He must have liked what he grew up with."

"Tried to talk him out of it, but he wouldn't listen." Birenbaum looked up from the chart that Gabe had filled out in the waiting room. "Rina tells me you're a pianist?"

"On my exceptionally good days."

"And you hurt your hand in a fight?" The doctor looked disapproving.

Rina said, "He was attacked by a mugger."

Birenbaum looked up. "Wow. That's scary. Did he hurt you in places other than your hand?"

"No, just my hand. And that was from punching him. I think I overdid it."

"Well, thank goodness it was fists and not a gun." Gabe didn't bother to correct him. "No other health problems?"

"I'm in good health except for my zits. I like had this major breakout attack."

The doctor regarded his forehead. "It would help if you cut your hair."

"Probably."

"I can give you a scrip for a cream." He put down the file. "I'm just going to do a quick exam."

He took Gabe's blood pressure and his heart rate, listened to his chest, checked out the eyes and the ears and the throat. Rina was impressed by his thoroughness. Birenbaum said, "All right, young man, let me see the damage."

Gabe gave him his left hand. The doctor regarded the flesh. "Big hands. How tall are you?"

"Six feet."

"And how old are you?"

"Almost fifteen."

"So you still have some growing to do." He flipped the hand over and then over again. "A little bruised, that's for certain." He flexed the fingers and rotated the wrist. "Nothing's broken." He pressed and pulled, trying to find tender spots, noting when the boy made a face. "Any numbness?"

"No."

"Any pain when you stretch your arm or fingers?"

"No."

"Have you tried playing the piano?"

"Not since I hurt my hand." He paused. "I really haven't touched the keyboard in five days unless you count accompanying the school choir, and I don't count that."

Birenbaum smiled. "I specialize in professional musicians. I have an instrument room including a piano with electronic hookups. When the musicians play, the readout gives me an idea about their hands and fingers, the deficits and strengths. If you are a serious musician, I'd like to monitor your hands as you play."

"Sure."

The doctor brought them down the hall and into a soundproof room. On the walls were a violin, a cello, a guitar, an oboe, a sax, and a trumpet. The piano stood in the middle of the room. It was a Steinway, but the white keys had colored patches on them: the C's had red, the D's were blue, the E's were green, and so on up the spectrum. Birenbaum said, "I also use the piano for a lot of my patients who don't play. That's why the keys are colored. If you can tolerate the distraction, I'm going behind the window, where I have all my equipment, and listen to you play. Don't start until I tell you, okay?"

"Sure."

He took Rina into a booth that looked like an engineer's studio. Sitting on one of the chairs was a man in his sixties, bald except for a gray ponytail. He was of medium height with a round face and dark intense eyes. Birenbaum introduced him as Nicholas Mark. The man stood up and offered Rina his chair.

"I'm fine," Rina said.

"Please, sit."

Rina sat down. Birenbaum fiddled with a few of his controls. He talked through a microphone. "Can you hear me, Gabe?"

"Sure can."

"The piece I usually ask pianists to play is the Fantaisie-Impromptu because most of them know it fairly well and it's long enough to give me a good readout. There's sheet music in the bench for that, and other pieces if you don't want that one. If your hand hurts at any time, stop."

"Okay."

"The sheet music is in the bench," he repeated.

"I know the piece." Gabe adjusted the bench so he could comfortably operate the pedals. He took off his glasses, rubbed his eyes, and put the specs back atop his nose. His hands flew up and down the keyboard. "Nice piano."

"You can start whenever you're ready."

The kid didn't answer, just stared into space for a few moments. Then he lifted his left hand, his eyes half closed as he launched into a series of arpeggios.

Rina's mouth dropped open.

For the next five minutes and fourteen seconds, she was transported to another world. She had attended a few classical music concerts, but not being very musical, she couldn't even remember them. But with the boy, there was something different. Never had she heard the piano played with such technique, touch, and feeling.

When it was over, no one spoke. Nicholas Mark, the ponytailed man who was in the room, said, "Matt, ask him if he knows any of the Chopin Opus ten Etudes."

Through the mike, Birenbaum cleared his throat. "Your finger strength is registering well. Do you know any of the Chopin Opus ten Etudes?"

"Sure." The boy thought a moment. "How about the Liszt Transcendental Studies?"

Mark nodded. Birenbaum said, "Liszt is fine."

"Or how about the Grandes études de Paganini? 'La campanella.' I like the piece, and that should tell you a thing or two about my hand's strength."

Mark said, "Tell him if he has any pain to stop playing immediately."

Birenbaum said, "That's fine, Gabe, but watch your left hand. If you feel any twinge of anything, stop playing. Your hand is what's important here."

"Sure." Again, Gabe stared into space for a few moments, readjusting the bench for his feet. The etude started out with a few light touches, but then quickly progressed into an exquisite series of bell-like passages with the boy's right hand moving a mile all the way up the keyboard to a series of lightning-fast trills, and ended with a rousing climax. It was a beautiful and complex piece of music that traversed an emotional spectrum, but Rina felt that Gabe chose it because, more than anything, it showcased virtuosity. Four minutes and thirty-two seconds later, again, she was stunned into silence.

This jewel that had been entrusted into her care.

Gabe rubbed his eyes behind his glasses. "A little dicey. Not my best, not my worst. I made some mistakes. My left hand's definitely off. But it should heal, right?"

Birenbaum cleared his throat into the microphone. "It should heal fine. I'll be out in a minute, Gabe." Matt turned to his pony-tailed friend. "That was weird."

"You might say that. Where'd he *come* from?"

They both looked at Rina.

"It's a long story."

"So what do you think, Nick?" Birenbaum asked.

"What do I think?" The man shrugged. "The kid's a freak."

CHAPTER THIRTY-THREE

IT WAS THE first time that Rina had seen the boy display unfettered emotion. Too bad it was anxiety. His eyes got big and his breathing quickened. His gaze was on Nicholas Mark. "Were you listening to me?" He regarded Rina. "Did you set this up?"

"Set what up?" she asked.

"No one set anything up. I just happened to be here getting my hand checked," Mark told him. "Dr. Birenbaum invited me to listen."

Gabe said. "I can do better than that. That stunk!"

"Stank," Rina corrected.

"Stunk. Stank. I can do better than that. I swear I can. My hand's off. Not that I'm making excuses. It's just that I know that I can do better—"

"Relax." Mark put his hand on the boy's shoulder.

"I know I made mistakes. It wasn't my best at all—"

Rina said, "Excuse my ignorance, but are you a pianist?"

Birenbaum said, "Nicholas Mark is not only a renowned pianist, but he is at the forefront of modern composition for the piano."

"That's great," Rina said. "We're looking for a piano teacher—"

The boy spoke through clenched teeth. "Uh, I don't think Mr. Mark needs to be bothered with our trivial problems."

"Relax." Mark put his hand on Gabe's shoulder again. "It's okay. Take a deep breath."

Gabe nodded, took a deep breath, and let it out.

"Better?"

"I'm fine." Gabe suddenly felt dumb for being so nervous. "I'm okay."

"Good. First of all, who have you studied with?" After Gabe rattled off a half-dozen names, Mark asked, "What happened? You kept outgrowing teachers?"

"Yes, that happened. And I was sort of at my parents' transportation whims since we didn't live in the city—in Manhattan. I'm from back east. We lived about thirty minutes away in the burbs."

Mark looked at Rina. "How are you two related?"

"We're not," Gabe said. "I'm a foundling—"

"You're not a foundling," Rina said. "His parents are unavailable at the moment. He's staying with my family. When he hurt his hand, I thought of Matt. We go to the same synagogue and he's the best."

"You make me blush," Birenbaum said. "But not too hard."

Mark smiled. "You *are* the best." To Rina he said, "How long is Gabe staying with you?"

"That's up to Gabe and his parents. As far as I'm concerned, he can certainly bunk down with my family, especially if it means having the teacher he wants."

"Where are your parents?"

Gabe turned bright red, but Rina was very calm. "That's at issue right now. We don't know where his parents are, but his parents do know that Gabe is staying with us. Professionally, what can you do for him?"

The boy slapped his hands over his face. Mark smiled. "I said relax, okay. It's not a prerequisite of American citizenship to know who I am." He turned to Rina. "What I can do for him . . . is . . . this. I want you both to know . . . that I'm not looking for students. With my teaching at the university, my composing, and commuting each weekend to and from Santa Fe, I don't have a lot of free time."

"I can move to Santa Fe," Gabe blurted out.

"You're not moving anywhere," Rina said.

Again, Mark laughed. "I have a waiting list a mile long and to bump him to the top would be unfair."

"Of course," Rina said. "Maybe you can recommend someone?"

"Hold on a minute. I said it would be unfair . . . if I decided to take him on full-time. But since this looks like a temporary situation, I'd be willing to see him for a few lessons."

Rina said, "That would be really nice of you."

Mark said, "This is the deal, Gabe. I don't demand one hundred percent perfection in your playing. But I do demand . . . one hundred percent dedication. If I make time for you, you'd better be prepared." He took out his BlackBerry. "I can only see you once . . . no, let's make it twice a week at . . . ten in the morning at USC. I have no other time. I don't know how that affects your schooling."

Rina said, "We can work around that. What days?"

"How about . . . Tuesday and . . . and if I move this and move this appointment there . . ." He played with his PDA. "Let's try out Monday and Thursday at ten—sharp."

"I teach," Rina said. "I have to be in school by nine—"

"I can take the bus," Gabe said.

Rina ignored him. "My husband or I will drop him off early. I'm sure he can figure out something to do."

"It's a university with a major music department," Mark said. "There are practice rooms." He regarded Gabe. "You don't drive or you don't have a car?"

"He's too young," Rina told him. "He'll be fifteen in June."

"Younger than I thought. Even better. What kind of piano do you have?"

"We don't have a piano," Rina said. "Do you have a recommendation?"

"A good piano is tens of thousands of dollars."

"That would be very pricey," Rina said.

"I'll see if I can loan you something from the university," Mark told her. "But no playing until your hand is completely healed and you get the okay from Dr. Birenbaum."

"It should take about a week before all the bruises are gone," the doctor told him.

"So let's make our first lesson a week from today if you're still around." He entered some data in his PDA. "What etudes do you know?"

"All the Chopin ten Etudes, some of the twenty-fives, and some of the Liszt Transcendental. I have the sheet music for those and the ones I don't know by heart."

"Bring them with you. We'll start with that." He offered him a business card. "You did a pretty good job with 'La campanella,' but I definitely want you to lay off that until we do some of the etudes. Call the night before if you can't make it."

Gabe took the card. He was beaming. "Thank you so much, Mr. Mark, for this opportunity."

"Of all of your teachers . . . the only one I know is Ivan Lettech. I'm going to give him a call. Anything you'd like to tell me before I speak to him?"

"He taught me for almost a year. I think it went okay. He told me I needed to enter more of the major competitions to make myself known."

"Did you?"

"Uh, the family situation at that time made it a little hard. But I'm older and things are better. Or maybe not better. Maybe more stable. Well, I don't know if 'stable' is the right word. Am I rambling?"

"A little bit," Rina said. "Whatever guidance he needs would be appreciated."

"Not a problem."

Gabe looked down. "I think Mr. Lettech was angry when I left for California." His eyes went to Mark's face. "If you do speak to him, please tell him again that the move wasn't my idea."

THE MASKED MAN with the whip wasn't Aaron Otis. The tats, as small as they were, didn't match up. Aaron continued to study the pictures. "It's not Greg, that's for sure. It *could* be Garth. I really can't make out the tattoos. Could you enlarge the pictures?"

Decker gave the snapshots to Marge.

"Have someone scan it into the computer and see if we can bring up a larger image." After she left the interview room, Decker said, "Recognize the girl?"

"Doesn't look like Adrianna."

"Do you think you might recognize her if we enlarged her face?"

Aaron shook his head. "Honestly, Lieutenant, she doesn't look familiar." The young man raised an eyebrow. "Too bad. Looks like she might have been fun."

Decker failed to find the humor in two corpses and a missing woman. He remained flat-faced and Aaron turned red.

"Sorry."

"And you haven't heard a peep from Garth?"

"Nothing. I'd tell you if I did. I love Garth, but if he's mixed up in something bad, I don't want any part of it."

Oliver came in. "Can I see you for a moment, Lieutenant?"

Decker excused himself. The two of them talked outside the interview room.

"Marge is still scanning in the photographs," Oliver told him. "Greg Reyburn walked into the police station about five minutes ago. I put him in room number three. Do you want to talk to him or should I do it?"

"You can do it."

Oliver took out his notebook and read from a list. "Find out where he's been for the last twenty-four hours, check out the alibi, ask him again about Garth and their camping trip, show him the snapshots I found in Mandy's apartment, ask him to identify the tattoos, then lastly about Mandy Kowalski. Anything else?"

"That about covers it. Aaron claims he doesn't recognize Mandy in the photo as someone he knows or has seen around."

"Do you think he's lying?"

"He's been cooperative. He's clearly not the masked man, but he could have taken the pictures. He even made a joke about it. Said it was too bad he didn't know her. She seems like a lot of fun."

"Rim shot," Oliver said, miming a drummer hitting a cymbal.

"Indeed, it was a joke of poor timing and poor taste. Aaron needs to revamp his material."

GREG REYBURN LOOKED at the enlarged pictures with tired, red-rimmed eyes. "That snake up his arm with the wings . . . it's like the medical symbol."

"The caduceus," Oliver said.

"Yeah, Garth has one just like it." Reyburn raked his black curls with his hand and made a face. "I'm no prude. I like a good time just like anyone. I could see me doing something like that maybe once or twice . . . like if I was piss-drunk . . . but even I don't think I'd take pictures of me acting like an ass no matter how drunk I was."

Oliver nodded. "Do you know if Garth has played dress-up before?"

"If it is Garth. I mean, a lot of people could have that cadu . . . what did you call it?"

"Caduceus."

"I'm sure that's a common tat with the doctors."

Oliver hadn't known too many inked-up physicians in his lifetime, but who knew around the younger set. It was a new world out there. "Do you recognize any of the other tattoos?"

"Well . . ." Reyburn sifted through the pictures again. "This one." He pointed to a black widow in her web. "He has this one, too."

"So let's assume it's Garth," Oliver said. "What about the girl?"

Reyburn shrugged. "I can't place her."

"You never met her at one of Garth's and Adrianna's parties?"

"Maybe." He gave the photographs back to Oliver. "They sure partied a lot, entertained some strange people. I don't remember any girl wearing a leather collar with spikes and a bustier, but I didn't check out everyone."

Oliver gave the pictures to Greg. "Look at them one more time."

Reyburn cooperated. One pose—the masked man riding her back—caught his interest. "Maybe yes, maybe no. That's the best I can do right now."

"Any idea who took the picture?"

"Not me."

"How about Adrianna or Crystal?"

"I'd just be guessing." He shook his head. "Can I go now? I'm pretty fucked up right now. Crystal and I were friends, you know."

"How close?"

"Did we have sex? Yeah, we did." His eyes moistened and he tried to cover it by rubbing them. "Crystal was a free spirit."

"Did her freedom include Garth?"

"Probably."

"Probably or definitely."

"Definitely. I remember once . . . when Garth was completely blitzed . . . I think he suggested a threesome with her."

"And?"

"Wasn't my thing." He stopped. "At least not with him. Maybe if it had been Adrianna and Crystal, but not Garth and Crystal."

"Let's get back to Adrianna. Did you ever do her?"

Greg shook his head. "No . . . not that I woulda said no if the situation came up, but we never got around to it."

"Aaron did her."

Reyburn shrugged. "Good for him. I didn't."

"How did Garth feel about Aaron fucking Adrianna?"

"Never talked to him about it." He scratched his stubbly face. He had broken out over his forehead and chin. "Garth knew that Adrianna was screwing around. And Adrianna knew that Garth was screwing around. And both of them were kinda jealous of the other one. Why they stayed together was a big question mark."

"I heard Adrianna was giving Garth play money and that's why he stuck with her."

"Yeah, she gave him a couple hundred here and there."

"What did he do with it?"

Reyburn shrugged "Took it to Vegas."

"I heard he spent a lot more on women than on gambling."

"Maybe. Garth liked his pussy."

"So maybe that's why he stayed with Adrianna. She gave him money." When Greg's eyes darted back and forth, Oliver said, "What is it?"

Reyburn threw up his hands. "You're going to think I've been holding out on you . . . but I just thought of something. It could be that Adrianna wasn't the only one giving Garth pocket change."

"Go on."

"I say it could be because I never really believed Garth." Reyburn sighed. "So here's the deal. Once when he was drunk, Garth told Aaron and me that he had a couple of cougars in Vegas that gave him money. Way more money than Adrianna. That's why he went to Vegas so often."

"Okay," Oliver said. "Do these women have names?"

"He never told me names. He mentioned this only once, and when he was blotto, and that was like over a year ago. Aaron and I decided it was bullshit. I don't know why I just thought of it . . . maybe because you said that Adrianna gave him money."

Oliver said, "Did he tell you anything about the women?"

Again Reyburn ran his hands through his hair. "He told us that the women were like married to Mob guys, and when their husbands were away, he'd fuck them for money. We pressed him for details, but he said he couldn't tell us any more. That it was all very secret, and if their husbands found out, he would be killed. That's when we decided that the whole thing was crap. We could see Garth screwing women . . . we could see Garth screwing women who gave him money. But the whole Mob thing . . . I mean, c'mon! You're a fucking radiology tech, Garth. Get over yourself."

"So you didn't believe him."

"Not the Mob part. Garth said a lot of stupid stuff when he got drunk. He'd . . . embellish things. But who doesn't say stupid stuff when you're bombed."

"Where'd you stay when you went to Las Vegas?"

"Garth went a lot more than we did. When we went together, we'd go to the Luxor or MGM. They were a little cheaper but still on the Strip."

"And you have no idea who these women are?"

"I don't know even if they're real."

"Would you excuse me for a moment?"

"Can I go now?"

"Greg, I think it would be best if you stayed for a little bit longer. Until I talk to the girl you were with last night. She is your alibi."

"Then can I go?"

"One thing at a time. You want some more coffee or a soda or something to eat?"

"I want to go home and go to sleep."

You and the rest of us, Oliver thought. "I'll only be a minute. Just hang on, okay?"

Reyburn's answer was a doleful shake of the head. Oliver left the interview room and went to look for Marge. When he didn't find her, he headed for the Loo's office. Decker was on the phone but motioned Oliver in. A minute later, he hung up. "That was Sela Graydon. She and Kathy Blanc are coming to the office tomorrow. That should be a real yuck fest."

"Why are they coming in?"

"For an update on the recent events, to cry on my shoulder, to yell at me, to curse the world: pick any one or all of the above." He blew out air. "What's up?"

"Is Aaron Otis still here?"

"No, we kicked him loose about twenty minutes ago."

"Damn."

"What's going on? Should we pick him back up?"

"I'd like to talk to him." Oliver told him Reyburn's story about Garth and his cougars. "Sounds fanciful to me, but it did give me the idea that maybe Garth is holed up in Vegas. Maybe he and Mandy are making new lives for themselves as Mr. and Mrs. Dominator/Dominatrix whatever."

"Contact Las Vegas Metro PD."

"Or Marge and I can take a little journey to the east."

"Even if you do, you still need to contact the local law."

"What do you think of the story?" Oliver asked.

Decker shrugged. "I've learned over the years to reserve judgment."

Wanda Bontemps knocked on the doorframe. "I have Eddie Booker on line two."

"Who?" Decker said.

"That's all he said. He's Eddie Booker and he's returning your call."

"My call?" He picked up the phone. "This is Lieutenant Decker."

"Hi, Lieutenant. Eddie Booker. My mother-in-law said you called a couple of days ago and wanted to talk to me."

Decker's mind was racing. Luckily, Booker helped him out.

"I woulda called sooner but there wasn't any communication on the ship."

Ship . . . cruise ship . . . the security guard at the hotel where Terry was staying. "Yes, Mr. Booker, thank you very much for calling back. Hold on, one minute." He turned to Oliver. "Get hold of Aaron Otis and see if he verifies the conversation. Then call up Las Vegas Metro and I'll see about sending you and Marge over there. I've got to take this call."

Oliver nodded and left.

Decker told Booker why he had called. "For the sake of completeness, we are interviewing everyone who was working at the hotel the night that Ms. McLaughlin disappeared. We understand you were on duty that night and left . . . actually quit the next day."

The line was silent.

"We understand that the hotel offered incentives to anyone that would leave early."

"They did."

"And that's why you decided to leave your job?"

Again, there was silence. Decker said, "We'd like to talk to you . . . find out if you saw Ms. McLaughlin or perhaps heard anything unusual."

There was a third pause.

Decker said, "Maybe it would be better if you came down to the station house. Since you live in the Valley, I think I'm closer to you than West L.A. Could you make it here in an hour?"

Booker's voice was shaky when he decided to talk. "I didn't know that Ms. McLaughlin went missing on Monday."

"Since Sunday night, actually."

"No one told me."

"So now you know. We're asking for everyone's help."

"I knew I shoulda *said* something."

"About what?"

The man didn't answer. Decker was sitting on anxiety and frustration. "How about if I came by your house and we could talk there?"

"No, I'll come in to you."

"Great. When?"

"Where are you? Devonshire?"

"Yes, sir."

"I could be there in a half hour."

"I'll be here. Thanks for your help."

"She seemed okay," Booker said. "I swear she was okay when I left her."

Soothingly, Decker said, "I'm sure she was okay. She still might be okay. We're just putting pieces together. That's why we're asking for your help—"

"What about the boy?" Booker asked. "She has a son."

Decker laughed to himself. "The one thing I can tell you with certainty is that the boy is okay."

CHAPTER THIRTY-FOUR

EDDIE BOOKER CARRIED a burden. The former security guard should have looked rested from cruising the open seas. Instead his face oozed stress. He was a tall, rawboned man in his fifties with tired dark eyes. He had a wide mouth and tightly knit gray hair. He came in dressed in a white button-down shirt and brown slacks. He was sweating and the interview hadn't even begun. Decker had originally called him up for the sake of completeness. Now he wondered if he wasn't looking at a suspect.

"Would you like some water?"

"No, I just want to get this over with." Booker took a nearby box of tissues and used one to mop his brow.

"Tell me about it," Decker said.

"I knew it was wrong." A sigh. "I worked in this business for thirty-six years and nothin' like this has ever happened before. I don't know what in hell I was thinking."

Decker nodded.

"My wife thinks I should get a lawyer."

"Why?" Decker asked.

"That's what I was telling her. I'll just return the money and that'll be that. But now you tell me that Ms. McLaughlin's missing, it might look like trouble." His eyes were wet. "I swear this was the first and only time I ever did something like this. And I only took the money because she told me to."

"Ms. McLaughlin told you to take the money?"

"Yes, sir."

Decker pulled out his notebook. "Mr. Booker, let's back it up. Start with the time. When did all this happen?"

"It was about . . . three, three-thirty in the afternoon."

"Sunday afternoon?"

"Yeah, Sunday afternoon. I was doing my rounds. Just checking the grounds, and I heard the arguing coming from Ms. McLaughlin's hotel room."

"Okay." Decker kept his face flat. "When you say 'arguing,' could you define it?"

"Yelling."

"Who was yelling?"

"Both of 'em."

"Ms. McLaughlin and . . ."

"I don't know the man's name. He never did say it. Just offered me the money, and like a damn fool I took it. Only reason I took it is because she said for me to take it."

"Ms. McLaughlin did."

"Yes, sir. Boy, she was angry. Angry at him . . . but she looked angry at me for bothering them." He reached in his pocket and pulled out a wad of hundred-dollar bills. "I didn't even spend it. I knew it was wrong." He thrust the bundle in Decker's face. "Just take it from me. That stuff is poison!"

"I can't do that, sir."

"Well, I sure as hell don't want it." He threw the money on the table.

The bills started to uncurl. Decker didn't make a move to take them, but he knew later on that he'd bag the money as evidence. Maybe it was payoff from Donatti to do something bad. "Let's backtrack a little, Mr. Booker. You were doing your rounds. It was about three, three-thirty on Sunday afternoon."

"Yes."

"You heard some arguing coming from Ms. McLaughlin's room."

"Yes."

"Then what happened?"

"I knocked on the door. I called out her name, asking her if everything was okay."

"What happened after you knocked and called out to her?"

"Well, for one thing, the arguing stopped. The yelling. After I knocked, no one said a peep."

"Okay. Go on."

"I knocked again, calling out her name. I started to put my pass-key into the door, but then she opened it up before I had a chance."

"How'd she look?"

The man's skin darkened. "She was a beautiful woman."

"I mean what was her emotional state?"

"Angry."

"Angry and afraid?"

"No, sir, just angry. If she woulda looked afraid, I wouldn't have gone away. She just looked pissed, pardon my French."

"So what happened after she answered the door?"

"She told me . . . let me see if I can get this exactly right . . ." He took another dab at his brow with the Kleenex. "She said thank you for my concern. That she was sorry they were making a racket, but everything's fine."

"Did she look like she was roughed up at all?"

"Roughed up?" The guard looked horrified. "Like she was beaten?"

"Well, was her hair messed up, did she have any marks on her face—"

"No, no, no. Nothing like that. If I would have suspected anything, I would have called my supervisor or even the police."

"What was she wearing?" Decker asked.

"Wearing?" Booker looked pained. "I gotta think a minute. She had something red on . . . like a loose red top. She was wearing dark pants. Her hair was down. She kept swishing it off of her shoulders. She had on big diamond studs in her ears."

"Was she wearing makeup? Like lipstick or mascara?"

"I don't remember."

"Did she look like she'd been crying?"

"Her eyes weren't red or anything like that. Nothing dark running down her face. She just looked mad. Which was different from other times I saw her. Normally, she was very nice and social. Not this time."

"Did you happen to see who she was arguing with?"

"Yeah, of course. He was the one who gave me the money."

"What did he look like?"

"Very tall. Big, blond guy. Spooky eyes. I was worried for her."

"And she didn't look scared?"

"No. Not scared, not crying, just angry. When he offered me the money for my 'troubles'"—Booker made air quotes—"I almost called the police. But then she told me to take it. She said, 'Take the money, Eddie. And keep this little incident to yourself. It would be embarrassing for me if you told someone.'" He furrowed his brow. "She said something about that the man was the boy's father and they were having a difference on how to raise him right. That's why I asked you about the son. Is he really okay?"

"Yes, he's fine. Do you think that's what they were arguing about?"

Again, Booker looked pained. "I couldn't say yes and I couldn't say no. If you're asking for my opinion, I think the arguing was more personal than raising a boy."

"How is that?"

Booker blew out air. "I heard him call her a lying little bitch. She called him paranoid and crazy. That's when I knocked on the door and everything got quiet. Those kinds of words . . . to me, that doesn't sound like they were arguing about their son. I knew I shoulda said something, but . . ." He shook his head in shame.

"What?"

"This is gonna sound bad."

"Tell me anyway."

He covered his face. "He gave me a thousand dollars. I could really use that money. But there was no question in my mind that I wasn't gonna keep it. Just as soon as I got back from the cruise . . . I was gonna give it back."

"So why'd you take it?"

"You're not gonna believe me."

"Try me out."

"I took the money because Ms. McLaughlin . . . well, how do I say this? Like I said, she was a beautiful woman with this beautiful, soft voice and a lovely smile. She smiled at me whenever I passed her. Always addressed me by my name and took the time to say a couple of words to me. She always treated me like a person instead of a piece of furniture."

"I heard she was very friendly."

"Friendly but never flirtatious. Just a good soul. And like I said, she was so pretty." He looked down. "I had kind of a crush on her. I took the money because I didn't want her to be mad at me."

"YOU LET HIM go?" Marge asked.

"What am I going to hold him on?"

"Maybe he sneaked back in after Donatti left, and killed her."

"He gave me a complete schedule of his movements. The only way he could have murdered her and disposed of the body would have been if he did it on the grounds. And too many people saw him in between the time he took the money and the time that Gabe got back home and discovered his mother was gone."

"Maybe he murdered her, stuffed her in a closet, and came back to dispose of the body."

"He left for home after six-thirty and arrived forty minutes later. He claims he was with his wife the whole time, packing for his vacation. I checked his face, his hands, his arms, and his legs. He even showed me his back and stomach. There were no scratches anywhere. He agreed to take a polygraph. You saw the room. Was there anything to indicate that a struggle took place inside?"

"Loo, he admitted having a crush on her. Maybe she rejected his advances."

"If he got physical, she didn't fight back, and I find that hard to believe. I had nothing to keep him on. He doesn't have a record, he's got a sterling history of employment, he pays his taxes, he sends his kids to Catholic school. You get a gut feeling about a person. I believed him, so I let him go."

"I don't like the part where he said he had a crush on her."

"She's a charming woman. He probably wasn't the only one."

Marge regarded his face. "Including you?"

"I remember her as a little kid, so to me she's always a little kid. Objectively, she's alluring. And I think she played it to the hilt. Not with me, though. With me, she used the helpless-female dodge. 'Please, Lieutenant, you're the only one I know that can control him. I feel safe when you're around.' And moron that I am, I bought it."

"You sound angry."

"I'm an idiot. But at least I was smart enough to ask my wife's opinion about helping her out before I agreed to do it."

"And Rina said yes?"

"Rina said she'd back me either way. But we both knew that I'd agree to do it because of Donatti's potential for violence. It could be something terrible happened to Terry, but I'm beginning to think that she planned this all along and I've been had. And now I got a teenage boy living at my house and my wife is renting him a piano."

Marge laughed. "She's renting Gabe a piano?"

Decker looked sour. "She heard him play this morning. Apparently, he's some kind of piano genius. Now she's got him a teacher and I don't know what else. All I know is it's going to cost me money." He hit his forehead. "I'm ready to retire. What the hell did I get myself into, Marge?"

"You're not going to retire. You'd die."

"Maybe not *retire* retire, but I was certainly ready to kick back. How did I get bamboozled into letting this kid into my life?"

"You're asking me? I adopted Vega and haven't slept a night since." She paused. "It's better now. But I still worry until I get that phone call, telling me 'good night, Mother Marge.'" She threw up her hands. "Some people take in stray cats. We take in two-legged creatures. It's not so smart, but at least we don't deal with litter boxes."

OLIVER HUNG UP the phone. "That was Las Vegas." He looked at his notes. "Detective Silver. He said he'd stop by the hotels but not to expect anything. The hotels keep their registries pretty damn private unless there's a warrant or an overriding reason to expose their patrons."

Marge said, "How about two dead girls?"

"That's why I got the kind of cooperation that I did. But until we have more evidence, we'll be hitting a brick wall."

Marge said, "We could go there and hunt around the hotels ourselves, but I don't think we'll get much. Could be Garth is using an alias. Vegas is a place where people come to reinvent themselves. And each hotel is enormous, with lots of wings and hundreds of rooms."

"Needle in a haystack."

Marge shrugged. "What are you doing this weekend?"

"Nothing."

"Neither am I. I've never seen *O*."

"It's good." Oliver shrugged. "I'll see it again."

"I'll check out who has the cheapest seats possible." Marge readjusted her purse over her shoulder. "I'm off to see Yvette Jackson with a six-pack ID lineup. Wanna come with me?"

"Yeah, sure." Oliver stood up and put on his jacket. "We should run our Las Vegas junket by the Loo. I'm sure we could get some recompense for it."

"We could make a good case for it," Marge said. "Except the *O* tickets."

"Then we just have to figure out a good way of presenting it to accounting. How about . . . how about a refresher course in emergency medicine and CPR?"

Marge laughed. "And how do figure that?"

"All those women underwater . . . what if one of them suddenly gets a cramp?"

"Uh-huh, and how do you propose to help?"

"I'm very good at deep massages."

CHAPTER THIRTY-FIVE

I**T WAS ONE** in the afternoon, but Yvette Jackson was still in her robe—a dusty rose satin dressing gown. Her apartment was a studio done up in Old Hollywood. Her daybed was dressed in heart pillows and a pink satin comforter. She also had a camel-back white couch with silk pillows, and a glass-and-chrome coffee table adorned with a vase of lilies. Her kitchenette was tiny. A lone coffeemaker sat on the counter. With Yvette's blue eyes, her buxom build, and her white-blonde hair that fell carelessly at her shoulders, she could have been the heroine of a screwball comedy from the forties. Except her eyes were red-rimmed and her expression was somber.

"Thanks for seeing us," Oliver told her.

"I agreed before I found out." She flopped on the white couch and drew a blanket over her chest. "I called in sick. I'm not going back to that place until I know what's going on. I'm scared."

"Who told you about Crystal's murder?" Marge took out her notebook.

"One of the bartenders—Joe Melon, who heard it from Jack

Henry—one of the owners of Garage." She tucked the blanket under her chin. "At this point, I don't know how smart it would be to get involved."

Marge said. "We don't know who we're dealing with. If it has something to do with Garage, the sooner we get identification, the better it is for all of us."

"You really think it's someone from the bar?"

Marge evaded the question. "Do you know if Crystal was having any trouble with anyone from Garage?"

"A patron or someone who worked there?"

"Either, both," Oliver said.

"Not that I know of." Yvette was quiet. "Crystal didn't have a lot of boundaries. She'd take a liking to a guy and comp him drinks. Maybe somebody took it the wrong way." A pause. "I don't know what that would have to do with Adrianna. She didn't work there. So it could be their murders had nothing to do with Garage."

"Absolutely," Oliver said. "Crystal and Adrianna had very active social lives that had nothing to do with Garage."

"I'm sure they had lots of friends in common," Yvette said.

"And that's the main focus of the investigation," Marge said. "That's why if we could just take a few minutes of your time, we'd like to show you a photo pack of some men and ask you if any of them look familiar."

She got up from the couch. "Could I make some coffee first?"

"Of course."

"Would you like a cup? It's just as easy to make for one as for three."

"I wouldn't mind," Oliver said.

"Good." She trudged into the kitchen. "It's the only thing I know how to make." As if to underscore the point, she opened the refrigerator and all that was inside were different types of coffee and several bottles of sparkling water. "Oh, I also have water. Would you like water?"

She was stalling before she took a look at the photos. Another few minutes weren't going to matter. Marge said, "Coffee's fine."

As Yvette took out the coffee and the filter, Oliver asked, "How well did you know Crystal?"

"We were coworkers, not friends." She filled the machine with water. "This is going to sound snobbish, but the job to me was just a job, a way to earn money until my singing career takes off. Being a hostess to Crystal . . ." She took out three mugs and placed them on her empty kitchen counter. "For her, it was a profession. The best she could get." She turned to the police. "Cream or sugar?"

"I'll take a little cream and Splenda if you have it," Marge said. "Did you meet a lot of Crystal's friends?"

"I met Adrianna. And her lawyer friend. She was a nice woman. I don't know what she was doing hanging around those clowns."

"What about their guy friends?"

"Yeah, I met a few . . . the one I remember is Garth." Yvette rolled her eyes. "Not bad-looking, but a piece of work."

"How's that?"

"He just thinks he's all that. When it was clear I wasn't interested in joining his fan club, he got hostile . . . well, maybe 'hostile' is too strong a word. He got peeved. Started being a prick, shouting out orders like . . . 'Hey, can we get some more nuts around here.'" She shrugged. "But he was a customer and I played along . . . like I give a damn what he thinks."

Marge said, "Did you happen to see Garth the night that Adrianna was in the bar?"

"Not that I remember." She poured the coffee out, handed a mug to each of the detectives, and sat back down on the couch.

Marge took a sip of coffee and looked around for a coaster.

Yvette said, "Just put it on the table. I don't have coasters because I rarely serve anyone. I don't cook and there's a coffee shop around the corner. It's my home away from home."

"Sounds convenient," Oliver told her. "Are you ready to look at the photos?"

"I guess."

Marge offered her the six-pack that she had made this morning. There were six men with similar facial features—three on top and three on the bottom. Tinsley was on the bottom, right side.

Reluctantly, Yvette took the card, her eyes scanning the images. Then they widened. "Oh my God, it's this one." Her finger was on the right bottom. "This is the guy that Adrianna was talking to."

Marge and Oliver exchanged glances. "You're sure?"

"Positive. If you knew, why are you asking me?"

"We didn't know until you told us," Oliver said.

"But you put him in the picture," Yvette said. "You had to have known."

Marge shrugged, but Yvette wasn't having any of that. Her hands started shaking. "He *saw* me, Sergeant! He saw me and I waited on him. Now I'm identifying him. Do I have to be nervous?"

Feigning a casual air, Oliver shook his head. "Nah, we'll pick him up and talk to him. We know where to find him."

"How do you know? Who *is* this guy?"

"That's what we aim to find out."

AFTER THE DOCTOR'S visit, Rina took Gabe shopping. He insisted on paying and she didn't argue. He was happy about that. Rina had a way of making him feel calm but not smothered. She didn't try to parent him. She let him make his own choices, but if he had questions, she'd offer advice. She also had a great sense of humor. She was kind of like your favorite teacher. By the time they were finished, Gabe had two bags of clothes and two new sets of sneakers. She told him that she had stuff to do at her school, so she dropped him off at the house, giving him his own keys.

He went into the room and started to straighten out the closet again, emptying a few shelves for his meager things. It wasn't like he was moving in, but he was trying to make himself a bit more comfortable. Afterward, he read until his eyes felt strained. He tried to sleep but to no avail. Bored and lonely, he picked up the guitar, knowing that he shouldn't be fingering a fret board with a sore left hand.

WTF . . . just a few little bits won't hurt. Just don't overdo it, he told himself. Restraint . . . something he never lacked.

If anything, he needed to infuse his music with as much feeling as technical prowess. That's what Lettech used to tell him.

An ear worm was coursing through his brain, a song they'd heard on the radio. "Crossfire"—a blues song made immortal by Stevie Ray Vaughan. He liked Stevie Ray. Not only was he a great guitarist technically, he was incredibly tasteful and could milk a note like no man. He loved the way Vaughan used his guitar as a response to his singing, as if he were having a conversation with the instrument.

He had jacked up the amp. The instrument was a piece of crap, but the amp was decent quality and somewhat compensated for the tinny electronics of the guitar. As the song repeated in his head, he began to copy Stevie Ray note by note until he had the fills to the vocals down pat. Now it was just a matter of the solo. He was so absorbed in his music that he didn't hear the door open. When he did look up, two guys in their twenties were staring at him. He didn't know who the sandy-haired one was, but the dude with the black hair and blue eyes was the image of Rina.

Dude said, "Do I know you?"

Sandy Hair gave Dude a look. "I'm Sam, he's Jake—"

"Yeah, we live here," Jake said.

Sam said, "And you are . . ."

"Gabe Whitman." He knew he was blushing. He stood up, turned off the amp, and put the instrument on the bed. "Sorry about messing with your stuff."

Jake said, "Are you kidding? My guitar never sounded so good. Certainly not when I played it. You rock, kid."

"Especially compared to us," Sam added. "This family doesn't have a musical bone in its body."

Jake threw his duffel on his bed and opened the closet. "Clean and organized." He looked at Gabe's clothes and held up a pair of cargo pants. "Definitely not my size."

The boy was still red. "I'll move my stuff."

"Nah, you don't have to do that," Jake said. "The question is, what's your stuff doing here in the first place?"

"It's a long story. The short version is your parents have been nice enough to let me stay here."

"How long have you been here?" Jake asked.

"About five days."

"And how long are you staying?"

"That remains to be seen."

Sammy said, "We're just in and out for the weekend. Just keep your stuff where it is and we'll work around you."

"Uh, last time I counted, there were only two beds," Jake said.

"I can sleep on the couch," Gabe told him.

"Yonkel, you know that there's a trundle," Sam said. "We can squeeze in for a couple of days."

"I'm not sleeping on a trundle," Jake said.

"I'll sleep on the trundle," Gabe offered. "Or I can give you guys some privacy and sleep on the couch. Or I can sleep on the floor."

"Nonsense," Sam said. "Jake and I will flip for the trundle."

"*What?*"

"You know that Eema won't let him sleep on the couch. Stop postponing the inevitable. Rock, paper, scissors. If you don't play, you forfeit and automatically sleep on the trundle."

"Since when do you make all the rules?"

"Yadda, yadda, yadda. Are you in or out?"

The two guys sat on the bed and did the first RPS. Jake's paper lost to Sam's scissors.

"Two out of three," Jake told him.

"You're kidding."

"C'mon."

The next time Jake's rock lost to Sam's paper.

"Shit. Three out of five."

"I'll sleep on the trundle," Gabe insisted. "Actually, you don't have to bother. I can just stay with my aunt for the weekend. It's not a problem."

"Who's your aunt?"

"Who's my aunt?"

"What kind of a question is that?" Sammy said to Jake.

"It's a reasonable question. Maybe she's a felon and that's why he's not staying with her in the first place."

"Her name is Melissa and she's not a felon."

"So why aren't you staying with her?" Jake asked.

"Yonkel, are you trying to torture the kid or are you just nosy?"

"Both."

Gabe was still red. "She's going to Palm Springs for the weekend with a group of her girlfriends. She invited me to come, but I begged off."

"Why?"

"Why? She and her friends are party girls. I'm fourteen."

"And the problem is . . ."

"As tempting as it sounds, it's not for me."

"How old is your aunt?"

"Twenty-one."

"Is she cute?"

"She's very cute."

"I've got a great idea," Jake said. "Why don't you stay here and I'll go with Melissa."

Sammy hit him. "Help me move the lamp and the nightstand."

"I'll do it." Gabe unplugged the lamp and lifted the stand with the lamp still on it. "Where should I put it?"

"Put it in the corner," Sammy said. "Let's get this sucker out."

The two brothers bent down and yanked at the trundle that was stowed underneath one of the twins. When they liberated the apparatus, the frame and mattress popped up with a vengeance. Jake swiped at the top. "Relatively clean."

"Get the linens," Sammy said.

"You get the linens," Jake told him.

"I rented the car, you get the linens."

Gabe couldn't help himself. He just started laughing—first time in over two months and it felt good. "You know, I do know how to make up a bed. Where are the linens?"

"I'll get 'em," Jacob grumped, and stormed off.

"I know," Sammy said. "We're ridiculous. I'm getting married and graduating from med school in two months, he's got a degree in neuroscience. We go home and we're ten and twelve again. Guess who the oldest is."

"No question about that," Gabe said. "Where do you go to med school?"

"Einstein. That's in New York."

"I know Einstein. I'm from New York. My mom is a doctor."

"What's her specialty?"

"Emergency room medicine. What are you going into?"

"Radiology. Are you interested in medicine?"

"No, thank you. I don't want anything to do with people."

Sam laughed. "That eliminates a lot of jobs."

"Not music."

"Yeah, Jake wasn't lying. You sound really pro on that thing."

"I'm actually a pianist. Uh, that sounds pretentious. Piano is my main instrument."

"We don't own a piano."

"I know. I think your mom might be getting one on loan for me."

"So you're here for a while?"

Gabe felt his face go hot. "I really don't know. Your parents are very nice people."

"Actually, they're gems."

Jake came in and threw the linens at Gabe's chest. He caught them and started to make up the trundle.

Sammy said, "He's a pianist."

"Really?" Jake asked. "Are you any good?"

Gabe shrugged. "Not bad."

Jake sprawled out on his bed. "Seriously, kid, what are you doing here?"

Gabe stopped. "My mom is missing and your dad is looking into the case." No one spoke. "Your father thinks that my father might have killed her. I don't think he did. Your dad wants to talk to my dad and my dad isn't making himself available."

"Wow," Jake said. "Sorry I asked."

"It's messed up, but I'm used to that."

Sammy said, "So how did you get here . . . with my parents?"

"My mother knew your father from like when she was a teenager. So when the two of us came out to California, she left me his cell phone number in case of an emergency. When my mom didn't come home last Sunday, I called him. It was late at night and I didn't have anywhere to go, so he took me to his house. They're letting me stay here until one or both of my parents show up. My dad definitely knows I'm here. I suspect my mom's alive and she knows that I'm here, too."

"What about living with your aunt?"

"I love Melissa, but she doesn't have the same standards of cleanliness that I do. I have a real hard time living in messy surroundings."

"Another compulsive." Jake high-fived Gabe. "Maybe you can help out our sister? I can't go into her room."

"Neither can I," Gabe said. "It makes me anxious."

Sammy said, "We're going out to get a pizza. You want to come?"

Gabe was hungry, but he declined. "I'm okay. I'll unpack your bags, if you want."

"No one touches my things," Jake said.

"Sorry," Gabe said. "I won't play your guitar anymore."

"I'm ribbing you." Jake jumped up from the bed. "You can have the guitar. I mean that. I never play it anymore. Never really played it much to begin with. Come with us, kid." He gently whacked Gabe in his hollow stomach. "You look like you can use a couple of extra calories."

Gabe felt his skin grow warm. "Thanks. Can I ask why you're here?"

"Other than the fact that I live here?"

Sammy said, "We came in to surprise our dad."

"Technically, he's our stepdad. But after enduring all of the grief I gave him, he has earned the title of Dad."

"The Loo is turning sixty on Sunday," Sammy said. "We're surprising him and our mother and sister. We've got a massive dinner planned at the station house today at seven. The only one who knows about it is our stepsister and her husband."

"That's Cindy and Koby, right?"

"You sure made yourself at home in a short time," Jake said. "As long as you're here, you can help us pick up the food."

Sam said, "We ordered enough to feed the entire station house. We're picking it up at five. What time is it?"

Gabe checked his watch. "Two-thirty."

"Any idea where our mother is?" Jake asked.

"I think she's at school. She said she'll be home around four."

"Perfecto," Jake said. "We should be home just in time. Are you coming with us for pizza or not?"

"Sure. Thanks." Gabe got his wallet and stuffed it into his pants. "That's cool. I didn't know that the Loo was that close to sixty."

Then again, why on earth should he know?

He kept forgetting that he was a stranger.

CHAPTER THIRTY-SIX

OVER THE MONITOR, the detectives saw Chuck Tinsley fidget and twitch, his meaty right leg bouncing up and down. He was also muttering, his thin lips making sounds that didn't quite articulate into words. Although he had come in willingly—the cops had used the ruse that they needed his help—his facial expression said: *Lemme outta here*. Dark eyes set into a seamed face swept the room, failing to focus for more than a second or two. His muscular arms and chest were covered in a gray T-shirt. Faded jeans and athletic shoes completed the outfit. A lightweight black nylon jacket rested on his lap.

"He's nervous," Decker said to Oliver and Marge. "Like he's guilty of something. Hang tight in case I need reinforcements."

"We're not going anywhere."

As soon as Decker left, Oliver said, "When is the food for his party coming?"

"Around six-thirty. We were supposed to get him out of the station house by six."

"It's four now. You think he'll be able to wrap this up in a couple of hours?"

"Don't know how hard he'll be to crack. Let's hope that the Loo is at the top of his game."

TINSLEY'S COMPLEXION WAS almost as green as the first time Decker had seen him. Maybe he should have brought in a barf bag. "Thanks for coming in." He placed a cup of coffee in front of the foreman, along with some whitening powder and a couple of sugars. "Thought you could use something to do with your hands."

Tinsley picked up the coffee. "I look that nervous?"

"More like you have better things to do with your time."

"That's true." Tinsley took a sip of coffee, made a face, and then added the whitener and the sugar. "I don't know what I could tell you now that I didn't tell you the first time. Tell you the truth, I don't wanna remember." He lowered his head. "It was horrible. How do you do that, day in and day out?"

"I like getting bad guys off the streets." Decker took the chair next to him. "You're a little calmer than the first time we met. Maybe some details might come back."

"What kind of details?"

"I don't know." The Loo took out his notebook. "Why don't you start at the beginning?"

"Like when I got to work or when I first saw her?"

Tinsley had given Decker an opening. "Well, let's start with when you first saw her." A noncommittal smile. "When was the first time you saw Adrianna Blanc?"

Tinsley cleared his throat. "I came to the site around one forty-five. I noticed the body around five minutes later."

"Tell me exactly what happened?"

The recitation came by rote. He got to the Grossman project around one forty-five. He wanted to clean up before the inspector came later in the afternoon. He started picking up trash, noticed a spot with a lot of flies, saw the body, dropped the garbage bag, and heaved. Lastly, he called 911. His story—from start to finish—lasted five minutes.

Good and fine except Yvette Jackson had ID'd Tinsley from a six-pack as the man Adrianna was talking to at Garage. It was now almost four o'clock. Decker didn't know how long they would dance around the truth, but he knew that Tinsley would crash sooner than later. The Loo stared at his prey for a few seconds, trying to unnerve him.

"Mr. Tinsley, I didn't ask you for the first time that you saw Adrianna's corpse. I asked you when was the first time that you saw Adrianna Blanc."

Again, Tinsley cleared his throat. "I don't understand. I saw her hanging up there about five minutes after I came onto the property."

"I'm not arguing with you. I'm sure you did see the body hanging from the rafters at about one-fifty in the afternoon. But that's not what I'm asking. Listen carefully." Decker leaned over. "When was the first time you saw Adrianna Blanc?"

"At around one-fifty that Monday afternoon." Tinsley's leg was going a mile a minute. "I don't know what you're getting at."

"Why do you think I'm getting at something?"

" 'Cause you keep repeating yourself."

"That's because you're not answering my question. When was the first time you saw Adrianna Blanc?"

"I am answering your question. Around one-fifty in the afternoon."

"And that's your story?"

"Whaddaya mean that's my story?" His hands were shaking. "That's the truth. I thought you wanted my help."

"I do want your help. That's why I asked you to come in here."

"So I came in. Now why are you giving me a hard time?"

"I don't mean to give you a hard time, but we have a little problem."

Tinsley looked stricken. "What kind of problem?"

"Let me start with another question. Where were you the previous evening?" Decker gave him the date to refresh his memory. "It was Sunday night. Do you remember where you were between seven and ten P.M.?"

Without hesitation, Tinsley said, "I wanna lawyer."

"We can get you representation." Decker stood up. "Or you can get your own. In the meantime, you'll be booked and printed—"

"What do you mean booked and printed?"

"You can have your lawyer meet you here. The arraignment will probably be sometime tonight—"

"Arraignment for what?"

Tinsley bolted up. Decker was bigger than the foreman, but a physical confrontation was that last thing he wanted. "Could you please sit down, sir?"

The foreman looked around as if he hadn't realized he was on his feet. "What the fuck is going on? What're you charging me with?"

"I have a number of choices: obstruction of justice, lying to the police, maybe murder—"

"Whoa, whoa, whoa!" Tinsley shot back in his chair, a horrified look on his face. "Wait just a fucking minute! I didn't murder anyone!"

"I'm not saying you did. You just asked what I was going to book you for—"

"You're not going to frame me for this bullshit!" He was panting and sweating. "I didn't have nothin' to do with her death."

"You can't speak to me, Mr. Tinsley. You asked for your lawyer."

"Just let me say something—"

"You asked for a lawyer," Decker repeated.

"What if I say I don't want a lawyer now? Can I ask for a lawyer later?"

Decker said, "Mr. Tinsley . . ." He sighed. "Chuck, can I call you Chuck?"

"Call me whatever the hell you want to call me. Just let me say something."

"If you want to talk to me, you have to sign a waiver that you've been advised of your rights and you waive your right to an attorney."

"But I can ask for one later."

"You can ask, sure."

"So where do I sign?"

"Let me advise you of your rights first."

"I'm not signing anything until you tell me what you are charging me with."

"Let's start with obstruction of justice—"

"I didn't obstruct anything!"

"Let me tell you your rights. Then you can decide what you want to do."

"I didn't *do* anything!"

"Just shut up and listen, okay?" Decker finally got the Miranda out. He asked Tinsley if he understood his rights.

"Do I look like a moron?"

"Yes or no?"

"Yes."

"So sign here."

Tinsley inked the card. "Can I talk now?"

"Do you wish to waive your right to an attorney? Yes or no?"

"Yes."

"Even though you asked for one before, now you don't want an attorney?"

"I just want to talk to you for a few minutes. Then I'll ask for my lawyer."

Meaning he wanted to figure out how much the police knew. Decker said, "Are you waiving your rights to an attorney even though you asked for one five minutes ago?"

"I already told you yes."

"So sign the card right here. That says that you're willing to talk to the police without an attorney present. And you know that anything you say can be used against you in a court of law."

"Fine, fine." He signed the card again. "Now can I say my piece?"

"Say anything you want, Mr. Tinsley. I'm all ears."

"I didn't murder anyone! That's bullshit!" He sat back and folded his arms. "And that's all I wanted to say."

"Chuck . . ." Decker started out. "Did you really think that you could go to Garage and flirt with Adrianna for over an hour without someone recognizing you?"

"I didn't kill her."

"I didn't say you did. All I said is, Do you really think you could flirt with Adrianna for over an hour without someone recognizing you?"

Tinsley didn't answer.

"Chuck, you had buddies there. They called out your name. Chuck, over here, Charley, pick up a cold one for us. People recognized you, Chuck. You're not a moron, but neither are cops. We've all been doing this for a very long time."

"I didn't kill her. I was sick to my stomach when I saw her hanging up there."

"So how'd she get up there?"

"The fuck if I know! I didn't put her there!" His eyes watered. "Someone's trying to frame me. Honest to God, she left before I did . . . way before I did. Someone musta . . ." He clamped his lips shut. "I didn't hurt her. I've never hurt a woman in my life!"

"So tell me how Adrianna wound up in your construction site?"

"If I knew, I'd tell you!" He wiped his forehead with the hem of his T-shirt. "I shoulda said something in the beginning, but I knew that you wouldn't believe me."

"Start from the beginning, Chuck. Tell me everything. It'll feel good to get it off your chest."

The man slunk down in the chair. "I never been to Garage before."

"So what brought you down there?"

"A buddy of mine suggested it. I musta got there around seven-thirty. Adrianna was already there. I noticed her right away."

"What was she doing?"

"Talking to one of the hostesses. I think her name was Emerald. She was cheap-looking—not Adrianna, the hostess. I got the feeling that I coulda taken her home that night, but she wasn't my type. Now I wish to God that I did. She coulda been my alibi."

Decker immediately thought of two reasons why that wouldn't have worked: (1) Adrianna Blanc was murdered the next day, not on Sunday night, and (2) Crystal Larabee was dead. Tinsley didn't know how lucky he was, not taking her home. "And this was around seven-thirty?"

"Yeah, around that."

"Go on."

"So I was drinking with my buddy Paul. Have you talked to Paul yet?"

"He's next on my list," Decker lied. "What's Paul's last name again?"

"Goldback."

"Sorry to interrupt. Keep going."

"So I was talking to Paul, but looking at Adrianna. And she was talking to the hostess but looking at me. You know that kind of thing. We both knew there was some kinda spark."

"Okay."

"So after I finish my beer, I go over to her. I offered to buy her whatever she was drinking."

"What time was this?"

"Maybe fifteen, twenty minutes later."

"So around ten to eight."

"I guess." Tinsley paused. "I thought she was a recovering alcoholic. She was drinking club soda. But then she told me that she had to go to work, so that's why she wasn't hitting anything heavy. She told me she was a nurse and worked with babies and that the one thing she promised was that she'd never drink right before she'd work. I thought that was really honorable, you know."

Decker nodded. "I agree."

"Then she said that she knew Emerald from high school, and if there was anything that I wanted, she could probably talk Emerald into giving it up for free."

"I don't know anyone working at Garage named Emerald, Chuck. Do you mean Crystal?"

"Yeah, Crystal. Adrianna was talking to me about Crystal and her work as a nurse and so on. I was talking about my work. We musta talked for over an hour. Crystal kept coming over, offering me free refills of my beer. Finally, she said she had to go to work. Adrianna did."

"What time was that?"

"A little before ten. I asked her where she was working tonight and she said St. Tim's. I told her I was working at a site right near there. I asked for her phone number and suggested lunch or dinner."

"What'd she say?"

"She asked me for my phone number instead. I didn't think twice about that. Lotta women check out guys before they go out with them. So I gave her my business card. It had my cell number and my e-mail address. But I remember very clearly writing down the address of where I was working . . . to show her I really was working close to St. Tim's and not giving her a line."

"You wrote down the address of the Grossmans' house?"

"Yeah, exactly."

"We found her purse, Chuck. We didn't find any of your cards in it."

Tinsley's face turned white. Decker waited him out.

"My card was in her coat pocket when I found her. I took it out."

Decker stared at him. "Do you still have the card?"

"Yeah, I think so."

"You think?"

"It's in the nightstand of my bedroom. I'll get it for you." Tinsley spoke intensely. "Don't you get it, Lieutenant? Someone found my card in her purse or pocket and hung her up on my construction site to frame me."

No pun intended, Decker thought to himself. "That's a possibility."

"It's what happened! Do you really think I'd be stupid enough to murder someone, then put her somewhere that was connected to me. I'd have to be a *moron*."

The jails were filled with stupid criminals. Decker said, "You know that when you removed the card, you tampered with material evidence."

"I knew that if the cops found it, it looked bad for me."

"It does look bad for you right now, Chuck."

"Look, I admitted to removing the card. Would I be stupid enough to leave a body where I was working? I'll answer that. The answer is no. Someone left the card in her pocket to make me look bad."

"Could be. Because right now, the focus is on you."

"Lieutenant, I swear she left the bar alive and that was the last time I saw her until I found her body at the construction site."

"Let's backtrack a little bit. What did you do after Adrianna left?"

"I talked to Em . . . to Crystal for a little bit. Then I talked to some chick named Lucy. No chemistry there. I left Garage's at about eleven, and went straight home. I don't remember what I did. I usually go to bed between twelve and one."

"You live alone?"

"Unfortunately I do."

"So tell me about the next day. Monday, the day you found the body. What time did you wake up?"

"Seven-thirty. That's when I always get up. I went to another one of Keith's jobs. The Rosen project on Chloe Lane."

"What time did you arrive at the Rosen project?"

"About eight-thirty. I was there all morning. Mrs. Rosen was there all morning. She brought me out some coffee. She can tell you I was there."

"When did you leave the Rosen project to go to the Grossman project?"

"Around twelve-thirty, I left the Rosen project. I stopped off at Ranger's to eat lunch. That's a deli. I ate a corned beef sandwich with mustard. That I remember because it's what I threw up. I can't eat corned beef anymore and I used to love corned beef. The whole thing is fucked up."

"How'd you pay for your meal?"

"Like I pay for all of them. In cash."

"That doesn't help me."

"Sorry," Tinsley mocked. "Didn't know I would need receipts to get me out of criminal charges."

"What time did you leave Ranger's?"

"About one-thirty. I came straight to the Grossman project. It's about fifteen minutes away. You can clock it yourself."

"What did you do while you ate your sandwich at Ranger's?"

"I dunno. I just ate. I mighta caught up on some phone calls. Sometimes I do that."

"On your cell?"

"How else? I didn't borrow the landline."

"Do you have any objections to my going through your cell phone records?"

"Be my guest."

Decker said, "Better yet, how about handing over your cell?"

Tinsley shrugged. "Fine." He fished into the pocket of his nylon jacket and gave Decker the cell.

"Give me a couple of minutes with this." Decker stood up and left, returning to the video room, where Marge and Oliver were still studying Chuck on the monitor. Tinsley had laid his head between his arms on the table and appeared to be going to sleep.

"Check this out, Marge." Decker handed her the phone. "What do you two think?"

Oliver said, "I'm always suspicious of a guy who tries to nap after being grilled by the police."

"He said that the card that he gave Adrianna is in his night-stand," Marge pointed out. "Why don't we see if we can get him to agree to a search of his place?"

"Good idea."

"He could be lying. But I don't think he is. If his story checks out, he wouldn't have had enough time since he was accounted for from eight-thirty until he called the police."

"If you believe him," Oliver said. "Besides, how long does it take for a quick screw?"

"If it was only a quick screw, it wouldn't take too long," Marge said. "But if it's a screw with games that resulted in murder and stringing her up with cable wires on the rafters all the while looking around to make sure that no one's watching, I'd say it could take a hell of a long time."

CHAPTER THIRTY-SEVEN

WHILE MARGE WAS checking out Tinsley's phone, Decker went back into the interview room and sat down at the table. "What did you and Adrianna talk about?"

He sighed. "Just stuff. We had a good rappaport."

"Rapport?"

"Yeah, rapport. I don't even know what I'm saying." Tinsley paused. "We talked about a lot of stuff."

"Can you be more specific?"

Tinsley blew out air. "I talked about my job . . . how I liked working with my hands and seeing that I'd actually done something at the end of the day."

Decker nodded.

"She said she really liked her job for the same reason . . . that she felt she was doing something important." He attempted to collect his thoughts. "She said her job was real stressful . . . taking care of sick babies." Another pause. "Oh . . . now I remember. She said something about her job being more stressful 'cause she was in the process of getting out of a bad relationship. But she still had to work with the guy."

"Did she mention the man by name?"

"No . . . only that he worked where she worked. They didn't always bump into each other, but it was enough that when they were fighting, it was awkward."

"I get that," Decker said.

"Yeah, yeah, it's comin' back." Tinsley was getting excited. "She said she was about to break free. All she needed was an excuse."

"What did you say to that?"

"I think I said something dumb like . . . I hope I'm your excuse. She laughed." He looked pensive. "She had a nice laugh. She was a pretty girl. I had a good time." He dropped his forehead in his hands. "Seeing her like that . . . it still makes me sick to think about it."

The man's feelings may have been legit, but that didn't mean he didn't kill her. "Chuck, you've got a couple of choices right now."

"I don't like the sound of this."

"I can either book you for tampering with material evidence and obstruction of justice. Or I won't do anything just yet, if you agree to cool your heels here in the police station until we can check out your phone and get a timeline for where you were the day of the murder."

"That's a choice? Either way I'm here."

"You're here but not in jail."

Tinsley thought about that. "How long do you think this is going to take?"

"It might take the better part of the evening. I can get you some dinner if you're hungry." Tinsley's response was a shrug. "Where did you find the business card that you gave Adrianna?"

"In her pocket."

"And now it's in your nightstand drawer?"

"Last time I checked."

Decker wondered why he didn't just throw it away. Maybe he kept it as a trophy. "Would you mind if we go inside your apartment to pick up the card? It could have forensic evidence on it."

"Like my DNA or my fingerprint?"

"You took it, so both are a possibility."

"Yeah, go get the card. Maybe it'll help me."

Decker said, "While we're in your apartment, do you mind if we look around?"

"For what?"

"I'll know it when I see it."

"I have a couple of ounces in my bottom dresser drawer." He threw up his hands. "I don't know why I just told you that. I must be in the mood for confession after all these years of being a lapsed Catholic."

"If a couple of ounces are the worst of it, you'll be okay. So is it a yes or a no?"

Tinsley reached in his pocket and gave him the keys. "Help yourself. Maybe you can be a pal and do the dishes while you're there."

"Maybe not. Is your apartment alarmed?"

"Nah, don't have all that much to steal. Just a flat screen. But I get the sports package. The Lakers are playing tonight. When you get back, don't tell me the score. I've got it on DVR. I'll watch it when I get home . . . whenever the hell that is."

LIKE ANYTHING CHOREOGRAPHED, timing was everything. The food arrived ten minutes after Decker went back into the interview room with Tinsley. Everyone pitched in to set things up and all was ready for the Loo just as the interview was drawing to a close. When Decker came out of the room, he was assaulted by a raucous "surprise" by family and coworkers. Totally disoriented, he looked around and saw what everyone had done for his birthday. Rina came up and hugged him. "Happy big one, Lieutenant."

Decker realized with a gasp that his sons were present. "What are you guys doing here?"

"I'll go anywhere for the free food." Jacob hugged him fiercely. "Happy birthday, Dad."

Sammy was next. "Happy birthday, Dad." He gave him a bear hug. "Like they say, till a hundred and twenty."

"So I guess I'm at the halfway mark." Laughs all around. Decker was still dazed. "Is this all for me?"

"No, it's for Chuck Tinsley," Marge said.

"He wants a hamburger, by the way."

"He'll have to make do with corned beef on rye."

"Corned beef makes him sick. Try turkey."

Another round of laughs. Marge clapped her hands to get everyone's attention. "Time's a-ticking and some of us have work to do. Grub is served, so dig in."

Decker spent the next twenty minutes shaking hands, hugging his family, and accepting congratulations on his upcoming birthday as his coworkers formed a long line to the makeshift buffet. There were platters of roasted chicken, corned beef, pastrami, smoked turkey, bologna, potato salad, coleslaw, chopped liver, olives and pickles, onions and tomatoes, and baskets of sliced breads—rye and challah.

Decker turned to Rina. "How did you plan this without my knowing?"

"I didn't plan it. The boys and Cindy did everything. What I can't understand is how they did it without *my* knowing."

"You should have seen the look on the ladies' faces when they saw us," Sammy said. "Eema was funny, but Hannah was priceless."

"I did kinda freak when I saw them." Hannah rested her head on Sammy's arm.

Decker said, "How's Rachel, Sam?"

"Studying for finals. She sends her regards."

"Ilana sends her regards, too," Jacob said. "She really wanted to come, but she also has finals."

"Next time," Decker said. "You're staying the weekend? Of course you are."

Jake said, "We even pulled out the trundle because it appears we've been supplanted by a younger model." When Gabe turned red, he added, "Go eat some corned beef, kid. You need some protein."

"I'm still full from the pizza."

"Well, then go make me a sandwich. I'm hungry."

"Excuse me?" Rina said. "Is that how I taught you to talk to guests?"

"He's not a guest, he's an interloper."

"It's fine." Gabe smiled shyly. "What kind of sandwich do you want?"

"Pastrami and smoked turkey on rye, mustard, no mayo, and all the sides."

"Got it." Gabe turned to brace himself for the onslaught at the buffet.

When he left, Jacob said, "Nice kid. I understand he's dealing with a couple of issues."

"Aren't we all?" Decker threw his arm around his sons. "Thank you, Yonkel. Thank you, Shmueli. I will never forget this day."

"I love you, old man," Jacob told him. "Now can I have the car?"

Cindy came up to her father, munching on a drumstick. She kissed his cheek. "Happy birthday, Daddy. You deserve all this and more."

"I love you, princess." He kissed her cheek, peeking at her abdomen that had blossomed into a nice bump. "How are you feeling?"

"I'm always famished around this time."

"When's the big day?" Jake asked.

Cindy said. "Christmas or New Year's . . . something like that."

Jake laughed. "You don't know the due date?"

"I wasn't listening too closely once the test turned up positive." Cindy mussed up her stepbrother's hair, then took another bite of chicken. "Wow, this is good. Koby, can you get me another drumstick?"

Koby finished off his turkey on rye and wiped his hands on a napkin. "Not a problem. I'm ready for seconds anyway. Anyone else want something?"

"I'll take another sandwich," Sammy said.

"Hannah?" Koby asked.

"Smoked turkey on rye."

"Rina?"

"Same as Hannah."

"Lieutenant?"

"I'm okay."

"But you haven't eaten anything," Rina said.

"I'm still trying to figure out how all this happened."

"You figure it out," Koby said. "I'll get the food."

"There are going to be lots of leftovers," Rina announced. "You guys will have to take all this food off my hands."

"Why don't we eat it for Shabbos so you won't have to cook," Sammy said.

"This is like the first time in years that all my family is going to be together," Rina said. "Do you honestly think I'm going to serve you cold cuts for Shabbos?"

Decker said, "How about if we let the guys and gals who work here take the food home to their families?"

"I think that would be a dandy idea," Rina said.

"So if the cold cuts are vetoed for dinner, can I put in a vote for rack of lamb?" Jacob said. "Medium rare with green beans and garlic mash?"

Rina rolled her eyes. "Anything else, Yonkel?"

"A nice apple pie never hurt anyone."

Koby brought Cindy a drumstick, which she polished all off in four bites. "I love you all, but we can't stay. Both of us have to go back to work."

"Wait," Sammy said. "You have to stick around for the cake."

"A cake?" Decker said. "You're not actually going to sing me 'Happy Birthday'?" He turned to Rina for help. "Don't let them do this."

"It's not my decision."

Decker was getting desperate. "I have to get back to work. I've got a possible murder suspect sitting in the interview room wondering what's going on."

"Actually, I just checked in on him," Oliver said. "He's very happy with his smoked turkey on rye."

Sammy said, "Go get the cake, Yonkel."

"You get the cake."

Marge said, "I'll get the cake." She turned to Oliver. "C'mon, Detective, let's go embarrass the Loo."

The cake was brought in, looking more like a welding torch than a pastry. There were sixty candles plunged into chocolate icing. Decker braced for the misery as the entire squad room erupted into an off-key rendition of "Happy Birthday." The only saving grace, in his opinion, was that he was able to blow out all the candles in a single breath.

As Rina was cutting the cake, Decker took Marge aside. "What's going on with Tinsley's phone?"

"Well, Chuck did make some calls on that Monday during the time he was supposedly at lunch at Ranger's. I've got someone checking on the towers to see where the calls were bounced from and then we'll work backward."

"Is the cell tower for Ranger's the same cell tower for the Grossman project?"

"I'm checking that out as well."

"Tinsley gave us permission to get the business card that he took off of Adrianna's body and also to search his house."

"Good job, Rabbi. Now I know why you're in charge."

"You know, I really need to get started on that. I won't be able to keep stalling him forever."

"No, Pete, you need to stay here with your party guests. Oliver and I will go over to Tinsley's apartment." Marge held out her hand. "Keys, please?"

"You're not cutting me a break, are you?"

"To every season, there is a time." She clamped a hand on Decker's shoulder. "Loo, this is your time."

A SEARCH OF Tinsley's place revealed the business card in the nightstand, a few ounces of cheap weed, and most important in the detectives' eyes, a bag of women's jewelry. Tinsley swore that the baubles belonged to his late mother, but Decker knew that killers often took trophies. He needed to make sure that none of the trinkets belonged to Adrianna Blanc and that meant calling up Kathy Blanc and asking her if she could identify any of the pieces. Tomorrow was going to be a hellish morning.

Tinsley was run through the local system—no wants or warrants—then his prints were submitted to AFIS. Nothing popped up. He gave a buccal swab for DNA. Decker now faced a dilemma. He could either arrest Tinsley on lesser charges, which would guarantee no further cooperation on his part. Or he could spring him from the station house, thereby keeping the lines of communication open. Decker chose to let him go, keeping Tinsley in the crosshairs, assigning a cruiser to keep watch on the man.

Both Ranger's (the deli where Tinsley ate) and the Grossman place (the site where he worked) used the same tower for cell phones, so that was a bust. The next best option—and far from optimal—was to go to the eatery and see if anyone could put Tinsley there at twelve-thirty Monday afternoon for lunch.

It was after one in the morning by the time Decker finished the paperwork and made it home. He was still on a high from his party, but it was tempered by the full schedule he knew he had tomorrow. He hoped to get a little bit of solitude before he dropped off to sleep. The house was quiet when he opened the door, lit with a lone living-room lamp. He expected to find Rina reading, but it was Gabe bundled up in blankets.

"What are you doing up so late?"

The boy took off his glasses and put down his book. "It was really cramped with the three of us in the bedroom, so I offered to sleep on the couch."

"Nice of you, but you're not sleeping."

"No, I don't do that too much these days."

"How's your hand?"

"It'll be fine." He rubbed his arms. "That was a stroke of luck . . . hurting my hand. No way I could have gotten an audition with Nicholas Mark. He's got a waiting list for students that stretches to the moon."

"You must have impressed him."

"I don't know how. I made mistakes. Probably fewer than if I knew he'd been listening." He drew his knees up to his chin. "Can I talk to you for a minute?"

"Sure." Decker sat down. "What's up?"

"You know that I did talk to Chris on Tuesday. I was reluctant to tell you everything because I promised him I wouldn't tell you about the conversation until three days later. He wanted time to get out of L.A."

Decker paused. "And that's what he said? He needed time to get out of L.A.?"

"More or less. You probably think he's gone into hiding. I think he was trying to shake you off so he could find my mom without you bugging him."

Decker was quiet.

"Anyway. You can look at my stuff. All the bank and phone records. I don't care. I kept my promise to him and my conscience is clear. Maybe now I can fall asleep."

"As long as we're on this topic . . . I spoke to a security guard from the hotel today. He had a lot to say about your mother and father."

"You mean about the fight?"

"So you know about it."

"Chris told me. He said it was a bad one. He said you'd find out about it. He swore to me that Mom was alive when he left."

"And you believe him?"

"Yes, I do. Chris also told me that he offered the guy some money and the guy took it. So how reliable could he be if he was bribable?"

"The guard felt guilty about it. He gave it back to me. I think his account is pretty reliable." Decker chose his words carefully. "But he did tell me a few things about your mom that makes me wonder if Chris is telling the truth or not. The security guard told me that your mother looked more mad than scared when he interrupted them."

"Mad or upset?"

"Mad as in angry, which is the word he used. Your mom was angry at the guard for barging in on their argument. And it does sound like a bad fight. He heard your dad call your mom a lying bitch and he heard your mom call your dad crazy and paranoid. The point I'm making is that your mom didn't look scared to the guard."

"That's odd . . ." Gabe licked his lips. "Chris was under the impression that he had scared the shit out of her."

"He told you that?"

Gabe nodded.

"Interesting," Decker said. "Because . . . I'm just wondering if . . . maybe after all these years . . . your mom has finally learned how to snow people. In my opinion, Chris would be far more likely to leave her alone if she appeared scared rather than angry."

Gabe was quiet.

"I would really like to talk to your father. I'm on the fence about his guilt and innocence and it would help me to hear his point of view. If you could call him up and ask him to come in just to talk . . . maybe take a polygraph, which he could probably pass even if he did murder your mom." Decker thought a moment. "If Chris didn't do anything to her, I want to concentrate on other leads. And if she vanished of her own accord . . ." *Like with a rich doctor to India.* "Well, it would be nice not to waste departmental resources on finding people who don't want to be found."

"Lieutenant, I can't call Chris and ask him favors. He'll act like I'm betraying him or something." Gabe rubbed his eyes. "Just wait for him to call me."

"What makes you think he'll call?"

"Because I know my dad. He's going to want to know what you know and the best way to find that out is through me. Then I can tell him, 'Decker wants you to come in and take a polygraph.' He'll probably say 'fuck that' or something equally pithy, but at least I can plead your case without looking like a traitor."

A fair compromise. "Okay. I'll wait until he calls you. When he does call you, let him do most of the talking."

"He's onto that. Chris uses silences as efficiently as his Mauser.

But I can handle him." Gabe rubbed his eyes. "I'm going to have to give him something—my dad."

"Give him Atik Jains. He probably knows about it anyway. Don't say anything about your mom knowing an Indian doctor."

"Did you get a chance to check out the names I gave you?"

"I did and I might have some information." He paused. "How much do you want to know, Gabe? Because if you know stuff, then you might have to lie to your dad."

"You're right. I'm better off not knowing." He folded his arms across his chest. "Besides, if she left on purpose, then why should I care?" Anger in his eyes. "Let her start a new life without me. It's her prerogative."

"I'm sure that if she did that, she felt that you were best off without her."

"Yeah, isn't that what all mothers say when they give up their babies for adoption."

"You're not a baby. You're an independent guy. She knew you could handle it."

"And here I am . . . handling it."

"She stuck it out for almost fifteen years. After the beating, she probably didn't feel safe anymore."

"I know." A sigh. "You're right. She probably did feel like this was her last shot at freedom. She had all the right reasons for doing what she did, but that doesn't help to ease the pain."

CHAPTER THIRTY-EIGHT

THE JEWELRY TAKEN from Tinsley's apartment was neatly laid out atop a clean plastic sheet on Decker's desk. He explained to Kathy Blanc where they were in the investigation and the purpose of the identification. She became livid when he got to the part about letting Tinsley go. "You let this monster walk out of here a *free man*?"

"He's not in jail but he's under watch," Decker said. "We can pick him up at any time once we get evidence on him."

"A woman from the bar identifying him as the man my daughter spoke with isn't enough? His business card in my daughter's coat pocket isn't enough? Finding my daughter dead at his place of work isn't enough? What do you jokers need to arrest someone?"

The questions were rhetorical, but Decker answered them as if they were sincere. "If *we* would have found Tinsley's business card in her purse, I might have kept him under lock and key. The truth is that he told us about the card. Otherwise we wouldn't have known about it."

Kathy was coiffed and bejeweled, dressed in gray slacks and a red cotton tee. Her complexion matched the hue of her shirt. "He threw you a bone and you lapped it up."

"He's on our radar. I have cops on him. Unfortunately, I need hard evidence. I've talked to the D.A. this morning. She won't take it to a grand jury unless I have more."

"Then she's an idiot."

"Mrs. Blanc, what I have on Tinsley is easily explained away by his story. Plus, Garth Hammerling and Mandy Kowalski are still missing. Why Garth hasn't shown his face is anyone's guess, but it sure makes him look bad."

"You told me that Garth was five hundred miles away when it happened."

"No, I said that Garth was five hundred miles away when Adrianna went to work at St. Tim's Sunday night. We know he came back to L.A. What we don't know is if he saw Adrianna or not."

"So why can't you find him? Isn't that your job?"

"Yes, it's our job. And we're doing everything we can to find him and Mandy Kowalski. If he's with Mandy, that might be worrisome."

Kathy folded her arms across her chest. "I never trusted that girl."

"Interesting you should say that. She lied to the police at least once. Can I ask you why you never trusted her?"

"I don't know." She had lowered her voice. "She appeared nice, but she was very serious." Her eyes watered. "If she would have been Bea's friend, I might have felt differently. But Adrianna didn't have friends like her. She liked her friends like herself—freewheeling. Also I felt that she was . . . disapproving of my daughter."

"If so, why do you think they became friends?"

"This is going to sound terrible . . . and it's based on nothing . . ."

"Go ahead," Decker said. "I like conjecture."

"I sensed that Mandy liked Adrianna because she could feel superior to her, like mentoring her through nursing school. And she did help her. But once Adrianna stopped being . . . dependent on Mandy, I think Mandy became bitter."

"Was it you who told me that Mandy introduced Garth to Adrianna?"

"I think so." Kathy paused. "Maybe that's why Mandy was bitter. Maybe Mandy liked Garth. In any case, Mandy was certainly not like Adrianna's other friends."

"Not like Crystal Larabee, for instance?"

"Poor Crystal." Tears raced down Kathy's cheeks. "Her mother is coming in this afternoon. I've invited Pandy to stay with us until both of the girls . . ."—sobs now—"are laid to rest."

"That's very kind of you."

Kathy dried her eyes with a tissue. "Are you coming to the memorial service?"

"When is it?"

"Tomorrow at eleven."

The date was not only on Shabbat, but was the first weekend in years when his entire family would be together. He said, "Of course."

"That would be nice." Another swipe at her eyes. It did little to stanch the flow. Her eyes focused on the gold pieces. "What exactly should I do?"

"We found these in Chuck Tinsley's apartment. He claims the pieces belonged to his late mother. I'd like you to tell me if any of the items might have belonged to Adrianna. If you need to touch anything, I'll give you some latex gloves."

She studied the pieces with her hands in her lap. "These are all yellow gold. Adrianna never wore yellow gold. She thought yellow gold was very old ladyish."

Decker noticed the yellow gold chain around Kathy Blanc's neck. "So . . . as far as you know, none of these items is Adrianna's."

"As far as I know, that is correct. I don't know all of her jewelry, but these pieces aren't her style. Maybe my style, but not hers."

"That helps a lot. Thanks so much for coming down." He studied the jewelry for a few moments more than he should have. Something was catching in his brain.

Kathy said, "Would it have helped your case against Tinsley if I would have identified one of the pieces as Adrianna's?"

"Of course. It would have helped the case immensely."

"And you would have arrested him?"

"Probably."

"I should have lied. I should have picked out an item at random and told you it belonged to Adrianna." Her expression was furious. "Stupid of me. Tinsley should be behind bars."

"Only if he did it." Decker stopped bagging the jewelry and looked at her. "Kathy, you have to believe me on this one. You don't want to be responsible for putting the wrong man in jail."

"I don't know, Lieutenant." She smacked her lips. "The way I feel right now, I'd rather have the wrong man than no man at all."

BACK IN MISSION Control, officially known as Central Security for St. Tim's, Peter the tech was as mute as ever. But his light eyes twinkled as he nodded to Marge and Oliver, indicating that they were now buddies. Ivan Povich seated the detectives in front of a blank monitor and poured coffee from a glass carafe into four Styrofoam cups.

"Fresh," Povich said. "Peter just made it."

Marge took a sip. "It's good. Is there anything that Peter doesn't do well?"

The silent tech saluted her.

"It's Kona," Povich said. "Less caffeine, less acid. Peter, can you bring up the original tape from the emergency vehicle lot . . . the one before the enhancement."

Peter began sorting through the cassettes and slipped one into the machine slot.

"How'd that go?" Marge asked. "Any of the features recognizable?"

"You will see everything for yourself." Within moments, black-and-white images blossomed onto the monitor. "This is the original." Povich zeroed in on the lone female figure lurking on the loading dock. With each twist of the dial, she grew in size. "Everything blurs as the image gets bigger, no? Now watch. Peter, put in the enhanced tape."

When the new images came onto the screen, Marge was delighted. She could see the differences: sharper angles, clearer delineations. "Wow. That makes a difference."

Povich advanced the enhanced tape until he came to the frame of interest. Again, everyone concentrated on the figure in the corner of the loading dock. He turned the dial until the gray, grainy face came into maximum size and focus.

Marge stared at the screen. "Looks like Mandy Kowalski to me." She turned to Oliver. "What do you think?"

"Wouldn't bet my life on it." Oliver sat back in his chair. "But I'd bet money on it."

Marge said, "What's the time on the tape?"

"Eleven fourteen A.M.," Povich said.

Oliver said, "And Tinsley found the body at one forty-five?"

Marge nodded. "Plenty of time to string up the body at the construction site. St. Tim's is a hop, skip, and jump away. Ivan, can you back up the tape?"

"How far back?"

"A couple of minutes?" Marge explained, "We're interested in Mandy because we're thinking she might have had something to do with Adrianna's murder and she used the dock to load the body."

Povich said, "So like you're looking for a body bag?"

"Body bag, trash bag, a big box . . . something." Marge shrugged. "If Mandy or Garth was carting away a body on the sly, he or she would probably be savvy enough to avoid the security cameras. I suppose I'm looking for something less obvious . . . like a car or a person that doesn't fit the scene."

Povich said, "Maybe it would be better to view this in the station house."

"When can you bring the tape in?"

"You can keep this one. It is a copy. Peter made it for you."

Marge turned to the mute. "You made a copy for us?"

"He did," Povich said. "But don't tell the hospital." He popped the cassette out. "Here you go. Good luck."

"Thank you very much, gentlemen." Marge placed the cassette into her oversize purse. "Thank for the help and the cooperation."

"Yeah, thanks," Oliver said.

The two detectives got up and shook hands all around. As they left, Marge gave Peter a firm pat on the back—her silent way of saying "job well done."

"RIGHT . . . HERE!" Marge pointed to the rear of a car with its trunk open. "Keep an eye on this because it's relegated to the corner of the monitor."

"Now look what happens," Oliver said.

Decker watched the cassette frame by frame as a man in a gray uniform slid in and out of view. At one point, he was holding a black industrial garbage bag, which he hoisted—with effort—into the open trunk. Then he closed the lid and walked out of view. A few moments later, the car left.

Marge turned on the lights and removed the cassette. Today she had dressed in a navy sweater and tan slacks. "While this guy was schlepping the bag and hauling it to the car trunk, we have Mandy popping into view at eleven fourteen. Then the car leaving around two minutes later. Unfortunately, it's impossible to get a license plate. We have a good shot of the trunk. I'll visit some car dealers and see if someone can identify the make and model."

Oliver said, "The guy in the uniform appears to be about the same height and weight as Garth, but that's as close as we can come to identifying him."

"Get some pictures of Mandy and Garth and go back to the people who were working the emergency dock on Monday. Ask them if they remember seeing either or both of them." Decker rubbed his temples. "Anything else?"

"Not right now," Marge said. "You okay, Pete?"

"Yeah, I'm fine . . ." He raked his hand through his hair. "Maybe it's just turning sixty. Anyway, I sent Wanda Bontemps down to Ranger's Deli to see if I can find anyone who could corroborate Chuck Tinsley's story. She found a waitress who knows him. She says he eats there all the time. She thinks he was there on Monday around twelve-thirty, but she can't be sure."

Marge said, "Maybe Tinsley's telling the truth. That someone found his business card in Adrianna's pocket and set him up."

"Could be."

Oliver said, "You don't like Tinsley, do you?"

"He calls in the body, and he met her for the first time the night before. He doesn't tell us about it. No, I don't like him." Decker smoothed his mustache. "Something's off with that guy. If he were locked up, I'd feel better. But he's not in custody and I'm missing something."

"It'll come to you."

"Yeah, it will. Let's just hope it doesn't come too late."

CHAPTER THIRTY-NINE

THE DECKER HOUSE was much smaller than Gabe's home in New York, and with everyone coming in and out, the space had become crowded. The brothers had called up a bunch of their old friends, and within hours, dudes were occupying every inch of usable space. The cramped conditions and the noise were making him nervous. When he tried to take refuge in the kitchen, he found it a mess of pots and pans, although the cooking smells were wonderful. Rina was wearing an apron, her forehead moist with sweat. Out of politeness, Gabe asked if he could help. He was relieved when she declined the offer.

"In that case, maybe I'll go out for a walk."

"It's pretty insane around here. Even I'm not used to it anymore." Rina handed him notepaper and a pencil. "Write down your cell number just in case. And put my cell number into your phone. You should have it in case of an emergency."

"I'll do it, although I think I'll be okay."

"What if your mugger comes back for revenge?"

Gabe took out his iPod and smiled. "I still have my right hand. Can I pick up something for you while I'm out?"

"No, I'm covered." Rina tousled his hair. "Don't get lost in your music."

"Actually, it seems like a perfect thing to get lost in."

He left the hubbub and hadn't been gone more than ten minutes when he felt the vibration of his phone against his leg. He retrieved the phone, looked at the window, and saw that the number was restricted. He knew that the Deckers' landline phone was unlisted. It was probably Rina checking up on him. He debated letting it ring, but she'd probably keep calling until he answered. He took out his left earbud, clicked the green on button, and said, "Hi. I'm still alive."

"That's good to hear. What happened to your hand?"

The deep voice on the other end wasn't Rina. "Chris?" Gabe started shaking. "Where are you?"

"Answer the question. What happened to your hand?"

"Nothing. I'm fine."

"Then why'd you go to a hand surgeon?"

The man had eyes in back of his head. "It's nothing, Chris. It isn't even worth talking about."

"Talk about it anyway."

"I got in a fight. It was a little sore. It was fine, but Rina . . . Mrs. Decker insisted I go to the doctor. How'd you know about it? Where are you?"

"You got into a fight?" The line went quiet. "You're the most nonconfrontational person I know. What the hell happened?"

"Someone tried to grab my briefcase. I fought him off."

"Why the hell did you do that?"

"Because I had all the stuff you gave me in there."

"Gabriel, all that shit is replaceable. Your hands aren't. Are you out of your fucking mind?"

"Well, I didn't know how replaceable the stuff was, seeing you've been hard to reach lately and you get very piqued when I bother you."

"So I get piqued. It's better than ruining your life. Don't fuck around with your hands, okay?"

"I didn't do it on purpose. Where are you?"

"I've got to go."

"Decker thinks you're innocent."

Donatti gave out a mirthless laugh. "He's feeding you shit. He wants to fry me."

"Maybe. He wants you to come down and take a lie-detector test."

"Fuck that."

"He thinks it'll clear you. He said you could pass it even if you did murder Mom."

This time, Donatti's laugh was genuine. "He's right about that. Tell him to fuck himself."

"How about if I say you're not interested. He's going to know about this phone call. He checks my phone records. What do you want me to tell him?"

"Whatever you want."

"What's going on with Mom?"

"Ask your pal Decker. He's been following in my footsteps. What else has he been telling you?"

"Lemme think . . ." *Note to self: pretend to think.* "He knew you were in town on Tuesday. He said you're both on the same path, only he's a couple steps behind you."

Silence on the other end. "Go on."

"Decker thinks that maybe he's found Mom's car. He said you were looking for it at the same spot as he was."

"And?"

"The car he found wasn't registered to Mom. So maybe it wasn't her car. He's looking into that. Did you find Mom?"

"No, Gabriel, I have not found her. What else did he say about the car?"

Note to self: try not to sound rehearsed. "He said that the car was owned by some Indian guy. Indian Indian. He told me the name but I forgot it."

"Atik Jains."

"Yeah, that's it."

"Name sound familiar?"

"I don't know the guy. What about you?"

"No." Donatti paused. "So you never saw Mom with an Indian man? You were with her a lot more than I was."

Here was the part where he really needed to sound convincing. "I didn't see her that much. I was either in school or locked up practicing. The only reason we saw each other at all was because my lessons were in the city."

"Interesting, Gabe, but you didn't answer the question. Did you ever see her with an Indian man?"

"I don't remember Mom being with *any* man, let alone an Indian," he lied. "I mean I'm sure I saw her talking to men, but nothing that sticks out as weird."

There was a long pause. "Okay. If you find out anything, you'll let me know, right?"

"Of course," Gabe lied again. "Are you in L.A.?"

"No. I'll call you if I find your mother." Donatti was silent. For a moment, Gabe thought he'd hung up. Finally, Chris said, "You okay where you are?"

"They're real nice for perfect strangers."

"When the dust clears, you can come live with me. If you want to go back to New York, I'll get you a housekeeper. Personally, I think you're best off where you are."

"I agree mainly because I found a teacher."

A pause. "Who?"

There was real curiosity in his father's voice. He and Chris had only two things in common: Mom and music. Both were dominant factors in their lives.

"Nicholas Mark."

Again, Donatti was silent. "How the hell did you wangle that?"

"His doctor is the hand surgeon that saw me. By accident, he heard me play and afterward he agreed to take me on for a few lessons. I'm hoping my dedication will convince him to take me on permanently. I'll need someone of his caliber if I have any hopes of doing the Chopin International in five years."

"What'd you play for him?"

"Fantaisie-Impromptu and 'La campanella.'"

"You played 'La campanella' with a sore left hand?"

"Yeah. I made mistakes but it wasn't too bad, considering. I was relaxed. I didn't know I was playing in front of Nicholas Mark. The main thing is he agreed to give me a few lessons."

"Maybe you're finally reaching your goddamn potential. I always told you if you quit fucking around, you could be one of the greats."

"Thanks for the compliment—I think."

"Don't be a snot nose." A pause. "Guys like Mark can't come cheap. If you need more money, call up one of my places and I'll put more cash in your accounts. As nice as it's been to chitchat with you, Gabriel, duty calls. I've got to go."

But Gabe wasn't ready to hang up. "Aren't you worried about this call being traced?"

"They trace cell calls by relay towers. And towers can get scrambled if you have the right equipment."

"If you find Mom, please don't hurt her."

"I'm not going to *hurt* her. I'm done with that." Said more to himself than to Gabe. "I'm pissed as hell, but I'm not without insight. I'm impossible to live with. If she needs to get something out of her system, I can handle it. I want to find her mainly because I love her. But also all my businesses are in her name. I've got taxes coming up and she's got to sign papers or I'm screwed."

"Why don't you forge her signature?"

"I do that all the time. That's not the problem. The problem is if she's officially missing—not dead, just missing—she can't sign anything. That means everything she owns is in limbo until there's a legal resolution. I'd rather have her alive. But I'd rather have her dead than missing. If she was dead, you'd own everything. I could deal with that. If you need something, call up one of my places in Elko, okay?"

"What do you mean, I'd own everything?"

"You're her legal heir, not me."

"But it's not mine, it's yours."

"But legally it would be yours."

"So like do I have to sign something to hand it over to you?"

"Gabe, I can't own brothels and casinos. I'm a felon."

"I thought you were pardoned."

"I was let out of prison but I still have a record. I'm not worried about my assets being in your name. You're not going to steal from me. That would be really stupid. If you need money, it's the one thing I can give you. Take care of yourself. And lay off the fighting." A pause. "I can't believe you fought off a mugger. That's so unlike you."

"Maybe I've got more Whitman in me than either of us thought."

"Maybe." Chris was silent. "So maybe you actually are my kid."

Gabe laughed. "You have doubts?"

"You're the only carelessness that led to an accident and I've been careless all my life."

"Thanks for relegating my existence to a fluke."

"Stop being such a wuss. I support you, don't I?"

"Take a paternity test, Chris. I'm willing."

"Maybe you are, but I'm not." A pause. "You have blood relatives, Gabe. You got a mom and an aunt and a grandfather. You have a father—whoever he is."

"You know you're being ridiculous—"

"Who knows?" Donatti continued. "I'm betting that in the future, your mom will conceive a kid from someone else and you'll have a sister or a brother. Even more so, unlike me, you'll probably have your own children."

"You know that I'm commonly called your son—"

"Me? I got no one. I got no mom. I got no dad. I got no brothers and no sisters and no grandparents. Both my parents were only children, so I have no aunts, uncles, cousins. I have no known blood relationships except you.

"If I found out that you weren't mine, that your mother had cheated on me and fucked some other guy while I was penned up, I'd say adios and eat a gun. To me, it's better to die than to live out life as an extinct species."

MARGE KNOCKED ON the open door sash, then walked into Decker's office. "From what the dealers say, it's a 2004 Honda Civic. Same car that Garth drives."

Decker pointed to the seat across from his desk. "We've already got a BOLO on it in California. Call up Vegas Metropolitan and ask them for help. Tell them it might be part of a crime scene."

"Already done." Marge sat down.

"Were they cooperative?"

"Not too bad. I think that Detective Silver would take us more seriously if we went down in person. I've talked to Oliver. We'd like to drive down and hunt around over the weekend."

"Fine with me. I'd go with you except that my whole family is in town and I've got to go to Adrianna Blanc's memorial service tomorrow."

"Pete, if you want, we can drive down later and I can go to the service. I know how you feel about working on Shabbos. And how often do you have all your kids in one place?"

"Thanks for the offer, but I have to go. If I don't show up, Kathy Blanc will be pissed at me, and she's pissed enough as is. It's at eleven o'clock. I'll have plenty of time with my family in the afternoon. Besides I've got this irrational scintilla of hope that maybe Garth or Mandy will show."

"Delusions make life worth living."

"I can get you money for airplane tickets to Vegas if you don't want to drive."

"Thanks, but we both decided that driving will probably not only be less of a hassle but will probably take less time. Plus we won't have to rent a car. We'll save our gas and hotel receipts for reimbursement."

"Fair enough. Where is Scott?"

"He's still at St. Tim's trying to track down someone who might have seen Mandy or Garth at the emergency vehicle dock. He's talked to some of the EMTs who were on shift that Monday. The guys and gals he talked to said they were too busy concentrating on what they were doing to notice a few strays."

"Good to know that EMTs take their jobs seriously."

"Good for society, bad for us." Marge stretched. "I'll go make that call to Lonnie Silver at Vegas Metropolitan. Also, I have some information on the Beretta you gave me yesterday." When he looked blank, she said, "The one from Hannah's mugging?"

"Oh, right. Stolen of course."

"Of course. Two years ago. It belonged to . . ." She checked her notes. "Dr. Ray Olson of Pacific Palisades. We're running it through ballistics. I'll let you know if we get some hits."

"It would be nice if something positive came out of it."

"How's Hannah doing?"

"She seems okay." He shook his head. "What a terrible thing to go through. I should have been more sympathetic to her."

"Why don't you bring her some flowers. That's always a crowd-pleaser. There's a florist a few blocks away. I'll pick up something sweet like sunflowers."

"What would I do without you?"

"Don't even go there." Marge laughed. "By the way, Chuck Tinsley called. He wants his jewelry back."

His brain cells finally sparked. "Marge, where'd you find the jewelry?"

"Where?"

"Yeah, where in his apartment. Was it in plain sight?"

"I think it was in his underwear drawer."

"In a bag or what?"

Marge thought. "Yeah, they were in a paper lunch bag."

"And you itemized them?"

"Of course."

"And you gloved up when you sorted through them?"

"Absolutely. Didn't want to ruin any DNA if one of the pieces was from Adrianna."

Decker nodded. "Tell Tinsley we misplaced the pieces but we have a list of the items. If the stuff is permanently lost, we'll replace them for cash value. And at the current price of gold, he shouldn't complain."

"Are the pieces lost?"

Reaching into his desk drawer, he pulled out the paper evidence bag with the jewelry. "Look for yourself."

"What's up, Pete?"

"When did Tinsley's mother die?"

"I have no idea."

"Why would a guy like Tinsley keep his mother's jewelry? Some of these pieces look valuable. There's a big gold bracelet studded with rubies and there's a necklace pendant—an *R* made out of diamonds. Those could bring in some bucks. Does Tinsley look like the sentimental type to you?"

"You think he's a thief?"

"Something's not right."

"I'll have Wanda do an inventory cross-check with burglary. I'll also find out when Tinsley's mother died."

"Good idea. And while you're at it, find out Mama Tinsley's first name."

CHAPTER FORTY

WITH THE BOYS out of the house and Hannah rarely home, Decker had forgotten how cramped twenty-six hundred square feet could be. Rina liked euphemisms, referring to the situation as "compact" or "cozy." She was making last-minute adjustments on her Shabbos *tichel*—her special Sabbath scarf. In accordance with Jewish law, married women covered their hair. The one she had chosen was silk shantung interwoven with lamé threads. Her face was barely showing signs of age: laugh lines at the corner of the eyes, a wrinkle or two on her forehead. She still had some years to go before fifty, making her a filly in Decker's book.

"How much time do I have before Shabbos starts?" he asked her.

"About fifteen minutes." Rina applied a pale pink gloss to her lips. There was a pause. "It's nice to have everyone here together."

"It's terrific," Decker said. "The boys look good."

Rina's eyes got misty. "I don't see them too often. They're men."

"That they are. It was really generous of them to take the time out to come here."

"It was a special occasion."

"I suppose it was a convenient excuse. At least sixty is good for something."

"It's a celebration of life." Rina looked in the mirror. "Which is passing by at record speed. It's just lovely having everyone here."

"It is. And you know what's even lovelier?" He kissed the top of her head. "They're going back in a few days."

He thought Rina would admonish him. Instead she said, "I know what you mean: six strapping adults taking up space. Seven if you count Gabe. And he's eating here, so I guess we have to count him. I think I cooked enough, but I might have forgotten how much men eat."

"I'll take last," Decker said.

"No, you're the birthday boy," Rina said. "You take first. I made lamb. It's not only your favorite, but it's Yonkie's favorite, too. The boy is downright gleeful."

"Lamb as in rack of lamb?"

"Yes."

"Yikes. How many racks did you make?"

"When you french the bone, it doesn't leave all that much meat. So I needed a lot."

Decker made a face. "How much did all that cost?"

"You don't want to know." Rina stood on tiptoes and kissed his cheek. "You might as well eat it. I can't take it back. I also roasted an entire turkey. There will be enough for tomorrow and then some. I know you love sliced cold turkey sandwiches."

"I probably won't be home in time for lunch tomorrow."

Rina paused. "Probably or definitely."

"Adrianna Blanc's memorial service is at eleven. I'll try to be home by two."

"Don't rush, Peter. We'll wait for you." She slipped on her shoes. "Poor parents. What a brutal crime. What was she? Like Cindy's age?"

"A little older than Sammy. There's no good age for murder, but it really hurts when they're that young. Only thing sadder is children." He was quiet, then shook it off. "What's for dessert tonight?"

"If we were sticking to tradition, I would have baked you a cake. Instead, I baked pies."

"Good call. I love pies."

"Hence my decision. You have your choice of peach, strawberry, and cherry with or without pareve vanilla ice cream and/or pareve whipped cream."

"I have to choose between pies?"

"You may have all three," Rina told him. "It's the prerogative of the birthday boy."

"In that case, I will take all three. I'll probably stuff my face and get sick. You should have just made a salad."

Rina laughed. "My family is together for the first time in ages, and I should make a salad?"

"I have no self-control when it comes to your food."

"If you open the medicine cabinet, you'll note that it's fully stocked with Prevacid, Pepto-Bismol, and Tums. You know my slogan: eat, drink, and take antacids."

THE CHURCH SERVICE lasted forty-five minutes, and at the end, the minister invited anyone who wanted to speak to do so. There were about a hundred people at the gathering, none of them anxious to get up onstage. Finally, Sela Graydon braved the microphone, sobbing her way through a heart-wrenching eulogy of her two best friends. She had aged, with sunken eyes and a pasty complexion. Sela was followed by a woman named Alicia Martin, who introduced herself as Kathy's best friend. Then another friend took the microphone, followed by another friend, and then another. By the time the service concluded, it was a few minutes past one.

Decker didn't want to intrude on the grieving parents, but it had seemed important to Kathy that he make an appearance. He waited patiently behind a line to offer words of solace and condolences. Kathy, as usual, was dressed in style—a knitted black dress with a gold belt, black pumps, and tortoiseshell sunglasses. She saw Decker hovering in the back and waved him forward. Although he could see her clearly—he stood above most of the mourners—it wasn't easy for a big man to weave through the mass of human flesh. When he finally made it up to the front, Kathy took his extended hand with both of hers.

"Thank you for coming." Kathy's eyes moistened. "The burial is just for family. I hope you understand."

"I do. You need your privacy to say good-bye."

She looked away and dabbed her eyes with a Kleenex. Then she returned her gaze on Decker's face. "This is Pandora Hurst." She was referring to a woman on her right. "Crystal's mother."

Decker offered his hand, which she took. "I'm so sorry for your loss, Ms. Hurst." The woman looked him over with pale, dry eyes: long nose, thin lips, and a ghostly complexion. She remained silent.

Kathy said, "Will you excuse me for a moment?"

"Of course," Decker answered. "Please offer my condolences to your husband."

"I will." Kathy walked a few steps and collapsed into the arms of Alicia Martin, sobbing on her shoulder.

Decker returned his attention to Pandora Hurst. She wore a long black dress that bordered on a witch's costume. Her gray hair was in a bun secured with several ivory combs. "If there's anything that you need right now, Ms. Hurst, please let me know."

"You can call me Pandy." Her voice was emotionless. "When are you going to release my daughter for burial?"

"I'll check with the people who are in charge."

"I want to take her back to Missouri with me." Pandy crossed her arms. "They gave me all sorts of paperwork to fill out. I was never good at that kind of thing under the best of circumstances."

"I'll see that someone helps you out with the forms."

"When would that be?"

"Whenever you want. Monday would work best for me, but I can do it sooner."

"Are they going to release my daughter on Monday?"

"I don't know. I have to call and find out. Sometimes things slow down over the weekend."

"No one dies on Saturday or Sunday?"

"The staff is usually smaller. If they can, they'll hold things over until Monday."

"So they work at *their* convenience."

"I'll call right away and let you know as soon as they call me back," Decker told her. "Also, I know this is a very hard time, but it might help me with your daughter's case if I could talk to you about Crystal."

"Not now." She shook her head. "Not now."

"How about tomorrow or Monday?"

"I suppose on Monday. You'll help me with the forms?"

"Absolutely."

"I want to take her back to Missouri." Pandy rubbed her arms. "She never liked Missouri, you know."

"I didn't know."

"Well, then . . . there you have it."

"I thought you raised Crystal in L.A."

"I did. I moved out here for my husband. Then he left me five years later to chase young men. I was either stupid or in denial when I married Jack. When he came out to me, I told him no hard feelings. But I think it was hard on Crystal."

"Divorce usually is."

"That and finding out your father's gay." She shrugged. "After Jack and I split up, I took Crystal back to Missouri to visit my folks. I wanted her to know her grandparents. She just hated it. She complained about the heat, she complained about the bugs, she complained about the humidity, she complained about the camp I sent her to, she complained about the kids. When I moved back, she was flabbergasted. Why would I want to live in a swamp with a bunch of hicks? I tried to explain to her that I missed my family. That as I got older, I wanted to be around people who cared about me."

"I understand," Decker said.

"You may understand, but she sure didn't. But that was Crystal. She never really got the concept of intimacy and relationships. Everyone she met was her best friend."

THE DRIVE TO Vegas on the I-15 was a direct shot: around 270 miles that should have taken about four hours had they not stopped at one of Oliver's favorite diners. The place was noted for cheap prices, big portions, and clean bathrooms—the trifecta of the open road. Scott decided to treat himself to a cheeseburger and fries, while Marge selected a tuna melt. Both had apple pie for dessert.

They rolled onto the Strip around two in the afternoon. Not a cloud sat in the sky and the mercury danced around eighty-five. As they tooled down Las Vegas Boulevard going north, the sun was fierce, reflecting off the Four Seasons onto the gold glass walls of Mandalay Bay, the glare following them as they drove down the Strip. The gigantic hotels did little to shade the heat since they arose straight up like monoliths, their verticality even more pronounced because they had been erected in the middle of the Mojave Desert. Oliver had booked a small but serviceable motel off the Strip. The lobby was a brightly lit atrium that held coffee-shop tables, a reception desk, and a bank of slot machines that beeped and flashed even when no one was playing them.

After checking into their respective rooms and unpacking, Marge plopped down onto the bed and called Detective Lonnie Silver on her cell. "Sergeant Dunn here."

"Welcome to Vegas. How was traffic?"

"Not bad at all. Weather is accommodating."

"Yeah, it's beautiful outside. Way too nice to be bogged down in homicides."

Marge said, "Any news at all on Garth Hammerling?"

"I haven't found him or the woman. But something interesting came through the wire about an hour ago. It's good that you came down."

"That sounds ominous."

"Interesting, not ominous. Not yet. I'm right in the middle of fleshing out a lead on another homicide we're working on. How about we meet in a couple of hours?"

"Tell me where."

Silver asked Marge where she was staying. "I'll come to you, give you a call when I arrive. There's a coffee shop in the lobby. We can talk there."

He hung up. A moment later, Oliver knocked on the door between their adjoining rooms. Marge got up and opened it.

"We have a meeting in a couple of hours. He hasn't located Garth Hammerling, but he was glad we came down. Something interesting just came through the wire."

"What does that mean?"

"I don't know, but I suppose we'll find out soon enough." She checked her watch. "We've got some time. Weather's perfect. I think I'll take a dip in the pool."

"Have fun."

"What are you going to do?"

"I've been sitting for the last five hours. It's beautiful outside. I think I'll take a walk around. See what's happening in town."

"You know what's happening in town, Oliver. Gambling, gambling, and more gambling. How much money did you bring to flush down the toilet?"

"Since when did you become so judgmental?"

"I don't care if people gamble. I just don't want my friend and partner to lose his shirt." She held out her hand. "Give me half. You'll thank me later, after the gambling rush has died down and your pockets are empty."

Oliver thought about it. Then he peeled off five one-hundred-dollar bills and stuffed them in her palm. "I don't know why I'm doing this."

"Maybe because I'm right."

Oliver grumbled. "I'll be back in an hour. I'm going to play the tables. The ante is cheaper in the daytime. I've got this new system I want to try out. And by the way, I don't intend to lose."

"No one ever does, Scott. That's why the masses keep piling in and the hotels keep getting bigger."

OUT OF HABIT, Decker turned on his cell phone after he left the memorial service for Adrianna Blanc, and as always, there were messages. He figured he might as well clear them so he could eat lunch and enjoy his family in peace. Dinner last night was noisy and opinionated, with the younger set talking a mile a minute. There were times when he felt as if he were at a tennis match with his head moving back and forth to catch the flow of conversation. But the energy was great. He enjoyed it because he knew it was temporary. By Monday, he'd have his semiquiet house back to himself.

There were two messages on his voice mail.

Number one: *Hi, Loo, it's Wanda. I'm sorry to disturb you on your Sabbath, but something's come up that you'd want to know about. Give me a call as soon as you can.*

Number two: *Hi, Lieutenant, it's Gabe Whitman. Detective Bontemps left a message on your home machine and is trying to get hold of you. She says it's important. Rina said that you should go to the station house and not worry about lunch. She'll eat with you whenever you come back. I was elected to call you since I'm not Jewish. It's nice to be good for something.*

Although Gabe's humor made Decker smile, the contents of his message made him sigh inwardly. He turned the car around and headed for work.

CHAPTER FORTY-ONE

AS SOON AS Decker walked into the station house, Wanda Bontemps got up from her desk, a stack of papers tucked under her arm. Decker gave her a wave and grabbed a cup of coffee from the communal pot. He unlocked the office door, turned on the light, and offered Wanda a seat. She wore a long-sleeved lime green shirt over black pants, and rubber-soled shoes. Gold hoops adorned her ears, and her long nails were painted medium brown, matching her skin tone.

Decker was still in his black suit and uncomfortable loafers. He had taken off the tie in the car and elected to remove his jacket and hang it over his chair.

"How was the service?" Wanda asked Decker.

"Sad. Kathy Blanc introduced me to Crystal Larabee's mother."

"How'd that go?"

"Sad. Her name is Pandora Hurst and she's coming to the station house on Monday. She's been living apart from her daughter for a while, but there's always something new to learn." Decker leaned back in his chair. "So what's up?"

Wanda took the papers from under her arm and laid a colored jpeg on Decker's desk. "Look familiar?"

Decker was staring at a yellow-gold diamond-crusted *R* on a gold chain; it sat around the neck of a girl with shoulder-length dark hair and brown eyes that gazed off to the side. The photograph was a torso shot and the girl was in a dark boatneck sweater against a sage green background. "High school senior picture?"

"Yes."

"Who was she?"

Using past tense, Wanda noted. "Roxanne Holly—a twenty-six-year-old bank teller who was murdered by strangulation. Her mother gave the detectives this picture of her because it showed the necklace clearly. Roxanne wore it all the time, but it was missing when they found the body."

"How long ago was this?"

"Three-plus years."

"Where was the homicide?"

"Oxnard. I looked up the case when this came through. She went out drinking and never came back. Her body was discovered a day later by a homeless man named Burt Barney, a chronic alcoholic, who died a year ago from cirrhosis of the liver. He had always been the primary suspect, but police had never amassed enough evidence to charge him with the crime. There was no shortage of suspicious characters. It's an agricultural city, but it's pretty big—around two hundred thousand people."

"A big city and parts of it are very tough. Lots of migrants, lots of day laborers."

"Lot of construction people who probably like to go out drinking . . . like our friend Mr. Tinsley."

Decker studied the picture. "How'd you get hold of this?"

"I ran through statewide homicides linked with jewelry. This popped out."

"Did anyone find out the name of Tinsley's mother?"

"I did. It was Julia."

"Interesting. Have you contacted Oxnard PD?"

"Not yet. I wanted to talk to you first. I can do that right now, if you want."

"Right now, what I want is an increased watch on Tinsley."

"Done. Sanford and Wainwright are on him."

"Good." He drummed the table. "Okay. Playing devil's advocate for the defense, I would say that there must be hundreds of necklaces out there like this one. Just because Tinsley has the jewelry doesn't mean he killed anyone."

"But it makes him a liar since Julia doesn't start with an *R*."

"It's also possible that Tinsley's just a thief. He stole a necklace that looks like the one Roxanne wore. He could be a fence."

"If he's a fence, why is the necklace still in his possession and he's still holding on to eight pieces of jewelry?" Wanda licked her lips. "I'm not locked into anything, but we'd have to be idiots not to consider that these are trophies."

"We could bring Tinsley in. And we could question him." Decker's head was spinning. "But it would be hard to *hold* him on something."

"What about the marijuana you found in his apartment?"

"That's a misdemeanor possession. He's out in an hour. When I say 'hold him,' I mean *hold* him. He gave us a buccal swab. Let's get a DNA profile. Is this the only piece that you found on the computer?"

"So far, yes."

"All right." He thought a moment. "Has Tinsley lived in the area all his life?"

"I have him paying taxes in California for the last ten years."

"So look at all unsolved strangulations in the region. Call up the detectives on the open cases you find and ask if there was any missing jewelry associated with any of the victims. Since this one was found in Ventura County, direct the search up and down from L.A. If we find that Tinsley has another piece of jewelry that's linked to another murder victim, we'll talk to the D.A. and I'm betting that would be enough for us to hold him for a while. Tinsley could explain away one necklace as a coincidence. But it would be hard for him to explain away two."

"Do you want me to call up Oxnard?"

"Yeah. Ask them if we can get the file and a DNA profile of the victim. Tell them we're investigating a strangulation—a hanging specifically—and we're going up and down the coast. Don't tell them about the necklace yet. I want to keep a tight lid on this."

Wanda wrote down his instructions. "You know the business card that Marge and Oliver found in his apartment? That could have been the trophy."

"Maybe." Decker tried to organize his thoughts. "Let's send the necklace to the techs. If Tinsley yanked it off Roxanne's neck, he could have broken her skin and there may be blood on it. Also, let's swab the chain for DNA. The neck area is a prime sweat location. Skin cells slough especially in the heat and Oxnard can get very hot in the summer. If, by luck, the victim's DNA happened to be on the jewelry, Chuck would have some major explaining to do."

"I'M IN THE lobby."

Silver's voice. He had called just as Marge was toweling off her chlorine-saturated hair. "Be right down."

"See you then."

Marge checked her watch. It was close to five. She knocked on the door that joined her room with Oliver's. "You there?"

She heard muffled footsteps and then the door opened. There was a wide smile on Scott's face. "I'm here."

"Silver's downstairs, waiting for us." She regarded her partner's face. "You won?"

Oliver stuffed a wad of money in her hand. "In keeping with what we did before, this is half of it."

Marge fanned the bills. "There's over a thousand dollars."

"One thousand two hundred seventy-eight, to be exact. How about dinner tonight, Ms. Dunn? I'm nothing if not a gentleman."

"Sure." Her smile was genuine. "Good for you, Scott. If I keep what you gave me, even if you spend the rest, you'll still leave with a profit in your pocket."

"Too late. I blew it all."

She laughed. "On what?"

"Two premium tickets to Cirque du Soleil's *O* and a new pair of Gucci loafers. Plus, we are going out to dinner and it's all on the house." He pointed to himself.

"Thank you, my man. Let's go see what Detective Silver has to say about Garth Hammerling."

"Probably something good."

"I like your unexpected optimism, Scott. Stay that way."

"Sweetheart, the way I'm feeling, I could turn Detective Silver into Detective Gold."

THE ONLY PATRONS of the motel coffee shop were two middle-aged men dressed similarly in short-sleeved white shirts, dark slacks, and loafers. The men were average build and weight, with one having slightly more hair than the other. Marge waved at the men and they waved back. Introductions were made all around.

Lonnie Silver was the bald one in blue pants. He was drinking coffee and working on a piece of apple pie. Rodney Major had a bald dome surrounded by gray, curly hair. He was in the brown pants, wolfing down a chicken sandwich with fries. As soon as Marge and Oliver sat down, a stick-thin waitress with bouffant gray hair came over and brought them menus. Marge and Oliver ordered coffee and a blueberry-bran muffin at Silver's suggestion.

Small talk ensued.

How was the ride over? How long you here for? Gonna see any shows? Go to Delucci's for dinner. All the chitchat allowed them time to finish the food and get down to the real reason for meeting. Silver spoke up first.

"When you called a couple of days ago and asked about Garth Hammerling, frankly, I didn't give it much thought. Lots of people run to Vegas to reinvent themselves. Maybe your guy is here and maybe he isn't. One thing's for certain. It's gonna be hard to find him. You want to hide, you come to Vegas, although if this guy is truly a bad guy, we can track him down. Problem is, you don't know if he's a bad guy, so it's hard to justify resources on a maybe."

Marge said, "That's why we came down in person. We figured we could do some legwork. All we're asking for is a little direction."

"We can help you there." Major spoke up.

"Yeah, way more than I thought," Silver said.

"I like the sound of that," Oliver said.

Silver said, "See, once I get a bug in me, it's hard to let go. So I get to thinking on how to look for this guy. We obviously can't go knocking on hotel-room doors in the big casinos. And I can't ask them for guest rosters. We're dealing with thousands of people and you don't even know if this Hammerling guy actually did anything. Besides, I know all the homicides on the Strip and none of them sound like your guy."

"What kind of homicides?" Marge asked.

"Bar fights, gang fights, robberies gone bad," Silver told them. "And none of them took place in the big hotels. The big hotels police their clientele way better than we could do with our budget. They got the money, the motivation, and the manpower to keep the crap out. I'm not saying it couldn't happen . . . it has happened . . . but the hotel corridors are patrolled pretty well. Someone screaming or someone dragging a body out of one of the rooms would likely be noticed."

"They got more security cameras than the Pentagon," Rodney Major said. "They got people looking at them night and day. Funny stuff goes on between individuals behind closed doors, they don't bother with that. But if the powers that be see any hint of a prostitution ring or drugs being dealt out of a room, they're gonna bust it up with their own people and keep it quiet. The owners aren't gangsters anymore, haven't been for forty years. They're savvy businessmen. Why would they want the illegal crap when they can rake in billions doing legal gaming?"

"I'm not saying that Garth ran a prostitution ring," Marge said. "But we did hear from his friends that he goes to Vegas all the time, spending way more money on women than on gambling."

Silver said, "You told me that, and it got me thinking."

"He's dangerous when he's thinking," Major said.

"Yeah, you can smell the wood burning." Silver smiled. "Anyway, a lot of the young bucks who spend a lot of time here, like every weekend or every other weekend, they just don't have the wallet size to stay at the big hotels. If they want cheap action, they go outside the Strip. From my standpoint, that's easier to handle because the scale is smaller."

Marge and Oliver nodded. Silver had a story to tell and there was no sense rushing him through it.

"So I start making calls," Silver said. "I call up downtown . . . that's still pretty glitzy and hard to get a fix on. No luck there. I call up Boulder City. They've got a small strip there, but I still don't get anywhere with that. Then I start on the smaller places like the one you're staying at. These establishments don't have a posse of soldiers behind them like the big hotels do. They rely on police. I have a good relationship with them. I still don't get any hits, but I can't let go. I get that way sometimes . . . that I'm moving in the right direction, like this invisible hand pushing me. After so many years in homicide, you learn to respect your intuition."

Marge said, "Absolutely."

The waitress came by and refilled coffee cups. When she was gone, Silver said, "So I'm thinking about where else could this guy have stayed. And then I think of North Las Vegas and my buddy Rodney."

Major said, "If you want cheaper thrills, North L.V. is your kind of place."

"North Las Vegas isn't handled by Las Vegas Metro."

"Yeah, we're like the dot over the big *I* of the Las Vegas Strip. We've got our own casinos and they're cheaper than the Strip in Vegas proper."

"I call up Rodney and ask him if he can talk to his people and find out if Garth Hammerling was a regular in one of his places."

"I make my calls and guess what?" Major said. "He used to be a regular in a couple of my places."

Marge and Oliver exchanged glances. Oliver said, "You found him?"

"No, I'd tell you that right away," Major said. "There are about seven major places on my strip and they tell me he hasn't been around for a while."

"Yeah, I was pretty disappointed about that," Silver said. "So I ask Rodney, you know, I'm not familiar with all of your homicides like I am with my district. Have you had any unusual recent murders . . . like a hanging?"

Major laughed. "And I say, if we had a hanging, you'd hear about it."

"Yeah, the town's not *that* big. A hanging would make the local news," Silver said.

"A hanging made *our* local news," Marge said. "It's unusual."

"Right," Silver said. "So then I ask Rodney, have you had any recent murders by strangulation? Because hanging is essentially strangulation."

"And I say, not that I can recall."

Marge laughed. They had a real comic thing going.

Major said, "Most of our homicides are from knives, guns, and broken bottles that were smashed over some drunk's head."

Silver said, "So I was about to give up. But then you called and said you were coming down. And then you tell me that Garth might be traveling with a woman named Amanda Kowalski."

"That's what we're thinking," Oliver said. "Because she's missing, too."

"Right," Silver answered. "So I call Rodney back up. Because by now, I found out that Garth likes his district better than mine. So I tell him that Garth might be traveling with a woman. So could he check out any couples traveling together?"

"I told him I'd do that," Major said. "His curiosity has become infectious. So I take the picture of Garth and go around the casinos and hotels and motels ask them about couples with this guy. His name is Garth Hammerling, but he could be going under another name. No luck. I call the smaller motels and ask about couples named Hammerling. No luck with the hotels. Then I think a little. Maybe the guy got into a car accident. I call up HP and ask if any bad accidents went down in the area in the last week. Well, I don't have any luck finding Garth Hammerling. But there was an accident a day ago: a one-car crack-up in the middle of the desert. A couple of boys were dirt-biking and came across the wreck with a body in the driver's seat."

"Oh dear," Marge said. "That's not good."

"It was a miracle they found the car, but that wasn't the biggest miracle. When the HP got there and took a pulse of the body, they found out that the passenger—a woman in her twenties—was still alive."

Silver said, "The poor woman was a wreck. Burns on her lower body, broken bones, but she was breathing on her own."

"Weaving in and out of consciousness," Major said. "She was rushed to the burn unit at Las Vegas Medical Center. She's in a medically induced coma. The coroner's immediate thought is a one-car suicide. But we really don't know squat because she didn't have any ID on her. And she can't talk because she's unconscious."

"What about the car?" Oliver asked.

"It's a Toyota Corolla—older model—'02 or '03. It's a tangle of metal and burned at spots, but it hasn't been gutted by fire. It's at the forensic lab. We haven't been able to get an owner off of the VIN number, if that's what you're asking."

Marge spoke up. "What about burns on her face?"

"As far as I know, it was just her legs. She was wearing her seat belt, so she's got some bruises from the air bag deploying. But she'd be recognizable. Do you know what Amanda Kowalski looks like?"

"We do," Oliver said.

"That's what I thought," Silver said. "So I called up one of the doctors this morning and asked about her. She was still in a coma, although the doctor—her name is Julienne Hara—is optimistic. Then she tells me that the woman had Xanax in her system, enough to cause death. So it's beginning to look like a suicide. She took a fatal dose of Xanax, put her foot on the accelerator, and that was that."

"We think our murder victim was drugged before she was hanged," Marge asked.

"We haven't gotten the complete tox back on her yet," Oliver said. "But she didn't have any defensive wounds. It looks like she was sedated before she was strung up."

"Interesting," Silver said.

"Really interesting," Major said. "Because then the doc tells me a 'by the way.' I like 'by the ways.' It's always something juicy. The doc says that someone might have attempted to strangle her. Since some of the swelling went down, she might have seen bruises around the neck. She said we should come over and take a look. She said, if it wasn't an accident or it wasn't a suicide, it could have been an attempted homicide."

"Meaning the police should be involved," Silver said. "We figured you should come with us to the hospital. Ordinarily I'd ask you to send a picture of Kowalski. But you're here and she's bruised up. You could make a better ID."

"It may not be anything," Major said. "But if so, you can stick around and ask your own questions about Hammerling. I can help you out with the local hotels here."

"Hey, even if this doesn't pan out, we owe you one," Marge said.

"How about Delucci's tonight?" Silver said. "I'm in the mood for Italian and the place is open until one."

"Sounds good," Oliver reached into his pockets and pulled out two tickets. "We were supposed to see O tonight. That's not gonna happen. You want the tickets?"

"O's terrific," Silver said. "Don't miss that."

Major said, "Yeah, you gotta see O."

Silver said, "Do the ID—either yes or no—and then just make the time for it. Your questions will hold for a couple of hours."

Major said, "Yeah, the gal in the hospital isn't going anywhere soon. It's Vegas. You ever notice the casinos don't have clocks? That's because the city never sleeps."

CHAPTER FORTY-TWO

TYPING THE PARAMETERS into the computer—"homicide," "female," "strangulation"—Decker, Wanda, and Lee Wang pulled up a dozen unsolved but currently open cases within the jurisdiction of LAPD. When Wang entered the data into the files of the Cold Case Homicide Unit, the numbers climbed significantly. And that didn't even factor in cases from other nearby police departments: San Fernando, Culver City, Beverly Hills, Oxnard, Ventura, San Bernardino, San Diego, and a slew of other smaller departments up and down the state. There were no shortcuts. Cases had to be reread, lead detectives had to be contacted, questions had to be asked.

Among the things they were hunting when reading the files were: Chuck Tinsley's name as a witness or a suspect, and jewelry associated with the victims. Decker didn't need Sherlock Holmes. He needed detectives like Wanda and Lee who could read for hours and focus on details. It was tedious work, which generally produced more headaches and eyestrain than results.

By five in the afternoon, Decker was ready to pack it in when his cell rang. Restricted number and that made sense. No one he knew well would call him on Saturday. "Decker."

"It's Eliza Slaughter."

"Hey, Detective, how's it going?"

"Nothing big. I just wanted to tell you that the techs went through the car that Donatti rented. We sprayed luminal throughout the car and the trunk and under the carpet in the trunk, in the wheelbases, under the carriage. There's no evidence of blood. The car was cleaned by the rental company, but not immaculately. We picked up a lot of hairs and fibers. We'll check them out to see if any belonged to Terry, but honestly, I don't expect much."

"Okay. What about the Mercedes that was junked?"

"I have nothing on Atik Jains. He may have owned the car, but he doesn't have a California DMV license. I'm checking out-of-state licenses. I put him into the system, but nothing came back. Earlier this afternoon, I went back to the hotel and questioned what's left of the staff. No one saw Terry leave in her car. I don't know what to tell you. Could be her getaway was planned way before Sunday and she could be anywhere."

"That is true."

"I know we haven't tracked down her husband, but without a body, a crime scene, and witnesses, our leads are thinning. It's sounding like either the husband did it or she disappeared on her own."

"I'm beginning to favor the disappearance."

"Why?"

"I spoke to Gabe and he told me something interesting. He once found his mother talking to an Indian doctor—an older man, a visiting cardiologist whose father's a maharaja in India."

"Does that mean he's wealthy?"

"I would think so."

"Do we have a name?"

Decker fudged on this one. "Gabe never knew it."

"Why did the doctor stick in his mind? I'm sure his mother talked to a zillion doctors."

"That's just it. She didn't. All he said was that there was just something about the way the two of them were talking that tweaked his antenna. You know how perceptive kids can be to that kind of thing."

"Did he say anything to his mother?"

"He asked who she was talking to. That's when she told him he was a visiting cardiologist whose father was a maharaja."

"And?"

"That was it."

"You think she was having an affair with this guy?"

"Could be. And if she did run off to India, it sounds like the man is wealthy and well protected. She'd need both to escape her husband."

"So where does that leave us?"

"It's an open case. If she is alive, eventually she'll try to make contact with her son. So from my perspective, we wait."

"Where is the kid?"

"With me."

"Okay."

"Yeah, let's leave it at that." Call waiting beeped in. Marge's number in the window. "I've got a call that I have to take. Keep me posted."

"I will. Bye."

He depressed the button. "What's going on, Sergeant?"

"Sorry to disturb you on Shabbos," she said. "We found Mandy Kowalski."

Decker sat up. "Dead?"

"No, she's alive, but not in good shape. She has burns on fifty percent of her lower body. She's in a medically induced coma."

"That's awful." Decker felt his heartbeat race. "What happened?"

"She was brought into Las Vegas Medical Center as a Jane Doe, the victim of a one-car crack-up in the middle of the Mojave. The original thoughts by the police were suicide because only one car was involved and there was Xanax in her system. After we ID'd her as Mandy Kowalski, we're considering homicide."

"Like someone depressed the accelerator and let her fly?"

"Maybe. She doesn't seem like the type who'd be drag-racing in the desert."

"How'd you find her?"

"I didn't. Las Vegas did all the legwork." She filled him in on the details. "They said they went the extra mile because we went the extra mile and came down."

"Are you sure it's her?"

"Positive. Her lower body is burned but her face survived relatively unscathed. She has bruises from the air bag deploying, but definitely recognizable."

"If it was a homicide, wonder why the killer didn't disable the air bag?"

"Maybe he's not so clever. And of course, it could have been a suicide. Maybe she witnessed something that she couldn't live with—like the murder of her friend."

"Could be."

"Mandy's mom, Frieda Kowalski, is a widow. She lives in Mar Vista. I don't have the address, but I do have the phone number." She gave it to Decker. "Could you send someone out to let her know what's going on?"

"I'll do it. I'll want to talk to her anyway. What about Garth Hammerling?"

"No bead on him yet, but we haven't even started talking to people. I do have a list of hotels that he frequented. Scott and I will talk to as many people as we can. Mostly he stayed in North Las Vegas."

"I thought one of his friends said he stayed on the Strip."

"He could have stayed there, too. Maybe he likes to hop around."

"When is Mandy due to come out of her coma?"

"They'll start waking her up tomorrow, but even once she's conscious, she'll be doped up for a while. The doctor says she'll be out of it for days. Plus, there's a good chance that she won't remember much about the accident or what led up to it."

"Will she remember Adrianna's murder if she was there?"

"I have no idea how the accident will affect her memory. I'm not a doctor, but even the doctors don't know. We're all hoping against odds that she'll be able to shed some light on Garth Hammerling."

"Do we know for certain that she was traveling with Garth?"

"No, we don't know that. But we found Mandy and she's alive and maybe she can tell us something."

"Amen to that," Decker said. "I'll talk to Mrs. Kowalski. When she hears the news, she's going to want to go to Vegas. I'll find out her schedule. You pick her up and take her to the hospital."

"I can do that."

"You and Scott work over the weekend. I'll come relieve you on Monday. I want to be there when Mandy is able to speak."

"Come down whenever you want. No shortage of hotels." Marge thought a moment, then said, "Why are you working today? Isn't it your birthday?"

"Actually, it's tomorrow. And I'm going out with the entire brood to dinner. But I'll probably be working during the day." Decker brought her up-to-date on Roxanne Holly's murder and her missing necklace. "There must be more than one necklace identical to the diamond *R*, so we're looking through other strangulation cases, trying to find another piece of jewelry in Tinsley's stash associated with a murder."

Marge said, "So Tinsley's right back up at the top of the list."

"Absolutely. He was with Adrianna and Crystal at Garage on Sunday night. We're still trying to get a timeline on him for the day of the murder."

"Where is he now?"

"He's walking around under twenty-four-hour surveillance. Kathy Blanc wasn't happy about that. If she knew what we've discovered, she'd probably kill me. I'll call you if I find anything else on Tinsley."

"Likewise on Garth. Oh, I forgot to tell you. My phone will be off between eight and ten tonight. We're going to see *O*."

"The Cirque du Soleil show?"

"Yeah. Silver and Major, the cops helping us on the case, insisted we go to the show. Then we're going out for dinner. But I'll turn my phone back on when we eat."

"Glad you've scheduled in R and R," Decker said flatly.

"I suspect, Rabbi, that you're being sarcastic," Marge said. "But being the naive dolt that I am, I'm going to take your words at face value and simply say thank you."

TALKING TO FRIEDA Kowalski got him out of the office and that was the only positive aspect of the visit. When he broke the news about Mandy, her mother gasped and put her hand to her chest, stumbling backward. Decker helped her with her balance, sat her down on her floral sofa, and brought her a glass of water, which she sipped. No tears in her eyes, but her freckled pale face had turned ashen. He waited until she could find her voice. The woman appeared to be in her early fifties, with a nest of teased red hair and dark eyes. She was a pixie; she probably weighed about a hundred pounds.

When she finally did talk, she asked for details. Decker told her what he knew, minimizing any gore, then helped her book a flight to Las Vegas.

"Sergeant Dunn from my team is over there now." Decker gave her Marge's cell phone number. "She'll pick you up at the airport and take you to the hospital."

"Thank you," she whispered.

"I know this is a hard time, but anything you can tell me about Mandy would be helpful: her hobbies, her friends, her boyfriends. Did she drink? Did she take drugs?"

The woman looked stunned. "I rarely heard from her except for a dutiful call once every two weeks on Sunday. Tomorrow was the day." She looked at Decker's face. "It's not that we didn't get along. We're just so . . . different. I was a single mom. I might not have done the best of jobs, but I took care of her."

"I'm sure you did."

She nodded. Still no tears. "The truth is, even as a little girl, Mandy kept to herself. She was very secretive with friends and certainly about boyfriends."

"So there were boyfriends?" Decker asked.

Frieda thought about that. "She went to the prom with a boy. I think that was the first and only time I ever saw her with the opposite sex."

"Do you remember his name?"

"Not at all."

"Could it be Garth Hammerling?"

"Garth who?" Frieda was kneading her hands together.

"He's a tech that works at St. Tim's—where Mandy works." Still no response. "Garth is missing. We'd like to talk to him."

"What does he have to do with Mandy?"

"We're not sure if he has anything to do with her. Right now, he's just a person of interest."

"I can't help you. I didn't know much about Mandy when she lived with me. I certainly don't know much about her since she left me . . . left home."

"Does she have a father?"

"Everyone has a father. He took off when she was six months old. I don't know where he is and he never sent me any child support. I think there was a time when she wanted to find him. I told her to go ahead, but leave me out of it."

"What's his name?"

"James Kowalski. I don't know if she found him, and if she did, I don't know what he told her. I figured if she ever did catch up with him, she should draw her own conclusions." She stood up. "I should get some rest. It's going to be a long day tomorrow. Thank you for being so helpful."

"If you need anything, please call me." Decker gave her his card.

"Is she in a lot of pain?"

"I'm sure they'll do everything possible to keep her comfortable. I'll be coming into Las Vegas on Monday to talk to Mandy. I'll probably see you at the hospital."

"When are you coming?"

"Sometime Monday afternoon."

"We may miss each other." When Decker didn't answer, she said,

"Mandy never liked when I . . . crowded her. Besides, I've already missed a lot of work with my own medical issues." She opened the door. "Thank you again. Bye now."

Still no tears in her eyes. She'd probably cried them dry a long time ago.

CHAPTER FORTY-THREE

BY NINE IN the evening, Decker's eyes were buggy from staring at the computer and he was reaching diminishing returns. When Rina knocked on his office doorjamb, holding a big paper bag, he was grateful for the interruption. He rolled his chair away from his desk and stood.

"Hey there." He gave her a kiss. "What brings you into the bowels of purgatory?"

"How about seeking wit and charm?"

"Then you definitely came to the wrong place."

Rina sat down in front of her husband's desk. "We had lots of leftovers from lunch. I thought you might be hungry."

"I should be. All I had today was coffee and this morning's cereal." He looked at the clock and sat down across from her. "I'm sorry I never made it home. It's especially disappointing because the boys came all the way out to see me. Are they upset?"

"Not at all." Rina sat down. "We had a fine time, actually."

Decker was heartened and disheartened at the same time. "Yeah, everyone's so used to my being gone it's like 'what's the big deal?'"

"It's not that we didn't *miss* you. We toasted you in absentia." She opened the bag and handed him a wrapped package. "Turkey sandwich on rye with horseradish and mustard. You will make it for dinner tomorrow, right? It's in your honor."

"Absolutely."

"Then we're all fine. What are you working on that's consuming so much time?"

"We found something suspicious at Chuck Tinsley's apartment. We're trying to find more suspicious evidence. I've been on the computer for the last four hours, but haven't turned up anything useful. It's a wonderful machine, don't get me wrong, but it's always open for business."

He unwrapped the sandwich and took a bite.

"Wow, this is good." Another bite. "Eating is making me hungry."

"Sometimes it works that way."

"Delicious. Have anything to drink?"

Rina reached into the bag. "Coke Zero or Dr Pepper?"

"How about both?" His wife handed him the cans and he popped open the Dr Pepper. "On the plus side of the day, Marge and Scott also found a missing woman in a hospital in Las Vegas. A one-car crack-up. She's in guarded condition, but alive."

"You don't mean Terry, do you?"

"No, not Terry." Decker gulped down half the can of soda. "She's still missing. I don't reckon I'll find her any time soon. It comes down to this. Either Donatti did it and since he's a pro, we'll probably never find her, or she's in India with a billion other people. I'm certainly not going to look for her there. I already told the West L.A. detective on the case that if Terry is alive—and I think she is—she'll eventually make contact with her son."

Rina nodded.

"How's Gabe doing? Did he eat with the family?"

"Where else is he supposed to eat?"

"Just wondering how he's integrating himself. Are you getting him a piano?"

"Renting him one. He's paying for it with money his father gave him. It makes him feel like he's pulling his weight."

"Is it a problem for you?" Decker countered. "Keeping the kid?"

"Honestly, I'm okay with it. What about you? You seem to still have doubts."

"Of course I have doubts. There goes retirement and travel."

"Retirement would be very bad for you, and how much travel are you really going to do with your first grandchild on the way?"

"Maybe not so much," Decker admitted. "Cindy'll need her gun to keep me away."

Rina smiled. "That's my guy. So, since you're not going to retire and a world cruise isn't on the immediate horizon, we might as well give the kid a home."

Decker sneered. "As long as he doesn't do drugs, doesn't drink, doesn't smoke, doesn't make a pass at my daughter, and doesn't steal me blind, I suspect it'll be okay."

"You know, it's funny," Rina said. "It's not that I feel exceptionally compassionate. I'm okay with Gabe because he's not a bother. He does his own thing and pops his head out once in a while to get fed." Another pause. "You should hear him play, Peter. It transforms him into something otherworldly. Then he stops and he's fourteen again."

"That's right. He doesn't drive yet. Terrific. That means one of us is going to have to take him to school." Decker thought. "He's not going to want to continue at a Jewish school. What are we going to do with his schooling?"

"He's got lessons arranged with this hotshot piano teacher in the middle of the school week at USC. He practices six hours plus a day. We should consider homeschooling him. Not you or me personally, but someone. He's bright. I'm sure he could finish the high school curriculum in a year."

"Yeah, he said something about going to Juilliard next year."

"He also told me that he'd like to go to a regular university like Harvard. Because of his talent, he has lots of options. If his mother is alive, she's going to eventually try to reunite with him. He's not only exceptional, but he is her only child."

Her only child. Decker raised an eyebrow. "I suppose we can deal with him living with us for a year or so—as long as he isn't a psycho like his dad."

"Time will tell. So far, I don't see any indication," Rina told him. "Who's the missing woman in the hospital?"

"She's a nurse—a former friend of Adrianna Blanc. Both of them worked at St. Tim's. She disappeared a few days ago. While looking for Adrianna's boyfriend in Las Vegas, Marge and Scott talked to a couple of cops who told them about a Jane Doe in the hospital. A one-car collision in the middle of nowhere could be an accident, suicide, or possible homicide. Whatever it was, she knows way more than she told us in our original interviews." He finished his sandwich. "That went down well."

"You want dessert?"

"No . . . well, what do you have?"

"Apple pie."

"Leave it with me. I may succumb." He checked his watch. "I'll try to be home in an hour."

"That means two hours. So I'll see you around eleven, okay?"

"Fair enough."

Rina stood up. "I saw Wanda and Lee at their desks when I came in. There's also half a chocolate cake in the bag for you to share."

"No wonder everyone loves you. No one cooks or bakes like you. You're the candy man—the candy woman."

"That's me." Rina grinned. "I spread good cheer and calories wherever I go."

THE HIT CAME a little before eleven on Wanda's computer: an opal ring surrounded by diamond chips set into gold plate. The piece was a high school graduation gift to Erin Greenfield from her grandparents.

The young woman had just turned twenty-two when she was found in a vacant lot, strangled to death in Oceanside, California, two years ago. According to her roommate, she had gone out the night before and didn't come home. When she didn't show up for work the next day, the search was on. Her nude body was found that afternoon in a commercial flower field.

With gloved hands, Decker regarded the ring from Chuck Tinsley's stash, comparing it to the badly reproduced photograph printed off the computer.

Wanda said, "I counted the amount of diamonds surrounding the opal. Both the ring and the photograph have nine. What struck me was the gold plate. I examined the ring for a fourteen-K stamp and I didn't find any. The stones look like real stones but not set into real gold. I would think that would be unusual."

"I don't know a thing about jewelry," Decker said. "I would like a better image of the ring on Erin's finger."

"I'll see what Lee can do," Wanda said. "I looked up Oceanside. A nice little beach resort, but it's near Camp Pendleton. Lower-than-average murder rate but slightly higher rape and assault rates. Quite a few bars catering to the Marines. A single guy wouldn't stick out that much."

"He might blend into the crowds even more if he was wearing a uniform."

"Good point. Uniforms also inspire trust."

"Doesn't Oxnard have a naval base?" Decker made a few clicks of the computer. "Yeah, here's something—NBVC—Naval Base Ventura County. There's also a Point Mugu Naval Air Weapons Station. There's a Port Hueneme Naval Base. When you looked up Tinsley, did you happen to know if he served in the military?"

"Don't remember. I'll see what I can do on the computer, but it's too late to call any agency."

"Do what you can." With the ring still on his desk, Decker dialed up Marge's cell. She answered on the third ring. "How was O?"

"Beautiful."

"Are you actually working or still digesting linguine?"

"We are actually working. And you?"

"We found another piece of jewelry in Tinsley's stash that might be a match to a strangled woman."

"That's big."

"It could be. When you searched his apartment, did you or Scott find any kind of a military uniform?"

"I didn't. Let me ask Scott. I got to find him first. Let me call you back."

"Right." As he waited, he phoned his wife. "Can I have an hour extension? I have a lead I really need to look into."

"It's fine. I'm up anyway, talking to the kids. We're having a lot of laughs."

"And probably most of them at my expense."

"When do you realistically think you'll be home?"

"In an hour."

"I'll see you at midnight. Don't turn into a vampire."

"I'd love to be a vampire. They suck blood; I wallow in it."

OVER THE PHONE, Oliver said, "You know, there was something in his closet—more like a Halloween costume than an actual uniform. It was army green with bars sewed onto the shoulders, but made out of cheap material. Clearly not standard army issue."

Decker explained the circumstances.

"It wasn't a real uniform, but I suppose if you're in a dark bar, trying to make time with a drunken chick, she might not know the difference."

"I'd love to bring it for testing," Decker said. "Can we find a way to get back into his apartment? He's probably not going to give us access again."

Oliver said, "I'll ask Marge and maybe we can come up with something. You know, Tinsley wasn't wearing a uniform when he was talking to Adrianna."

"That's because macho army man doesn't really fly with the super-edgy L.A. chicks," Decker said. "Although Adrianna's murder fits the profile of the two unsolved cases, there are some differences. The two other bodies were found in wide-open spaces—one in a lot and one in a flower field. Not in the middle of a residential area, hanging from a cable cord."

"So what are you thinking?" Oliver asked.

"Tinsley is definitely a candidate," Decker said. "But Garth is still missing and Mandy's in the hospital. I'm wondering if Garth and Mandy murdered Adrianna and Tinsley had the bad luck to find her body. Or it wasn't luck at all. Garth set Tinsley up because he found his business card in her pocket."

"So how does Tinsley's jewelry figure in?" Oliver asked.

"Maybe we accidentally stumbled on a serial killer."

"If Tinsley's a serial killer, why did he agree to let us search his house?"

"Because we were looking for things associated with Adrianna's death and he didn't kill Adrianna. You know how these guys are. One mold. They're arrogant as hell. Who bagged the jewelry from Tinsley's apartment?"

"Marge did."

"Good move. Wanda and Lee Wang just came into the room. I'll keep you updated, and you do the same." Decker hung up and pointed to the chairs. Wanda had rolled up the sleeves on her lime green shirt. Wang was dressed in a black polo shirt and khakis.

After they sat down, Wang said, "Almost all military information sites are off-limits without a password. It's better to wait until morning to start delving into this."

"It'll keep as long as we have an eye on Tinsley. Besides, I'm not positive he actually served." Decker recapped his conversation with Scott.

"Okay," Wanda said. "So he could be a pretender like the Boston Strangler."

"Albert DeSalvo," Decker said.

"What's the next step, Rabbi?"

"As it stands, we can't say for certain that the jewelry belonged to the victims."

Wang said, "So we're not pulling Tinsley in?"

"Not yet." Decker smoothed his mustache. "We'll keep him in the crosshairs and hope that the techs can get DNA evidence from the pieces. If we can get DNA that matches up with Erin Greenfield and Roxanne Holly, then we can put their jewelry in Chuck Tinsley's hands. That'll take a couple of weeks. While we're waiting, one of you should call up Oxnard and the other take Oceanside to get the details of the murders." He exhaled loudly. "I'm exhausted. Let's all go home and get some sleep."

Wang rubbed his eyes. "Sounds like a good idea. Want me to put the jewelry back with evidence?"

"That would be great, Lee. Thanks."

"So you really think you just stumbled across a serial killer?"

"Maybe yes, maybe no."

"That would be weird," Wanda said. "In literature, that's called poetic justice."

"In Jewish law it's called *Midah kenneged midah*."

"What does that mean?"

" 'Manner begets manner.' What goes around comes around."

CHAPTER FORTY-FOUR

TWELVE STRETCHED TO one in the morning. At half past, Decker pulled into his driveway, spent and depressed. It was his official birthday and his sons had flown in from the East Coast just to be with him, and not only had he disappeared for most of the day, he had done it on Shabbos. He wondered why he kept at it. Crime was never going to vanish. There would always be that "just one more case" sitting on his shoulder. But then there was the flip side. Why stop working, taking with you years of experience, to putter around, trying to figure out how to make yourself useful when you're already doing something useful in the first place?

He quietly closed the car door. Rina insisted that she'd wait up, he insisted that she should not. Who knew who'd be the winner of that little bet? As he approached his front door, he saw a big manila envelope sitting on the welcome mat. He picked it up. There was handwriting on the front—a name but not his.

Gabriel Whitman.

What was *that* about?

He placed the key into his door, opened it, and stepped inside.

Rina was up and wrapped in a cotton robe. She had her fingers on her lips, and then she pointed to the couch. Gabe was sprawled out, one foot dangling over the sofa, sleeping soundly. The two of them went into the kitchen. Decker showed his wife the envelope. "This was on the front porch."

"It wasn't there when I came back from the station house," Rina said. "I would have noticed it. Would you like some coffee or tea?"

"I'd love some herbal tea. I'll make it. I'm antsy. I need something to do." He filled the kettle with water and placed it on the stove. Then he opened the tape end of the envelope with a knife but didn't look inside. "If it concerns Terry, Gabe would want to know. I need to wake him up."

"Okay. Want me to wait here?"

"No, I want you to come with me for moral support."

Together they went back into the living room. Decker sat down on the edge of the sofa but even that didn't rouse the teen. Finally, he placed a hand on his shoulder and gently shook him. "Gabe." Again: "Gabe, it's Lieutenant Decker."

The boy bolted upward. "I'm up, I'm up." He rubbed his eyes and groped for his glasses on the end table. When he found them, he put them on. "I'm up."

"I need to turn on the light," Decker said.

"Go ahead." Gabe squinted with the illumination. "What's going on?"

Decker handed him the envelope. "Sorry to wake you, but this was sitting on my front door when I came in tonight. I thought you'd want to look at it. I opened it up but I didn't take anything out of it."

"What is it?"

"I don't know."

Gabe slowly removed the papers. There were a stack of them—something about power of attorney to his dad for his businesses. But then he saw the handwritten letter. His hands started shaking as he read the note.

My dearest love, Gabriel:

By the time you read this, I should be far away, unreachable and safe. There are no words to tell you what happened and why I did this, but I can only say that I truly felt I had no other option. Do not try to look for me, and if Lieutenant Decker is searching for me, please tell him not to waste his valuable time trying to locate me. I am gone and do not want to be found.

With all my heart, I apologize for what I've put you through, not only for the past week, but for the past fourteen years. You are so special and so exceptional, you deserve only good things and happiness. I hope I have left you in a safe place, away from the conflict that your crazy parent had foisted upon you. You may not understand my motivation now, but I hope sometime in the future, when you are an adult, I can reconcile with you and explain what I have done and why I did it.

I believe that living with the Deckers is something that your father might approve of, and hence, leave you there. I have cast an incredible responsibility onto the Deckers and I hope they don't despise me for it, but they are the only people to whom I could entrust my jewel. Please try not to hate me, as I'm sure you do. Just know that I love you more than anyone in the world and my heart aches to write this and to be separated from you. But I feel that circumstances have placed you with a family that will finally give you a shot at the life you deserve. Even a selfish fool like your mother realizes that you merit your chance to shine.

I know that you are in contact with your father. I know that you will call him as soon as you receive this packet. Please give him these papers. They will allow him to run his business until our sordid mess can be straightened out.

With all my love,
Mom

Wordlessly and with trembling fingers, he handed the letter to Decker. Then he lay back on the couch, his glasses still perched on his nose, staring at the ceiling. When Decker finished the letter, he handed it to Rina. Then he said, "I'd like to have a handwriting expert go over it with some of your mother's known samples—"

"It's her handwriting."

"Just in case. You never know."

"It's her handwriting. More than that, it sounds like her. That's one of her favorite expressions—'sordid mess.'"

"Your father probably knows her favorite expressions as well."

"It's not my father writing for my mother. It's my mother. Face facts. She dumped me and she dumped me here. Sorry."

Rina sat beside him. "I already rented the piano, so you might as well stay."

Gabe gave her the briefest of smiles, but then his eyes watered up. "Thanks." He rubbed them furiously. "I should tell my dad about this. Chris called me yesterday. I would have told you sooner, but you haven't been home."

The tea-kettle started to whistle. Rina stood up. "I'll get it. Do you want some tea, Gabe?"

"I'm okay, thanks."

"Take some anyway."

Gabe nodded. After Rina left the room, he said, "I'm glad my mom's alive, but fuck her. Fuck the both of them. They don't give a shit about me. Why should I give a shit about them? The only thing I feel bad about is you being stuck with me." He looked at Decker with moist eyes. "I really can go live with my aunt."

"You're staying here. We'll work out the details. How's your hand, by the way?"

"It's fine. This, too, shall pass."

Decker didn't talk, giving the kid a few moments of silence to start digesting the horrific breach of trust. Then he said, "When you spoke to your dad, did he tell you anything?"

"Nothing you didn't already know. He knew about Atik Jains. He asked me about other men she was with. I told him I didn't know anything, which is the truth. I mean, I don't know that she ran off with an Indian doctor."

Decker was quiet.

"I bet my dad's in India right now chasing her down. Well, good luck to the both of them. Neither one is my concern anymore."

"Why do you think that Chris is in India?"

"I dunno. I just get the feeling that he's out of the country and knows where she is." He looked at Decker. "I mean, do you think she's in India?"

"I don't know, Gabe. That's the God's honest truth."

"You know, all she had to do was tell me: 'Gabe, I'm going to India. Don't try to find me. I'll write to you when I can.' All she had to do was let me know."

"Maybe she was afraid you'd tell your father."

"I wouldn't tell my dad. Plus, he'd find out anyway. She didn't have to be so dramatic."

Rina came in with tea. "Here you go, Gabe."

"Thank you." He sipped the cup. "Thanks. It feels good."

"You're welcome." Her eyes darted between Gabe and Decker. "It's late. I think I'll go to bed."

Decker gave her a peck on the cheek. "I'll be in soon."

Rina mussed her husband's hair. "If you say so."

When she was gone, Decker said, "Gabe, I don't know where your mother is and I don't know why she didn't tell you. But I think whatever it was, she probably didn't want you to know until you're a bit older."

Gabe looked angry. "Why do you say that?"

"Because maybe if you find out why she left at this stage of your life, you wouldn't be able to forgive her."

"Wouldn't forgive her?" Gabe laughed angrily. "What'd she do? Rob a bank? Rape a goat?" When Decker was quiet, he said, "Seriously, what could she have done that I wouldn't forgive her? Cheat on my dad? Leave my dad? She should have done that a long time ago."

Decker licked his lips. "Do you remember what your parents fought about when your dad beat her?"

"Of course. Chris thought she had an abortion instead of my aunt."

"What would you say if I told you that your aunt didn't have an abortion? That the papers weren't your aunt's papers but your mother's papers."

"No way." Gabe shook his head. "Mom was seriously pro-life. She'd never get an abortion."

"I think you're right. If your mother ever got pregnant, she'd keep the baby. The problem was . . . and what your dad suspected all along . . . that if she got pregnant, it probably wasn't going to be his child."

Gabe was quiet.

Decker said, "I think the paper your dad saw wasn't an abortion receipt, but an OB checkup billed as an abortion for your mom's own protection. When your dad hit the roof, your mom calmed him down by saying it was for your aunt and not herself. And she even registered under your aunt's name. But for whatever reason, she kept her own middle name. If your dad would have checked—and maybe he did—he would have found out pretty easily that your aunt's middle name is not Anne, like your mom said, but Nicole."

Gabe looked sick. "Do you know this for certain? That she was pregnant?"

"No, I don't. It's all conjecture. But I did notice when I saw your mom that she was wearing loose clothing and her face was a little rounder. Like you said, she would have never had an abortion. She could hide a lot of things from your father, but she couldn't hide a pregnancy. And she couldn't pretend the child was Chris's when the actual father was a dark-complexioned Indian. She had a decision to make and she chose the life of her baby."

Gabe started to speak but couldn't. Tears pooled in his eyes, then ran down his cheeks. Then he whispered, "Dump one, get another. She wanted a new start without Chris but also without me."

"She would have taken you if she could have."

"So why the hell didn't she?" He was enraged.

"Gabe, your father might let your mom go, but he'd never let her take you. You're his only child. The only thing he has in this world."

"Chris doesn't give a shit about me!" Gabe sputtered out. "You know he doesn't even believe I'm his biological son. And after what you told me, maybe I'm not."

Decker looked at him intensely. "You can't seriously believe that."

"It's what Chris thinks and maybe he's right."

"Your dad was wrong about a lot of things. Chris never thought your mom would have the gumption to fall in love with another man. He never thought she'd have the nerve to leave him. He never thought she could hide from him, and he never thought she could lie. He was wrong about all those things and he's dead wrong if he thinks you're not his kid. The Terry back then is not the Terry now. Your mother was completely smitten with him. Back then, in her eyes, your father walked on water. For better or worse, Gabe, you are Chris Donatti's son."

THE NEXT MORNING, and with Gabe's permission, Decker went through the papers Terry had sent him. He wasn't interested in the power-of-attorney documents, just who prepared them and who notarized them. He wanted verification that Terry's signature was from Terry and not some proxy. At eight A.M., he called up the law firm and spoke to the answering service, telling them that he had an emergency situation and needed to talk to Justin Keeler right away. He got the call back two hours later.

"This is Justin Keeler."

"Lieutenant Peter Decker with the LAPD. I've been working on a missing persons case for the last week. Her name is Terry McLaughlin—"

"You can stop right there, Lieutenant. You must know that I'm going to invoke attorney–client privilege."

"So she is your client."

"I can't tell you that."

"I'm in possession of some papers given to her son, Gabriel Whitman, that she supposedly signed and notarized. They were prepared by you and notarized by a Carin Wilson. Does she work for you?"

"Carin Wilson works for us. How'd you get the papers?"

"Gabriel is living with me and my family. The envelope was on our doorstep last night. The papers didn't come in the mail. Someone delivered them by hand. All I want is verification that Terry McLaughlin signed these papers and it's not a forgery."

"If they're notarized by Carin Wilson, I guarantee you that the papers are not a forgery. She's fifty-two and has been a notary for twenty years."

Decker paused. "I'm still a little squirrelly about this, Mr. Keeler. I'm sure someone with Terry's ID signed the papers. I want to make sure that the woman you think is Terry is the real Terry McLaughlin. Can I come down and show you a picture of her?"

"To say yes or no would also be a violation of attorney–client privilege. How about if you mail me the picture. If there's a problem, I'll let you know."

"Mr. Keeler, all I'm trying to do is give the poor kid some information about his missing mother. Terry's husband is a violent guy, capable of murder. I just want to make sure she's not dead."

Keeler sighed. "She's not dead." A pause. "I shouldn't have told you that. But if her son read the letter in the packet, he already knows that she's alive."

"So Terry McLaughlin really did write the letter?"

"I can't tell you any more."

"You obviously know the contents of the letter."

"I can't tell you any more. Just read the damn letter."

"I did."

"So respect her damn wishes. And if you care about her, get her violent husband off her back." Keeler hung up the phone.

Decker massaged his temples just as Gabe walked into the kitchen. He was still wearing pajamas. His face was pale and pasty and his forehead, despite the cream he had slathered on it, was still broken out. "Bad time?"

"Not at all." Decker smiled forcefully. "Have a seat. What's up?"

"I just wanted to let you know that I called up my father's main secretary. She told me that he wasn't there, but she'd let him know that I called. So I guess we wait."

"Okay. Just tell me when he calls back. I'd still like to talk to him."

"I will." He scratched his forehead. "So . . . is Chris like off the hook? I mean if Mom's alive, he obviously didn't kill her." Gabe scratched his forehead again and it began to bleed. He mopped it up with a napkin. "God, I must look like garbage."

"You're a good-looking guy and you come by your looks honestly. You could, however, use a little more rest. I'm going to work and Rina and the kids are going to visit their grandparents in an hour. You'll have the house all to yourself. Put on some shades and go to sleep. How's your hand?"

"I'll be okay for my first lesson with Nicholas Mark. That's all I care about."

Decker drummed the table. "I just got off the phone with the attorney who prepared your mother's papers. He couldn't tell me anything because of attorney–client privileges, but between the lines, I think those papers are legit. I think your mother wrote the letter. So in answer to your question, Chris is off the hook. And you can tell him I said so. I'd still like to talk to him, find out what he knows. I'm a curious guy."

Gabe looked away. "I mean, this isn't like a trap or anything."

"No, Gabe, it isn't a trap. I believe your mother is alive and is probably in India."

"Her and a billion other people. A billion and one counting her new baby. But, hell, I'm not bitter." Gabe stood up. "Thank you, Lieutenant, for taking me in—you and Rina. I really, really mean that. I promise you I'll be an easy tenant."

"You're not paying rent, so you're not a tenant. You're just a mooch."

Gabe smiled, but it was laced with sadness. "I'll be a good mooch."

"You call my wife Rina. You can call me Peter."

"Thank you, but I prefer to call you lieutenant, if you don't mind."

"No, I don't mind." Decker shrugged. "Can I ask why?"

"I still don't feel comfortable calling you by your first name. Also . . . this is going to sound a little wacky. But calling you lieutenant. I don't know . . . the sound of the word. It makes me feel safe."

CHAPTER FORTY-FIVE

WHEN DECKER WALKED into the station house at eleven, Wanda Bontemps snapped her fingers to get his attention. She was on the phone and pointed to an unoccupied extension. Decker punched in the lit button and quietly picked up the receiver.

"I don't understand how you could lose a whole bag of jewelry!"

It was Chuck Tinsley. Decker took up a notepad. Wanda said, "I'm sure it's not lost, Mr. Tinsley, just misplaced. I just want to assure you that all the pieces have been photographed and described. If we have to replace them, you'll get full monetary compensation."

Decker gave her the thumbs-up. She smiled.

Tinsley said, "I don't give a rat's ass about compensation. The items were sentimental. They belonged to my late mother. How are you going to replace heirlooms, huh?"

"I'm sure they'll turn up—"

"You know, I never had much respect for the police. And you know why? You guys have no respect for the people you serve. I mean, you treated me like a criminal and meanwhile the real jackass who murdered Adrianna is still out there. You guys are a bunch of clowns, you know that?"

"I know you must be frustrated, Mr. Tinsley—"

"What'd you do with my stuff? Take it home for yourself?"

"I will let you know when we find the pieces."

"Yeah, right. In the meantime, give me cash."

"Do you want cash compensation for the items?"

"No, I want the items. But if you can't find them, give me money. And don't take all year to cut me the check, if you know what I'm saying."

"I will put in for the money right now, if you want."

There was a silence over the phone. "Then what happens if you find the pieces?"

"I give them back to you and you return the cash."

"You should give me the pieces and the cash for all the aggravation you're putting me through." He hung up abruptly.

Wanda and Decker put down their respective receivers. She said, "He wants his trophies back."

"He certainly seems attached to them."

"Put to rest the lie that he's just a thief. If that was the case, he would have been thrilled about the cash. He wouldn't have to bother with a fence." She stood up and stretched. "I've been here for a couple of hours. Need a change of scenery. I'm going to bring the jewelry over to the lab myself. Want an update?"

"Always."

Wanda flipped through her notepad. "Spoke to Oxnard PD. I'm going up tomorrow to look at the file and compare notes. The primary detective isn't working today. I left a message. It would be great if Tinsley's name showed up in the Oxnard file."

"One can wish. What about Oceanside PD?"

"Lee Wang has contacted them. You'll have to talk to him about that. We've also been looking for a military connection with Tinsley. That hasn't happened yet."

Decker said, "The way Tinsley's acting, we're not going to get near his place."

Wanda said, "I'm also wondering if somewhere in the back of his mind, that maybe he suspects that we're onto him."

"Keep in close touch with his surveillance team."

"Of course, but . . . I'm also wondering . . . I don't know, Loo. That if the jewelry was his trophies, now that he thinks the pieces are lost, maybe he might try to find a few new ones to replace the old ones?"

"Let's put another team on him."

"Yeah, that would make me feel a little better."

OVER THE PHONE, Marge said, "Frieda Kowalski is with her in the ICU. She's holding her hand."

"How's she faring?"

"Mandy or Frieda?"

"Both."

"Mandy's going to make it, but she'll be in a lot of pain. She has burns on her lower half, a broken arm, and a bruised and swollen face from the air bag."

"And the mother?"

"She's a bit . . . reserved. She told me first thing she and Mandy weren't close. I mean I'm not that close to my mom, either. But if I were suffering from burns and broken bones, I don't think those words would be the first thing out of her mouth."

"She sounded numb when I spoke to her. Could be shock. Are they bringing Mandy out of sedation today?"

"Yes, but it's a slow process. She'll be out of it for days. The doc told us not to expect anything before tomorrow afternoon. Maybe by the time you get here, she'll be awake enough to babble."

"How's the search for Garth?"

"On that front, we made some progress. After pulling an all-nighter, we came away with several IDs that yes, he and Mandy were here in North Las Vegas. They were IDed by a waitress at Gold—one from the restaurant of the New Lodge Inn. That was on . . . hold on . . . on Wednesday night. And also on Thursday . . . let me check . . . they were spotted at the bar of the Gin and Rose

Pub and Casino. But . . . neither Scott nor I have found where they actually stayed. We'll keep at it."

"What car was Mandy driving when she had the accident?"

"She owns a 2002 Corolla."

"If Mandy cracked up her car, what is Garth driving now?"

"Don't know. He does have his own car, but I don't know where it is."

"Did they drive out separately?"

"Maybe. Or maybe he sold his car for cash. We'll hunt around."

"Okay. When was the last time Garth stayed in a hotel in North Las Vegas?"

"A long time ago . . . seven months maybe."

"But he's been to Vegas many times in the last seven months."

"I know, and that got Scott and me thinking. Maybe he rented an apartment or a condo. The monthly rent would be less than what the hotels would charge for a nightly rate if he went often enough."

Decker thought about that. "If Garth has his own place, he could be keeping his car down there."

"A car or a dirt bike maybe," Marge said. "Oliver and I would like to stay for another day. It'll take some time to check out apartment buildings, and honestly, we'd like to be there when Mandy starts talking."

"I can get you another day. I'll meet you there tomorrow either midmorning or in the afternoon. I need to clear a few things first."

"I'll pick you up from the airport."

"Nah, don't waste time. I'll take a cab."

"Sounds good." Marge smiled, although he couldn't see it. "If you want, Pete, we can all drive back together. Been a while since I've taken a road trip."

"I don't think I could survive four and a half hours in a confined space with Scott Oliver."

"It's not so bad. He does snore in his sleep, but at least he doesn't smell."

Decker laughed and hung up. It was almost two in the afternoon. Dinner was scheduled on the early side since the boys had red-eyes to take them back east. He decided to make a break for it and got halfway out the door when his desk phone rang. Decker threw up his hands and took the call.

Wanda said, "You got a minute?"

"Of course. What's up?"

"When the tech was examining the necklace for evidence, she found a tiny hair stuck in the clasp of the diamond *R* necklace. She said that microscopically it looks like one of the fine hairs around the neck that are so pesky when you put on jewelry."

"Wow. That's a stroke of fortune."

"Even better is that the hair has a root."

Decker felt his heart start to beat. "So we can get DNA off of it?"

"Possibly. Lucky for us that Tinsley was storing his jewels in a paper bag. Less likely to deteriorate."

"How fast can you get a turnaround, Wanda?"

"I put a rush on it. Soonest would be a few weeks."

"Tinsley gave us a buccal swab. Let's get it to the lab ASAP. If the hair belonged to Tinsley's mother, his DNA profile should be related to the hair's DNA. If not, we catch him in his lie. And if it is Roxanne's hair, what is he doing with her necklace? Did the primary on her case ever call you back?"

"Yes. His name is Ronald Beckwith. We're meeting tomorrow at ten."

"Call Beckwith back. Find out if Roxanne's DNA is on file."

"I did. It is."

"Also ask him if they picked up any foreign evidence that could generate a DNA profile of the perpetrator."

"Got it."

"Let's get on the stick with this. Tinsley is still out there and it's making me more and more nervous."

Once again, Decker hung up the phone. He rubbed his eyes, and then rubbed his neck. He was tired, but it was turning out to be a productive couple of days. Garth had been spotted with Mandy, so they were on the right track with Vegas. And Mandy, although in guarded condition, was still alive. Eventually she'd be coherent enough to talk.

And how lucky was it to have a hair with its root in the clasp of the necklace. A DNA profile would solve a lot of problems.

Things seemed to be coming together, but there were still a lot of fundamental unanswered questions.

Where was Garth?

What were the events that led up to Adrianna Blanc's death?

What were the events that led up to Crystal Larabee's death?

Were the two women's deaths related?

And was Chuck Tinsley a serial murderer?

So many crimes, so little time.

WIPING THE SWEAT from her face, Marge looked up at the glaring sky. The desert sun that had been so perfect yesterday when she was lazing around the pool had now turned into the enemy as they schlepped around in ninety-degree heat from apartment building to apartment building.

And, man, Clark County sure had a lot of apartment buildings.

It had apartment buildings, condos, housing developments, and seedy hotels with long-term rentals available. They had been going at it for hours before the two of them finally broke for dinner. The only thing open at five in the afternoon was an all-day storefront that advertised the best barbecue in town. They didn't lie. The ribs were messy and spicy, just the way Marge liked them. When she was done, she cleaned up with a premoistened towelette.

"That was good."

Oliver was still munching on a bone. "Damn good."

"What do we have left?"

"If you insist on working, we've got a slew of condo developments within a few miles."

"How many is a slew?"

"Five developments and each one has about thirty condos. Two of them have a management company on-site."

"So let's start with them." Marge signaled the waitress for the check.

"We're looking for something that might not exist." Oliver paused. "Kind of like love."

The waitress came over—a stout lady with gray teased hair. "No dessert for you?"

"Wish we could," Oliver told her. "We've got to go back to work."

"Working on Sundays? What do you do?"

"Cops." Oliver produced his badge. "For real."

She stared at the shield without examining it too closely. "In that case, I'll wrap up a couple of doughnuts to go. On the house."

"Thank you very much, but we can pay for it," Marge said.

"I wouldn't hear of it."

Oliver gushed with sincerity. "That's so kind of you."

"You betcha." She gently touched Oliver's shoulder and left.

Marge said, "What some people won't do for a free doughnut."

"We offered to pay. She refused."

"*I* offered to pay," Marge corrected.

"Yeah, you're the good cop, I'm the bad cop. We've already established that. Can we move on, please?"

Marge smiled. "Make sure she puts in a maple cruller."

"I have to make sure?"

"You're the lady-killer, Scott. If you ask nicely, I bet she'll put in two."

CHAPTER FORTY-SIX

THE GROUP HAD just polished off the chocolate cake—with half the restaurant joining in for an off-key happy birthday—and was sipping coffee when Cindy clinked her spoon against a water glass to get the table's attention. Decker regarded his first daughter and all of his children with love and pride. The time had gone by too quickly. Even Cindy's pregnancy seemed to be flying by. Over the past week, she had popped.

She said, "As the eldest of the Decker clan, I thought I'd go first." She and Koby exchanged smiles. "I'll make this quick because I know that the boys have a plane to catch. As you all know, Koby and I are expecting."

"Here, here," Decker said, hitting the table. His skin felt moist and he was in a jolly mood, no doubt from the wine. But it was his birthday and a big one. Rina insisted that she'd drive home so he should enjoy himself.

Jacob said, "And it's about time, I might add."

"You should talk."

"What do you mean? I'm not married."

"Exactly. Your brother got with the plan. What's your excuse?"

"I'm psychologically immature."

"It hasn't stopped me," Decker joined in.

Rina said, "Can Cindy finish, please?"

"Thank you, Rina," Cindy said. "We have some other news."

Decker perked up. "About what?"

"About the baby, of course."

The table went silent.

Cindy said, "Last month when Koby and I went to the OB for my routine visit, the OB picked up two heartbeats."

"Oh no!" Jacob said. "Your baby has two hearts?"

This time she slugged his shoulder. "I'm having twins."

The group erupted into a hearty round of mazel tovs. "What a wonderful birthday present!" Decker exclaimed. "You may have taken your time, my girl, but you sure did it right."

"Thank you, Daddy."

"I am so happy!" Decker exclaimed.

"I'm glad." Cindy laughed. Dad was a little tipsy. "We have other news. Do you want to tell them, Koby?"

"You do all the work. You tell them."

Okay." Cindy paused. "The babies are sharing the same placenta."

Rina said, "So they're identical twins."

"Oh my God, that's crazy!" Hannah exclaimed.

"Crazy?" Decker asked.

"Crazy as in so neat!"

"Neat for you, but expensive for me," Koby said.

"You save money on the hospital stay," Sammy pointed out. "A two-for-one."

Koby said, "That is a good point."

"Are you doing natural childbirth?" Hannah asked. "Can I be your doula?"

"We'll find some role for you, Hannah banana," Cindy said.

"Are there twins in your family?" Rina asked her husband.

"Not in my family," Decker answered.

"My uncles are identical twins," Koby said. "Also, I have identical twin cousins."

"So there you go," Decker said.

"Can I finish, please?" Cindy said.

"There's more?" Jacob asked.

"Yes, there's more."

"Are you giving birth to the family dog as well?"

Cindy said, "I'm trying to say something important."

"Uh-oh," Koby said. "Do not aggravate her. That can be very bad."

"Okay, I'm all ears," Jacob said.

"As long as you're not all mouth."

"Ooo . . . dis!"

"Will you let her finish!" Rina ordered.

"Please?" Cindy patted Jake's shoulder.

"I'll shut up."

"Okay. Here we go. Koby's custom, unlike Ashkenazi custom, is to name the baby after the grandparents even if they're still alive . . . especially if they're still alive. Which I think is much nicer. Anyway, the first boy or girl is named after the paternal parents. The second boy or girl is named after the maternal parents. So if it's two girls, the names will be Rachel after Koby's mother, and Judith, which is my mom's Hebrew name. But . . . if it's two boys, the babies' names will be Aaron after Koby's dad and Akiva." She looked at her father. "After someone we all know and love."

Decker grinned. "So I guess I'm rooting for boys."

Cindy said, "Okay. So here's the deal. Because I'm over thirty-five, we did a CVS a few weeks ago, which will show any genetic problems. And since there is only one placenta, we only did one procedure, so that worked well. I'm happy to report that everything looks great."

"And you know the sex," Sammy said.

"Yes, we do," Cindy told him. "At first we decided to keep it to ourselves, but since we're all here and that doesn't happen too often, I thought it befitting the guest of honor to let him know that yes, we are having boys. So, Daddy, you have the honor of being named after without dying. Happy birthday." She leaned over and kissed Decker on the cheek. He reciprocated by giving both Cindy and Koby kisses and hugs.

Koby said, "You are truly a prince of a father-in-law and you're very handy with tools. That is the best."

"Speech, speech," Jacob said.

All eyes went to Decker. He felt his throat get tight. "I'm . . . thrilled." He suddenly became overwhelmed and his eyes moistened. "I'm at a loss for words."

"Would you like me to speak on your behalf?" Jacob said.

"Sure, wise guy." Decker wiped his eyes. "Go ahead."

"Actually, I don't want to speak for you, I want to speak to you." He looked at Sammy. "Can we go out of order?"

"Just make it quick or we'll run out of time."

"Okay, okay." Jake rubbed his hands together. "I just want to say thank you for being my father. And unlike most fathers, you had a choice of whether or not to adopt Sam and me—"

"He didn't have a *choice*," Rina blurted out. Everyone laughed. "I would have killed him if he said no."

"Can I wax a little sentimental, please?"

"You, sentimental?" Cindy said.

"Yes, even I have a soft side. What I was trying to say is that you came into our lives—Sammy and me—after a rather dicey situation. I remember . . . when I first met you . . . thinking that you had to be the coolest guy on earth."

"Boy, did that change quickly," Decker said.

"Actually, it didn't." Jacob bit his lip. "You're still way up there in the cool factor. Just thanks for being there for me and Sammy and Eema at a difficult time." He looked at Cindy. "Your kids are going to be major cool. They've got coolness on both sides."

"Thank you, Yonkie."

"Happy birthday, Dad." He turned to Sammy. "Is that quick enough?"

"Unusually abbreviated." Sammy paused. "I guess it's my turn. So here goes. You might not have had a choice to adopt us, Dad, but you certainly had a choice to be a father or not. And you aced that test. You're not our biological father, but in terms of blood, sweat, and tears, you certainly are our real father. And even though I'm Ashkenaz, I'm really happy that you're getting one of your grandsons named after you. It's a well-deserved honor."

Decker kissed his sons and hugged them fiercely. "Thank you, boys."

Everyone looked at Hannah. "Well, with this red hair, I guess there's no doubt that you are my biological father. I'm really excited about going to Israel and college, but I know I'll miss you and Eema soooo much. You'd better visit me a lot." Her eyes got wet and tears ran down her cheeks. "I love you so much, Abba. Happy birthday."

Decker gave her a bear hug. "I love you, Pumpkin. And we will visit you a lot."

"Well, I guess I'm next," Rina said. "I'll keep it brief as well. I don't want to get all mushy in front of the kids, but I've been so blessed to spend these years married to someone I love so much. I've also been blessed to have this wonderful family, including my beautiful stepdaughter and son-in-law and my grandsons-to-be. Peter, I love you very much and I'm counting on many more years for us to be together. I've always been very proud of you. You are simply the best."

The group aahed as Rina gave Decker a big smooch on his lips.

"Speech from the guest of honor," Jacob said.

"Nah, you said it all for me," Decker said. "I'm just basking."

Jacob nudged Gabe, who'd been quiet throughout the evening. "Now's your chance to talk or forever hold your peace."

Gabe turned red and Decker said, "Yonkie, leave him alone."

"Sorry," Jacob said. "You know I'm just teasing you."

Gabe said, "Actually, maybe I should say something." The table grew quiet. The boy pushed his glasses up on his nose. "First, congratulations to Cindy and Koby."

"Thank you," Cindy said.

"You're welcome," Gabe said. "Second, happy birthday to the lieutenant."

"Thank you very much," Decker said.

"Sure," Gabe said. "And third . . ." The boy tried to collect his thoughts. Ideas were buzzing around his brain like a chain saw. "Like . . . like even though my parents aren't religious . . . at all." *Between the two of them, they've probably broken every commandment in the book.* "Uh . . . anyway, I don't know why, but they sent me to Catholic school." A pause. "And we were taught stuff by the nuns . . . although I don't remember that much of what they said."

"That's okay," Hannah said. "We don't listen to the rabbis."

"Hannah!" Rina said.

"Just getting a little empathy going."

Gabe smiled. "Anyway, the big thing . . . the nuns' big thing . . . was all about being good and nice and turning the other cheek and things like that. But when I think about it, it wasn't really about being good and nice. It was about being obedient. Being good . . . what does it mean? It's like an abstract concept. Anyway, *I* didn't really know what goodness meant because . . . frankly, my parents are a little crazy . . . they're a lot crazy. And being good doesn't seem to be a high priority for either one of them. Maybe my mom a little." He shrugged. "Anyway, after staying with the Loo and Rina—and Hannah—for even this brief time, I'm getting an understanding what good might be. Honestly, Lieutenant and Rina and all of you, thanks for being so nice."

No one spoke.

Again Gabe turned red. "That's it."

"Thank you, Gabe." Decker saluted him. "I'll make you the same deal that I did with all of my kids. You put up with me and I'll put up with you."

"I can handle that," Gabe said.

Sammy checked his watch. It was almost nine. They had an eleven o'clock back to New York. "I hate to leave, but we need to get going. We have to return the car."

At that moment, Decker's cell buzzed in his pocket. He let it go once, then took it out and glanced at the window. It was Marge's number. That sobered him up quickly. "This might be important. Do you mind if I take this?"

"Some things never change," Rina said.

"Very funny." Decker punched the green button. "Hi. Can I call you back in ten?"

"Okay. But do call back."

His curiosity got the better of him. "What's up?"

"Sorry to interrupt your dinner, Pete, but we have a situation here."

"A *situation*?" Decker said.

"This doesn't sound promising," Rina said.

"No, it doesn't," Decker said. "Marge, I'll call you right back. My boys are leaving for the airport. I want to say a proper good-bye."

"Why don't you hitch a ride with them to the airport?"

"You want me down in Vegas?"

"As in right now."

"You found Garth Hammerling's body?"

"No, Loo, Garth is still MIA. But as far as bodies go . . ." A pause. "Let's just say you might want to see for yourself."

CHAPTER FORTY-SEVEN

AS DECKER WAITED to board his flight to Las Vegas, Marge gave him a recap. Talking like a speed demon, she was breathless. Decker could hear sharp intakes of air as she spoke.

"This is the deal," she said. "Scott and I have been scouring apartment buildings, condo complexes, and housing developments all day. No results, but that's what we expected. We stopped around six, ate dinner, and decided to hit a couple of cheap housing developments nearby. One last shot. This was around seven."

Decker looked at his watch. It was almost eleven. "Okay."

"You've got to picture that we're out in the middle of nowhere. I mean this is the boonies. These particular units abut the desert, and after that, it's miles of empty space. To buy into the development is no money down and small monthly payments. Plus, about two-thirds of the houses have yet to be erected. Scott and I don't see any signs of building going on. We figure it's a perfect place for a loner without a lot of cash."

"I can see where this is heading."

"Yeah, and it's not a good place. Anyway, there's a model home office. By sheer luck, there's a woman inside. This is Sunday, mind you, and there's nothing going on. She tells us that it's late and she's about to lock up. We tell her we just need a few minutes. We ask her about Garth Hammerling. No response. Then Oliver shows her the pictures we have of Garth. Her face lights up, but she's trying to hide it even though she's giving off a tell that a blind man could read."

"A tell like in poker," Decker said.

"Yeah. Exactly. After all, we're in Vegas. Anyway, we press the lady . . . her name is Carlotta Stretch." She spelled it out. "We press Carlotta and she admits someone who *looks* like Garth bought a house in the development about six months ago. How amazing is that?"

"Very amazing."

"Yeah. Exactly. But we got a couple of problems. The guy who bought the house isn't named Garth Hammerling. His name is Richard Hammer. Scott and I call up our buds Lonnie Silver and Rodney Major and ask them what they think. They're good guys. They come right down. Carlotta wants to go home, but we keep stalling. So we all confer and we decide that with Carlotta's ID of Garth, any reasonable person would conclude that Richard Hammer is Garth Hammerling. But we still got a few problems. First, Garth or Richard isn't in default of anything, and second, we don't really have anything on Garth Hammerling except that he's missing under peculiar circumstances."

"So you don't have a good reason to enter the property."

"Yeah. Exactly."

"What about imminent danger?"

"That's what we all came up with. Garth and Mandy went missing roughly at the same time. Mandy nearly died, so Garth may be in trouble. It would be negligent not to check out the house. Silver calls up a judge. He says it's good enough to get into the house and look around as long as we don't trash the place. No opening drawers or anything like that. If we see something in open view, we can go for it. Other than that, we're pretty much hog-tied. It's about eight when we finally went in.

"Everything seems fine. We do see a couple of pictures of Garth, so we know that we're in the right place. We're dying to search the drawers, see if there are any more masked pictures of him and Mandy, but that's clearly off-limits. We shrugged and figured: that was that."

"My flight's starting to board, Margie. I've probably got another ten minutes before I have to go onto the airplane."

"I'll make it as quick as I can. So we're weighing our options. Should we put a police car on the house in case Garth comes back? But then we agree that any idiot would make a tail. There's no place to hide out here. We're still mulling over ideas when I get a call from Frieda Kowalski. I told you they were bringing Mandy out of her medically induced coma this morning, right?"

"Right."

"Okay. So Frieda calls me up, clearly very upset. She starts telling me stuff while we're still at the development, trying to plan our next step. Plus we're under time pressure. Carlotta Stretch wants to lock up and go home."

"What did Frieda tell you?"

"Okay. Here goes. The doctors started bringing Mandy Kowalski out of the coma at around nine in the morning. By early evening—Frieda told me it was around seven—Mandy regains consciousness enough to open her eyes and recognize her mom. She knows she's in bad shape. She's really agitated. Her blood pressure's sky-high, her heart's beating a mile a minute, and she's shaking like she's in the throes of a seizure. The docs thought that they may have brought her out of her sedation too quickly. Or maybe she was feeling intense pain from her burns. Because according to her mom, she was writhing in agony."

"That's horrible."

"Man, I was relieved that I wasn't there to see it." A deep breath over the line. "So Frieda starts asking for pain medication for her daughter, but before they can knock her out again, Mandy starts mumbling words. At first, Frieda couldn't make out anything distinct, but then Mandy kept repeating herself. Finally, Mom thinks she hears the word 'dungeon.'"

"Oh God!"

"Yeah, exactly. Frieda had the presence of mind to repeat the word 'dungeon' back to her daughter. And that really spikes Mandy's blood pressure. The girl becomes super agitated and buzzers start going off. The nurse rushes in, and is about to lace her IV with dope, but thank God for Frieda. She stops the nurse. The nurse and Frieda have words. Frieda wants a doctor to administer the sedation. The nurse gets all insulted and walks out in a huff and the doctor is paged."

"Bravo for Mom."

"You said it, because before the doctor could get to Mandy's IV line, Mom managed to make out a few more words: 'dungeon,' 'house' . . . 'murder.' Then Mandy starts saying over and over: 'the girl, the girl, the girl.' "

"Good Lord!"

"Yeah. Exactly. By this time, the doctor has come in and he's really upset with Frieda. And Frieda is upset with the doctor and the nurse. So everyone is upset with everyone, but finally the doc puts Mandy under, she quiets down, and all is well in Sin City. It's around seven-thirty by now. Frieda is finally calm enough to think. She decides it would be a good idea to call me up and tell me what Mandy said in her delirium. When I picked her up from the airport, I gave her my card, my cell number, and Scott's cell number. She decided to give me a buzz."

"It's amazing she had the presence of mind to call."

"Yes, it is, and not a moment too soon. Because all this is going down just as Carlotta's walking to her car and about to take off. With the words 'dungeon,' 'house,' 'murder,' and 'the girl,' we think we have a very good reason for a second look and maybe a more intense search. Scott runs after Carlotta and we catch her just as she's driving off. Matter of fact, she almost hit him. I can't tell you how frenetic things were."

"I can picture it. Marge, I'm boarding the plane now. I'll have to turn off my cell in a few minutes."

"I'll speed it up. We go back into the house and poke around. At this point, we're trying to find a trapdoor or a dummy wall or something that might indicate a hidden room. We come up empty. We check the garage. Nada. So I'm outside in the back looking around. Now mind you, this isn't a ritzy development."

"Got it."

"All the houses have small properties with low cinder-block walls to divide one house from the next. And you can see into your neighbor's yard if you look over the wall. I'm peeking into the neighbors' yards, figuring that maybe Garth saw us coming and was hiding out in one of the houses. It's like desperation time. Then I happen to notice that the two neighboring properties on either side of Garth's property have cement slab patios. Garth's patio is brick. I'm thinking to myself, 'Why would anyone bother with the upgrade out here?' Then I take a closer look. It's a brick patio, but there isn't any mortar or cement, Pete. It's just bricks laid into sand and the bricks on the right side aren't lying so neat."

"Oh dear."

"Yeah, you can see where I'm going. Since Mandy mentioned something about a girl, a dungeon, and murder, we start throwing off the bricks. Underneath the patio, dug directly into the ground is a . . ." A pause. "Like a bomb shelter. It's made out of cinder blocks with a trapdoor with a padlock on it. Rodney Major shoots it off the metal, we open the trapdoor, and the stench hits us immediately. It's a fucking cesspool down there—pitch-dark and fetid. Silver has a flashlight. I take it and volunteer to go down first. I'm shaking like Jell-O. You know how I feel about dark, confined places."

Decker knew too well. Ever since Marge had rescued a group of children from a cult that used tunnels as escape routes, she's been claustrophobic. "Good job, Dunn."

"Yeah. A pat on the back for me. Because on top of the dungeon being small and black, it really stinks. At this point sheer adrenaline is guiding me. I jump down . . . it's a good eight feet." A large sigh. "I find the girl, Pete. She's nude, wrapped up in plastic garbage bags with a ligature around her neck. By my rough calculations—judging by the time Mandy had been in the hospital—she's been that way for at least two days."

Marge's voice had cracked.

"I take her pulse . . . didn't feel anything. It was cold down there and she felt cold. But not ice-cold. She's not moving, though. I assume she's dead. I mean why should she be alive? Then I shine a light in her eyes. She fucking blinks!"

Decker couldn't talk. How could he?

"She's unconscious but alive. I tear the ligature from her neck. We call the paramedics. They get her out and rush her to the hospital. As of right now, she's in critical condition. We don't know if she'll come out of it. But for the time being, she's still among the living. How do you figure something like that?"

"You don't. Does Mandy know who she is?"

"Mandy's still under sedation. We'll have to wait until it wears off before we can talk to her."

The airplane door was closing. Decker had about thirty seconds. "You mentioned something about a strong stench. Was there anyone else in there besides the girl?"

"There are two other bodies down there in various stages of decomposition. The coroner's investigators have pulled out one body so far. It's bloated and filled with maggots and most of the skin has peeled off. It's gruesome. And that's the best of the two."

"Oh, my word! How long do you think it'll take before they clean the place out?"

"I don't know, Pete. They've still got a corpse to go. After that, they'll get to work on the ossuary. The bodies were sitting atop a pile of bones."

WITH NOTHING TO obstruct the horizon, the sun rose in its full glory— a hot, gold disk pulsating with light. By seven in the morning, the outside spots that had allowed the investigators to work through the night were shut off, although the lights set up inside the bunker were shining full blast. It took many more hours before all the biological material could be properly removed from the cement grave.

An APB was sent out for Garth Hammerling. North Las Vegas

police also composed flyers and faxed them not only to Las Vegas Metro, but to most of the police departments in the state of Nevada, with emphasis on Reno and the Silver State's side of Lake Tahoe. NLV police also faxed flyers to the poker clubs in Southern California and the casinos in Atlantic City. Everyone knew they were merely scratching the surface because there were thousands of Indian casinos and offshore gambling establishments throughout the nation. How to approach the situation was as confusing as it was dire. After discussing the matter, the consensus was that Garth wasn't much of a gambler. What he liked was what went along with gambling: loose women whom he could pick up, seduce, and then murder.

The house in the desert made headlines. The search for Garth Hammerling widened into a nationwide manhunt for a serial killer. Hopefully, he'd be caught before his compulsion to kill again became overwhelming.

By Monday afternoon, exactly one week after from the gruesome discovery of Adrianna Blanc's body, Mandy started talking, albeit unsteadily. There were so many queries that needed to be asked by so many detectives, it would take days if not weeks before the full story would come out.

Four days after Mandy was pulled out of her medically induced coma, Decker was on an evening Southwest flight headed back into Burbank. At the same time, Marge and Oliver were on I-15, on their way home. The three of them had come away with a story told from Mandy's perspective. Decker had cobbled together an unbelievable tale: a four-day odyssey of murder and destruction. There were gaps and some things didn't make sense, but there was a narrative that could be followed from beginning to end. He wrote down the following summary as he flew back home.

TEN DAYS AGO, at around eight-thirty in the morning, Mandy saw Adrianna slam down the phone at one of the nurses' stations, and bury her face in her hands. Since she seemed so very upset, Mandy went over to ask her what was wrong. Adrianna began to cry.

Mandy was surprised to see Adrianna still at the hospital because her shift had ended at eight. But she was there, and Mandy, being a good friend, sensed she needed some help. She told Adrianna to wait for her in the hospital cafeteria. She signed out on a break, showing up at the cafeteria ten minutes later to talk to her friend.

Adrianna told her that she was furious with Garth, his endless trips that didn't include her, and his pissy attitude in general. She was breaking it off for good this time. Mandy congratulated her. Adrianna was too good to put up with Garth's nonsense. But then Adrianna broke down. During their telephone call, Garth had begged her to reconsider. He said he really loved her and would prove it by canceling his trip to Reno and coming down just to talk to her. Adrianna told Mandy that she didn't know what to do. While she wanted to break up, there was part of her that still loved him. Mandy, who was playing the wise therapist, encouraged her to stay firm in her decision.

Of course, it came out fairly soon into the interview that Mandy had more personal reasons for wanting Adrianna gone. The truth was that Garth had never planned to go with his pals to the mountains. His intentions all along were to come back to L.A. and sneak off with Mandy for a couple of days—just the two of them.

Mandy was in love with Garth.

Mandy suggested that Adrianna needed to go home and sleep. Adrianna wanted to go home, too, but Garth was coming in. They were going to meet at the hospital, so she couldn't leave. Mandy "volunteered" to deal with Garth. Again she told Adrianna to go home and sit on her emotions for a couple of days. Then, with a clearer mind, she could deal with Garth. But Adrianna insisted on staying and meeting with her boyfriend.

That was the first mistake.

Now Mandy was getting agitated. For the last six months, she had been planning this tryst and she was inwardly enraged at the prospect of having to cancel everything. Adrianna's timing couldn't have been worse. She had been putting up with Garth's womanizing for two years. For once, she had decided to show some spine and it was totally messing up Mandy's romantic getaway. She had to get rid of her. Not kill her, Mandy told them: that never entered her mind. Mandy just wanted Adrianna to go home and sleep for a very, very long time.

Since Adrianna insisted on staying at the hospital, Mandy suggested that she go into one of the empty "on-call" rooms and grab a couple hours of sleep before Garth came in. Adrianna concurred. Then Mandy looked up and saw her head nurse giving her the evil eye in the cafeteria. She knew she had to act quickly.

Mandy quickly found Adrianna an empty room. She attempted to give her friend an Ambien so she could get some good sleep, but Adrianna resisted, saying that Ambien would put her out for the next twelve hours. All she needed was a few hours rest. Instead Mandy gave her a couple of tabs of short-acting Benadryl. It would help her sleep but wouldn't knock her out for the day.

After Adrianna was tucked away, Mandy went back to work, stewing about how Adrianna was ruining her life. She knew that Garth put up with Adrianna because she was his cash cow. Mandy accepted that. Garth needed money. But she wasn't about to let Adrianna screw up her few measly days alone with her secret lover. Garth would be arriving at the hospital in a couple of hours and all Mandy wanted was for Adrianna to be "indisposed." Then she'd tell Garth that Adrianna left and didn't want to be contacted. The two of them could go on their planned getaway. Garth would probably go back to Adrianna, but at least they'd have their time alone.

Since Mandy worked in an ICU, she decided to knock Adrianna out with a strong muscle relaxant used in surgery called Pavulon. The drug, whose generic name is pancuronium, is used for muscle paralysis and is administered before a patient goes on a ventilator. Muscle paralysis usually takes place between two to four minutes after administration and the clinical effects usually last about an hour and a half. Full recovery in healthy adults comes anywhere from two to three hours later.

Decker had some familiarity with Pavulon because it had been one of the drugs of choice for a serial-killer respiratory therapist named Efren Saldivar. The man had used Pavulon to murder his patients in a decade-long spree when he had worked at Glendale Adventist Medical Center about ten miles away from where Decker worked and lived. The local case was sensational and made national news. It had been a long-drawn-out affair that included confession, recantation, and exhumation of bodies. Most important, Decker knew that the drug did not show up on a routine tox exam.

While Adrianna slept, Mandy, a deft nurse with a gentle touch, injected her with the drug in the neck. The coroner didn't pick up on it because the cable ligature had broken some of the skin and had obscured the puncture wound. When Garth arrived, Mandy made excuses, but Garth didn't buy them. When he became threatening, Mandy finally confessed that Adrianna was sleeping in one of the on-call rooms.

How was he threatening? Decker had asked her.

Not threatening . . . she had whispered . . . just he knew some embarrassing things about her. With that confession, Mandy's monitor started beeping. Her blood pressure started spiking and the nurses came rushing in. Mandy had talked enough for the day.

End of interview.

Decker came back the next day. It took a while to get back to where they had left off but finally he brought Mandy up to speed—that Garth had just gotten her to admit that she had knocked out Adrianna with Pavulon.

Mandy continued the saga.

Once she confessed that Adrianna was still at the hospital, Garth insisted that the two of them go to the on-call room together to wake her up. By now two hours had elapsed and the drug's effects should have been wearing off, but when they tried to rouse her, Adrianna was unresponsive. In truth, she appeared to be dead.

Mandy was in a full-blown panic. Garth calmed her down and said he'd help her out. He told her that the best way to handle the situation was to make it look like Adrianna was murdered. At first, Mandy was appalled. They needed to go to the police and explain what happened—that it was an accident. But Garth told her that they'd book her for premeditated murder and that's when she really lost it. When he gave her an out, she took it. He explained his reasoning.

Adrianna was dead. Nothing they could do would bring her back. If she was "murdered," they'd both have alibis and be cleared of any wrongdoing. His alibi was he was away camping with his friends. Aaron and Greg would cover for him. Her excuse was that she was on shift working.

The first thing they needed to do was to get the body out of the hospital. They stuffed her into a doubled plastic garbage bag, and as they did this, Chuck Tinsley's card fell to the floor. Mandy picked it up and they both realized it was a card that some guy had given to Adrianna. The card had his name, his occupation—contractor—his home address, and on the back were his cell number and his work address—some house near the hospital. Reading the card seemed to make Garth angry. Mandy thought that was good. The angrier Garth was at Adrianna, the more he'd help to dispose of the body.

The two of them then filled the bag with other trash—discarded papers and the like—just in case someone asked them what was in the bag and they had to open it up.

But no one questioned them as they schlepped the bag onto the loading dock at the emergency vehicle location. Garth pulled his car up to the dock, popped the trunk, and loaded the trash bag. He told Mandy that he'd call her and they'd meet up later on. Mandy never even thought about the security cameras on the dock—a major slipup that got the police looking in the right direction.

When Adrianna's murder hit the news—that the body was found swinging from a rafter—Mandy knew what happened. Garth had put Adrianna's body at the address on the card, placing the focus on Chuck Tinsley. When Tinsley wasn't immediately brought in for questioning, the two of them figured there was a screwup.

Decker looked up from his writing. Fate had intervened. Chuck Tinsley had been the first one at the construction site and had come across the body. He had found his own card in her pocket and had swiped it so the police wouldn't know that he had seen Adrianna the night before. Decker went back to his notes.

The next day was Tuesday. Garth and Mandy rented a motel while the two of them figured out their next step. By Wednesday, things were spinning out of control. They needed to get out of L.A. They needed to think without the police breathing down their necks. Garth said that he owned a place in Vegas. They could lay low there.

The two of them hit the road.

From that point on, it all got fuzzy in Mandy's mind. The days and nights were filled with sex, a lot of booze, and copious amounts of drugs. Somewhere in the back of her mind, she remembered Garth bringing home a young girl—a runaway. The three of them took drugs and Mandy remembered Garth having sex with the girl. Then things became really out of focus. Mandy remembered the girl disappearing . . . but not murdered. She just went away. She also had no recollection of her car crash.

All very well and fine, Decker thought, but there were some major holes big enough to walk an elephant through.

Namely Crystal Larabee.

Oh yeah, Mandy said. Crystal.

She was even fuzzier on Crystal's death than on what had happened with the runaway. Garth initially went to Crystal's place just to ask her about Adrianna's investigation. When Crystal told him that the cops were looking for him, he got really worried. Then Crystal started talking about this guy that Adrianna was talking to at Garage. She told Garth that she felt that the guy was a suspicious character and that he had come on to her after Adrianna left the bar. Crystal felt that he probably had something to do with Adrianna's murder. It didn't take a genius to figure out that Crystal was referring to Chuck Tinsley.

Then Garth got a bright idea. He thought that if Crystal was found murdered, it would really point the finger at Chuck Tinsley. Tinsley had chatted up both women and now both of them were dead. So Garth killed Crystal.

Just like that.

Although Mandy felt bad for Crystal, she bore no guilt. She didn't know Garth's plan, and wasn't there when it happened. Crystal was not her fault. And she didn't seem to feel much guilt about Adrianna, either. Mandy was quick to point out that the whole thing—meaning Adrianna's death—was just a terrible "accident."

And yet here Mandy was, embroiled in a scheme that would certainly end in her being sentenced to do hard time, and maybe forever. Why did she agree to go along with Garth's plans? How did he convince her to participate in such horrible things?

"He'd . . . expose me," she told him.

The BP monitor beeped loudly. Decker knew he was working on borrowed time. "But you knew it would come out, Mandy. That you gave Adrianna Pavulon. Why compound your mistake? Why not just go to the police? That was your first instinct and it was a good one."

"It wasn't just Adrianna," she moaned. "It was the other . . . he'd expose me."

Decker said, "You mean the snapshots of you in leather?"

Again, the BP monitor started beeping. She was silent.

Decker took a logical guess. "And there were sex tapes, too."

"He'd . . . expose me."

The nurse came in. Again, he was asked to leave.

Decker was going back to L.A. in a few hours. It was now or not for a long time. He said, "Who took the pictures and the tapes, Mandy? It might help your case down the road. It's important that we know."

"Crystal Larabee," Mandy whispered. "The bitch . . ."

CHAPTER FORTY-EIGHT

AT SEVEN IN the morning, Decker thought he'd have the squad room to himself, but Wanda Bontemps was already at her desk, her attention focused on the computer. She didn't even look up when he came through the door.

"Good morning," Decker said, out loud.

Wanda greeted him with a smile that opened up her face. It wasn't one of those "nice day, isn't it" kind of looks, but a "we got the bastard" grin. "Have a minute?"

Decker motioned her into his office. Wanda was wearing a hunter green blouse and black slacks, with Vans on her feet. Under her arm was a case folder. He closed the door and the two of them sat down. "What do you have for me?"

She laid the papers on his desk. "A copy of Roxanne Holly's homicide file."

"It's very thick. Want to cover the highlights?"

"You've got it." Wanda took out her notes. "According to Roxanne Holly's roommate, Latitia Bohem, Roxanne went out for drinks at a local restaurant called El Gaucho and never returned.

The place was about four blocks from Roxanne's apartment. Lots of locals go there. It was a balmy night, so she decided to walk."

"Alone and in the dark?"

"Yes."

"Never a good idea."

"It wasn't in her case. After her body was discovered, the bartender and waitresses on staff that night were interviewed. They put Roxanne in the restaurant from about ten to midnight, but it was crowded enough that no one really remembered exactly when she left. The place closes at one."

"So how do they know she left at midnight?"

"Her tab was paid around twelve. She could have lingered longer, but let's assume she left around that time. The bartender did recall her talking to people—guys and gals. She seemed to be having a good time. There was nothing mentioned in the case files about servicemen or anyone in a uniform."

"That could be a dead end."

"Agreed. The detectives returned to El Gaucho several days later for a second round of interviews with the staff and local patrons. Among those who remembered Roxanne being there was a guy named Chuck Tinsley."

"Whoa!" Decker was amazed. Things didn't routinely fall that way. "Go on."

"Chuck was working at a lumberyard. He was living about six blocks from the El Gaucho and ten blocks away from Roxanne's apartment when she was murdered."

Decker raised a brow. "What did Chuck have to say for himself in the files?"

"He claimed he knew her from the area, maybe talked to her a couple of times at El Gaucho. Casual kind of thing. The kicker is that a patron recalled them talking the night that Roxanne disappeared."

"That's indeed notable."

"Chuck's alibi was that he was at the restaurant until the bar closed up. And that was verified by the bartender."

"So he's saying that if Roxanne was attacked at twelve, it couldn't have been him because he was still at the place until one in the morning."

"Exactly. But if things were busy and no one remembered Roxanne leaving, Tinsley could have easily left and come back. I mean honestly, Loo, what was he doing with Roxanne's necklace?"

Decker thought a moment. "Maybe we'll be lucky enough to pull some DNA off the hair and it'll be a match with Roxanne. Then we can say that Tinsley had her necklace. It's still circumstantial."

"A little more than circumstantial."

"Sure. Putting Chuck in the vicinity is both good and bad. You can make a case that Tinsley was involved with her murder. Or you can make a case that Tinsley found her body after she was dead and ripped the necklace off her neck." When Wanda gave him a look, Decker said, "It's what his attorney will say."

Wanda said, "Remember the primary suspect, Burt Barney?"

"The homeless guy who found the body."

"Yes. Oxnard police grilled him for hours. They asked him over and over what he did with the necklace. He never gave it up, Loo. He swore he didn't kill Roxanne, and when he found the body, there was no necklace."

"A lawyer could say that Tinsley took the necklace before Barney found her."

"That's stretching." Wanda threw her arms open.

"We need beyond a reasonable doubt and this is my problem. Tinsley looked like a potential serial killer when we thought he had something to do with Adrianna Blanc's murder. But we know what happened to Adrianna and Crystal, and Tinsley didn't have anything to do with them. That was Garth Hammerling." A pause. "Who is also a serial killer."

Wanda shook her head. "How many serial killers have you come across in your career?"

"In my thirty years of police work including Florida, I have dealt with three serial killers, although one case was iffy because there were charges against him for only one murder. It was just suspected that he may have done others. They're out there for sure, but not with the frequency portrayed in the media. To have one serial killer involved as a witness in a murder case committed by another serial killer is crazy. That's why we need to proceed slowly . . . so we don't make a mistake."

"So what do we do with Tinsley?"

"If we get Roxanne's DNA off of the necklace, we can arrest Tinsley on stolen property—which is how he's going to plead. He saw Roxanne's body in the open lot and made a bad decision. It would be great to find a witness who saw Chuck and Roxanne leave together. Anyone in the files look promising?"

"I have to reread the pages."

"You might want to check out Tinsley's buddies at the time. Maybe he confessed to someone, although if he truly is a serial killer, I'd have my doubts."

"I'll go over the files again."

"What's going on with Lee Wang and Oceanside PD?"

"He's still looking. We've sent the ring found in Tinsley's possession to the lab. Maybe we'll get lucky and get a DNA match for Erin Greenfield."

"Was Tinsley in Oceanside at the time Greenfield was murdered?"

"I don't know. I'll call up Lee and compare notes."

"One piece of jewelry is circumstantial," Decker said. "Two pieces with DNA that matches two murdered girls can't be explained away easily. Right now all we can do is cross our fingers and put our faith in science."

AFTER THREE WEEKS in the hospital, Jacqueline Mars, the sixteen-year-old runaway whom Garth and Mandy had abducted, strangled, and wrapped up in a garbage bag, had recovered sufficiently to be discharged from the hospital. Unfortunately, her memory of what happened during the period of time in question was even fuzzier than Mandy Kowalski's. At present, she still has no recollection of those fateful days she spent in a stupor.

Mandy Kowalski was arrested for the first-degree murder of Adrianna Blanc, and the attempted murder of Jacqueline Mars. She escaped charges in the murder of Crystal Larabee. She is assumed innocent of all the charges until proven guilty.

After the news about Garth Hammerling and Mandy Kowalski's drug-induced crime spree broke open, St. Tim's started examining routine deaths that had taken place during their shifts. Mandy's cases came up clean, but there were several suspicious deaths during Hammerling's years of employment. One month after the grisly discoveries at Hammerling's Vegas condo, those hospital cases that Garth handled still remained under investigation.

Decker finally did receive a copy of the tox report on Adrianna Blanc. It took a little longer than usual because the pathologist had to reorder a blood screen for Pavulon. And while the drug was found in her system—and might have killed her—the amount in her blood was not considered a lethal dose. A more likely case was that Adrianna was alive but paralyzed when Garth had strung her from the rafters at the construction site. The coroner's ruling was death by asphyxiation from the hanging.

It could have been that Garth genuinely thought she was dead. But Decker and his detectives thought otherwise. They all concluded that even if Garth had known that Adrianna was still alive, he would have followed through with his plans. As evidenced by Crystal Larabee and the two bodies and piles of bones found in his Vegas house, Garth simply enjoyed killing.

Six weeks after Tinsley's jewelry pieces were sent to the lab for DNA, the reports came back to the police with distinct DNA profiles. The necklace contained Tinsley's DNA as well as DNA from a hair root that belonged to Roxanne Holly. The ring took a while longer because of the scant biological evidence. The tests involved repeating the same sample of DNA over and over. Eventually two profiles were extracted: Tinsley's and that of Erin Greenfield.

Chuck Tinsley was arrested the following day. The timing couldn't have been better for Lydia and Nathan Grossman, the property owners. They had just passed final inspection.

The murders of Roxanne Holly and Erin Greenfield had taken

place outside Decker's jurisdiction. He was aching to be part of Tinsley's interrogations, but the whole thing became moot once Tinsley asked for a lawyer.

Although there was cause for a cautious celebration in Tinsley's arrest, there were also problems. Tinsley had allowed the detectives to search his apartment, but that was only in regard to gathering evidence in the Adrianna Blanc case. The jewelry, his lawyers pleaded, was inadmissible because it had nothing to do with Adrianna Blanc. And without the jewelry, there was no case against Tinsley in the Holly and Greenfield homicides.

The district attorney argued that the police had taken the pieces with Charles Tinsley's permission in order to see if any of them belonged to Adrianna Blanc. When the two pieces showed up in the files as identical to jewelry belonging to two other murdered women, it would have been negligent not to test them for DNA. And since the jewelry was obtained with Mr. Tinsley's permission, nothing illegal was done.

After many continuances, the first judge sided with the D.A. The jewelry was admissible. Tinsley's legal team appealed. Months later, the appellate judge sided with the first judge. First-degree murder charges were levied against Charles Michael Tinsley for the deaths of Roxanne Holly and Erin Greenfield. Tinsley is presumed innocent until proven guilty.

Garth Willard Hammerling still remains at large. Anyone having information to his whereabouts is requested to call the Los Angeles Police Department and/or the North Las Vegas Police Department.

CHAPTER FORTY-NINE

WHEN TRAUMA HIT, Gabe did what he always did.

He adjusted.

His father never did call him back. Gabe stored the papers in his closet, figuring he'd hear from the old man sooner or later. He proceeded to go about his business. Within a week's time, Rina found him a permanent tutor so he could be homeschooled. He finished tenth grade in a month. The only thing he couldn't pick up from the tutor was his language courses, but even that turned out to be okay. Rina spoke Yiddish, so he was able to practice his German with her. The Loo spoke Spanish, which Gabe picked up in a heartbeat. And while it wasn't the same as Italian, it was close enough to keep his ear trained.

Whenever he had spare time, he'd take in concerts and operas. A couple of times, Hannah went with him. Other times, he went by himself. He loved opera—the primary reason he wanted to learn German and Italian. He wanted to figure out how to mix the words with music, and the only way to do that was to speak the language of the libretto.

Most of his time was spent at the piano. His music had always been his lifeline, but there was always something desperate and rushed in the way he played. After living with the Deckers and taking lessons with Nicholas Mark, Gabe discovered actual joy in learning. Every meeting with Mark put him one step closer to being a real pianist. He could move a little slower, listen a little more carefully, linger at the keyboard a little longer because for the first time, he was living with predictability. Everything was on time and without drama. Not that there was anything wrong with drama, but it was better handled in the arts than in real life. He had always had freedom, but now he had freedom without fear. The autonomy made him generous. He often came with Hannah to her choir practice to accompany the singers—just to be nice. As graduation approached, Mrs. Kent had begged him to play something special for the evening. After much cajoling from her and from Hannah, he relented.

Why the hell not?

Originally he decided to do something technically challenging like Rachmaninoff—something that would wow an audience. But thirty minutes before the actual ceremony was to begin, he changed his mind.

This wasn't a piano concert: it was a *celebration*. People were happy. Some parents actually loved their children and took pride in their accomplishments.

At the last moment, he found a working computer and printer in the synagogue where the graduation ceremony was to take place and downloaded eighteen pages of Liszt's Hungarian Rhapsody no. 2 in C-sharp minor. It was a familiar piece to him and to most people because it was used in all the old cartoons whenever there was a chase. He knew he could sight read it without problems. When he was due to play, he lined up the first five sheets of paper on the piano stand, and had Mrs. Kent feed him the next one as he brushed away each used sheet onto the floor. With the papers flying about, especially at the end with tempo going at lightning speed, it had an unintentional comical effect which he incorporated with great flair.

Everyone was laughing. He had made a happy audience even happier. He learned another important lesson. Playing in public wasn't just about skill, it was about entertainment.

He never stopped thinking about his parents. It was wrong to compare them to the Deckers, but he did it anyway. He used to rationalize that their crazy behavior stemmed from their deep profundity. That was total horseshit. The Deckers were stable people, and just as—if not more—complex than his mom and dad.

Rina and the Loo had taken him in with grace and made him a part of their lives. It was brought home to him when they insisted he come with them to New York for Sammy's medical school graduation. They included him in Sammy's wedding. They also took him to Israel when they moved Hannah into seminary: paid for his ticket, gave him his own hotel room and his own personal tour guide. He and the guide went everywhere around the Holy Land as well as Petra in Jordon and the pyramids in Egypt. He explored ancient civilizations, finding out that the cliché was still true; it was a whole big world out there.

Neither of the Deckers tried to be a substitute parent. They were facilitators, and because they were kind, he tried not to be a pain in the ass. No, Rina was not his mother and the Loo was not his father. But truth be told, he knew at this stage in his life that it was far better to have Rina and the Loo than Mom and Dad.

BY MID-NOVEMBER, NEW York was awash in freezing rain while Chicago was experiencing its first snowfall. L.A., on the other hand, was clear skies and sunshine. The air had turned colder but it was far from cold and there was still color left on some of the trees. But what surprised Gabe was that the city was still green. Back east, the chill of fall was turning into the frost of winter. But Rina had a *garden*. It was weird.

But not as weird as the phone call from his dad. Chris's voice was a monotone. "You have papers that belong to me."

No introduction. Gabe had been expecting the call, but his

father's voice always made him stumble. "I do," he answered. "Where should I mail them?"

"I don't trust the mail. I'll come to L.A. and pick them up. Besides, I'd like to see you. What's your schedule like?"

"Aside from Mondays and Thursday from ten to twelve, I'm completely open."

Donatti paused. "You dropped out of school?"

"Rina set me up with a tutor. I'm being homeschooled, which is great. I should be done with high school by next June."

"I haven't seen any tutoring bill on your credit card."

"It's a couple of hours every week, Chris. I pay in cash."

"What's going on between ten and twelve on Mondays and Thursdays?"

"I have my piano lessons with Nick at USC."

A pause. "Nick as in Nicholas Mark?"

Donatti sounded a little peeved. Gabe smiled. "You're welcome to sit in and see him bust my balls."

"You should be used to that."

"He's a piece of cake compared to you."

"No need to get nasty. I'll be by tomorrow at two."

Tomorrow was Thursday. Gabe said, "I can't make it home by two on a bus. You could meet me at SC."

"We'll meet at SC. I'll call you when I get there." Donatti hung up.

According to Gabe's phone, the conversation had lasted one minute and twenty-eight seconds. Nothing remarkable had transpired, but one sentence rang in his brain.

Besides, I'd like to see you.

Not, I *need* to see you, but I'd *like* to see you.

It shouldn't have made a difference, but it did. It made him feel good.

THE PHONE RANG exactly at two. "I'm at an open air café on campus," Gabe told his father. "Is that okay?"

"It's fine."

Gabe gave his father directions. Five minutes later he saw Chris Donatti walking toward him—tall, tan, built, and handsome. The man turned heads wherever he went and today was no exception. Every time he passed a female, she'd look backward. Chris was wearing a white shirt, brown cords and a tweed jacket. He looked like every co-ed's fantasy professor. There were so many things to despise about Chris, but on a gut level, Gabe was proud to be Chris's son.

His father—for better or worse.

When Chris reached the table, he held out his hand. Gabe gave him the manila folder and Chris sat down and opened it up.

"Are you hungry?" Gabe asked.

"Get me a cup of coffee."

"Do you mind if I get something to eat?" Wordlessly, Donatti pulled out a hundred-dollar bill. Gabe said, "I wasn't asking for money."

"Take it."

"I'm really okay."

"Don't be an idiot. Someone offers you money, you take it. Now shut up and let me read."

So much for sentimentalism. Gabe took the cash, waited in line and bought a burger, fries, a Diet Coke and a coffee. He sat back down and started to eat. A minute later, Chris was glaring at him. He wasn't eating particularly loud, but his dad was in one of *those* moods where everything bothered him.

Gabe said, "Uh, maybe I'll eat at another table." He moved to the table next to his dad and was eating peacefully while reading Evelyn Waugh—one of Rina's favorite writers. It was a beautiful day and he felt happier than he had in years. He knew he was calm because his zits finally cleared up. How good was it to be chomping on a burger and reading a great book. The only thing missing was maybe a little Mozart—strings pieces only, and please, definitely no piano. He had become so absorbed in his reading that he didn't hear the old man clearing his throat until Chris was clearly annoyed. Gabe looked up and moved back to the first table. "Everything okay?"

"Get me another cup of coffee. Large."

"Sure."

When Gabe brought the second cup back, Chris was straightening the papers and putting them back inside the envelope. "It looks in order. I'll take the papers to my lawyer. See how we move on from there." Chris looked at Gabe. "Do you know where your mother is?"

"If I were to guess, I'd say somewhere in India judging from the owner of the car. Her letter also said that she was far away. I put a copy of the letter in the envelope."

"I saw it. And yes, she is in India. Uttar Pradesh, to be specific." Chris pulled out several photographs and spread them on the table.

Gabe sorted through the snapshots. "When did you find her?"

"Months ago."

"And you didn't tell me?"

"You knew she was alive. What difference would it have made?"

That was true. He stared at the photographs. "Man, she's ready to pop."

"She already has." He took out a final picture. "Meet your new sister."

The infant was round and chubby with a thatch of black hair. "Where'd you get this?"

"None of your business."

Despite himself, Gabe smiled. Babies were cute. No jealousy because his mom was lost to him anyway. "Do you mind if I keep it?"

"Go ahead. To me, she's just a little bastard. You're not surprised by any of this. Did she send you another letter?"

"If she had, I would have called you." He looked into his father's flat blue eyes. "She only contacted me once. Since then I haven't heard squat from her." Gabe adjusted his glasses. "Decker figured that she was probably pregnant and that's why she left so suddenly."

"Did she tell him that when she met with him way back when?"

"No. He just figured it out later."

"And you believe him?"

"Decker wasted a lot of time looking for Mom. He wouldn't have done that if he had known that she had wanted to disappear."

Donatti thought about that and decided it was the truth. "How's Decker?"

"They're nice people and nice to me. I'm okay if that's what you're asking."

"So Decker figured it out." Donatti drummed the table. "Your mom managed to hide *your* bastard origins from me, but she couldn't pretend with an Indian baby."

Gabe didn't take the bait. "Does Mom know that you know about her?"

"Not yet."

"So what are you going to do?"

Donatti shrugged. "Gabriel, I've thought about everything from doing nothing to killing the bitch."

"And?"

"In the end, I don't fucking care anymore." Donatti took out a pack of cigarettes and lit a smoke. "That isn't true. I do care. But I don't care enough to ruin my life even though I could get away with it. I'd like to kill her, but I don't want her dead."

"Not that you asked me, but I think that doing nothing is a very wise decision."

"Besides I have the best revenge of all. She's in India." Donatti smiled, but it wasn't a pretty one. "But you're here."

"So what? She doesn't give a damn about me." Said more to himself than to his father. "If she did, she would have taken me with her."

"Oh no, no, no, no." Donatti wagged his finger. "She didn't dare take you with her. Maybe I'd let her go—there are lots of women in this world—but bastard or not, you're still my only kid. If she had taken you away, it would have sealed her death warrant."

He crushed out his cigarette and lit another one.

"I know your mother very well. She's got herself a little bastard baby girl, but her *real* baby is right here with me. She's in incredible psychic pain and that makes me very happy." He stood up. "Let's get out of here."

"Are you taking me home?"

"You mean back to the Deckers?"

"Home is the Deckers." Gabe grinned. "But you'll always be my only dad."

"Yeah until you find out who shot his wad in your mom that summer."

Gabe ignored him and stood up. "You know, I can take the bus if it's an inconvenience to drive me into the Valley."

"Nah, it's fine. Besides I want to hear all about your progress with your new pal, Nick. "

"He's my teacher, Chris, not my pal. He tortures me every time I see him. But I guess that's the price of getting better."

"You'd better be improving after spending all my money on lessons." Donatti grabbed the nape of his neck and none too gently. "This way."

A stretch limo was waiting. That wasn't a surprise. His father usually needed room for his long legs. What was a surprise was a wisp of a girl sitting in the backseat. She looked fourteen although he knew she was at least eighteen. Chris didn't mess with underage girls anymore. She was cute in a pixie way—small upturned nose, dimples in her cheeks, and curly auburn hair. There was intelligence in her brown eyes.

"Talia." Chris pointed to the girl. To her, he said, "This is my kid."

"Gabe Whitman." Gabe offered her his hand.

"It's nice to finally meet you." She shook his hand back. "He talks about you all the time."

"No, I don't." Donatti looked annoyed and then proceeded to ignore her the entire ride home, listening intently as Gabe spoke about his lessons, his music, his composing, what he was studying, what he was learning from Nicholas Mark, and finally about upcoming competitions. Donatti smoked cigarettes and drank coffee, his eyes focused on Gabe's face the entire time, his gaze never wavering. Before Gabe could even catch his breath, the limo was outside the Decker house.

Never had time raced so fast.

Gabe said, "Well, I guess this is my stop."

"Call if you need anything."

"I will." He turned to Talia. "Nice to meet you. Take care of him for me."

"Blah, blah." Donatti handed him his empty coffee cup filled with cigarette butts. "You know how I hate crap in my face. Dump this out for me."

"Sure, Chris." He got out and the car took off before Gabe reached the front door.

Chris giving him shit. How metaphoric.

He stared at the garbage in his hands.

Huh.

He unlocked the door and headed for his quarters—not really *his* room, but after seven months he was more than a sojourner. Once inside his space, he sat on the bed and turned on his computer.

THE KNOCK PISSED him off. Donatti hated doing taxes and he hated being interrupted. "What?"

"Can I come in?" Talia's voice. "Being as you fucked up my concentration, you might as well."

She opened the door. "Sorry."

"No, you're not. What do you want?"

A small smile grew on her lips. "I brought you some coffee." She placed it on his rosewood desk. Chris's office was walnut paneled with a stone fireplace. It was filled with good art and the smell of leather and tobacco. He had shelves of the finest Scotch and cut crystal tumblers. The place looked like something that belonged in an English castle, not the office of a man who owned whorehouses. In the corner was a *huge* Christmas tree that she had decorated. Underneath it were piles of presents sent to him by happy clients. Talia never adorned a Christmas tree before she had met Chris. It was an assignment she always enjoyed.

Donatti looked her up and down. She was holding a wrapped package. "Just put it under the tree."

"It's from Gabe."

"Oh shit! I've got to get him something. What's the date?"

"The nineteenth."

"Okay. We got time. Go out and buy him a motorcycle."

Talia stared at him.

"What?" Donatti said.

"Chris, he doesn't drive. He's only fifteen."

"He's fifteen already? Shit, I missed his birthday."

"Don't worry. I sent him a card and a shirt."

Donatti stared at her. "You sent Gabe a shirt for his birthday?"

"You were out of town. And what's wrong with a shirt? He wrote me a thank-you card, so I guess he liked it."

She was pouting. Donatti kept forgetting that she wasn't much older than Gabe. "Thank you for sending my son a shirt. Let's aim a little higher this time. Get him a Ferrari."

"A *Ferrari*?" Talia exclaimed.

"Yeah, a Ferrari. Do you want me to spell it for you?"

"I know what a Ferrari is. Stop being so sarcastic." She paused. "Can I say something?"

"No." When Talia didn't talk, Donatti exhaled in disgust. "*What?*"

"We're going to Paris for New Year's. Why don't you ask him to come with us? I bet he'd like that even more than a Ferrari."

"I don't want him to come."

Talia looked perplexed. "Why not?"

"Because I don't want him to come, okay?"

Talia shrugged. "Okay."

"Look, Talia, Gabe is doing all right and I'm doing all right. Not a good idea to mix it up."

"Whatever you say." She paused. "What should I do with the present?"

"Give it here."

She handed him the wrapped box. "Where do I find a Ferrari dealership? This is Elko, not Las Vegas."

"You're right. Tell you what. We'll go to Penske-Wynn tomorrow and buy one together. Set up the jet. We'll leave at eleven if I can ever get enough peace and quiet to get my taxes done." He gave her a small wave. "Good-bye."

"You're welcome for the coffee."

"Thank you and good-bye." When she finally closed the door, Donatti smiled. He didn't love Talia, but sometimes her innocence made him laugh. He regarded the gift from his son. Gabe was a good kid—got that from his mother.

He thought about Terry more often than he should have. She was gone, but it was far from over. They were still legally married and eventually they'd have to face each other one way or the other.

Someday, he thought. Someday.

He opened the ribbon on the box and lifted the lid. Inside was a stack of papers secured by a staple and a small note in Gabe's neat handwriting.

Merry Christmas, Dad.

The papers were from some kind of medical lab . . . some kind of medical test.

What the fuck?

As he rifled through the pages, Donatti skimmed the words.

DNA taken from a cigarette

DNA taken from a coffee cup.

Positive paternity match—99.9%.

Donatti threw back his head and laughed out loud.

The little *bastard.*

Or maybe not.

He picked up his phone and got Gabe's voice mail.

Leave me a message and I'll get back to you as soon as I can.

"Thanks for the papers. If I ever need a kidney, I'll know who to call."

Donatti hung up the phone and went back to his work.

An hour later, he picked up the phone and called Gabe a second time.

After receiving the same message, Donatti waited for the beep and said, "I'm going to Paris for New Year's. Someone over there is playing Bach's Organ Toccata and Fugue in D minor. I'm thinking about getting tickets. Talia has a tin ear and I know you have an unhealthy fixation with the pipe organ."

A pause.

"We're leaving on the twenty-seventh, so give me a call back right away. If your passport is current, you got nothing better to do, and you want to hear the piece, I suppose you can tag along."